Julie Shackman is a feel-good romance author and former journalist.

She lives in Scotland with her husband, two sons and their little Romanian rescue pup, Cooper.

julieshackman.co.uk

X x.com/G13Julie

instagram.com/juliegeorginashackman

facebook.com/julie.shackman

BB bookbub.com/authors/julie-shackman

D1100570

Also by Julie Shackman

A Secret Scottish Escape

A Scottish Highland Surprise

The Cottage in the Highlands

A Scottish Country Escape

The Highland Lodge Getaway

THE BOOKSHOP BY THE LOCH

Scottish Escapes

JULIE SHACKMAN

One More Chapter
a division of HarperCollins*Publishers* Ltd
1 London Bridge Street
London SE1 9GF
www.harpercollins.co.uk

HarperCollins*Publishers*
Macken House, 39/40 Mayor Street Upper,
Dublin 1, D01 C9W8, Ireland

This paperback edition 2024
1
First published in Great Britain in ebook format
by HarperCollins*Publishers* 2024

A catalogue record of this book is available from the British Library

ISBN: 978-0-00-861431-7

Printed and bound in the UK using 100% Renewable Electricity
by CPI Group (UK) Ltd

Chapter One

J ust ten minutes to go.

Ten minutes and there would be the announcement that I, Lexie Dunbar, was to become the new senior commissioning editor for romance and popular fiction, here at Literati Publishing.

My heart skittered against my ribs.

New tailored navy suit. Tick.

Lilac pussy-bow blouse. Tick.

I even had my long, straight, toffee-coloured hair blow-dried and tonged into a cloud of tumbling curls first thing this morning, thanks to the magical capabilities of my amazing hairdresser, Fabia. Tick.

I drummed my fingers against the edge of my maple office desk, before remembering I had treated myself to a professional manicure yesterday. I drew my shiny cranberry nails to an abrupt halt.

Around me, my colleagues were sliding knowing looks and

encouraging smiles in my direction. The clock trudged closer to eleven o'clock.

This was agonising!

I had worked here at Literati Publishing in Glasgow for five years as a junior editor and boy, had I paid my dues!

Ridiculous hours; taking minimal holiday entitlement; working through my lunch break or devouring a sandwich while up to my elbows checking edits; chasing up manuscripts; taking work home evenings and weekends; massaging the rampant author egos of the likes of Dame Alicia Kilroy and Sir Stephen Todd; tackling an inbox which bred emails every ten minutes.

But despite the incessant pressure, working in publishing had been all I had ever wanted to do, since I was little and able to hold a book.

I grew up in Bracken Way, a small Highland tourist town with a crumbling castle ruin and a beautiful loch, but moved through to Glasgow at eighteen to study English Literature at Glasgow University for four years and have lived here ever since.

Once I obtained my degree, I worked for the Scottish Civil Service for three years on one of their in-house newspapers, before hearing about the job of junior editor at Literati.

I knew I had to apply.

I ended up working under the auspices of senior commissioning editor Tabitha McGregor and learnt so much from her. When she retired recently, I knew her shoes would be considerable ones to fill, but it was what I wanted and had been working towards.

I turned my attention back to the office clock on the far wall.

Five minutes to go until our Executive Publisher, Grant Mullen, materialised to make the announcement about Tabitha's successor.

I shot out of my chair and paced backwards and forwards across the champagne carpet in my pearly heels. Well, when I say paced, it was more of a hobble. My toes were screeching out in protest but no other shoes matched my suit as well as they did.

Outside the panoramic office windows, Glasgow was a sea of stippled roofs, towering spires and winking glass in the Monday morning April light. The sun was pushing through the clouds.

Our offices were modern with floor-to-ceiling glass windows, situated in the trendy Byres Road area of the city. Surrounded by media types, students and struggling actors, Literati overlooked the emerald spread of the Botanic Gardens and their meringue-shaped glasshouses.

I returned to my desk and sat down again for what seemed like the twentieth time in the last couple of minutes.

I smoothed down my skirt. My light grey eyes shone back out at me, wide and expectant, from my laptop screen.

"How are you feeling?" hissed a familiar voice as she hurried past.

It was Rhiannon, my best friend and head of marketing here at Literati.

"Like I'm about to throw up."

Rhiannon flashed me a white grin. She was all peroxide-blonde bob, had just hit the age of thirty – the same as me – but seemed to possess far more confidence. "You're going to be a brilliant successor to Tabitha. Everybody knows it. Oh, stand by your beds, folks."

From the left, the doors swished open and Grant Mullen strode in, like an older, Scottish version of Pedro Pascal.

At once, chairs were squeaked back and bodies rose upwards, gravitating towards him.

Oh God. This was it. This was the moment.

With my legs resembling a newborn foal's, I managed to make my way across the office floor and joined the others in a semi-circle. Rhiannon glided up beside me and gave my arm a supportive squeeze.

"Good morning, everyone. I trust you all had a weekend full of fun and debauchery?"

There were ripples of polite laughter.

"I take it that's a yes then?"

There was a chorus of more sycophantic chortles.

"Right, down to business. You will be aware of Tabitha's recent retirement. This has, of course, left us with the senior commissioning editor vacancy for romance and popular fiction to fill."

I was aware that dozens of sets of eyes were drifting my way. Grant glanced over. He gave me a knowing look. My stomach rippled with apprehension.

"Finding someone who has the same drive, flair, experience and creativity as Tabitha has meant, as far as me and the board are concerned, that there was only one candidate for the job."

Rhiannon gave me a nudge and I grinned at her, rolling my eyes.

"And so, it gives me the greatest pleasure to introduce you

to our new senior commissioning editor. Please step forward, Anya."

A confused ringing sound went off in my ears.

What? Anya? Who?

I felt like I was trapped underwater. There were sounds around me, but they were distorted. My colleagues were muttering and Rhiannon made a weird, gasping noise. Then she ground out a string of expletives.

An impeccably dressed ice-blonde, who looked to be in her forties, emerged out of nowhere.

Heads turned to me for my reaction.

My stunned eyes swept over the woman. Her bleached wavy hair sat perfectly on her shoulders. Recognition punched me in the stomach. Shit. Anya. It was Anya Mills, from the top New York publishing house, Panache Publishing.

I was struggling to swallow. Was this some sort of twisted joke?

Grant began talking again, but my brain couldn't process what he was saying.

"Team, for those of you who might have been living underground for the past few years, I'd like you to give Anya Mills, our new senior commissioning editor, a very warm welcome. Anya worked as an executive editor for Panache Publishing in New York and her credentials speak for themselves."

I have no idea how, but I managed to force out a few awkward handclaps, before stumbling in the direction of the ladies' toilets, with Rhiannon in hot pursuit.

And there I huddled in one of the cubicles, a crying and snotty mess against Rhiannon's cerise blouse.

Chapter Two

I scuffed my dark leather ankle boots on the train platform and pushed my fringe out of my eyes.

Lugging my florally wheelie case behind me, I squinted around, until I saw Mum waving so hard at me from across the station car park, it was like she was performing semaphore. Her shoulder-length dark hair was being buffeted around her face.

My stomach sunk to the ground. I knew that once I confessed everything to Mum, she would be sprinting up to my old bedroom to turn it into a spa sanctuary for me, with soft towels and scented candles.

I had intended on telling her and my grandfather last week when I rang them to alert them that the prodigal daughter was returning home for three months, but the words lodged in my throat.

Instead, I'd mumbled something about the extended leave I'd decided to take to lick my wounds, as just being a "use it or lose it situation."

Oh God. Where was my life headed? That was the million-dollar question. What was I going to do with myself for the next twelve weeks? Did I really want to return to Literati? Did I want to stay here in Bracken Way permanently? Would that feel like I was going backwards, instead of moving on?

What now? Was I even thinking straight? According to Rhiannon, I had lost leave of my senses, when I'd whooshed up in the lift to HR after Anya Mills's appointment last week, to announce that I had accrued a ridiculous amount of leave entitlement and I would be taking it with immediate effect.

When they appeared reluctant, I pointed out I could take the money instead, to which they relented after working out the considerable sum involved and agreed yes, taking my accrued total leave of three months was the more sensible option.

I think looking like a terrifying, tear-stained poodle helped my case.

Grant had summoned me up to his ostentatious office after the announcement, to tell me that while my skills and abilities were much appreciated, the board had decided that Anya Mills's name carried more weight, which meant, "We would be in a better position to take on the other publishing power houses."

More swirling thoughts took over. The way I felt right now – cheated and foolish – I couldn't envisage myself returning to work there. But I loved the publishing world so much. Could I really turn my back on it?

I did have some savings put by, thanks to the money my late grandmother had left me in her will eighteen months ago, plus what I would make from temporarily renting out my flat in Glasgow for the three months I was back here in Bracken Way. The combination of both of those would keep me going if I did decide to hand in my notice, but it wouldn't last forever.

I tried to give my head a mental shake. Right now, I was struggling to decide between peppermint tea or camomile, let alone what I wanted to do about my job.

I set my shoulders, plastered on a smile and started to stride over to where Mum was, but she had already abandoned her zesty yellow Hyundai and was bearing down on me, arms flung open.

She enveloped me and planted a huge kiss on my cheek. The wind carried wafts of her Estée Lauder perfume towards me, warm and flowery. "Three months," she breathed. "I've got my baby girl home for three months."

Guilt tugged at my insides. I fought to make my voice sound jovial. "You'll want to see the back of me after a fortnight."

"That long?" she teased. "Come on. Let's get you home and you can tell us all your exciting news."

Right. Enough. I would tell her and my grandfather the truth, once lunch was out of the way. I couldn't carry on, bottling up my frustration like this.

Mum held up the fob to the car and it let out a series of bleeps.

While I dumped my wheelie case in the boot, I realised that it only seemed like five minutes ago, that I was in the midst of the hustle of Glasgow and now, I was being blasted by hypothermic winds. And this was April, for Christ's sake! Bracken Way was a romantic, rugged part of Highland

Scotland though, carrying echoes of the Vikings, so I guess the bracing weather was to be expected.

I buried my hands deeper into the pockets of my denim jacket, wishing I'd thrown on my thick pink fleece instead and clambered into the passenger side.

Mum began talking about Grandpa complaining about his new reading glasses. I hoped I was murmuring and nodding in the right places. I was struggling to focus. My thoughts were jumping everywhere.

She indicated out of the train station car park and took us in the direction of the main street, moving the conversation on to the bad snow that had hit the area last month. I could see visitors meandering up and down the hill towards Bracken Castle.

Clusters of chattering American tourists were entering the castle courtyard in an array of multi-coloured waterproofs and clutching maps.

Chilly, Scottish dappled sunshine rippled down through the exposed towers.

To the right, was the gift shop, selling everything from Bracken Castle embossed bookmarks to postcards and clotted cream fudge. To the left, was the entrance kiosk and office. I recalled coming up here on school trips to hear about the history of the castle, with its links to hidden treasure, smuggled ladies of nobility fleeing from arranged marriages and the rumoured ghost of a knight searching for his lost love.

I gazed out of the car window, drinking in the achy, buttery stonework, with its narrow, grinning passages and elaborate crenelations. Busty balustrades erupted at every turn, depicting frilly flowers and rearing horses.

If you ventured through the gift shop and out of the exit on the other side, you were greeted by a hillside of sloping green grass, which overlooked the shimmering loch.

My heart sank. It was as if my life was contained in a snow globe and someone had snatched it up, given it a prolonged shake and then handed it back to me and said, "Right then. How are you going to deal with this?"

Perhaps I should have ignored that voice in my head at sixteen, telling me to indulge my dream of becoming a book editor. Maybe if I'd chosen another career, I wouldn't feel so much of a withered, rejected husk right now at the age of thirty. Literati had chewed me up and spat me out.

It had been the love of our local bookshop, Book Ends, which had triggered my book obsession from an early age. From the moment I had stepped in there with my late grandmother Pattie, the world of books and publishing had cast its spell on me and there had been nothing I could do about it.

I stared up at the castle, as Mum eased us up to the traffic lights. This place was the voice of the long-gone characters who had drifted in and around these walls, who had drunk up the sunshine in the sprawling lawns and hatched and plotted in its chambers hundreds of years ago.

I bit back a swell of disbelief as I played over in my head again, Grant's burring voice as he introduced Anya Mills and her perfectly pressed checked suit.

"Are you alright, sweetheart?"

Mum's voice made me sit up straighter.

"You're very quiet."

I huddled deeper into my denim jacket. "I'm fine." Out came another brittle smile. "Just a bit tired."

She weaved her way along the street. "You work too hard at that place."

Yeah. And look where my hard work has got me.

I shot a surreptitious glance back towards the bustling gift shop and then to the kiosk, where Nigel Carter, the dashing, elderly stalwart of the castle, was holding court with a group of visitors. Nigel, suited and booted and with his dark grey hair combed, was pointing a gnarly finger towards the grounds.

I thought again about me returning home. My grandfather lived with my mother. I was looking forward to seeing him again too. They'd act like a morale-boosting tag team, and right now I really needed it.

No sooner had I got through the front door and deposited my case and jacket in the hall, than my grandfather embraced me. He beamed at me from under his white moustache. He smelled of tobacco and fabric softener. "I don't know how many people your mother is expecting for lunch."

I popped my head around the sitting room door to see the dining table at the far end of the room laid out with her best crockery, on a starched white tablecloth.

"I've made your favourite," she grinned at me, her eyes shining. "My chicken pasta bake."

"And then sticky toffee pudding and custard," added Grandpa.

I stared at the set table and at the familiarity of my old

family home. I couldn't hold it back any longer. My emotions swamped me. My face crumpled.

Both of them shot forward, concerned.

"Lexie. What is it? What's wrong?" asked Mum, shooting worried looks at my grandfather.

I gave my head a shake, as they guided me into the sitting room and my grandfather encouraged me to sit down.

His sympathetic, papery hands seized mine. "Come on, lass. You can tell us."

"How could they do it, Grandpa?" I gulped into his shoulder, not making any sense to either of them. "I've given them everything. I've worked so hard. I've sacrificed so much."

They exchanged puzzled looks.

And out it came: the kick in the teeth about the job I'd been led to believe was mine and which I'd worked so hard to earn, the appointment of someone who they believed held more gravitas than me.

My grandfather surveyed me with his intelligent eyes. His long, considered face was framed with bristly brows and a thick sweep of white hair.

My mum's sitting room, with its well-worn sofa and armchairs and chestnut-coloured cushions, gave me a shred of familiarity and comfort.

My father had walked out on us when I was seven years old to pursue a career in journalism. Working on the local paper, the *Bracken Way Observer*, hadn't been high profile enough. Niall Dunbar had far more lofty ambitions than that, wanting to cover international stories and win the Pulitzer Prize for intrepid journalism.

My parents got divorced a few years later.

I blinked several times, refocusing on my grandpa and my mother.

"This is just a blip. A bump in the road," he assured me.

"Yes. Well. It's a sodding big bump."

Grandpa pressed his lips together. "Things will sort themselves out in the end. They always do. You'll see."

Gerald Foyle was still a dapper man, even at eighty years of age, and had long possessed a penchant for snazzy waistcoats, which had endured from his twenties. Today, he was sporting a jade-green paisley style over a cream shirt and dark trousers.

He had been a real father figure in my life.

He had been born and raised in Bracken Way like me and had worked for a local boat building company for years, until his reluctant retirement fifteen years ago. He was also an eternal optimist.

I moved my tear-stained attention to Mum, who looked like she wanted to commit murder. She perched beside me on the sofa and reached her hand over to rest it on mine. "I can't believe the way you've been treated. All the hours and weekends you've given that company! I hope they have a good think about what they've done and offer you another post." She sniffed. "So, this American woman was given the senior role instead of you?"

I swiped at my face with the back of my hand. "Yes."

"And that's why you've taken this extended leave?"

I nodded and dabbed at my eyes with a clean hankie Grandpa had just handed me.

Mum's expression stiffened even more. "Still, with your experience and your ability, if you feel scunnered by the way they've treated you – I know I do – you should have no problem getting a position with another publisher."

My heart hammered in my ears. Saying the words out loud sounded alien – like it was someone else speaking. "Right now, Mum, I don't know if I ever want to go back to publishing, let alone Literati, but I love what I do so much. That's why this has come as such a kick in the teeth."

She raised her brows in surprise. "But... but I don't understand? That is all you've ever wanted to do, sweetheart."

"I know, Mum, but I had my heart set on that position. I'd been led to believe it was mine." I rubbed at my face. "I put my life on hold for Literati. I gave so much of myself to them and this is how they've repaid me. I don't know that I'm prepared to do that again."

She frowned. Then a sudden helplessness took over her features. "I just want you to be happy, love."

I leant over and squeezed her hand. "I know you do, Mum. I'm not sure what else I would do instead, though. If I did decide not to go back to Literati, I suppose I could offer freelance editorial services. That would bring in some extra income."

Mum mulled this over. "Well, you would need to think about your finances. What about your flat in Glasgow? What would you do about that?"

As I continued to sit there, thoughts tumbled through my head. God. There would be so many decisions to make. "I'm renting it out for the three months I'm here, to bring in some extra income and I still have Grandma's inheritance put aside."

Grandpa digested this for a few seconds and then gave me a confident nod. "Well, you know your own mind. In the meantime, don't make any decisions on anything. You'll know soon enough what you want to do."

I bent forward and gently clasped his weathered hands in mine, so grateful for his optimism. "I wish I had your confidence."

He gave a small smile. "You need time, lass. You don't know where you are right now or what you want. But you will."

Grandpa moved to speak again, but Mum got there first. "But what will you do, if you do decide you aren't going back?"

Maisie Dunbar could make worrying an Olympic sport. "Try not to fret, Mum. I'll just have to think about my options."

"Well, like I said, no making any decisions on your future right now," advised my grandfather, giving Mum a charged look. "You're still very upset."

I nodded, fixing a smile as Grandpa suggested that Mum put the kettle on.

She surveyed us both, sighed and vanished into the kitchen.

Once she was out of earshot, he lowered his voice to a whisper. "Once your mother has a cuppa and a biscuit, she'll be calmer and not quite as likely to want to go and rip the head off that boss of yours."

"It's going to take more than a cup of tea and a chocolate digestive to stop her worrying."

Grandpa nodded his head. "Och, like I said. A bump in the road, little dove. A bump in the road."

My heart constricted at hearing him call me what he had always called me since I was small, after we discovered an injured dove near the loch and fearing for its safety, we brought it home and nursed it back to health. I planted an affectionate kiss on his cheek.

Then I made my way through to the kitchen.

Mum was clattering around with the jar of tea bags. In the sitting room, my grandfather had switched on the TV for the lunchtime news. He had cranked up the volume, which made Mum pull a disapproving face. "I'm surprised they can't hear that television set in Dundee."

She opened the bread bin next and stashed a new pumpkin and sesame seeded loaf inside. "Lunch will be ready in a little while."

"Thanks, Mum." I tried to gather my resolve. "Promise me you won't worry. I know what you're like. I just need some time."

Mum swung round to face me. "Why didn't you tell us last week, Lexie? You phoned but never said a word about the real reason for all this time off."

"I thought it might be easier telling you and Grandpa face to face. I'm fine."

She picked up the kettle and moved to fill it from the tap. "You're not fine…"

"Maise! Maisie! Lexie! Get through here!" Grandpa's voice erupted from the sitting room.

Mum and I exchanged worried glances as she dumped the kettle by the sink and we both took off together back towards the sitting room.

"Dad. Are you alright? What is it? What's wrong?"

My grandfather's expression was tense.

I crouched down in front of him, still seated in his favourite armchair. "Are you ok, Grandpa? Aren't you feeling well?"

"No, lass, I'm fine," he managed after a pause, his attention focused over my shoulder at the burble coming from the TV. "Or at least I was until I saw that."

I gazed up at Mum from my crouched position, but she was also now staring at the television with a strange expression on her face. "Mum?"

I got up from the carpet and turned to look at the TV. "Please tell me all six of our lottery numbers have come up."

It took a few seconds for my eyes to register what I was looking at – or should I say, *who* I was looking at – in glorious colour. The craggy smile, pointed chin and sun-weathered complexion.

I blinked for several seconds. No. It couldn't be. It couldn't be him.

Chapter Three

I t was my father, reporting for the national news, with the dazzling White House and its swathe of lawns laid out behind him.

My eyes ricocheted from him, as I listened to his throaty voice, to the well-cut navy pinstriped suit, pale shirt and slick of silky olive-green tie he was wearing. He was talking about the US president's forthcoming visit to Europe.

Along the bottom of the screen, the ticker stated, *Niall Dunbar, Washington Correspondent.*

The last I heard, he was working for some big broadsheet newspaper in San Francisco, when he deigned to award me the odd phone call, birthday and Christmas card; that was when he happened to remember. I would read them with indifference, before shredding them and tossing them in the bin.

You don't miss what you've never had.

I gawped back at the image on the screen. I knew I resembled my father. My eyes mirrored his, a bright light grey, as did my quizzical brows and wide mouth. Sometimes, I caught Mum studying me when she thought I wasn't looking. No doubt seeing the echoes of her ex-husband in her only daughter.

Mum had paled. She pushed a hunk of dark hair behind one ear. "Turn it off please, Dad."

My grandfather stared up at her from his armchair.

"I said, turn it off. Now!"

Then she fled out of the sitting room and back through to the kitchen. Grandpa snatched up the remote control and jabbed it at the TV. My father's image vanished.

"For Christ's sake. Just when I thought we might have seen the last of that bastard… Pity this thing hadn't been a bloody light sabre," grumbled my grandpa under his breath. I watched him slam the remote back down on the little mahogany table beside him. "Still, looks like he finally got what he wanted: up the front on the telly. That man always had to be the centre of attention."

I shot a worried look towards the kitchen, where I could hear my mother muttering to herself and bashing things around. "I'll go and check on Mum."

"Aye, thanks, lass. I'll be through in a minute."

We'd heard through the journalistic grapevine that my father had had a few dalliances with glamorous colleagues over the years, but had never remarried. Neither had my mother.

Mum was thumping three mugs around in the kitchen, her expression pinched. "Can you believe that?" she shot over her shoulder. "Just when I think I've put him behind me, up he pops again like a bloody Jack-in-the-box!"

She swung round to face me. Her rich blue eyes threatened to leak furious tears. "It's been years. I think the last time I saw him was when he had that feature and his photo in *The Mail*." She returned to clashing the mugs. "I think it was some piece he'd written about politicians' expenses." Her voice wobbled.

I dashed over and slipped one arm around her shoulders. "If you bang those any harder, Mum, they'll hear you in Australia."

She thrust the kettle under the tap to fill it. "Well, looks like he's done well for himself. Swanning around in the States and on TV too." She fought to keep her voice steady. "Did you see that suit he was wearing? I bet that wasn't out of some cheap catalogue."

Then her shoulders dipped under her fitted top.

"Mum?"

She closed her eyes for a few moments. "Despite everything, despite him walking out on us like that..." Her voice faded.

"What?"

She forced a smile. "Oh, just forget it."

"No, come on. You were going to say something."

She started to talk about Mrs Hamilton's grandson passing his driving test. I folded my arms. "I'm going to keep asking you what you were about to say. And stop trying to change the subject."

She set down the kettle and surprised me with a short laugh. She dropped her voice, so Grandpa wouldn't hear, although there wasn't much chance of that anyway, going by the volume the TV had to be at for him. He was a stubborn bugger about wearing his hearing aid. Mum gave her head a sorry shake. "I know this is going to sound pathetic, but Niall Dunbar will always be the love of my life. There. I said it. Satisfied?"

"Tell me something I don't know."

Mum blinked at me. "So, you're not surprised?"

"Are you kidding? I've known for years how you still feel about him." I pursed my lips. "He doesn't deserve love like that."

Mum eyed me. "No, he doesn't."

I heard a puffing noise behind me.

Grandpa had materialised in the kitchen doorway, concern for us both etched into his features. "I wouldn't waste any more time or energy on that man. I know he's your father, Lexie but he's a waste of space."

Mum flashed me a guilty glance.

"He's not my father. Well, he is biologically, but that's as far as it goes." I offered my grandfather a soft smile as he stood there, hunched in the kitchen doorway. "You know who I think of as my dad. I'm looking at him right now."

He blushed a fetching shade of pink. "Och, away with you!"

Mum stood there, gazing out of her kitchen window at the stippled roofs of the other surrounding cottages. She wasn't hearing a word of what we were saying.

I shot a hot look back through at the sitting room TV. Bloody typical. If we'd been five minutes later switching on the news, we wouldn't have seen that dashing, tanned expression of his.

"Right. Enough about Niall Dunbar," I announced, pushing

forced joviality into my voice. "I'm looking forward to lunch, Mum."

The next couple of days rolled past to midweek.

Mum had been doing mad trolley dashes around local shops and had purchased some new fluffy towels for me to use, as well as a lavender-scented candle and a gorgeous set of rose-gold printed bedding.

I was meandering by the castle, when Mrs Dinklage from the gift shop, emerged out of nowhere, like an inquisitive tropical bird, with her penchant for multi-coloured dangly earrings and draped chiffon scarves. "I heard you were back, Lexie. Just a flying visit?"

I nodded and murmured in the right places. Blimey. You weren't allowed any secrets in Bracken Way. "Yes, something like that."

"No young man in your life then?"

"Nope. Too busy."

"That's the spirit. I bet that grand job of yours keeps you out of mischief."

I squinted against the sunshine. I didn't feel like explaining the whole, sorry situation.

Sweet and harmless though she was, I also knew that my conversation with Mrs Dinklage, would soon be public knowledge.

She opened her mouth to say something else, but I started to edge away. "Anyway Mrs Dinklage, nice to speak to you. Take care. Must go. Sorry."

I would have to move on from the Literati disappointment.

I had to. I couldn't sit and do nothing for the next three months. It would drive me insane. I was used to being occupied.

So, gathering myself together after breakfast the next morning, I phoned a couple of writing magazines for their advertising rates and began to compose a post to promote my editorial services on social media. The fact that I'd been an editor for a number of high-profile authors should be a real selling point, I reassured myself. Surely that would lure frustrated writers? It would also help me keep my hand in with my editing and copy-writing skills and boost my savings in the meantime.

Still dreaming of securing that publishing deal?

Attracting the attention of that agent?

I am a freelance editor with several years' experience in the book industry, editing for such prestigious authors as Sir Stephen Todd and Dame Alicia Kilroy.

Send me your first three chapters and synopsis and I will make suggestions and provide direct advice for your manuscript. I will also provide a three-page detailed report, indicating problem areas, as well as concentrating on your writing strengths and weaknesses.

Where I feel your story may require additional work, such as character development or scene setting, I will highlight this.

Once I receive your first three chapters and synopsis, I will confirm receipt and provide the detailed report to you within six weeks of submitting it to me.

Don't delay – start making your writing dream a reality today!

Once I'd posted the ad on my Facebook, Instagram and

Twitter accounts, I decided to leave Mum's and take a meander down the high street for some fresh air.

The high street was a mish-mash of browsing locals and spring holiday makers, milling around the shop windows and availing themselves of takeaway coffee or a dribbly ice cream cone. Others stood and admired the rippling, whispering rush of the loch shoreline and Bracken Castle gazing down at them from its majestic hilltop.

What a week it had been!

I recalled Mum's expression again, when she'd seen my dad on TV, pain and anger battling it out in her eyes.

Mum had been on a few dates over the years and had a couple of male friends who escorted her to the odd local function, but she always shied away from making anything more serious.

Whenever I had pointed this out, she would go all prickly, saying she preferred her own company with no complications. In other words, none of those other men were my father. *She should be delighted about that*, an irritated voice hammered in my ear.

My mum was a lovely-looking woman, with a wonderful smile and a kind heart. My erstwhile dad didn't deserve the feelings she still carried for him.

I couldn't remember the last time I'd had an actual, proper conversation with my father. I think it was around the time of my thirtieth birthday, so that would have been November.

I squirmed at the recollection. The call had lasted about a minute, as he said he was on a tight deadline with the newspaper he was working on at the time. We never seemed to have much to say to one another.

I had more camaraderie with Frank, our postman, than I did with my own dad.

I decided not to give my father another thought. He didn't deserve it. I had much more important things to think about, like what my future was going to look like. At the moment, I had no idea.

I tapped along the cobbled high street, the breeze whipping my ponytail around. I was used to having a plan, a focus. I felt like I was a little boat tethered in a harbour, bobbing about on the tide and not going anywhere.

"Lexie! Oh goodness! What are you doing back here? I thought it was you."

Oh shit. Here we go again.

Get used to it, whispered a resigned voice in my head. *You wanted to come back to your home town. You knew what to expect.*

Glasgow had the anonymity, but there were tainted memories floating around there now. At least here in Bracken Way, I had Mum, Grandpa and the freedom of its clean, sharp fresh air.

I whirled round with a strained smile plastered on my face.

Several intrigued expressions, led by Flora Simmonds, the retired school secretary from Bracken Way Primary School, came into view.

More questions came shooting towards me like a bullet. "How's your job in publishing?" barked Flora. "Just taking some holiday?"

I squinted through the spring morning sunshine. "Yes." Several pairs of eyes bored into me. *Oh, get it over with, Lexie.* Seeing me around the town for the next three months, would raise their suspicions even further. "I'm taking extended leave." I hesitated and gathered myself. "Actually, I don't know if I want to go back to my publishing job."

"But what would you do instead?" pursued a shocked Flora. "I don't think there's much going in the way of vacancies around here."

I was tempted to ask Flora if she'd ever considered motivational speaking. "I'm not sure. I'm going to do some editorial freelance work in the meantime."

Flora's expression became almost dreamy. "I've read all of Dame Alicia's books. They really are sublime. You edited them, didn't you Lexie?"

I nodded.

She dropped her tone to a conspiratorial level. "I don't suppose you have Dame Alicia's phone number? I would love to invite someone of her calibre for supper. I feel we'd have such a rapport."

I clutched my bag tighter to my side, keen to make a sharp exit and ignore her question. Dame Alicia would have me hunted down and flayed.

One of Flora's friends piped up from behind her like a meerkat. "There was a feature in one of those glossy magazines about Dame Alicia last week. Her home is spectacular. It reminded me a lot of what used to be the Stafford-Wells property. You know, that old house out on the coastal road."

Flora's expression became odd. "We're not idiots, Martha," she snapped. "We're aware of which house it is!"

Martha blinked in consternation. "Alright, Flora. Keep your hair on. I was merely saying Dame Alicia's house looked rather like the Stafford-Wells place, with its balconied—"

Flora cut her off. "Yes, you've already said that." She

fiddled around with her rose- imprinted scarf. "I'm sure Dame Alicia has more class in her little finger than that Stafford-Wells lot ever did."

Everybody else exchanged puzzled glances.

I saw an opportunity to escape while they were bickering. "Well, thank you once again for your kind comments. Now, I really must get on."

Flora gathered her nautical jacket around her, stuck in her own thoughts for a few moments. Then she rallied her troops. "Once again, Lexie, so sorry to hear about the demise of your job. Dear me. It's true what they say, isn't it? There's always something going on in one's life!"

"It's not a demise," I replied, my face tightening. "I'm just considering my options."

"Send our regards to your mother and grandfather," added Flora, thrusting out one arm to indicate to her squad it was time to go.

The cluster of well-turned-out women moved away, chattering and proclaiming in the windswept April sunshine.

I stepped to one side, allowing a harassed woman pushing a buggy to ease past me on the pavement.

Now that I was alone again, I decided to stroll along to the end of the high street and pop into our local bookshop, Book Ends. It'd make me feel closer to Grandma Pattie. The prospect of being surrounded by gorgeous books, with their vanilla scent and embossed covers, made me pick up speed in my urgency to get there. The whisper from the pages as you turn them over; the spines standing to attention on the shelves; the feel of someone else's thoughts and creativity, cradled in your hands.

Even though it felt as though publishing had turned its back on me, the lure of being in Book Ends was all-consuming. Nothing got my heart racing more than the thought of a bookshop. Ok, Ryan Reynolds did, but for different reasons.

I struggled to recall the last time I'd been in Book Ends, what with just snatching the odd harassed flying visit back to see Mum and Grandpa, while I lived and worked in town.

Book Ends was a mullion-windowed affair, with flower boxes and an old-fashioned swinging shop sign above the entrance. It also possessed an uninterrupted and enviable view of the loch.

Trevor Newman had owned it for the past thirty years. It was a treasure trove, deceptively large despite its bijou appearance from the outside and stocked every genre, appealing to everyone from literary lovers and romcom fans to amateur sleuths devouring crime, thrillers, and history buffs.

Grandma Pattie started taking me into the bookshop from the age of about four and she would sit and read to me or tell me stories about the books on the shelves. It seemed so sophisticated and grown-up. Other times, she would tell me tales about the authors themselves.

I devoured everyone from Judith Kerr and Enid Blyton to Wilbur Smith and Sydney Sheldon, all under the auspices of my book-loving grandmother and the magical, enticing atmosphere of Book Ends.

There had been a few scattered tables for book lovers to sit at, peruse their purchases or just relax and absorb the serene atmosphere.

Trevor Newman was a charming well-read widower, who was now in his late sixties, and who had encouraged me when

I was a self-conscious teenager, prattling on about how much I wanted to work in publishing.

He'd offered me a summer job during the school holidays and I would spend my lunch breaks on the shop floor, nibbling on the packed lunch Mum had made me and savouring the sights and scents of the books, fascinated by which novels customers were buying and imagining my name appearing in the acknowledgements from grateful authors, saying what a talented and encouraging editor I was.

The sign of the bookshop ahead spurred me onwards, its gold and chocolate lettering a welcome sight, as it gently swung in the breeze.

But as I negotiated my way around a couple of shoppers engaged in animated conversation, I noticed an odd triangular sign had just been erected and was jutting out above the bookshop door.

What did it say?

I drew up level with the entryway.

No. That couldn't be right. I must be imagining it.

Closing Down – Shop for Lease.

Chapter Four

F lora Simmonds and her collection of compatriots were standing a few feet away from me, after emerging from the nearby shoe shop.

They had noticed the sign too and were as appalled as I was.

"What on earth...?" gasped Flora. "Did any of you know about this?" There was a collective shaking of heads.

The man who had just put up the sign, had already scrambled down from his ladder and was beating a hasty retreat to his car.

Flora did her best to accost him, but he was sheltering inside his white Volvo, the words Carter & McKinlay Estate Agents running along each side of the vehicle. Without so much as a backward glance, he threw the car into first gear and shot off.

Flora finally noticed I was standing next to her. "Did you know about this, Lexie?"

"No," I managed, my throat tight. I stared through the

bookshop windows at the rainbow array of book spines, feeling thrown. "No, I didn't."

Trevor Newman had just finished tidying underneath the counter and I couldn't see any customers milling around inside despite the fact there was an "open" sign in the window.

On seeing the swell of shocked faces gathered outside the entrance, Trevor emerged from his shop. He took an apprehensive step backwards, as questions were flung at him from every direction. "Why are you closing down?" "When did you make that decision?" "What on earth are you doing that for?!"

He raised his hands, as though trying to deflect them. "One at a time please!"

"Why are you selling up?" persisted one of Flora's friends. "Book Ends has been part of the community here for donkeys' years."

Trevor's huge dark eyes were woeful behind his John Lennon spectacles. "Believe me, it hasn't been an easy decision." He glanced over his bony shoulder, as though to check the bookshop was still there. "It's not the same since I lost my darling wife, Naomi. I've struggled on for the last three years, but the early starts, not to mention the passion… It's just not there anymore."

My heart gave a jolt of empathy for him. It was like listening to my grandpa talk about my grandmother. But the loss of the bookshop, a comforting, familiar and traditional sight in our high street, would be a very difficult one for the town to come to terms with. It had opened the year I was born.

"And Tamsin isn't interested in taking it over?" asked the same woman.

Tamsin was Trevor and Naomi's only child, now married and living in Sydney with her husband and three children. "No. She has her interior design career and her life in Australia and has no interest in taking over the bookshop here."

More images of me and Grandma Pattie marvelling at the book covers together shimmered in front of my eyes. Then I saw myself in there as a blushing, awkward teenager, serving customers behind the counter and taking every opportunity I could to marvel at the new books as they arrived.

"So, you're closing down so you can retire?" I asked, not able to conceal the wobble in my voice.

He nodded. "Yes, Lexie. I think it's time." He thrust one thumb behind him. "Sales haven't been what they were for a long time now. What with online shopping and the supermarkets selling paperbacks, it seems like I don't have much choice."

Flora rolled her eyes. "Well, I think the Bracken Way community should have been informed first, before you took such a momentous step." With a purse of her lips, she and her friends marched away back up the high street, muttering like the witches in *Macbeth*.

Poor man. It couldn't have been a decision he had taken lightly. Anyone would have thought he had decided to close down Book Ends just to spite Flora Simmonds and her cronies!

I lingered, watching a myriad of emotions cross Trevor's face. He stuffed his hands in his trouser pockets and surveyed the closing down sign again.

"Are you alright?"

He watched the chattering tourists as they ambled past. "Ach. I'm not so sure about that."

I followed him inside the bookshop, leaving behind the echoes of children's laughter, the trickle of traffic and the throng of tourists.

The interior of Book Ends was a world away from the crumbly castle and shimmery loch shore. The shop smelled of beeswax and vanilla.

Heavy dark rosewood bookcases ran the four sides of the shop interior, broken up by Formica cream tables and chairs and a couple of squashy bean bags.

The wooden counter, also in rosewood, was situated along the back of the left wall.

Light, playful jazz interchanged with Scottish bagpipes through the concealed speakers. The place hadn't changed at all.

Trevor observed me out of his gold-rimmed, round spectacles. "Anyway, enough about my woes. The Bracken Way gossip machine tells me you're going to be around for a while."

I hooked my straw bag from my shoulder and dumped it down by my feet onto the scuffed, hardwood floor that looked like it was desperate for some tender loving care and a slick of varnish. I let out a defeated sigh. "Yes. Three months. I've taken all the leave I've built up at work. I don't know how I feel about going back." I rubbed the back of my neck. "I was overlooked for the role of senior commissioning editor. They gave the role to an American high-flier."

"Dear me. I'm so sorry, Lexie. That must have hurt." He stared around himself. "We spend so much of our time at work, I should know. You have to enjoy it, otherwise what's the point?" And as if to articulate what he was saying, he gestured around Book Ends with a flip of one gnarled hand. "This place means the world to me but it's time." Sadness clouded up again in his dark eyes.

"Yes, sometimes you just have to move on," I agreed.

"Lexie, I'm so sorry. What can I say?"

"There's nothing you can say, Trevor." I turned to appreciate the bookshop's enviable vista, watching the mirrored surface of the loch. The scenery rose and fell behind it and clotted bursts of heather in pink and purple were studded on the hillsides. "My pride has taken one hell of a mauling, but I'll just have to try and put it behind me."

"That's the way," encouraged Trevor. "So, what's your plan?"

"Plan?"

"What are you going to do?"

I found myself running my fingers up and down the polished counter. "To be honest, I've no idea."

He gave a brief nod. "Well, I'm sure that whatever you decide to do next, it'll be successful. And you do have some time to weigh up your options."

"I do. Thank you."

Trevor's voice dragged me back. "You've got a very impressive track record in the book industry."

I halted my fingers as they sought out the knots and grains on the counter. "That's very kind of you to say that." I gave a small smile. "I'm going to offer freelance editorial services to writers."

"That's good. It'll keep you out of mischief," he teased.

I glanced out of the shop windows. The sun was fighting

through some cloud and was stippling over the top of the loch water like little gold stars.

"I'm sure there are quite a few frustrated Dan Browns and Danielle Steeles out there, who'll keep a great editor like you busy. You've been warned, Lexie!"

Then his expression drifted into something more wistful. "It only seems like last week that your Grandma Pattie would bring you in here for a browse."

I blinked at him as I took in the bookshelves again, creaking under the weight of the grinning novels. "She used to buy me a new book every time we came in."

Much to my embarrassment, a sudden wave of emotion came out of nowhere and caught me off guard. It was a painful, biting cacophony over not getting the senior editor job, my dad's sudden appearance on TV and now the loss of this gorgeous bookshop. It was morphing together into one giant lump and I felt like I was being crushed under the weight of it. I could feel it pushing down, draining me of any shreds of optimism I might have had.

Hot tears stung the corners of my eyes.

Trevor didn't say anything. He reached into the pocket of his brown cords and plucked out a freshly washed and ironed hankie. He handed it across the counter to me.

I snuffled into it. "Thank you. I'm sorry."

"There's no need to apologise."

"I'm really going to miss this place." I swallowed, forcing out a grim smile. "I hope whoever buys it keeps it going as a bookshop."

Trevor looked cynical. "That would be wonderful, but I think unlikely. Like I said, too much competition from the online retailers and the supermarkets now." He sighed. "No doubt it'll be transformed into some upmarket homeware shop, selling candles for sixty pounds a pop."

The thought of Book Ends not being here anymore, made my stomach twist. My late grandma would have been heartbroken too. "So many people will miss this place and not just because of all these amazing books. It's been such a large part in people's lives around here."

"Aye. I know, lass. I feel so guilty about it, but what can I do? Folks don't have a lot of disposable income nowadays and unfortunately, visiting their local bookshop drops down their list of priorities." He lowered his voice, agonised." All things considered, I think it's time me and Book Ends parted company."

A preoccupied look took over his despondent features again. He turned his attention to some ten pence pieces in the till.

I gazed around, my attention flitting from the mullioned, gleaming windows to the embossed spines of the hardbacks and paperbacks lined up on the shelves.

My head returned to the horrified comments from Flora Simmonds and her entourage about the bookshop closing. Perhaps if the locals had been more supportive of Book Ends in the first place, Trevor wouldn't feel like he had no option but to call time on it.

I took in the unmistakeable scent of print and paper. I could see my teenage self as though it were yesterday, in my trainers and tight jeans, tugging out the steps and clambering up them to fetch novels from the higher shelves. I had plaits and my feet felt like they were too big for the rest of my body. Working here during the school holidays, had been my idea of heaven.

This couldn't really be the end of Book Ends, could it?

I surveyed the interior. It was like a Tardis in here. A modest appearance from the outside, but inside, it was big and brimming with potential. All that extra space towards the back of the shop too.

Book Ends had so much more to give, not just to the locals of Bracken Way, but to the tourists, day trippers and second homers who flocked here. It was just stuck in the past. For thirty years, it had been a part of the community, but it hadn't evolved. The old-fashioned furnishings and drab, weary decor confirmed it.

If only Trevor would decide not to close up and give Book Ends a makeover instead. Inject some twenty-first century pizazz into the place?

"What about not giving up yet?" The words were out of my mouth before I knew it. I flushed shocking-pink.

"What do you mean?"

I stared around myself at the tired Formica tables. Oh well. I'd started now. "What if you gave Book Ends an upgrade? Perhaps you could give the interior and exterior a fresh lick of paint; update the shelving; modernise the furniture; undertake some advertising?"

Trevor stared at me with a mournful expression from behind his glasses. "I think it might take more to rejuvenate the shop than that."

"Then do more." I pinned him to the spot with my growing enthusiasm. "You could run book-based competitions and events; hold book signings for prominent authors; have themed displays in your windows."

I carried on. "I know you won't like this suggestion, but I'm going to make it anyway. You could create social media accounts for Book Ends."

Trevor let out an agonised groan. "Oh God, no. All that faffing around." He gave a theatrical shudder. "I did take a look at all that Twitter and Insta-whatsit once, but I ended up with a migraine."

"But all the faffing around would be worth it."

Trevor listened as I described the ever-growing community of book bloggers, readers and authors on the likes of Instagram and Twitter. "You're missing out on so much engagement. You have to remind everyone that Book Ends is still here. I know it can be a bit intimidating, but all businesses need that sort of presence now. If you don't, you get left behind."

He rolled his eyes, unimpressed.

"You could always get someone to assist you. They could post details about Books of the Week, read-a-longs and competitions."

He stared around himself at the familiar jaded paint and shabby tables and beanbags.

"You could put up details about three for two book offers; authors who are making a splash; ask followers to talk about what books they remember from their childhood – that kind of thing."

Trevor digested the suggestions that were tumbling out of me in a torrent of growing excitement.

"You could organise reading sessions with authors and

charge a small fee for people to attend." Another idea struck me. "Do you have a Book Ends loyalty card?"

Trevor flushed. "No."

"That sort of thing is very popular with shoppers. Buy six books and get the seventh free, or customers could accumulate points towards future purchases."

"Er. Right."

"And do you have a Book Ends gift card?"

There was that embarrassed flash of colour in his cheeks again.

"People can come in and if they aren't sure what book to buy someone as a present, they can have the card loaded with a certain amount of money and the receiver can choose what book or books they want."

Trevor gazed at me, his black arched brows rising even further to his receding dark hairline. The shelves of books were reflected in his spectacles. "What else would you do, if you were in charge?"

"*Me?*"

"Yes. You."

Oh God. I hoped I hadn't offended him with my torrent of suggestions. But if there was any way of making Trevor see that giving up might not be the best solution, then perhaps some ideas might make him reconsider.

I eyed the bookshop windows, which were decked out in short, brown, frilly tie back curtains. "I would run seasonal themes. You could have pink and red covered books in the window on Valentine's Day; blue and yellow buckets and spades with yellow and blue toned books during the summer, with piles of romantic beach reads surrounding them."

"Right. I see." He gestured around himself. "And you mentioned giving the place a freshen up. So, what would you do there?"

"I'd repaint the walls and the front door, something bright and eye-catching, have new shelves installed, have the floor revarnished and remove the Formica tables and chairs you have."

"Oh?"

"I'd have a few chairs around, but not replace the beanbags, because the children always like those. You want people to feel welcomed and be fascinated with the books, but not treat Book Ends like a café by sitting down and not buying anything."

I pointed to the once-cream bean bags. "Maybe go for ones in primary colours though, rather than that shade, which can look dirty in no time."

I suspected I knew the answer, but I decided to ask Trevor anyway. "Do you still employ Esther and Wilf?"

Trevor nodded.

I dropped my voice, even though there was no one around. "Please don't think I'm being harsh, but I'd suggest you rethink your current staff." Esther Potts and Wilf Mackie were both retired, pleasant people and former members of the Bracken Way community council. They'd been helping Trevor out for years in the shop on an ad hoc basis, serving and replenishing the bookshelves.

"I know they're both long-time friends of yours, but if I were you, I'd think about taking on a couple of new members of staff."

Trevor looked anguished.

"I don't mean straight away," I clarified. "I think you'll

need at least one full-time person and maybe another on part-time hours."

I tried to stem the hot lava of ideas that were coursing through my head all of a sudden. "Sorry. I'm going on rather a lot."

"Not at all, Lexie. You're enthusiastic. Anyway, I asked you." He reddened. "To be honest, it'd be a relief to escape from Esther's tales about her musical theatre grandson."

I turned to drink in the view from the bookshop windows. Nothing ever stayed the same.

Trevor narrowed his eyes at me. "Are you alright?"

I cleared my throat. "Yes. Thank you. I'm fine." I gathered myself together. "I'll be sad to see this place go. It can't have been an easy decision for you to make."

My eyes swept up to the ceiling. "I know Naomi loved this place every bit as much as you do."

He looked troubled. "Yes, she adored it."

I offered what I hoped was a sympathetic smile. "Then she would understand why you feel like you've no option." I bit back a lump in my throat. "Sorry again for wittering on like that."

I took one final forlorn glance around and then hurried out of the shop and back down the high street. I marched past the florist's, its window wreathed in sunshine-coloured blooms. Despite my frantic suggestions for improving Book Ends, I got the feeling I'd been wasting my time.

No more Book Ends in Bracken Way. The very idea seemed preposterous.

Chapter Five

I arrived back at my mum's house.

I was glad to be returning to somewhere comforting and familiar. The news about Book Ends had thrown me.

Grandpa was pottering about in the kitchen.

Mum was always out on a Friday morning, when she would pop by for a coffee with a disabled, elderly lady, Fiona, who lived round the corner.

"Only me!" I called, after opening the front door with my spare key, clattering it shut behind me and shrugging off my denim jacket. I hung it up in the hall and made my way into the kitchen.

The familiarity of home wrapped itself around me, like one giant hug.

"Aye, it's only you," beamed Grandpa, planting a bristly kiss on my cheek. "Want a cup?" He indicated to the kettle.

"No thanks."

I leant against Mum's pine kitchen worktop, taking in the lime hessian blind at the window and her ceramic mug tree.

Grandpa slid me a look. "What is it, lass? You want to talk about something."

My cheeks flipped with guilty colour. "You know me so well."

Grandpa rattled his teaspoon and abandoned it in his empty mug. "So come on then, Lexie. What's bothering you?"

I stared down at my trainers, before looking back up and into my grandfather's expectant face. "Did you know Book Ends is closing down?"

He widened his crinkly pale blue eyes in surprise. "Is it? Are you sure? Bloody hell! That's the first I've heard." He looked thoughtful. "I know Trevor has had a tough time of it since he lost his wife." He paused. "I know how that feels." He appraised me. "That's such a shame, though. Och, Bracken Way will be the poorer for losing it. Pattie loved taking you there."

"I know she did. And I loved going in there with her, even when I grew up."

He eyed me again with curiosity. "So, what is it you wanted to talk about?"

"Oh, Grandpa. I don't know."

He gestured to the kitchen table and we both sat down next to one another.

I slumped back in Mum's kitchen chair, as if the air and fight had been sucked out of me.

I could hear Mum's sitting room clock delivering its subtle click from above her stone fireplace across the hallway.

My grandfather studied me. "Well, you must have wanted to talk to me for a reason. I know I'm scintillating company."

I laughed, despite my inner turmoil. "To be honest, I don't

know what I'm doing anymore. I don't know where I'm headed and then hearing about Book Ends; I suppose I'm feeling a bit off-kilter right now."

Through Mum's kitchen window, lunchtime sunshine was managing to punch its way through a bank of surly cloud.

Grandpa digested what I'd just told him. "I can't say I'm surprised, sweetheart." He offered a supportive wink. "But things have a habit of working themselves out in the end."

One corner of his mouth hitched up under his silver moustache. "I must say though, I'm stunned that Trevor has decided to call it a day. Grandma Pattie used to adore reading the romances she bought from there."

I smiled at the images in my head I had of her, scrambling to scoop the latest Dame Barbara Cartland, Loretta Chase and Julie Garwood from the Book Ends shelves.

A knock on the front door, made me almost bang my knees on the underside of the kitchen table.

"That'll be your mother. She said she was going to drop by the corner shop on the way back from Fiona's for a few bits." He rolled his eyes. "But we know what the definition of a "few bits" is with your mum. She'll have emptied poor old Eric Robertson's shelves like she's taking part in *Supermarket Sweep*."

"Well, let me come and help."

I followed my grandpa's tall, thin frame towards the door.

He eased it open.

It wasn't Mum though, laden down with bulging groceries and looking harassed.

It was Trevor, out of breath. His complexion was flushed.

He exchanged a few pleasantries with my grandfather.

"So, Trevor, what can we do you for?" asked Grandpa.

Trevor pushed his glasses up his nose. "Actually, it's Lexie I've come to have a word with, Gerald."

I was bemused. "Me?"

Trevor glinted behind his spectacles. "Yes." He shot me a bashful expression. "It's about Book Ends." He inhaled a mouthful of air. "I've been thinking long and hard about what we were talking about; you know, improving the shop, giving it a new lease of life and purpose, dragging it kicking and screaming into the modern day. That goes for me too, I suppose."

I frowned at him, thrown by his endless rush of excited words. "Oh. Right."

Trevor's shining dark eyes glinted with anticipation. "Sorry. I'm probably not making much sense at the moment." He struggled to steady his voice. "The thing is, what you were saying started to make a lot of sense to me."

"Oh good." I brightened, feeling stunned. "That sounds promising." I angled my head to one side. "So does that mean...?"

"I've decided I'm not going to close down after all."

A delighted smile broke out across my face. At last! Some good news for a change. "Well, that's great."

"I didn't want to give up the shop. I felt like I had no choice. But not anymore."

"Now, you can see a possible new direction for Book Ends?" I grinned. "Wow. Well, I'm thrilled for you. That sounds great."

"Well, it will be great," he continued, looking awkward.

"Or it could be." He hopped from brogue to brogue on my mum's front doorstep. "That rather depends on you."

"Sorry?"

Trevor looked hopeful. His fingers kept tumbling over one another. "I'd like you to manage the bookshop for me, Lexie." He took a step closer, his expression brimming with hope. "Come and turn Book Ends around."

Chapter Six

My grandpa looked almost as shocked as I did.

He jerked his head from me to Trevor and back again, risking giving himself a crick in the neck.

"What?" I croaked, my mouth flapping open in a spectacular fashion. "Sorry?"

My grandfather's brows rocketed upwards. "Goodness me. Well, you had better come on in, Trevor," he urged. "Don't stand out there."

Trevor sat himself down in one of Mum's armchairs. He couldn't contain himself. "After Lexie left a short while ago, all I could think about was her wonderful suggestions for updating and revamping Book Ends."

He shot forward in the armchair. "The more I thought about your ideas, the more they made sense." Trevor rubbed at his sharp, clean-shaven jaw. "I don't want to give up Book Ends. Of course, I don't. There are too many memories of Naomi in its four walls." His voice drifted off. "But I can't do this alone, Lexie. I'm too much of an old fart, set in my ways for that." He knotted his long fingers together in his lap. "Book Ends hasn't moved with the times. It's still stuck in the past. So am I."

He offered me an encouraging smile as his legs crossed and uncrossed, as though they were struggling to decide what to do with themselves. "But if I keep it on and you become manager, I think you could be onto something." Trevor glanced across at my grandpa, residing as usual with his mahogany table at his side. "Those ideas you have about the displays, promotions and Insta-Twit…"

I let out a small, stunned laugh. "It's Instagram and Twitter."

He was asking me to take over the revamp of Book Ends? Manage the shop? A place that had been part of Bracken Way for thirty years? This was crazy! I couldn't do that. Imagine the responsibility, the weight of it pressing down on me, the judgemental looks from the likes of Flora Simmonds.

Trevor's imploring voice crashed through my rambling thoughts. "See what I mean? I haven't a clue about that kind of thing. But you do."

I was struggling to take this in. This was ridiculous. I'd never managed a business before. My hands rose and fell. "Look, I'm very flattered, but Trevor, this is out of my comfort zone."

"It didn't sound like it when you were telling me all your ideas and suggestions." He paused, his face breaking into a hopeful expression across from me. "And you're right about Esther and Wilf. They're good friends and were very kind to me when I lost Naomi, but they don't belong working in Book

Ends. The shop needs new blood and enthusiasm." He rubbed his hands together nervously. "I wouldn't be here if I didn't think you could turn the fortunes of my bookshop around."

Trevor flapped out the hem of his raincoat. "I have the funds in place to do this, to give it a good go." His dark eyes flashed. "My intention would be to hand the day-to-day running of the shop over to you and we'd discuss rebranding, changing the decor, starting up social media accounts, introducing the gift card and loyalty card schemes you mentioned." Trevor gave my grandfather an encouraging glance. "You would manage the full overhaul of the shop, Lexie. And when – not if – business improves, we can think about recruiting a couple of new members of staff."

My grandpa's brows fenced. A smile flirted at the corners of his mouth, lifting his silvery moustache. "Well, well. It all sounds very exciting, my lass."

Everybody knew how book obsessed I was and had been since I was a child, but taking on something like this... well, what if it didn't work out? What if I made a colossal mess of the whole thing? The locals would hunt me down with pitchforks.

Grandpa fixed his light gaze on me. "Lexie?"

Self-doubt gnawed at me. This was happening so fast; it was as if I was struggling to jump from a speeding merry-go-round. I opened and closed my mouth a few times. "You're putting so much faith in me, Trevor. Please believe me, I'm very flattered. Really. I just don't know if I could pull something like this off. It's such a big undertaking."

Trevor's dark eyes flashed with brimming optimism. "We won't know unless we try. Let's see what you can do." He gave me a look. "My other option is just to close down and call it a day. Lease the shop. If Naomi were still here, you know what she'd say. She would tell us to at least give it a go."

My thoughts travelled to Trevor's sweet late wife. "That's unfair," I choked. "Mentioning Naomi."

Trevor gave an embarrassed shrug. "But it's true though."

I could hear my grandmother's strong, dignified voice in my head. *Och, if there's a chance the bookshop can be saved, you must take it! If you don't, you'll always wonder what if?*

I wasn't thinking straight. Was I actually considering doing this? My heart hammered faster. Managing the local bookshop – and a failing one at that.

My grandfather sat forward in his chair. "You're keeping us both in suspense here, Lexie, and I haven't got time on my side at my age."

I hesitated and blinked, lost in my own thoughts.

"We work on rebuilding the community spirit ethos of the place," carried on Trevor, undeterred. "That is what any good, local bookshop should be about." He pinned all his attention on me. "We give those online retailers and the supermarkets a run for their money."

I opened my mouth to speak, but he carried on. "I think the modern word is reboot?"

"Trevor, I'm not sure…"

He pushed his glasses back up his nose. "Tell you what. Why don't we give this arrangement with you taking over as manager a year and if things don't work out as planned, then so be it. Would that make you feel more comfortable?"

"A year?" I repeated.

"Aye. That way, we'll have given it a good old try and if

things don't work out as we hope, you can move on after twelve months to something else and I'll admit defeat and close down."

Managing Book Ends and trying to turn it around in a year? It would require a lot of hard work and creativity. It would be a huge gamble.

Cold, hard reality started to kick in. Hang on. Anyone would think I might actually be giving Trevor's job offer serious consideration!

I had to get a grip. I wasn't thinking straight. So much was happening, twisting and turning in my life. I needed to give my head a serious wobble. "I really appreciate you coming to speak to me about this, Trevor, but the answer is no."

I shot up from the sofa and tried to ignore my burrowing guilt at Trevor's crestfallen expression. "Thank you so much for thinking of me and for the job offer, but after what's happened, my confidence is rock bottom and I don't think I could be…"

"I think it's a great idea."

I stared down at my grandfather. "Sorry?"

He performed a casual shrug. "You know what books sell, Lexie. You're full of ideas. I think you could make a real go of this."

I started to protest, but my grandfather kept talking.

"Much better Trevor here keeps Book Ends and you give it a go for the year. At least you can try, rather than it be turned into some pretentious coffee shop."

The pale light was spiralling through the sitting room window now, nudging its way across the barley-coloured carpet. "It could still end up being turned into a pretentious coffee shop, Gramps."

"Yes, but there's a chance it won't be if you agree to help me," insisted Trevor.

"I know your grandmother would approve." Grandpa's eyes carried a faraway look. "And like Trevor just said, if he puts a twelve-month deadline on Book Ends' fortunes turning around and things don't go to plan – well, you haven't lost anything."

Now I had the two of them ganging up on me. Talk about defenceless. "You do realise this is emotional blackmail?"

Trevor almost hid a smile. "Maybe it is. But I can't even begin to make a go of this without you, Lexie."

The fact that I was even giving Trevor's job proposal consideration was freaking me out. My head was saying one thing and my heart was screaming another. "I'm worried that I won't be able to improve things for you, Trevor," I faltered. "It's a big challenge."

Trevor looked at me warmly. "Do you honestly think I would be here if I didn't think you could do it?"

From down the hall, the front door creaked open, making the three of us start.

"Hi, Dad. You, ok?" called Mum.

I stared down at Trevor and Grandpa as the front door clicked shut.

I was tired of making everyone else happy at the expense of my own fulfilment. I was tired of putting myself through physical and mental exhaustion as a junior editor, in the hope of getting noticed and promoted.

What about me for once?

What about what I wanted?

How about I do something that meant a lot to me? That would give something back to the community and provide a challenge? Twelve months to reverse the bookshop's fortunes and then...?

An excited, but nervous smile began to break out across my face.

Trevor's eyes grew behind his glasses. "Is that a yes?"

I stared back at Trevor and my grandfather.

I was going to undertake some freelance editing, but that wouldn't occupy all my time.

Was I going to take a chance on this? I needed to believe in myself more.

I found myself blowing out a cloud of air and answering before I had time to change my mind or debate it any longer. I would drive myself crazy if I did. "Yes. Alright. You win. I accept. Thank you."

Trevor gawped at me.

"I'll hand in my notice to Literati and I accept your job offer."

Realising what I'd just said, Trevor clapped his hands together with delight and sprang out of Mum's armchair.

Grandpa let out a small cheer.

"Wonderful," said Trevor, overflowing with renewed vigour. "Thank you, Lexie. Thank you so much."

We shook hands and then Trevor gave me a grateful, fatherly hug.

He tried to gather himself together. His voice cracked. "Right. No time like the present."

Mum was gawping at the three of us in confusion in the

sitting room doorway and still clutching her shopping bags. "What's going on here?"

Trevor beamed at her as he dashed past and headed for the front door. "Hello, Maisie. How are you? Now you can tell your mother your good news, while I ring the estate agents and have that closing down sign removed!"

Chapter Seven

The last week of April evaporated in an initial haze of joyous but terrified euphoria, before realisation started to kick in.

I had a tough job ahead of me, re-establishing Book Ends, and the last thing I wanted to do was disappoint Trevor.

Mum had been speechless at first by my job announcement, but once the initial surprise had worn off, she was soon enthusing about it. "Well, I don't see why you couldn't make a go of it." She'd cupped my face in her warm hands. "And as long as you're happy, that's all I care about." Then she'd scooped me into her arms and wished me the best of luck, before insisting on cracking open a bottle of bubbly she located in the dining room cupboard.

My mind was already cartwheeling with potential ideas. Visions of paint colour charts flitted through my head. I would suggest that we abandon the heavy claret walls and go for something more modern.

I would set aside time with Trevor to discuss new colour

schemes, the launch of the social media accounts, as well as advertising and promotional ideas.

I'd decided though, that my first priority should be a makeover for the shop.

And so later on that day, I gave Trevor a call and we arranged for me to drop by Book Ends at ten o'clock the following morning to discuss my ideas for the revamp with him.

Then I composed an email to Literati's Human Resources department on my laptop, informing them I was giving my notice and fired it off, before contacting the Glasgow estate agents renting out my flat. I asked them to put it up for sale instead.

There was one lone student in the corner, hammering away on his laptop when I entered Book Ends the next morning.

A frisson of nerves rattled through me. I'd spent an excited but fretful night trying to sleep. Every so often, pictures of the bookshop entered my head, together with the judgemental expressions from the likes of Flora Simmonds and company.

I gazed around myself at the dark walls and the rows of books, begging to be picked up and browsed through.

Trevor grinned at me in delight, which made me feel worse.

Had I thought about what I was taking on here? Twelve months to turn around the *Marie Celeste* – like Book Ends – and transform it into the thriving, colourful bookshop I remembered from years ago?

"So, let's get started, shall we?" he said, clapping his hands.

"Yes, why not?" I grinned back manically, putting my bag behind the counter and fetching from it a notebook and pen.

Through the bookshop windows, the water of Loch Bracken glided this way and that, like an accomplished dancer showing off her moves in a silvery dress. At least the view was perfect.

First, I gestured to the array of books. "I suggest we have a fifty per cent off sale of any stock that isn't selling so well. That'll clear the way for us to bring in new books."

I glanced down at my notes. "We can go through the stock together and have a big clear out. If we have this sale on for two weeks, we can then begin having the refit and revamp undertaken after that."

I gave Trevor an encouraging look. "We need to make sure any books that aren't selling within three months are returned to the publishers." I pointed my pen at the bookshelves. "That'll stop Book Ends from being clogged up with titles that aren't performing and it'll mean you won't have to foot the bill to return them."

I wandered around with Trevor, admiring some of the embossed book spines. "Once our discount sale finishes, we could give whatever books are left over to charity?"

Trevor was enthusiastic. "What a lovely idea, Lexie."

I moved onto the next set of notes I'd made. I pointed to the generous bookshop space. "How would you feel about incorporating floor-to ceiling bookshelves that run right around here? That would modernise the space and show off the stock. Books sell themselves."

I jabbed an excited finger at the additional space towards

the back of the shop. "We could see how things go, but it seems a shame not to use that space too. Maybe we could run monthly promotions on certain genres in that area; arrange the books and have promotional material surrounding them; props and that kind of thing?"

Trevor nodded his approval. "That's a great idea. It does seem a shame that all that space is going to waste."

I glanced out of the curtained bookshop windows, my mind whirring. "Having the shelving that way will allow more space too, as well as more light to come in, and people will have a much better view of the books from outside. How would you feel about having the curtains removed?"

Trevor's lips twitched. "I'm sure I could live with that."

"That's great. No distractions or anything obscuring the stock. Having a raised platform in the windows means we can arrange the books to their full advantage."

I then mentioned to Trevor having white and grey signage made up for the shelves, identifying each genre and category. At the moment, it was rather slapdash and disorganised.

Trevor stuffed his hands into the pockets of his loose trousers. "Well, I'm sure it'd be a big improvement on what I have right now."

"I think it would. And I was going to suggest we have the counter moved, so that it's facing the street and customers are greeted by someone the minute they walk through the door."

I delved one hand into my bag and produced my phone. I pulled up a colour chart. "I've been giving some thought to the decor too and I wondered about having the new shelves in white, with a soft dove-grey shade on the walls." I pointed to the books racing along the current shelves around us. "Books are so colourful, that you don't need to go crazy with bright paints. They speak for themselves."

Trevor examined the grey shade on the paint chart on my phone and beamed. "I see what you mean. That's very classy."

I eyed Trevor. "Do you still wrap up books when they're purchased?"

"Yes. I still use the black and white gift wrap."

I recalled the bland paper from my years working here during the holidays. I hoped my voice sounded respectful. "What do you think about having a new Book Ends gift bag made instead and ditching the gift wrap? It could be a white bag, with Books Ends embossed on it, in a swirling, silver typeface and we could have white and grey tartan ribbon for the handles? It would match the new interior?"

Trevor considered this. "What a lovely idea."

"Thank you. I hope all these suggestions are agreeable to you, Trevor."

His mouth split into an optimistic grin. "You're a revelation, Lexie."

I blushed hot-pink. "Let's just hope everybody else is as enthusiastic." I then turned to my notes from last night, about ordering new stock. "We can make sure we're signed up to all the publishers' online catalogues, so that ordering is nice and easy to keep track of."

Trevor gestured outside. "You seem to have thought of everything. Have you had any ideas about jazzing up the exterior?"

I pointed to the shimmering vista of the loch across the road. "I was going to suggest having the front of Book Ends repainted a gleaming white and the windowsills decorated with the same pale grey as the interior. I thought that might play well against the water just across the way."

Trevor had been very generous with providing funds for the shop revamp, which was a relief. We would no doubt need every penny!

The student, who hadn't purchased any books, gave us a brief smile as he packed up his laptop and vanished into the street. "That's the first thing that has to stop," I said, with an eye roll. "We're not a library."

Trevor shook his head, exasperated. "It's been happening a lot."

We both meandered outside, drinking in the tired shop facade, before hurrying back in, thanks to the keen breeze whipping in from across the loch.

I chose that moment to mention to Trevor about looking at the staff rota. "As you won't be working in the bookshop for ninety-nine per cent of the time, like I said before, I think we'll need a full-time assistant and perhaps one other part-time member of staff."

"Oh, I'm sure," agreed Trevor. "We'll be swamped with customers and will need all hands on deck!"

"I hope so," I said, my heart giving a nervous jolt. "Once we get the revamp underway, we can start thinking about advertising the two vacancies."

Trevor suggested we take a look at the bookshop office next and we agreed that just needed a lick of white paint to replace the dark burgundy in there, which would complement the biscuit carpet better and enhance the rectangular walnut desk. The fridge and microwave could remain in there for the staff to use.

I made more copious notes.

We closed the office door and stepped back out into the bookshop. Excitement zipped through me. "If you're happy, I can recruit the services of one of Mum's friends to undertake the redecorating."

"As soon as possible would be best," mused Trevor. "Now that the bookshop is off the market, I want to hit the ground running."

My attention fell again on the generous space at the rear of the bookshop. If things went well, we could think about expanding further.

I gave myself a mental check. *One thing at a time, Lexie.* I had twelve months to turn the fortunes of Book Ends around. One thing at a time.

As soon as I arrived back home, I set to work. Keeping occupied was helping me not focus too much on the task I was taking on, as well as the fact I'd told Literati where they could stick their job.

I moved on to pulling together ideas for posts for Book Ends' social media accounts, as well as advertising and promotion. I noticed Trevor developed a nervous twitch whenever I so much as mentioned Facebook, so I knew he wouldn't want to be involved in any of that side of things.

I'd already begun setting up social media accounts for Book Ends on Instagram, Facebook and Twitter. Now, it was just a case of pulling together exciting, enticing posts to load up on them!

I gave my lengthy to-do list another critical look as I

perched on Mum's sitting room sofa. Bloody hell! I wanted it to start looking shorter, not longer!

I wandered through to the kitchen, from where I could see a teasing glimpse of Bracken Castle's jutting turrets in the distance.

Tomorrow was the 1st May and Easter had vanished, taking with it the dusty lemon and lime daffodils on the castle hill.

I'd managed to place a couple more adverts in local and regional newspapers earlier that afternoon, as well as one in a writing magazine, advertising my editorial services.

I had to keep my options open. If Book Ends didn't work out in the next twelve months, I'd have to have something else to fall back on.

Mum and Grandpa had gone out to the local garden centre for a wander and a cup of tea. They'd tried to persuade me to go with them, but I knew I had to press on.

After rustling up a salmon, cream cheese and salad bagel for lunch, I returned to my action list.

The words "Speak to Rhiannon!" jumped out at me from the yellow, lined paper.

I wasn't looking forward to that. I'd texted her with my news, but it looked like she hadn't received my messages. I suspected she hadn't heard yet about me abandoning ship from Literati either, as she'd been away on holiday, visiting her sister who lived in a remote part of Canada. She would've called me otherwise and tried to change my mind if she'd known.

I procrastinated for a few more minutes by sticking on some washing, watching videos of wild dolphins on my laptop and admiring the latest photos of Ryan Reynolds on social media, before I managed to harness enough courage to ring Rhiannon.

When she heard my voice, hers rose several panicked octaves down the line. I asked her how her sister was and if the Canadian weather had been kind to her. But Rhiannon wasn't in the mood for small talk. "I've just received your texts," she gasped. "What the hell is going on, Lexie?"

"I've handed in my notice. I've got a new job. I'm now the manager of my local bookshop."

There was such a deafening silence, I wondered for a moment if she'd passed out and was lying in her carpeted, glass-desk office, with her red-soled Louboutin's in the air.

There came a couple of stutters. "Well, that's great," she choked, struggling to find the words. "Really. I mean… it's a shock."

"What, me getting another job?"

"No, of course not. Just you quitting like this and the type of job it is. You know…" Her voice withered. "You managing a bookshop."

"So, you don't think I'm up to it?" I said with forced laughter. Oh shit. Right now, I was wondering the same thing. I dragged my socked foot backwards and forwards on Mum's sitting room carpet.

"Don't be daft. Of course, you are. I'm pleased for you. I'm just a bit stunned, that's all. I've just got back from Canada, I'm jet-lagged to hell and now this."

If Rhiannon was pleased for me, I wish someone had told her voice. But then she couldn't help herself. Like a Scottish Highland wind, she breathed long, low and hard into my ear, before she launched into familiar territory again. "Look, I don't mean to rain on your parade Lex, but we're struggling. A lot of the authors are revolting."

A laugh shot out of me. "You'd better not let Dame Alicia hear you say that, although there were a few that were already revolting when I started working there."

"Oh, ha ha!" she shot back. "I'm glad you're finding this so amusing. You never used to be like this."

"Like what? You mean more relaxed?"

"Sarcastic."

"I was. I just didn't have the time or energy to be sarcastic when I worked at Literati."

Rhiannon let out a grunt.

"Look Rhi, I never envisaged handing in my notice, but things happen. I gave everything to Literati, but it wasn't enough."

After a few more moans, Rhiannon conceded defeat. "Alright. Alright. I get it. I guess our loss is this bookshop's gain then."

I bloody well hoped so.

The first weekend in May was on the horizon and already, a number of the second-home owners in the area were arriving on the Thursday afternoon, their vehicles topped with bikes, canoes and surfboards.

The refitting of Book Ends was underway. The local joiners I recruited were streaming in and out, removing the old bookcases, as well as preparing to install a platform at each of the two shop windows and John McColl, Mum's painter and decorator friend, had rung me to say he and his team from

Brush Strokes were cracking on with the repainting and would begin in the bookshop office.

The tradesmen were hopeful that with all possible hands-on deck they could have everything achieved over this bank holiday weekend.

We had opted for 25th May, the big bank holiday weekend, to officially re-open, which was now only three weeks away. That prospect was thrilling me but terrifying me in equal measure.

I thought that opting for that long weekend might mean we could draw upon curious visitors to Bracken Way, as well as the returning second homers.

After breakfast and showering, I threw on my jeans, trainers and a sparkly pink T-shirt with a matching cardigan on top. The temptation to go and take another look at the progress being made at Book Ends was too much to resist, despite the persistent rain.

I decided to pop down, take some photographs of the revamp progress on my phone and then I'd upload them on social media, under a "Taking a sneak peek" post.

I slipped on my waterproof and grabbed my bag, before heading out the door. I was so glad, on a day like this, that Mum lived just a ten-minute walk away from the shop.

It might be the beginning of May, but it was the Scottish Highlands and anybody who didn't carry something to protect them from the rain was viewed with bemusement by the locals.

Sure enough, no sooner had my trainers set foot onto the pavement, but the rain started to dart down.

Hardy souls, though buffeted by the fresh breeze,

remained by the railings that looked down onto the loch shore. They continued to take pictures of the castle, now slick with rain and pummelled by the wind. Miserable but atmospheric!

My heart quickened and I realised I was beaming as Book Ends morphed into view.

As I drew nearer, I could see John had strolled out of Book Ends, his white overalls splattered in a rainbow of paint. He was engaged in what looked like a heated conversation with another man.

The man he was talking to was tall, with curly, shoulder-length dark hair pushed back behind his ears.

"Hi." I smiled, my attention travelling between the two of them.

The dark stranger whirled round and scowled down at me with striking green eyes that reminded me of the Bracken Way hillsides on a dappled summer's day.

I'd never seen him before. I would have remembered if I had. He was very handsome and looked in his late thirties. He made me think of an Italian Renaissance artist.

He possessed thick, dark brows and a proud, regal nose. His jaw was peppered with black stubble. John disappeared back inside Book Ends, while the stranger glowered down at me. "Are you Lexie Dunbar?"

I blinked up at him. "Yes. That's me."

He jerked his head at the bookshop window, where John had stuck a sign up on my behalf:

Book Ends Bookshop – Grand Re-opening 25th May, 10am!

"What on earth is that about?" he snapped.

"Excuse me?"

"That." He was struggling to keep his deep, brisk voice on an even keel. "A re-opening?"

"It's as it says on the notice," I explained, noting the irritation in his voice. "Book Ends is undergoing a makeover and is re-opening on that date." I hesitated. "Sorry, but I didn't catch your name?"

The man continued to stare at the notice in the window, as though he couldn't believe what he was seeing. He jerked his strong profile round to look at me again. His face was all angles. "I'm Tobias Black. I'm Trevor Newman's nephew."

I blinked up at him. *Nephew?* I never recalled Trevor mentioning he had a nephew and I'd known him for years. A kernel of worry grew inside me, but I tried to dismiss it.

The man shoved his hands into the pockets of his dark jeans. He eyed the bookshop again. "I think there must be some mistake."

"Like what exactly?"

Tobias Black surveyed the written notice again, taped to the inside of the window. "I was told that my uncle was closing down Book Ends."

"Yes, he was," I replied evenly. "But he had a change of heart."

Tobias Black cocked one brow. "Why ever would he do that? I understand that footfall is well short of what it used to be."

"Yes, it is, but we're intent on changing that."

"*We?*"

I gave him a professional smile. "Trevor has appointed me manager. Together, we're going to turn the fortunes of Book Ends around."

Tobias Black looked like he'd been punched. He shook his dark, curly head, as he processed what I'd just told him. "No. I'm sorry, Ms Dunbar, but that's what you think."

A flicker of worry lit up in my chest. "What do you mean?"

"I'm going to have a chat with my uncle now. I need this shop for my own business."

It took a few moments for what he said to sink in. Why did I feel like I'd suddenly gate-crashed a private event? "But it's off the market," I stammered. "Trevor wants to keep it going as Book Ends."

He glowered at me, making me take a faltering step backwards. "Well, let's see, shall we? I'm sure he'll change his mind, once I've spoken to him." His cool gaze froze me to the spot. "I can be very persuasive when I want to be."

Chapter Eight

W hat?!

No. This couldn't be right. This Tobias Black was talking a load of bollocks. He couldn't be Trevor's nephew... could he?

But why would he say that, if it wasn't true?

Worry and panic revved up faster inside me.

I was at risk of giving myself a thumping migraine, turning this over and over in my head.

Could he be a conman? Maybe he was a crook who preyed on businesspeople? Was he trying to deceive Trevor and swindle him out of his business? Yes, that must be it. There was no other explanation. Ha! He could try! Trevor had been very good to me and I wasn't about to let him be swindled by anyone.

But then again, this man seemed very sure of himself.

I straightened my shoulders, as shoppers and visitors darted around us in the street, clutching their purchases and huddled against the weather. "Sorry. I think you've misunderstood. Trevor owns the bookshop and I'm the manager. It's continuing as Book Ends." I was determined to remain calm, even though my chest was fluttering with apprehension. "Did you just say you're Mr Newman's nephew?"

Tobias Black's annoyed gaze blazed back at me. "Yes. Is that so difficult to comprehend?"

God, if rudeness were a disease, he'd be dead!

He gestured to the open bookshop door, the smell of paint and a chorus of hammering and sawing shooting out. "What the hell is going on here? I arrive to visit my uncle at his shop and I find it's morphed into a doll's house!"

"It isn't a doll's house," I bit back, trying to rein in my growing dislike of this man. "It's still the bookshop. It's just undergoing a makeover."

"You must be joking." Tobias Black's voice was incredulous. He peered through the windows again.

"No, I'm not."

He stared me down. "Well, that's a matter of opinion. Where's my uncle? What have you done with him?"

"Done with him?" I let out a bark of laughter. "I haven't *done* anything with him."

I could see Tobias grind his jaw even harder.

He plucked his phone out of his jeans pocket and pulled up his contacts. "I'm getting my uncle down here right now to sort this mess out."

So, my initial faint hope that he might be bluffing was shot down in flames.

I folded my arms and tried to reassure myself. "Feel free to ring Mr Newman. He'll tell you what I just have."

One thick, dark brow arched up to his hairline. "Oh, don't worry, Ms Dunbar. I'm going to."

Trevor answered the phone after a few rings and Tobias swaggered down past the bookshop, to hold their conversation in private. Every so often, he discharged black looks over his shoulder at me. What an ignorant git!

What the hell was going on?

After a couple more minutes, Tobias Black strode back up the pavement towards me, with an air of triumph. He'd just completed a second call to someone else and had been extolling the virtues of paint staining, granulation and transparency. His jacket carried the remnants of rain. "My uncle is on his way. We'll soon have this mess sorted out."

I hoped I sounded far more confident than I felt. "Yes. We will."

John reappeared and made his way towards his van which was parked a few feet away. He cranked open the double doors to fetch more white paint and a roller.

Tobias eyed him. "Excuse me? What are you doing?"

John stared back. "I'm about to swim across Loch Bracken. What does it look like?"

Tobias Black pushed his mobile back into his rear pocket. "I'd appreciate it if you didn't undertake any more work on Book Ends until my uncle gets here."

I struggled to keep my voice level. What did he think he was doing? Who'd put him in charge? "Now hang on a second, Mr Black…"

"Tobias? Tobias! What's going on?"

Trevor was pushing his car keys into a pocket of his bottle green trousers and huddling into his quilted jacket. He was staring in disbelief down the pavement at his nephew.

None of this was making any sense. The prospect of losing the bookshop before I even had a chance to try and make a go of it made my stomach plummet.

I didn't know what to think or who to believe. Just as I thought my life might be starting to sort itself out, this happens!

Tobias Black and Trevor shook hands. Tobias then patted his uncle on the back. Trevor kept staring at him as though he couldn't quite believe his eyes.

The older man's smile was awkward. "Yes… Er… you look well, Tobias, but to say this is a surprise is an understatement."

The younger man gestured to the bookshop again. "Not as much as this is to me, Uncle. Mum told me Book Ends was closing down."

"That's right. It was." Trevor pushed his hands into his jacket pockets and continued to gawp at his nephew. "But as you can see, it isn't now. I changed my mind."

Tobias's expression glowered with disapproval at me. "Or someone changed it for you," he muttered under his breath.

My mouth sprang open with indignation. "Pardon? I hope you aren't inferring anything underhand."

Tobias ignored me. "Uncle, I'd appreciate a quiet word with you about this. In private please."

Trevor shot me a sideways glance. He opened and closed his mouth for a few seconds, before rallying. "Yes, of course. The three of us should go inside and we can discuss it further."

Tobias reeled. "Sorry?"

"Let me explain," insisted his uncle. He gestured for Tobias to lead the way. "Shall we?"

I trooped in after them, stung at this rude man's inference. He thought I'd coerced Trevor into keeping his business? How dare he!

As soon as we stepped inside the doorway of the bookshop, the cacophony of scents hit us again: wood panelling, paint and sawdust.

Tobias Black wasted no time in whirling round to confront his uncle. "So, can you explain what's happened to Book Ends?"

Trevor aimed a brief glance my way. "Nothing has happened to it, except for me upgrading it with Lexie's help."

Tobias Black looked like he'd trod on something sharp. "This is crazy. I had hoped there might have been some sort of mix-up." Disbelief gripped his stormy features. "And Ms Dunbar has been appointed manager?"

Trevor nodded. "That's right. For a year. We want to give it twelve months, to see if we can turn the business around."

There was an awkward silence that seemed to last forever, before Tobias let out a cross between a laugh and a snarl. "This is ridiculous! Why weren't Mum and I told about this?"

Trevor eyed his incandescent nephew out of his round spectacles. "I didn't tell your mother because it was – and is – none of her business."

Tobias shook his dark curls. "She's your sister-in-law. Apart from Tamsin, we're the only family you have left, Uncle Trevor." He flashed me a glance. "And if you haven't forgotten, I do have shares in the business."

Shares? My heart sank further.

"Aunt Naomi asked for my help a few years back when the shop was having a lean time and—"

Trevor cut his nephew off. "Yes, I'm aware of that and I appreciate it, but it's still my business." His face carried an odd look. "Naomi should never have asked you to invest in the shop in the first place." Then Trevor stunned me, by letting out a sudden rumble of sarcastic laughter. "But as for family? We never see each other or keep in touch." He pulled a wry smile. "Only when it suits your mother, that is."

Tobias's eyes burned. "What does that mean?"

Trevor didn't respond.

I shuffled from foot to foot. This appeared to be some sort of awkward family issue and I didn't want to intrude, but at the same time, I didn't want this Tobias Black trying to con his uncle. The fact that he also had a stake in the bookshop was gnawing at me. "Perhaps I should go," I interjected into an atmosphere so frozen it would give the Arctic a run for its money.

Trevor shook his fine head of swept back, dark hair. "I've appointed you manager of this place, Lexie. There's nothing more to discuss."

"Oh, but there is," growled Tobias, folding his muscular arms over his grey T-shirt and black leather jacket. "This shop has been struggling for a while. Mum heard there were rumours circulating around Bracken Way about Book Ends having a tough time of it and I'm looking for new business premises."

His uncle appraised him with a cool stare. "Well, news does

travel fast, doesn't it? The gossip hotline between here and your mother is obviously in full working order." Tobias moved to say something, but undeterred, Trevor ploughed on. "After your aunt passed away, I did think about closing down and leasing it, but I've come to realise it isn't what she would have wanted."

Then he turned to me with an appreciative smile. "Lexie here has made me see that Book Ends still has so much to offer the Bracken Way community."

Tobias started to protest. "But in the current economic climate, Uncle, do you think that's wise? What if your plans for the shop don't work? Wouldn't you be better calling it a day and retiring?"

"Certainly not. At least not for the time being. If there is any chance, however small, that Book Ends can be saved, then I'm willing to give it a try." Trevor aimed a measured look at Tobias. "That's why we're going to give it twelve months to turn the shop around."

Tobias's features dropped. "A year to improve its fortunes? Channelling money into a business that looks doomed to fail anyway? And then what?"

"If things haven't picked up by then, I sell it."

"But it won't come to that," I insisted with far more confidence than I felt.

Trevor's look was steely, which was unusual for him. "No. It won't."

My heart lifted in gratitude.

He offered his shocked nephew a measured stare. "Now, would you like us to update you on our plans?"

Tobias flicked a dismissive hand at the new paint and the

tradespeople going about their business. "And you're ok with this?"

"Of course, I am. Lexie and I have discussed and agreed everything."

My teeth ground together. He was doing it again, inferring that I'd forced Trevor's arm up his back about the changes.

What a bloody cheek, sweeping in here and throwing his weight around. "How many bookshops do you frequent, Mr Black?"

"A few."

I raised my chin a little higher. "I've worked in publishing for several years. I know my way around a bookshop."

"We'll see about that," muttered Tobias from under his tousled curls.

Outside Book Ends, a couple of gulls bickered over a piece of bread. Their cries and indignant shrieks reminded me of the heated conversation playing out right now between Tobias, his uncle and me. Except compared to this obnoxious man, the fighting gulls had better manners.

"Tobias, if I'd decided to continue with the sale of the lease, then of course I would have kept you informed and you would've had the opportunity to buy." Trevor paused for effect. "But not everything is about money."

I gave Trevor an appreciative smile.

Tobias muttered something under his breath and glowered around the shop interior. Behind us, there was the intermittent sound of hammering.

My annoyance was fast reaching a critical level. Talk about making inaccurate and sweeping assumptions. He might look like Kit Harington, but he was arrogant and judgemental.

Trevor adjusted his round spectacles. "Anyway, I'm rather confused. Why are you here in Bracken Way? Just visiting? We're not exactly close to Glasgow here."

Tobias's expression changed. He performed an awkward shrug. "I'm thinking about moving back."

Back? I studied him. Tobias was from Bracken Way too?

His uncle's dark eyes widened. There was an uneasy wobble to his voice. "What, here? You mean, permanently?"

Tobias shifted from foot to foot. "Well, I don't mean to Gotham City."

My optimism plummeted through the floor. If this nephew of Trevor's did relocate to the area, what would that mean for me? Would he be frequenting Book Ends, interfering in everything? I bloody hoped not!

His stunned uncle considered this for a few moments. "Right. I see. Well, that's a surprise. I wouldn't have thought Bracken Way would be your cup of tea anymore."

"Why?"

Trevor floundered around. "Too quiet and provincial perhaps."

Tobias fidgeted again. "I feel like I need a change of scene. And anyway, I do come from here, if you remember."

A strange expression flashed across Trevor's face. "Yes. Of course, I remember." He eyed Tobias from under furrowed brows. "But I thought you loved living in Glasgow. And what about your gallery there? You can't just walk away from that?"

Tobias's second shrug was another uneasy one. "I can set up a gallery here. I've been taking a look at those new flats on the outskirts of town and there's one I've expressed interest in."

Trevor's mouth dangled open. "What? You mean, you've been house-hunting already?" Alarm revved up in his eyes. "This is all rather sudden, isn't it?"

"No point in hanging around."

"Right," faltered Trevor, his eyes locked on his nephew's dark, brooding expression. "But moving back here after all this time… relocating… well, it's a big step."

"It's beginning to make more sense, the more I think about it," insisted Tobias. "Getting away from the city and settling somewhere quieter, where I can paint."

A concoction of emotions charged across Trevor's face. "So, have you identified a suitable location for a gallery here? I'm not aware of any of the other businesses for sale in the town at the moment."

"Exactly," replied Tobias, aiming another pointed glower at me. "Like I said, I would've been very interested in this place." He stared around at the interior of the shop.

Trevor's voice was laced with irritation again. "It was on the market for five seconds and then I changed my mind. If I'd proceeded with the sale, of course I would've told you." Trevor sighed. "From the minute the For Sale sign went up, I wondered if I was doing the right thing. I've just explained what the situation is."

"Oh, you've made that clear."

Tobias made a sudden move to leave the bookshop

"Tobias. Where are you going?" asked his puzzled uncle.

"I need to start shopping around for premises for my gallery." Tobias drew up. "Nice to see your loyalties lie with family, Uncle Trevor."

He offered me a lengthy stare. "Good luck, Ms Dunbar. Something tells me you're going to need it."

It was then that his mobile let out another demanding ring.

Tobias answered it and exchanged small talk with the caller, before launching into a description about using salt in his paintings for added texture. Then he was gone.

Chapter Nine

Trevor watched his scowling nephew retreat along the pavement, through the bookshop window.

His face still possessed a troubled edge.

"Ae you alright, Trevor?"

He frowned. "What? Oh. Yes. I'm fine, thank you. I just didn't expect to have Tobias turn up so unexpectedly."

"I take it you aren't close to your nephew and sister-in-law." I didn't want to appear nosey, but my curiosity was piqued.

Trevor squinted against the light glancing off the loch. "No. Not very. At least, we used to be." His voice tailed off.

"Families," I said. "You can choose your friends but you can't choose your relatives. I know what that's like."

"You can say that again."

"When was the last time you saw him?"

"Tobias?" Trevor screwed up his eyes with concentration. "My goodness. It must be about eighteen months ago now, at my sister-in-law's birthday party. She lives in Loch Muir, that little market town about forty-five minutes' drive from here." Trevor continued to explain. "I dropped by just to be polite, but didn't stay long." He flapped one hand in a dismissive gesture, as though the whole affair had been of little consequence.

I couched my words. "I hope this situation with me taking over as bookshop manager isn't going to cause you any undue friction with Tobias."

Trevor opened and closed his mouth several times. But his dilemma was cut short by the arrival of an older couple who were passing by with their two small grandchildren. He switched on a smile.

They popped their heads around the door, made encouraging noises about the revamp of Book Ends and wished Trevor good luck.

When they'd gone, Trevor stuffed his hands into the pockets of his trousers. "Nothing's ever straightforward, is it?"

"In what way?"

Trevor let out a pained sigh. "Tobias isn't happy about me changing my mind over the shop." A myriad of emotions crossed his pensive face. "But I have to do what I feel is right, don't I?"

"Of course, you do." My stomach clenched with irritation. That pain in the arse Tobias Black had managed to get to his uncle; he had thrown Trevor, made him feel conflicted, as though he was doing the wrong thing.

Trevor gathered himself. "Och, enough about me and my family dramas. Things still tense with your father?"

The bookshop windows reflected the rainbow mixture of waterproof jackets and baseball caps ferrying past. "That's being polite." I paused. "Mum, Grandpa and I happened to see my father on TV a few weeks ago, reporting from Washington for one of the lunchtime news shows."

Trevor's eyes popped in surprise. "Goodness me. That must've been a shock for you all."

"It was."

He shook his head. "He's missed out on so much, not watching you grow up." He fell quiet for a few moments. "And your lovely mum... how he could abandon you both like that."

We both moved towards the bookshop entrance and stared out at the view.

"It is what it is," I answered, gazing ahead of me again at the dancing sparkles of water on the surface of Loch Bracken.

I turned to him, the chatter and excited squeals from the ice cream shop a bit further up the road travelling down the pavement.

My worry began to bite again. "I won't lie, Trevor. I'm concerned about your nephew's reaction to us modernising Book Ends."

Trevor brushed off my worries. "Don't you take any notice. Like I said, I know Tobias has a stake in the business, but at the end of the day, it's my shop, not his."

I nodded. I would just have to throw everything at this and ensure that this time next year, business in Book Ends was brisk and that there would be no way Trevor could contemplate closing down. Now that I'd met that arrogant nephew of his, I was even more fired up about making the bookshop a success.

Trevor stuck his neck out further from his brown checked shirt. "I have to say I'm very surprised though."

"About what?"

"Tobias moving back to Bracken Way. He's an enterprising young man. I would never have thought he'd want to leave the city and return here."

"You said he's an artist?"

"Yes. A portrait painter and a very accomplished one." Trevor fiddled with one of the chunky buttons on his cardigan, deep in thought. "He was spotted by a prestigious critic doing street art in Glasgow a few years ago and his career took off." Trevor's expression changed. "No doubt I'll have his mother braying down the phone at me about getting my priorities wrong and not putting family first."

The faint lines around his eyes deepened. There was a troubled haze to his expression. Then it cleared. "Right. Seeing as I'm here, how about I treat you to one of Mrs Hegarty's lattes and a Danish pastry and you can tell me how things are going with your plans for Book Ends conquering the book world?"

"That would be lovely. Thank you. And we can start making plans to sort through the book stock, if that's alright?"

Trevor agreed.

"As it's the bank holiday weekend, I thought we might be able to begin selecting what books to sell and we could make a start on trying to sell those on Monday morning? Set up a table here? I've checked the forecast and there's supposed to be no rain."

Trevor broke into a smile. "Sounds like a plan. Now, let's go get those pastries and talk more."

I began the weekend by updating the bookshop's social media accounts with details of our new plans for Book Ends. I hoped that my exciting announcements would draw the curious – of all ages – to come by and take a look.

Book Ends will be back on 25th May – brighter and better than ever!

Come along to our grand re-opening at 10am, to see the new-look bookshop in your community.

It still has all the wonderful selection of authors and genres you know and love, but there are some new additions too, as well as enterprising and exclusive loyalty schemes to save YOU money!

*Pick up a Book Ends loyalty card. Have it stamped every time you make a purchase and receive your seventh title FREE!

*Stuck on what author or genre to buy for that special person in your life? Why not buy a Book Ends gift card? Have your chosen amount loaded onto the card and your loved one can come in and choose the book they want.

*You can now catch up with Book Ends whenever you want, wherever you want, on our new social media channels – check out Facebook, Instagram and Twitter for all the latest book news, author updates, as well as promotions and competitions. Take part! Post your reviews for other book worms!

*What would YOU like to see in the revamped Book Ends? Leave your comments and suggestions on any of our social media channels and you could win a gift card to spend in store.

I'd also received a couple of tentative email enquiries from frustrated writers, who were trying to secure representation with agents or get published, who had seen my magazine and press adverts for editorial services and wanted to improve their manuscripts.

I made a note to get back to them with more information and details of my rates.

Then I began pulling together ideas for the shop's official relaunch. I had just under three weeks till the re-opening and I knew the time would vanish in the run-up.

I decided to put any thoughts about that muppet Tobias Black to one side. Fingers crossed; I wouldn't have to have any further dealings with him. Maybe he'd have second thoughts about moving to Bracken Way, seeing as he couldn't get his ruthless hands on Book Ends for himself.

And like Trevor had pointed out, there weren't any vacant business premises he could snap up at the moment anyway, thank goodness.

I told myself to stop thinking about that grouchy man and instead, switched my attention to more arrangements for our opening event. I thought the idea of laying on glasses of champagne would be a nice touch.

Once I'd made notes to discuss that with Mrs Hegarty, whose brother-in-law owned an upmarket wine and champagne business in Perth, I rang Trevor and arranged to meet him down at Book Ends that afternoon, to begin sorting out books we could sell at a fifty per cent discount.

The interior of the bookshop was slowly morphing into what I envisaged. The joiners were hard at work, putting the finishing touches to the floor-to-ceiling shelves and solid, wooden platforms had materialised in each window, to support the book displays.

The bookshop office was now gleaming with snow-white paint and was far airier.

After rummaging through several boxes of books in there, Trevor and me identified a large assortment of books for our first wave of sales, which he admitted hadn't flown off the shelves.

They included everything from guidebooks and obscure memoirs to old cartography publications and autobiographies from Z-list celebrities.

I'd mentioned to John what we were doing and so he very kindly donated a huge pasting table for us to erect outside Book Ends. It was handy that we had the first of two bank holidays coming up this month, which we could use to entice people to peruse the books we were selling on discount. John's table would be perfect for arranging our first batch of tomes on. There were more where they came from, judging by the other cardboard boxes Trevor had lined up in the office!

Monday morning rolled around, so I got ready, snatched some toast and tea and then took myself down to Mrs Hegarty's tea room for opening time, ready to discuss our champagne requirements with her for Book Ends' official re-opening. I was hoping we could secure a discount!

Then it would be straight across the road to help Trevor set up the discounted books for sale. It was going to be a hectic bank holiday Monday.

. . .

It was still a little too early for the ardent shoppers and day visitors yet. There was a languid atmosphere and only the odd dog walker and keen fresh air enthusiast were about. Another hour or so and Bracken Way would be buzzing again.

A big grin flashed across my face as I spotted John painting the windowsills with slicks of the dove-grey paint. I'd made arrangements with Mrs Hegarty to have her brother-in-law supply us with bottles of champagne and glasses for the re-opening. Another job done!

One of John's younger colleagues, a tall, gangly lad with a ginger buzz cut, was gliding the same shade onto the shop door.

"Good morning," I grinned at them. "It's going to look so gorgeous when it's finished."

John stretched out his back. "I wondered if you were going to tell me I'd missed a bit."

"As a matter of fact…" I teased.

John suddenly slapped his forehead. "Och, before I forget Lexie, Trevor popped by a short while ago. He said he'll be back soon to help you set up. That cranky nephew of his was with him."

My buoyant mood evaporated.

Had Tobias managed to talk his uncle into selling the shop lease to him, after all?

John's voice broke through my concerns. "Trevor asked me to give him a ring when you turned up." He pulled his phone out of the front pocket of his overalls. "Is that ok?"

I struggled to look calm. *No, stop it, Lexie. You're jumping to conclusions.* "Yes, John. Of course, it is."

John stepped a few feet away and rang Trevor. After a few verbal exchanges, he rang off. "He said they'll be here in about ten minutes or so."

"Ok. Thanks." *They?* Oh, great. So, it sounded like Forrest Grump was coming along too.

I hovered outside Book Ends for a few minutes, appraising its new paintwork in progress, but was unable to concentrate on anything except speculating what Trevor wanted to discuss.

And why the hell was Master of the Dark Arts with him? Unless Trevor had roped him into helping us with the book sale this morning?

Suspicion coursed through me. Trevor was a gentleman, but as for that arrogant nephew of his... Ok, I hated to admit it. He *was* very good-looking, but he had all the finesse of one of Bracken Way's gulls.

I attempted to distract myself by reading over the contents of my pink folder of notes, but even my to-do list and imagining those gorgeous new window displays I was planning weren't able to dispel my niggling worry.

I shuffled my notes back into my folder, as the sound of Bracken Loch whispered behind me.

"Lexie? They're here now."

I snapped my head up on hearing John's voice. "Oh, ok. Thanks."

I hugged my folder to my chest.

Tobias and his uncle had stopped a few feet away along the pavement, their backs turned away from me. They were both appreciating the jagged blue hillside skyline.

I clutched my folder tighter, as I approached them. "Good morning, Trevor." My teeth ground. "Mr Black."

They both swung around.

Trevor smiled, but his eyes carried an edge of apprehension. Tobias gave me a stiff nod.

"Good morning, Lexie. Think the weather is supposed to get a little warmer later."

I noticed Trevor shuffle from foot to foot in his heavy lace-up shoes.

"Even brighter blue sky over there," I commented, for something to say. I aimed a suspicious glance at Tobias. "So, John tells me you're keen to have a word?"

Trevor opened his mouth, but Tobias was far too quick for him. "Yes, we do." His jade eyes slid down me, making me hold tighter onto my folder.

"Book Ends has a very generous amount of space, doesn't it?"

"It does," I frowned, wondering why Tobias was mentioning this and where this conversation was going. "It's a real little Tardis in terms of dimensions." I narrowed my eyes, struggling to read Trevor's awkward expression beside his nephew. "Why?"

Tobias took a step forward. "There are no other premises available in Bracken Way for me to open up as a gallery at the moment. Believe me, I've looked."

He gestured to the bookshop. There was a glint in his eyes. "That's why I'm proposing we share the space."

What space? Where? What did he mean? "Sorry?"

"It's more than big enough to accommodate two businesses."

A pool of dread began to swill in my stomach. What? Wait. No. Did he mean the bookshop? Was he being serious?!

"Half of the space would be for Book Ends and the other half would be for my new gallery." A triumphant expression played around his mouth. "So, what do you think of my suggestion, Ms Dunbar?"

Chapter Ten

W hat did I think? Nope. No bloody way. That space belonged to Book Ends and I'd earmarked that for expanding the bookshop, using it for the genre-themed displays I'd suggested to Trevor.

Was Tobias serious? It was the worst idea ever. Working alongside him every day? I would rather rip out my own fingernails.

Trevor couldn't be ok with this? But then again, Trevor said Tobias had invested money in Book Ends, so he did have some influence.

No. Trevor wouldn't support that. Tobias was trying to manipulate his uncle and pressure him into running with this crazy idea. Any moment now, Trevor would interrupt and shoot down his nephew's absurd suggestion.

I waited. And waited. And waited.

Trevor didn't say anything.

My eyes widened at this shocking and unforeseen turn of events. Tobias performed an officious nod, taking my stunned silence for capitulation. "Excellent. I can make a start on arranging for the transportation of my artwork."

I shot up one protesting hand. "Whoa! Hold on!" The words tumbled out of my mouth in a furious stream. "I haven't agreed to anything, Mr Black."

He blinked down at me.

"I'm now manager of this shop and was appointed by your uncle, in case you'd forgotten."

Tobias's stubbled jaw jutted out further. "You've mentioned that once or twice."

We exchanged heated scowls, until his uncle broke in. Trevor was struggling to make eye contact with me. "Lexie. Please just listen. My nephew has a proposal for you."

Did that mean Trevor was in favour of this suggestion? I stared at the older man, incredulous.

Was this some sort of twisted nightmare I was trapped in? Only a few days ago, Trevor was criticising his nephew and didn't even seem keen at the prospect of him moving back to Bracken Way, and now he was trying to help him secure gallery space? "Sorry, but I'm very confused by all this."

Tobias examined the snaking row of shops either side of the main street. "It's simple. My proposal is that we split Book Ends in two. You'll have plenty of room for the bookshop and I'll utilise the large space at the rear of the shop for my art gallery."

His mouth hitched up triumphantly at one corner, which irked me further. "And I won't be around all the time anyway, seeing as I'll be out painting commissions."

I thundered with incredulity. "So, if you're out, *who* will be looking after your gallery? I hope you're not expecting me to do that, Mr Black." He gave me a withering look.

"Certainly not, Ms Dunbar. I'll be recruiting staff – people who have a genuine love and knowledge of art."

I scowled up at him. What?! Five minutes ago, I was brimming with excitement and plans for Book Ends and now, this?! I struggled to remain composed. "Trevor, what's going on here?"

Trevor didn't reply.

"And it goes without saying I'll be paying monthly rent."

Tobias then reeled off a suggested figure to his uncle, which made both our eyeballs pop.

I gripped my folder tighter. This whole situation was not panning out as I imagined it would. Why was Trevor supporting this, helping Tobias, after what he'd said before?

My head was whirling. I narrowed my eyes at Tobias, my blood bubbling.

What the hell was this going to be like, having him prowling around in the background, judging and commenting on everything I did?

Trevor was one of the last people I wanted to upset or offend, I was incredibly fond of him, but this was ludicrous!

Then again, did I have any real say in the matter? Trevor still owned the bookshop.

I didn't want to come across as childish or uncooperative, but this was all I needed.

Tobias continued to tower over me. He offered me a cool look out of those glittery, forest green eyes of his. "My art gallery's going to give Book Ends a much-needed boost, Ms Dunbar."

Was he for real? "Excuse me?!"

"A renowned portrait artist sharing your business space – it'll give the bookshop gravitas."

I gripped onto my pink plastic folder so hard, I was at risk of puncturing holes in it. "Book Ends does not require additional gravitas, thank you very much. It'll prosper again on its own merits." My eyes blazed back at him. "You can't piggy-back off the success of Book Ends."

"I'd no intention of doing that."

"So you say."

Tobias's eyed burned. "And what the hell is that supposed to mean?"

"Ladies. Gentlemen. Please!"

We fell silent, snapping our furious faces away from one another to look at Trevor. His exasperated expression softened as he concentrated on me again. "Lexie. I want to stress that you don't have to agree to this, if you feel it would hinder Book Ends' new launch."

Tobias let out an audible growl. "What? Oh, you're kidding!"

Trevor shot his nephew a glower. "But let's be honest, Tobias's rent would help us out, going forward." Two spots of pink flourished on his cheeks. "And it would mean a great deal to me."

I frowned at him, willing him to explain his head-spinning change of heart in helping his nephew. Had they decided to resolve whatever disagreement they had? Perhaps Trevor's sister-in-law had managed to persuade him to help Tobias? Maybe she'd laid a guilt trip on Trevor, seeing as Tobias had a stake in the shop? Questions spun around in my head, but

Trevor was providing no answers. Instead, he just gazed beseechingly at me.

If I didn't agree to this, it could put Trevor in a more difficult situation with his sister-in-law and nephew. It sounded like they weren't exactly happy families, judging by Trevor's previous comments. And Tobias viewed his stake in the shop as a reason to throw his weight around, even if it was to contradict well-meaning plans for the benefit of the business. The last thing I wanted was to create any more problems for Trevor than appeared to be there already.

I was aware of both men staring at me under the scudding clouds of the Bracken Way sky. I had to make a decision. I shuffled from foot to foot on the pavement.

Across the road, Loch Bracken shimmered.

"I know I still own the shop," said Trevor interrupting my off-kilter thoughts. "But you're the manager now and I want you to be content about everything."

Out of the corner of my eye, I saw Tobias perform an exasperated eye roll.

If I did agree to this, was I making a huge mistake?

I had to give them an answer. I wasn't prepared to have Tobias think I was some ditzy young woman who couldn't make a decision if her life depended on it.

If I went along with it, I would just have to concentrate on the bookshop, work hard for Trevor and Tobias could do one. I'd ensure that I had as little interaction with him as possible. It wouldn't be easy though, sharing the same shop space as him.

This was not what I was expecting this morning. But what other choice did I have? The more I thought about the future of

Book Ends, the more I was starting to believe I might just be able to make a difference, in the long term.

I fired a steely glower at Tobias, before softening my expression for his uncle. "Trevor, you've put so much faith in me and I'm grateful." Trevor's tense expression relaxed as I nodded. "Yes, of course. I'm on board with it."

Tobias lifted one expressive brow.

Trevor let out a relieved sigh. "Thank you for being so understanding, Lexie. I appreciate it."

I whirled my attention back to Tobias. "Now, seeing as we'll be sharing business premises, Mr Black, I think the three of us need to discuss the practicalities of how this will work." Now it was my turn to be direct. "Oh, and you can help us set up our discounted books for sale as well."

Tobias's teeth clenched.

I gave him a wide smile. "No time like the present to start getting details finalised, is there?"

Chapter Eleven

I f someone had told me a few weeks ago, that I would be
managing my local bookshop, I would've laughed.

Good grief. Talk about your life taking an unexpected turn.

I was about to speak to Trevor about next steps, but he
began to move away from Tobias and me.

Alarm took hold. "Where are you going? We need to have a
talk about things going forward. Then we have to get the table
set up outside for the book sale."

Trevor observed me like a wise owl. "I won't be long. You
and Tobias can have a chat."

Tobias arched one brow at me.

"I thought I'd take myself off for a stroll and a coffee at Mrs
Hegarty's. You two will have a lot to discuss."

Great. I was going to be left alone with Tobias. "But Book
Ends is your shop," I insisted, mentally willing him to stay.
"You need to know what's happening."

"And I will. No, you two can sit in peace and sort things

out. Then you can give me a debrief and we can set up the books for sale. See you soon."

I watched with increasing dread as Trevor headed off up the pavement, which was now strobed with tentative patches of sun.

Come on, Lexie. Channel your inner tigress. You can handle Tobias Black.

I turned around. He was watching me intently.

I cleared my throat. "We can step into my office."

"I think you mean *our* office?" he corrected. "We'll be sharing the shop space, so surely we'll be sharing that as well?"

One of my brows flexed upwards. Tobias's expression didn't flinch. So, this was how it was going to be, was it? Every time I had something, he'd try to snatch half of it, like a spoilt toddler? How very mature.

I hoped I appeared crisp and professional. "The decorators have finished in the office now and I've put a couple of old chairs in there, so you can sit on one of those."

I moved ahead, striding into Book Ends. I was aware Tobias's emerald eyes were burning into my back. "Gee. Thank you," he growled.

Tobias took in the freshly painted walls; skirting boards and the finishing touches being put to the counter in its new position facing the door.

I approached the office. He followed me into the small space and closed the door behind him. He seemed almost too big for the room, his presence and ego taking up much of the space.

We sat down either side of the newly installed walnut

desk, me on the swivel black chair and he on one of the wooden kitchen chairs. I hoped it'd give him a splinter in the arse.

Before I had the chance to get myself prepared, Tobias launched straight into his ideas for the decor for his gallery. "I intend to have the walls in my section of the shop painted mint-green and have wooden blinds installed across the rear window. I'd like to distinguish between your bookshop and my gallery so I plan on having a semi-circular glass counter put in too."

I eyed him. "That all sounds very sophisticated. As long as your uncle is ok with that, then it's fine by me."

"Good."

His long, dark lashes fluttered as he concentrated on me. I shifted in my chair.

Then he moved on to talk about staffing. "I plan to place an advert in a few art magazines for at least one part-time member of staff to begin with and take it from there."

I nodded. "We'll be taking on a couple of new members of staff soon as well."

"And my uncle is aware of that?"

I managed to push out a strained smile. "What do you think? He still owns this place."

Tobias continued to gaze across the desk at me. "Glad to hear it."

My mouth flatlined.

"As for the name for my new art gallery, I've decided on Mirror Image."

"You don't hang around," I announced with a twang of sarcasm. "You seem to have everything in order already."

"Oh, I can assure you, Ms Dunbar, if I want something, I don't hold back."

Tobias's stare didn't waver.

A sudden, deep rush of adrenalin came out of nowhere and shot through me. The office felt like it was holding its breath. "Good. Excellent," I managed. "Wonderful. Ok." I straightened my shoulders. "So, what's the reason for your move back to Bracken Way?"

He raised a brow. "What do you mean?"

I'd done the same thing moving back here, but I reflected on Tobias's brittle reaction when Trevor had asked him the same question. "Quite a change, isn't it? Moving your gallery from somewhere buzzing like the city, back to a smaller town like Bracken Way?"

Tobias's steady expression remained. "Maybe some of the locals would benefit from a bit of culture."

I fired him a disapproving look.

"If you've no objection, I'll arrange for Mirror Image's official opening to coincide with yours on the 25th."

My brain skittered. The more I allowed myself to think about it, the more I was coming to the swift conclusion that this was going to be one car crash of a business arrangement.

I was aware of Tobias searching my face.

"That seems sensible," I managed.

Tobias indicated his head back towards the office door. "I'll speak to your decorators now and get the ball rolling. If they're too busy, I'll recruit someone else, but it makes sense to try and use the same people."

And with that, Tobias was on his feet and looming over me.

I stood up and he offered me his hand. His grip was firm

but soft, and his eyes never left my face. A shock of something went through me, unexpectedly, so I tugged my hand away first. I didn't want this. The more I thought about it, the more pessimistic thoughts crowded in on me. I yanked open the office door.

If I ensured I was busy with the bookshop and maintained my distance, it would be ok. Oh shit. Who was I kidding?

"After you," he murmured.

"Thank you."

I was relieved to escape from the confinement of the office and step back out onto the bookshop floor. My heart performed a leap of excitement as I took in the shop makeover being conjured up before my eyes.

Tobias's mobile started ringing. "Excuse me a second," he said, striding away from me towards the shop door.

My attention followed his retreating back.

"Everything alright?" Trevor's voice made me jump. "I knew I shouldn't have gone to Coleen Hegarty's. I think I've just eaten my own bodyweight in lemon cake."

I grinned at him. "With all the rambling you do, you'll soon burn that off."

"As long as you don't mean rambling of the talking variety."

He indicated to Tobias, who was still on his phone. "How did it go? No shouting matches or pistols at dawn?"

I explained about our agreement to share the same re-opening date. "And he already has plans to have his section of the shop redecorated. He's even chosen a name for his new gallery here; Mirror Image."

"Oh, he was always a very focused young man. Even when

he was small, he was very determined. You might even say pig-headed…" His voice tailed off. Then he recovered himself. "And is this alright with you, Lexie? I know it's all rather sudden."

Despite my festering apprehension, I nodded. "Don't worry. I'm sure it'll be fine." Ha. Maybe if I repeated it to myself often enough, I might start believing it.

Trevor swiped off his spectacles, gave them a thorough clean with a paisley cloth he produced from his trouser pocket and tucked it back in there after he'd finished. "I do appreciate this, Lexie."

"That's alright. It's the least I could do after the opportunity you're giving me."

Tobias was still prowling up and down outside the bookshop window, talking into his phone.

I offered Trevor beside me a brief glance. "I hope you don't mind me asking, but what made you change your mind?"

"Sorry? I don't follow."

"About helping Tobias. You told me that you weren't very close."

Trevor squirmed away. "It just seemed a sensible solution," he babbled. "On reflection. You know, all things considered, like his stake in the shop…" His voice tailed off. He let out a self-conscious cough. "Right. Let's get this show on the road. Ready to start selling books? I stashed the pasting table up in the loft."

"All ready when you are," I replied. Then I turned to Tobias, who had just finished his call. "Care to make yourself useful, Mr Black?"

. . .

I festered for the next couple of days about this awkward situation I found myself in, but focused on our continued book discount selling.

Some of the titles were more popular than others, but it was gratifying to see the book-loving public of Bracken Way making a point of dropping by to browse the discounted titles.

Deciding early that Wednesday morning that Tobias Black wouldn't get the upper hand or intimidate me from honouring my promise to Trevor, I took myself down to Book Ends for some thinking time, before we began day three of our discount book sale.

Unfortunately, someone else had been harbouring the same idea.

Tobias was peering through the bookshop windows and scribbling in a small notebook.

Oh shit.

My lips were rictus. I managed to grind out, "Good morning. What are you doing here so early?"

He appraised me. "Good morning. Well, seeing as I'm staying in Mrs Hopkirk's bed and breakfast just round the corner, I thought I'd make use of being close by. That's until my furniture is transported through from my rented place in Glasgow, of course."

Oh, wonderful.

"It shouldn't be too long until I can move into my new flat here."

I forced a strained smile. "You really have thought of everything, haven't you?" So, he *wasn't* staying with his uncle Trevor then. Very odd.

Tobias gestured to Book Ends. "I see we have the same idea."

I hoped I looked nonchalant. "And what idea might that be?"

"Getting our ideas together. Hit the ground running."

"I've already hit the ground running," I announced. "I know what I'm doing. This place will bounce back."

Tobias stuffed his notebook into the pocket of his jeans. He crossed his muscular arms. "Who are you trying to convince? Me or you?"

I squinted with irritation under the milky morning sky. "I'm not trying to convince anybody, certainly not you."

"Ouch. That's no way to talk to your business partner."

Oh, bloody hell! I wished he would just sod off. "We are *not* business partners, Mr Black. I think you'll find we just happen to share the same workspace." I found myself clutching the strap of my bag over my shoulder. Oh, how I wished Rembrandt wasn't here, with those scorching eyes of his.

I took an exaggerated look at my watch. "Shouldn't you be off somewhere, painting by numbers?"

Tobias let out a bark of deep laughter. "You wouldn't say that, if you saw my etchings."

A flood of colour took over my face. "No, thank you. I'm rather choosy whose etchings I look at."

He bathed me in his stare. "I'm glad to hear it."

Hoping he wouldn't notice my flaming cheeks, I marched away back up the street, not quite sure where I was headed. I would wait until he'd gone, before coming back.

Idiot!

. . .

Tobias informed us he'd opted for not one, but three part-time members of staff to run the gallery whenever he wasn't there.

Tobias's employees turned out to be three attractive young women called Octavia, Suki and Anais.

I was hardly surprised. They were all legs and long fringes.

Book Ends was finished now in terms of the refitting and redecorating and Tobias's team of decorators were putting the finishing touches to Mirror Image. John had been approached by Tobias about undertaking the decorating for him, but he'd already committed to a large job at a new, local fish restaurant. That meant Tobias had recruited a decorating firm from town instead, who probably charged him three times the amount but they did a very good job.

Silky mint-green paint now adorned the walls in Tobias's section of the bookshop and the delivery of his new-age glass counter was scheduled for the following day.

Both our shops signs were now also *in situ*, nestled side by side above the entrance: Book Ends with its sweeps of dove-grey and white paint and next to it, was Mirror Image Portraits, the lettering running along the silver sign in bold charcoal.

We stood outside Book Ends, gazing up at our respective signs.

"I think you'll find that you made the right decision," Tobias breezed. "The gallery will draw people in and Book Ends will benefit from that."

I swung round to him. "I think you're forgetting, Mr Black, that your uncle's bookshop has been here in Bracken Way for thirty years. If anybody should be grateful about this arrangement, it's you."

I found myself drowning in intense green again and jerked my eyes away.

"You seem to forget, Ms Dunbar, that you only have a year to make a success of this place. Not long in the scheme of things."

"It's long enough," I snapped. "Don't worry about that."

I wheeled back inside. Arrogant prat!

"Excuse me?"

A hesitant, female voice made me spin round.

She was, I suspected, in her mid-forties and attractive, with a riot of dark, curly, shoulder-length hair and a scattering of freckles dancing across her nose. "I wondered if you might be looking for bookshop staff?"

I gave her an encouraging smile. "Yes, we will be."

Her small white teeth flashed. "Oh, that's wonderful. I'd be very interested." She shot out one hand and we shook. "I'm Chloe Fleming. I live locally. I used to work full-time in a bookshop in Edinburgh."

My smile widened at her evident enthusiasm. "I'm Lexie Dunbar, the new manager. Wow. That must have been interesting. Do you work at the moment?"

Streaks of colour appeared on Chloe's creamy cheeks. "No. I have two teenage sons at Bracken Way High School and now that they're older, I'm keen to get out of the house and back to work." I drank in her bright trainers and the chunky silver rings on her hands. "I love reading and I'm a real book lover. I can supply you with references?"

Chloe proceeded to delve into her bag and produced a pale blue folder, which contained copies of references from her old bookshop, Chapters.

Chapters was a very prestigious bookshop in Edinburgh, located just off Princes Street. It featured vaulted ceilings, spiralling staircases and the sheer volume of books they sold was staggering. Their staff were well-trained and didn't get through the door unless they showed a real enthusiasm for reading.

I scanned Chloe's references.

They were exceptional and spoke about her being "very well organised", having "excellent communication skills" and possessing "a genuine love of books, which is infectious".

Talk about a blessing! I think I was looking right at one.

I read on about her winning employee of the month four times for her innovative ideas, which ranged from prize-giving read-a-thons to draw in younger readers to literary events up at Edinburgh Castle.

I could feel her trying to read my expression. I looked up and smiled. "The job is yours, Chloe. If you want it. It's a full-time position, though."

Chloe's face split into a huge grin and she began nodding her head so hard, her curls jumped everywhere. "Seriously? Yes please! Oh, thank you, Ms Dunbar. Thank you so much!"

"Please call me Lexie," I beamed back at her. "If you give me your contact details, I'll get back in touch with you. Would you be able to start straight away?"

There was more frantic head nodding. "Of course. You just tell me when."

We shook hands and I watched her virtually pirouette out of the shop. I almost joined in.

Chapter Twelve

Tobias and I managed to just about maintain a strained *entente cordiale*, but today, much to my relief, he was out organising the delivery of his artwork and was also busy arranging for his furniture and possessions to be transported from Glasgow to his new flat here.

It was only five days now till our grand re-opening and my emotions were rolling around like a pinball machine.

Luckily, the weather had held out and there was no sign of the familiar dreich days so far that Bracken Way was infamous for, so we'd been able to sell the vast majority of the discounted books out on the pavement from the pasting table. Any that were left, had been donated to a couple of local charity shops.

Mum, Chloe and I were busy dusting the shelves, wiping down the counter and steam cleaning the blond wood floor.

The excitement ramped up as a lorry trundled its way up the high street and pulled into the kerb right outside the shop.

It was the wholesalers with my new orders of the latest beach reads in romance, cosy crime and domestic thrillers.

A buzz of anticipation fired through me like a rocket. All these gorgeous new books! I couldn't wait to slide them onto our new shelves.

I'd been taking a surreptitious mental note of the books Trevor had been selling from before and while there had been some real treasures there, Trevor didn't seem to go in for as many novels at the commercial end of the spectrum as he should.

I hoped my suggestion of including more works from mainstream, popular authors, would help to entice a wider range of clientele through the doors.

I stuffed a duster into the back pocket of my filthy old jeans. "That's the new books here!"

Grandpa was seated behind the now gleaming counter, examining the electronic till and credit card machine as if they were about to lunge for his throat.

I thought getting involved in hectic preparations for Book Ends' rebirth might be a bit too much for my grandfather, but he insisted on helping out. "Don't be daft, lass. I can assist you with restocking the shelves," he had said. "I'm not sitting at home like some useless old relic, while you all graft away."

Grandpa's intrigued expression zoomed to the shop entrance and out of the mullioned windows.

"Ah. Just in time!" called Mum to Trevor, who had arrived. "I'll get the kettle on."

My heart quickened at the sight of the first batch of sealed cardboard boxes being off-loaded and ferried towards the shop entrance. "Delivery for Book Ends," exclaimed the driver, puffing out his red cheeks.

I leapt forward, angling the first few boxes onto the top of the counter, with the driver's kind offer of assistance. I dived underneath the counter and located a pair of scissors and began tearing open the brown tape. I was like a child on Christmas morning.

I marvelled at the rainbows of covers peeking out from under the box flaps.

Embossed foil lettering on the beautiful jackets, candy-coloured artwork, silhouettes of creepy houses, broody-looking heroes – which for some obscure reason, conjured up an image of Tobias – and pensive heroines, glossy pictures of moody castles, cosy cottages and intimidating shadows. I hoped I'd managed to cater for every reader's tastes.

My heart jumped even higher at the sight of the assorted book spines, as I began to ease them from their boxes. Chloe let out a series of dreamy sighs.

It brought back a tumble of memories about working in publishing. Some joyous and satisfying as authors held their latest book in their hands; others stress-filled, as I recollected the toiling hours and relentless pressure.

Trevor grinned over at me. "It seems much more real now, doesn't it? Like starting over again."

"It does."

Grandpa gave me a smile as he helped Mum and I lever out the novels, before I took a note of them on my laptop spreadsheet and he started placing pricing stickers on them. Then we proceeded to slide the new arrivals in alphabetical order according to the author's name, onto the glossy, towering shelves that snaked all around the bookshop walls.

The signs highlighting the assorted genres sat atop each partitioned section.

Another lorry grumbled to a stop outside on the cobbles.

Mum reappeared, manoeuvring a tray bearing six mugs of tea, which included one for the grateful delivery driver, who gulped his down before vanishing back out onto the main street to retrieve the last few boxes of novels.

"This is a hive of activity." Tobias's deep Scottish burr made me stop what I was doing.

Oh, just great. What pearls of wisdom was he planning on coming out with today?

I put down copies of the latest fiction titles with an eye roll and made my way round the bookcase. I tried to arrange my expression into something which resembled a polite one. "Good morning."

He pointed over his shoulder to the grumbling black lorry burring outside. "It would seem you're not the only one in receipt of stock today, Ms Dunbar."

"Oh?"

"That's my artwork arriving."

"Good for you," I replied with a cool smile. "And for goodness' sake, call me by my first name. It's Lexie. There's no need to be so formal around me."

Tobias flexed a brow.

Mum's cheeks flushed as I called Tobias over to introduce him to my mother, Chloe and my grandfather. "It's a pleasure to meet you all," he grinned.

Mum and Chloe couldn't stop staring up at him. He also

charmed my grandfather, with a firm handshake and a polite, "How are you, sir?"

Unbelievable!

Then Tobias spotted his uncle and they shared another odd handshake. Honestly! There were times when Tobias and Trevor made my family look like something out of a Disney movie.

Tobias disappeared out of the shop, appearing moments later carrying some personal possessions and what looked like a few knick-knacks. Amongst an assortment of pens poking out of a black chrome holder, tins of expensive-looking coffee and some Moleskine notebooks, was a *Guardians of the Galaxy* mug and a ceramic figure of cute little Groot.

When Tobias vanished out to assist the delivery driver to offload his paintings, Mum, still clutching her tea, came scurrying up to my shoulder. "My goodness. He's very good-looking."

A prickle of irritation shot through me. "Who? The lorry driver? Not my type, but hey, each to their own."

Mum tutted. "Och, stop being daft, lassie. You know full well who I'm talking about."

I busied myself with setting more books, a *Scottish Escapes* feel-good romance series, onto the shelves, which Grandpa continued to price up for me. "Oh, you mean Tobias? I suppose some women might find that arrogant, up-himself artist vibe attractive."

I could tell Mum was trying not to smile. "But not you?"

I jerked my head up at my mother's question and let out a ringing, theatrical burst of laughter. "Me? Are you joking?! Noooo! Goodness, no."

"Jings! That fine young man looks just like I did back in my youth," winked Grandpa, delivering another book onto the shelf in front of him. "Except I was even better-looking."

I laughed, but became curious by the sight of a series of paintings emerging out of the open doors of the black lorry.

Tobias was striding backwards and forwards in his dark jeans. He had thrown off his leather jacket and I caught a glimpse of the red and black Ghost T-shirt he was wearing.

My eyes popped in surprise. He was a fan of the Swedish heavy rock band? At least he had great taste in music. I loved them.

I brushed aside my ponderings about his musical tastes and carried on with perusing more of the new book arrivals. I did my best to ignore him. He was probably hoping I would head over there and start oohing and aahing over his artwork. As if!

I was so preoccupied with the new novels; I took a step backwards. I found my feet faltering, spun round, but collided face-on with another person.

I barrelled into a solid chest.

Tobias was holding another piece of artwork, concealed by a loose canvas cover. It slid to the floor as we connected.

I forced my eyes upwards. "Oh, sorry."

Tobias didn't move. He was staring down at me, bathing me in the glow of his stare again.

He cleared his throat. "Apologies."

I realised I was still standing there, looking up at him. Embarrassment took hold and I sprang away. I wrapped my arms tighter around the paperbacks I was holding and focused my attention on the bookshelves again.

Grandpa and Trevor were busy examining the gift cards

and loyalty cards we'd ordered. My grandfather set one of the cards down, suddenly more interested in Tobias and me. A little smile played around his mouth, before he returned his attention to what he was doing.

I noticed out of the corner of my eye Tobias bending down and retrieving the piece of canvas cloth that had slid off from the painting he was holding. My attention fell on the picture.

It was a portrait of a little girl with long, fair hair and a straight fringe, gazing down at a small, brown teddy cradled in her arms. You could make out the flecks of cornflower blue in her eyes and the faint dusting of freckles across her snub little nose. It was as if I could feel the pink ripples in her silk dress and the ragged texture of her beloved bear's ears. It was stunning.

The brush strokes were an alluring combination of deliberate, delicate and sweeping watercolours.

I couldn't stifle my appreciation of the glorious portrait. It looked more like a photograph. "That's gorgeous," I breathed, nodding at the painting in his arms. "It's almost as though I could reach out and touch her."

For a moment, Tobias looked confused, thrown even. He followed my eyes to the framed painting he was clutching. "Oh. Right. Thank you."

I admired the little girl's freckles again. "How did you manage to paint something so beautiful?"

"Is that your not-so-subtle way of saying you couldn't imagine an ogre like me being able to paint something like this?"

"No, of course not. I'm just a bit surprised."

"I got that impression."

Tobias leant the painting against the nearest wall. "I don't paint by numbers."

"I never said that."

"If I recall, you did. A couple of weeks ago."

Oops. I did. My cheeks lit up.

"I enjoy painting with water colours. I think they remind me of dancing; they possess a life and rhythm of their own." He angled his head to one side as he studied me. "But you do sound surprised that I painted this?"

"No," I clarified. "I suppose I'm surprised that you paint like that."

Tobias indicated his shoulder-length mane to another painting being transported past me by the delivery driver. This one was of a half-naked young woman with a messy raven bob, examining her reflection in a long, oval mirror.

"That's lovely too," I admitted.

His eyes shone. "It was a commission I was asked to do by the lady in the portrait. It was a surprise gift for her husband for his fortieth birthday. Camille, the lady in question, has given me permission to display it."

"It's beautiful," I said, before realising I was giving Tobias another compliment. That would have to stop.

He kept staring at me. "Thank you."

Chapter Thirteen

The day of the official relaunch of Book Ends and the opening of Mirror Image dawned with bright, sweeping sunshine that glittered on top of the loch like scattered pieces of gold confetti.

I'd had a restless night's sleep, my head filled with thoughts of the bookshop and niggling doubts about whether working so closely to Tobias had been such a great decision on my part. Only because he was so arrogant, I assured myself. For no other reason than that.

Oh well. It was too late to do anything about it now. I'd just have to get on with it and make the best of the situation.

Had I remembered everything? What if I failed? How would the Bracken Way locals react to the new look Book Ends?

Would the next twelve months see me able to make a success of the bookshop or was it a catastrophe waiting to happen? I really wanted this to work. Failure was not an option.

In the end, I became so agitated, I threw back my bed covers and padded downstairs to Mum's kitchen to make myself a cup of tea.

It was just after 5am and the dawning sky reminded me of treacle spilling across the amber silhouette of the town walls.

Realising my brain was full of so much turmoil I wouldn't be able to get back to sleep, I drained the dregs of my tea, managed a few bites of toast and then showered.

Mum, Grandpa and I had arranged to meet Trevor and Chloe down at Book Ends at 8am, so I took my time getting ready.

I also checked my emails from authors seeking my freelance editorial services.

I'd received a couple more enquiries from struggling writers, who had seen my adverts and were keen to speak to me, so I dashed off replies, asking for them to send me a synopsis and first three chapters of their novels. I also attached details of my rates.

One said she'd written a political romance that had received a torrent of rejections from agents and the other author, a retired man in his sixties, had completed the first draft of his Scandinavian espionage thriller, but felt like it needed an expert eye.

Another writer had also been in contact about his memoir of his times on an oil rig, but I replied with a polite decline, explaining that I was only dealing with fiction.

Then I gave him a couple of names of other freelance editors I recalled from my days at Literati, who he might be able to approach.

Once that was done, I decided to throw on my old

sweatshirt and jogging pants. I also piled my hair into a messy up-do and applied my make-up, so it would just require a quick retouch before we officially re-opened at 10am.

Last night, I'd fetched my floaty, sky-blue, daisy-printed summer dress from my wardrobe and slid that into a hanging suit carrier to protect it.

To accompany it, I chose my pale ballet flats topped off with yellow leather bows. Once we had everything in place and as it should be in the bookshop, I could slip into the staff toilets and change out of my scruffy clothes.

Mum, Grandpa and I made sure we departed at 7.45am and armed with my change of outfit and shoulder bag, I jumped into the back seat of Mum's car, with Grandpa easing himself into the passenger side. It would be a little too far for him to walk.

Bracken Way was basking in the early morning sunshine as we pulled up into one of the sought after and currently empty parking bays along the main street.

Trevor and Chloe were waiting for us outside the shop when we arrived.

Mum had decided to do the same as me, dressing down in her battered old jeans and a loose denim shirt, while her fancy outfit was covered in plastic sheeting and draped over one arm.

Grandpa, on the other hand, had decided not to bother with such trivialities and was already suited and booted in his best dark grey suit, white shirt and colourful, stripey tie. His papery mouth broke into a warm smile under his military-style moustache when he saw Trevor and Chloe standing there. Trevor was sporting a smart, naval-type blazer, white shirt and red tie, with matching dark blue trousers.

Chloe, meanwhile, looked charming and professional, in a black and white, slim-fitting dress and a matching monochrome band in her hair.

Grandpa gave me one of his supportive, big hugs. I got a comforting whiff of Brylcreem. "Well, little dove. Are we all set then?" he asked.

I pulled a face as I embraced Trevor, who turned red. I fished around inside my bag for the shop door key and unlocked the shop door. "Let's hope so!"

We spent the next half an hour having a cup of tea and reminiscing over Naomi and Grandma Pattie and how they would've loved to have been here, thrown into the middle of it all.

The bookshop felt like she was holding her breath. There were the packed and rejuvenated bookcases, glossy new window displays of the latest book releases, not to mention the multi-coloured beanbags for the children to relax on.

My attention then travelled to Tobias's gallery.

All his portraits, hanging on those chic mint-green walls, seemed to follow me whenever and wherever I moved. He had selected an eclectic mix of his work for his grand opening of Mirror Image, which included my favourite of the little girl and her teddy, not to mention the half-naked woman with the tousled hair.

There were a few of his other paintings of couples, expectant and embracing, and other pieces of work featuring elderly gents. Their expressions were lived-in and craggy, bearing their own individual stories.

The spotlights above each artwork were not yet switched on, but Tobias had assured me yesterday that he would be arriving around 9am.

Mum had insisted on giving the shelves and the counter a final dust, even though you could've eaten your breakfast off them.

Grandpa gave his head a bemused shake. "Dear God. I don't know who's the more bloody nervous, you or your mother."

Trevor, who had already given the shop windows a final once-over with vinegar and a cloth, aided by an enthusiastic Chloe, rung up a couple of book suppliers to order copies of an A-lister autobiography, and had already popped to the bank, smiled. His spectacles shone. "I might not look nervous, but inside, I'm quaking. I shall be celebrating with a drink at the end of the day – and I don't mean orange juice."

Grandpa's pale eyes lit up. "Och, that sounds like a fine plan, Trevor. The first round is on you." He creaked up from his chair behind the counter. "Oh aye. Look sharp, ladies and gents. It's Coleen Hegarty."

Bearing down on the shop entrance, accompanied by two of her waiting staff, was Mrs Hegarty. They were juggling boxes of bottles of champagne and elegant glasses.

She rapped on the door, before turning to gesticulate to someone lagging behind further up the street.

I hurried to the door, opened it and insisted on helping them inside.

Mrs Hegarty's husband Frazer was following up the rear with the trestle tables. "All hands-on deck!" she boomed. "The girls have managed to persuade their boyfriends to come along and give us a hand too."

"That's very kind of them." I smiled.

"Ken was going to drop this little lot off himself, but he's got an urgent order in for a fiftieth birthday party who've been let down by their caterers," explained Mrs Hegarty, taking great delight in directing operations.

She, together with her entourage, trooped in like clockwork soldiers on parade, wishing us all a good morning, before Frazer and the two strapping young lads set up the trestle tables outside the bookshop windows.

The champagne bottles and glasses were placed with the utmost care on top of the bookshop counter. I hoped the sea of glorious books and receiving ten per cent off first purchases on opening day would tempt lots of people in.

"I even brought three tablecloths along with me," announced Mrs Hegarty with self-satisfaction, widening her eyes in a meaningful way at the young girl with two long blonde plaits.

The teenager took her cue, delved one hand into a huge canvas bag over her shoulder and pulled out three lacy white tablecloths, each folded and wrapped up in protective cellophane.

"Oh wow, Mrs Hegarty You're a star. Thank you!"

She glowed with delight. "Aww away with you! Just thought it might add an extra touch of class."

"I do hope you can all manage to pop down at some point this morning to help us celebrate Book Ends' re-opening."

"We'll see what we can do. Bank holiday weekends are

normally manic for us in the tea room, but we'll try. Us local businesses must support each other!"

And with that, Mrs Hegarty, her puffing, out-of-breath husband and the teenagers disappeared back up the street in a haze of trainers and baggy T-shirts.

"It's happening," murmured Trevor. "It's finally happening."

I patted him on his jacketed arm. "No regrets about giving me a chance?"

He sucked in some air. "None at all."

I glanced at my watch. "Good. Right. I'll quickly go and get changed. Then we can set out the champagne and glasses."

I had just thrown off my old jogging bottoms and sweatshirt and jumped into my dress and ballet flats, when Mum's voice trilled through the door. "Sorry to interrupt you sweetie, but there's someone here to see you."

I finished stuffing my old clothes into a carrier bag and began reapplying my pink lipstick. "Who is it?" I called.

"Oh, some book sales rep."

I swung open the toilet door, to see Mum looking resplendent in an electric-blue fitted jacket and skirt. "You look lovely, Mum."

"Thank you darling. I just got changed in the office." She leant in closer to the door. "Can you come and have a word with her?"

I frowned. "What, now? We open in an hour. Can't you just take a note of her details and I'll get back to her next week? Or maybe Trevor could have a quick word with her?"

Mum shook her wavy dark hair. It bounced on top of her

shoulders. "I've already said that to her, but she was insistent. She asked for you."

I tutted.

"Just go and see her and then I'm sure she'll leave."

I teased my hair, piled on top of my head. "For goodness' sake. Oh alright. Let me drop this lot in the office first." I snatched up the bag containing my old clothes and trainers. What great timing!

I whipped open the office door and dumped the bag inside, before closing it again.

Mum joined me as I tapped down the shop floor. I could make out the silhouette of a woman standing with her back to me between two of the bookcases. I hissed out of the corner of my mouth. "I hope she gets the hint, Mum, and doesn't outstay her welcome. I want to have a final check of everything and…"

My voice died as the woman emerged. She was grinning at me and rocking a sophisticated, flared trouser suit in marigold.

It was Rhiannon. "Good morning, Ms Dunbar."

I let out a squeal and whirled round to look at Mum. "Did you know about this?"

"No. Not until Rhiannon arrived just now."

"It's true," she confirmed, striding towards me, with her hair more platinum than ever as it bounced against her cheeks. "I'd every intention of coming, but decided not to tell you. I wanted it to be a surprise." She pulled me into her arms. "As if I would miss my best friend and favourite editor's bookshop launch!"

I hugged her back. "I bet you say that to all the editors."

She winked. "Nah." She angled her head to one side. "Now,

please don't shoot the messenger, but I don't suppose you've given any more consideration to returning to publishing at some point?"

I folded my arms. "You're persistent, I'll say that for you."

"Good morning, Lexie. Ready for the crazy day ahead?"

My stomach lurched at the sound of Tobias's voice.

He strolled in, pushing a stray curl back behind an ear. He was wearing a checked herringbone waistcoat in sea-blue, with white shirt, dark tie and black trousers. He reminded me of a sexy, brooding poet.

His expression was one of cool efficiency. Then he spotted me in my summer dress and with my hair piled up, messy tendrils framing my face. His face changed. He fell silent for a few moments and then recovered himself. "Well... you look... um... very professional."

"Thank you." I gestured at him. "Likewise."

His mouth broke into a stunning grin, exposing his perfect teeth and my stomach performed an impressive backflip. Good grief! I'd never seen him smile like that before. It lit up his eyes. I felt like I'd been winded.

Mum, Trevor, Chloe and Grandpa, who was nursing yet another cup of tea by the counter, joined Rhiannon in exchanging meaningful glances with one another.

"I can understand what you meant when you said your mind has been on other things," hissed Rhiannon, giving Tobias an appreciative once over as he moved away to illuminate his gallery. "Who's the dishy Jon Snow lookalike?"

I hoped my face wasn't scarlet. "Tobias Black. He's the bookshop owner's nephew. He also owns the portrait gallery section just behind you, Mirror Image."

As if on cue, Tobias returned and introduced himself to Rhiannon. Her attention trailed after him, once they'd exchanged handshakes and a few words.

She observed him inspecting his paintings. Then she waggled her plucked eyebrows at me in a suggestive way.

I clapped my hands together for something to do and ignored her dancing brows. "We're work associates. He pays his uncle rent to use the space. That's it."

"How boring," joked Rhiannon. Her attention flitted in Tobias's direction again. "I wouldn't be getting any work done if I had someone like him to look at every day."

I waved my hand, keen to change the subject. "Anyway, enough about Tobias. I'm still reeling from you being here. When did you arrive? Where are you staying?"

She flicked some hair back from her face. "I drove up last night and I'm staying at The Drawbridge."

"And how long are you here for?"

"Till Monday afternoon. Thought I'd make the most of the bank holiday weekend." She threw me a cheeky smile. "We can catch up, have a laugh… discuss why a brilliant editor like you has left us in the lurch…"

I narrowed my eyes at her. "Don't make me regret having you as my best friend."

"Ok, ok," agreed Rhiannon with a dramatic sigh. "Point taken. The wine and chocolates will be on me."

Half past nine saw the arrival of Tobias's trio of gazelle-like members of staff. They trotted in, wobbling about in needle-thin heels, black shirts and tight trousers. They looked more like they were a superstar singer's glamorous backing vocalists.

Octavia was a highlighted blonde who swished her hair around a lot; Suki was a statuesque brunette with a gravelly laugh; and Anais had stunning looks and seemed far more interested in our books than Tobias's portraits.

They awarded us megawatt smiles from their lofty positions in Mirror Image, when they weren't flirting with Tobias.

Not that I was bothered about that, I assured myself.

10am arrived in a final flurry of activity and panic.

The trestle tables were covered in the brilliant-white fluttery tablecloths and glinting champagne flutes.

The bookcase contents were appreciated, browsed, examined and in many cases, purchased. People were relaxed and wreathed in smiles, appreciating the late May bank holiday weekend weather and the bustle of Bracken Way.

Some locals drifted around, savouring the atmosphere, appreciating the array of books and sipping their champagne.

Others took a few moments to examine the books they'd just bought.

Compliments flowed, as did the champagne and there was a general feeling of optimism and delight for the new-look Book Ends.

Mum was a godsend, making sure glasses were topped up.

My grandfather, meanwhile, joined Trevor, Chloe and me behind the counter, serving customers, chatting about the cricket on TV and sliding purchased books into our jazzy new gift bags.

The joint opening of Mirror Image saw arty friends of Tobias, critics and intrigued customers mingling and exchanging pleasantries with the bookshop customers. I overheard snatches of his conversations, discussing blending surfaces, intermediate colours and citrus turpentine.

Tobias observed a couple of ladies, armed with their purchased copies of two dark thrillers, stroll into his domain to admire his portraits and ask details about his work.

One even purchased a smaller print of his little girl and teddy portrait.

I turned, smiling, nodding and thanking others for their good luck wishes and enthusiastic congratulations as they mingled around. Business was brisk. Ok, curiosity would be playing its part, but nevertheless, Trevor was grinning from ear to ear, so my one-year timeline to improve Book Ends was off to a flying start.

A waft of recognisable, citrus aftershave emerged from behind me. My heart jumped in my chest.

It was Tobias. "Things seems to be going very well," he said, close to my ear.

I disguised the electric shock that shot through me as his breath touched my neck. "They are. How is it for you?"

Tobias took a sip from the champagne glass he was holding. "I have to say, it's all going very smoothly." He waggled his champagne flute. There was a devilish twitch at the corners of his mouth. "Can I tempt you?"

I whipped my attention away, before he could spot colour

flooding my face. Why the hell were my cheeks scalding like this? "Thank you, but no, I'd better keep a clear head."

Tobias twinkled at me from over the top of his glass. "Scared you might let your guard down?"

I prickled. "About what?"

His attention lingered on my mouth. "You tell me."

I jutted out my chin. "Not at all. In fact, alright. I will have a glass." I shot him a look. "Actually, I think that's a bit rich coming from you."

Both of his eyebrows arched up to his thick hair as he fetched a glass of bubbly for me and handed it over. "Sorry?"

"Thank you." I gathered myself together, clutched my champagne flute and pushed on. "Well, all this secrecy. Why did you come back here? Why did your uncle change his mind about helping you?"

Tobias switched his attention back to drinking his pale gold champagne. "I've no idea why my uncle did what he did. You'd have to ask him that." He took another gulp from his champagne flute. "Maybe he felt obliged to help me because of my investment in the shop."

Our conversation was interrupted by Rhiannon shimmying past with an attractive young spiky-haired blond man in a sharp blue suit and pillar-box red shoes.

She waggled her fingers in a jokey wave.

"Who's that Rhiannon's with?" I asked Tobias.

"Lester Graves. He's an immersive artist."

"Immersive?"

"Yes. It's a bit like stepping into a computer game. He's big on using water effects like dolphins, waves and jelly fish in his work."

128

"That sounds impressive."

"He likes to think so," glinted Tobias. "He's also an infamous womaniser."

"And does it take one to know one?" I remarked. Bugger! Why did I say that? I wasn't bothered about what Tobias did and with whom, so why ask the question?

I noticed Tobias was widening his green eyes. His mouth flickered at the corners. "Whatever gave you that idea?"

I pulled a sarcastic face as Rhiannon and Lester were swallowed up by the chattering throng. "You seem to have recruited three supermodels as your new employees."

Tobias shrugged. "I'm more concerned about them being good ambassadors for the gallery."

His attention followed Rhiannon and Lester again.

"I hate to admit it, but Mirror Image does look very classy."

There was a look of surprise on his handsome face. "Good grief. Another compliment. I should have these recorded for posterity."

I rolled my eyes. "Yes. Well. You've obviously worked very hard on the gallery."

"It's a jungle out there," replied Tobias, deadpan. "I always sleep with one eye open."

I couldn't help but laugh against my champagne glass. Then I got annoyed at myself for finding Tobias funny. I took a sip and caught a glimpse of Rhiannon flirting with her new artist companion through the bodies of people. Even if this Lester was a womaniser, he'd have met his match in Rhiannon.

· · ·

The morning vanished, more customers filed in during the afternoon and by closing time we were frazzled but happy.

So many books had been sold, a few of Tobias's pieces had also been bought and several others reserved, and the white tablecloths were adorned with abandoned, empty champagne glasses, which we had gathered together and washed before we returned them to Mrs Hegarty.

Mum and Grandpa looked happy but exhausted, so I ordered them home just before closing, so it was just me, Tobias, Trevor and Chloe who remained.

"That was a very special first day," exclaimed Trevor.

"And a lovely surprise that your publishing friend was able to make it too," piped up Chloe.

Yes, Rhiannon had delighted me by turning up like that.

Then a thought occurred to me and I glanced around at the empty floor space, which during the day, had been clotted with bodies. "Come to think of it, have any of you seen Rhiannon?"

"Not since she vanished with that young man earlier," said Trevor, frowning, as he replaced the roll of receipt paper in the till.

I turned and stared past the bookshelves and up towards Mirror Image.

Tobias was engrossed with his phone, frantically typing away.

"You don't happen to know where your friend Lester and Rhiannon have got to, do you?"

He slid his mobile into the pocket of his dapper waistcoat and strode down towards me. "Sorry, Lexie?"

I repeated my question to Tobias about Lester and Rhiannon's whereabouts.

"I can't speak for your friend, but Lester left about two hours ago on his own."

A kernel of worry about Rhiannon implanted itself. "Are you sure?"

"Absolutely. Why do you ask?"

I shot concerned glances at Trevor and Chloe. "We haven't seen Rhiannon since."

"I'm sure she's fine," assured Tobias. "She's probably returned to her hotel. Maybe she wanted a rest or forgot something."

"I'll give The Drawbridge a ring now," offered Trevor. "Find out if she's got back to her room yet." He headed off towards the office door and slipped inside to ring the hotel.

But a sudden loud knocking on the shop door made the three of us start.

It was Rhiannon, grinning.

A mixture of relief and irritation fired up inside me, as I marched over and unlocked it. "Where the hell have you been? You've been gone ages!"

Rhiannon swept in, her designer leather bag dangling from her shoulder. "I was having a drink in the local pub." Her eyes sparkled with a combination of alcohol and teasing.

"What? With a guy?"

"No, a dog. Of course, with a guy," she giggled. She hooked her hair back behind one ear and glanced over her shoulder. She dropped her voice to a tipsy hush. "He's just outside, round the corner."

I arched one brow at her. "So come on then," I urged. "Who is he? We've been worried about you."

Rhiannon attempted to steady herself in her white strappy

heels. "There's no need to worry about me, Lexie. I met this guy down by the loch, we started chatting and then he invited me for a drink." She flushed pink. "He's a bit of a charmer." She flicked me a coy look. "A little bit older than what I usually go for, but he's rather tasty." She let out another drink-induced laugh. "Hang on a sec. I'll invite him in. He was very interested in you and your bookshop."

She swung round and walked like a gazelle on stilts back out the shop door to retrieve her new drinking buddy.

"What's going on?" asked Trevor, emerging from the office. "I just rang The Drawbridge and they said your friend hasn't been back there."

I rolled my eyes. "Panic over, Trevor. Rhiannon is fine, if a bit squiffy. She met some charming guy at the harbour and he took her to the local pub. She's just popped back outside to bring him in."

"Thank goodness she's alright," said Trevor.

As if on cue, Rhiannon clattered back in through the shop door, with someone following up behind.

Tobias and Trevor watched, almost as curious as Chloe and me, keen to see who'd managed to charm my discerning friend.

Rhiannon let out another fruity giggle as a male figure emerged from behind her.

My expectant smile collapsed.

Oh, you had to be kidding.

This wasn't happening.

Chapter Fourteen

It took a few moments for my brain to catch up.

The air in Book Ends was still, a world away from this morning when it reverberated to the sound of clinking champagne flutes, chattering and laughter.

Was this some sort of joke? If it was, nobody was finding it bloody funny, least of all me.

Rhiannon observed me with bemusement. "What's going on? Why are you looking like that, Lex? Do you know each other then?"

My mouth contorted. I found myself fighting to speak." You could say that." The words lodged in my throat. "This charming man you've just met is my dad."

The colour drained from Rhiannon's face. "What?" She spun round to look at my dad. "You're kidding. You're Lexie's father?" Her red slicked mouth fell open. "But... but you said your name was Niall O'Connell."

I stood rigid, as though frozen in time. "O'Connell was my

paternal grandmother's maiden name," I managed after an agonised pause.

Rhiannon planted her hands on her hips. Her face was flushed, clashing with the bright blonde of her hair. She let out an embarrassed laugh. "I don't believe this. How sodding underhand can you get?! Why didn't you tell me the truth when I told you why I was here?"

My father made a half-hearted attempt to say something, but Rhiannon cut him off. "You let me ramble on like an idiot. I wondered why you were asking me so many questions about the bookshop and Lexie." She whirled back to me. Her face could have heated the National Grid of its own accord.

My father stood there, his dark hair lifting in the open shop doorway, the evening light highlighting his silver streaks. It was as though he'd just stepped out of the TV screen and planted himself in front of us like a magician. His grey eyes stayed glued to me. God, it was like staring in a mirror. I squirmed inside.

His accent, a concoction of Scottish-American, rang around the four walls of Book Ends.

"Lexie, I'm sorry but I didn't know what to do. I was desperate to find out how you were doing and then when Rhiannon told me she was your best friend, I thought that'd be the perfect opportunity."

I glowered, my eyes burning into him, and shook my head. "You just thought you'd trick her into giving you the lowdown?" My teeth gritted with disbelief. "And lying to her about who you were as well. Nice to see you haven't changed a bit, Dad."

My father flashed an apologetic look at Trevor, Tobias and Chloe.

Tobias, who I'd almost forgotten was also a witness to these stunning proceedings, stepped forward.

"Are you ok, Lexie? Anything I can do?"

His kindness made me start. I watched him through a confused haze. I managed to find my voice after a few seconds and gave him a watery smile of gratitude. "Thank you, Tobias, but no, I can handle this."

My lips puckered with disdain, as I returned my stunned attention to my dad. Outside, the loch shimmied under the sunshine and late browsers drifted past the shops. "How did you know we were re-opening today? You can't have just flown over from the States by coincidence."

Niall, his smooth tan enhanced by his buttercup-yellow shirt, adjusted his collar.

"Well?" I pushed, hurt clouding in my eyes as I looked at him.

Chloe was shooting me uncertain glances.

"No. It's not a coincidence. One of my old fishing buddies who I still keep in touch with from here told me about you and the bookshop."

I let out a burst of loud, sarcastic laughter. "No, don't tell me. Let me guess. It wouldn't happen to be that old reprobate Gilbert Guthrie by any chance, would it? That man couldn't hold his own water."

Dad gave a self-conscious nod. "Yes. Gilbert told me a few weeks ago that today was the official re-opening."

I couldn't disguise my sarcasm. "And you just thought

you'd fly across the Atlantic and turn up in Bracken Way today to wish us well. Pity you weren't so considerate twenty-three years ago."

Rhiannon rubbed at her eyes, embarrassment still gripping her. She let out an audible groan, as she shuffled from foot to foot in her trendy suit. "I had no idea who he was. I feel like this is all my fault. I'm so sorry." She dug her manicured nails into her bag. "He just started chatting to me. I think he must have overheard me talking about the bookshop opening to Lester and thought I could get him in here." She closed her eyes for a few moments. "If I'd known he was your dad, I would never have brought him here." She noticed my stormy expression. "I'm so sorry, Lexie."

"No need to apologise. My dad has always been a smooth talker. That was part of the problem."

My father flinched and struggled to look at me.

Rhiannon was still blushing. "I still feel awful about it though, especially today."

I rubbed at my exhausted face. "Look, let's forget it," I said with added emphasis. "It isn't important."

Trevor desperately tried to melt the frosty atmosphere. "We've had a lovely day and the relaunch has got Book Ends off to a wonderful new phase."

I wrapped my arms around myself, my shocked gaze now morphing into a furious one at my father. "Well, whatever the reason is that you decided to show up today, I want you to leave. Now."

My dad took a hesitant step towards me. "Lexie. Please. All I'm asking is for a few minutes to talk to you."

I was shaking my head so much; I was in danger of dislodging my up-do. "No. I'm busy."

It was then that Trevor suggested he and Chloe head home.

They both grabbed their things, eager to give my father and me some space.

I thanked them again for all their hard work. I got the impression that after the soap opera they'd just witnessed, they were relieved to leave Book Ends behind for the day!

I hugged Trevor and Chloe and watched them leave, exchanging smiles and chatter as they went.

Rhiannon, meanwhile, continued to shuffle awkwardly, apologising for the twentieth time, until I asked her to go and buy us a bottle of something crisp and white for later.

I gave her a reassuring squeeze. "Honestly, it's fine. He played you. He has an ability, don't you, Dad? Don't give it another thought."

My father blanched as we watched Rhiannon disappear up the sun-spilt high street and head back towards her hotel.

I swung round to face my father. "I don't want you here, Dad. We have nothing to say to each other."

I waited, but still he hovered.

"Lexie. That's not true. I have something to say to you."

I made a noise that was a cross between a laugh and a bewildered snort. "Whatever it is, I don't want to hear it. You've had a wasted journey. Now go."

A strained silence permeated.

"I think you should leave, sir." Tobias was polite, but his voice was laced with assertiveness. I'd momentarily forgotten that Tobias was still here with us.

Undeterred, my father pressed on regardless. "Please, Lexie."

I scowled.

"What bit of piss off don't you understand?" I shrieked, biting back a sob in my voice.

Tobias stepped forward. "Sir, you can see you're upsetting your daughter."

Dad's face dropped. "That's the last thing I want to do, believe me." His gaze levelled with mine. "Lexie, this might well be the last chance I have to apologise for what I did to you and your mother."

"Oh, stop being so melodramatic!"

"I'm not. I'm serious."

I frowned, swiping at my eyes with the back of my hand. His words made me draw up. "What do you mean? What are you talking about?"

Dad sucked in a mouthful of air. Behind him, life was playing out in Bracken Way, with its busy little shops and the traffic idling past. Bikes on top of car roofs glittered in the late afternoon sun. Agony reared up in his eyes. "I didn't want to tell you. Not like this. I'd planned to tell you and your mother together."

I sniffed. "Tell us what? Are you finally getting remarried, Dad? Tired of shagging your way around the newsrooms of the world?"

The atmosphere inside Book Ends was like a giant bubble preparing to burst. There was an electrified silence. He rubbed hard at his lined forehead, before staring down at the polished shop floor. He jerked his head back up to meet my gaze. "I'm ill, Lexie. Seriously ill."

I drank him in, trying to process what he was saying. "What on earth are you talking about?"

And for the first time I saw my father, normally so self-assured and confident, look agonised and lost. He set his shoulders.

"I've got dementia."

Chapter Fifteen

Tobias made his way to lock the front door before moving back into my shocked line of sight. "Lexie? Lexie. Do you want me to stay?"

I stared past him for a few seconds, struggling to comprehend what was happening. Today had been delightful, with enthusiastic sales and customers wreathed in smiles. Book Ends had been relaunched with a fanfare. Today was supposed to have ended on such a high.

It seemed a world away now.

A swirl of emotions whirled through me like a tornado. Dementia?

I refocused on Tobias's broad shoulders and the silhouette of his wild dark curls standing in front of me.

Dad's words rang around my head, like clanging church bells on a Sunday morning. He didn't feel like a father to me, but nevertheless, I wouldn't wish this on anyone.

I tried to unscramble my head. *Come on Lexie. Speak!* My

voice sounded like a faint echo. "Yes, please could you stay, Tobias."

He nodded and gave me a flicker of a supportive smile. "Sure."

Dad's face was pleading. "I'm sorry, Lexie. Like I said, I didn't want you to find out like this. I didn't plan on blurting it out."

I straightened my dress, before my hands started to tumble over each other again. "Dementia?"

"Yes."

"Are you sure?"

"My doctor confirmed it."

My thoughts jostled, as I tried to make sense of the news. Snatched, brief memories of my father from my childhood, shimmered in front of my eyes. His handsome silhouette reflected in the computer screen as he bashed out urgent copy for the local newspaper; his frustration that he couldn't land a post on one of the bigger publications; Mum's tears as he delivered a whole raft of excuses why he was walking out on us. I blinked across at my dad, struggling to focus. "But... but you're only sixty."

"Coming up for sixty-one now." He gave a shrug, fighting to look accepting of it. "Unlucky, I guess."

My thoughts were running in every direction.

I made my way to the counter and leant against it, my head bursting with so many sudden questions it felt as though it was about to explode. I cleared my throat. "When did you find out? About the dementia?"

"Two months ago." He opened and closed his tanned hands. "I noticed I was beginning to forget why I was going into a particular room a few months prior to that. At first, I thought it was just me getting on." An echo of a wry smile toyed at the corners of his mouth. "Then I found I was beginning to forget my lines when I was reporting; even the names of the guys who I've worked with for a few years now."

Dad gathered himself, as he described the battery of tests and examinations he had to go through – everything from mental capacity to blood tests and scans. "I was like a sodding pincushion." Dad gripped tighter to the jacket he had draped over one arm. "I had a lingering fear at the back of my mind that it might be dementia. But I convinced myself that it was just stress-related and me overdoing it."

He fiddled with his jacket, for something to do. "I'm not expecting you to forget me walking out on you and your mother. I didn't think you would throw yourself at me and tell me I was forgiven." His mouth gave a nervous twitch. "Although if you wanted to do that, I wouldn't object."

I didn't return his hint of a smile. I still felt like I was fighting my way through a fog. What was I supposed to do? How was I meant to handle this? Would other people react in this way, after receiving news like that about their father? How would they feel?

"I just wanted to tell you." His voice crashed through my thoughts. He hesitated, before carrying on. "I've taken a few weeks' holiday, so I'll be here in Bracken Way for a while."

The inference hung in the air.

I hugged myself tighter, trying to unscramble what he'd just told me and the meaning behind it.

"Anyway, thank you for hearing me out, Lexie. I'm sorry again for telling you like this. Maybe we could talk again?"

I slid a glance to my left. Tobias's dark features studied me.

One of my hands shot up to fiddle with the buttons on my dress. "I don't know, Dad. Maybe. This has come as a real shock, you turning up like this, not to mention what you've just told me."

I realised I was rambling and bit my bottom lip. "Look, I really am sorry to hear about your diagnosis, but why come back into our lives now? Is it because you want us to feel sorry for you?"

His quirky mouth moulded into a dry smile. "I don't want anyone's pity, Lexie. But I've had time to think and I want to try and put things right, while I can."

I stood there, feeling thrown off-kilter. "Like I said, Dad, I'm sorry."

"Not as sorry as I am." He jerked his head back over his shoulder. "I had better be off." He reached into the pocket of his jacket and pulled out a business card. "I'm staying at The Drawbridge, but you can reach me on my new mobile number."

I eyed his fingers sliding the white card along the counter. They remained on top of the card for a few seconds. "Maybe you could tell your mother for me. I had hoped she'd be here."

"She was. She and Grandpa left a short while ago."

He nodded, before making his way back out of the shop and heading into the melee of day trippers. He turned around, offered me an awkward, brief wave through the window and vanished.

For a few seconds, I thought I was handling my father's shock diagnosis. But a delayed weight pushed down on me, taking my breath from my chest.

Tobias was beside me in a couple of keen strides. "You, ok?"

I started, as though I'd almost forgotten he was still there. "Yes. I think so." I paused. "Actually, I'm not sure."

He nodded, as though he understood what and why I was rambling. "Right. We're going to take a walk now. You look like you could be doing with some fresh air."

"No, it's alright."

"No, it isn't alright. Now just for once, Lexie, will you please do as you're told?"

I glanced up at him, bathed in the glow from his eyes. I wanted someone else to tell me what to do for once. It was a lovely sensation. "Yes. Alright." I blushed through a shocked fog. "Thank you."

"No problem."

Tobias waited as I vanished into the office to collect my bag. He ushered me out and locked up the shop behind him.

I squinted against the May sunshine. What was I supposed to feel? How was I meant to deal with this? He was my dad – well, in the loosest sense of the word. He was ambitious and had loved his career – more than Mum and me. He was a clever and driven man. And yet, he'd been stricken with dementia?

Sensing so many questions bolting at breakneck speed through my head, Tobias kept pace beside me along the pavement. "Just say as much or as little as you want, ok? What do you want to do? Where do you want to walk to?"

I reached up and toyed with one of my silver stud earrings. "The castle," I murmured. "Bracken Way Castle. I always like to go up there when I have to think." I gave him an awkward blush. "When I was a teenager, that was where I always headed after an argument with Mum."

He almost smiled. "We've all been there. Ok. Let's do that then." He strode on beside me, shooting me frequent glances.

To the right, the loch waltzed under the evening sun. To the left, the castle erupted out of the hillside, reminding me of a medieval wedding cake, with its turrets and crenelations.

In silence, we strode up the steps until we reached the railings that ran around the perimeter of the castle.

I clung onto the peeling, painted rail, admiring the view down over Loch Bracken.

Tobias leant beside me, his strong profile inches away.

"Isn't there somewhere else you should be?" I asked him, noting the generous curve of his mouth and not sure what I was doing up here with him.

"Nope. I had been invited to a friend's art exhibition in Glasgow tonight, but I cried off." A corner of his mouth flickered. "After a hard day charming Bracken Way ladies into parting with their hard-earned cash, I figured I needed a break."

My lips hinted at a smile. "Yes, it must've been exhausting for you."

We mirrored each other, savouring the swish of the water. The castle had closed for the day and sat there behind us, as though discreetly listening to our conversation.

Tobias angled himself round. "You know, you don't have to feel raging emotions or guilt, Lexie, about your dad. You don't have to feel anything."

He swiped some hair away from his face. "I don't pretend

to know what things were like between you and your father, but I heard you say he wasn't there for you or your mum."

"You don't know the half of it."

"Go on then. Tell me."

I must have looked pained.

His voice was comforting. "Come on. Talk. It might make you feel better."

I shrugged my bag from my shoulder and set it down by my feet. I couldn't believe I was standing up here with Tobias, on the verge of confiding in him about my estranged father. "Ok. You'll regret saying that."

And he towered over me and listened, while I regaled him about my dad's obsession with a successful career in journalism and the painful debris he left in his wake. "He never looked back. He just vanished to London and then moved to the States."

Tobias considered this.

I shook my up-do, as though I was struggling myself to comprehend what I was saying. "He's never been a part of my life. He was too busy chasing his dreams to give Mum and me a second thought."

Tobias mulled it over. "Perhaps his diagnosis has made him realise what's important."

I pulled a dismissive face. "He should've realised twenty-three years ago what was important. He shouldn't need a degenerative illness to make him think."

A couple of small children rattled along the loch shoreline below, swinging their arms and pursued by their exhausted parents.

A guilty rush of feelings charged through me. "How am I

meant to feel, Tobias? I've never wished my father to come to any harm, but I pushed him out of my life years ago." My chest sagged under my dress. "Right now, I don't know anything."

He gazed down at me. "If I were you, I'd take time to process everything. You've had a real shock with him turning up like this, let alone the news about his dementia." He continued to hold me to the breezy spot by the railings with his magnetic expression. "Take some time to get everything straight in your head. Don't be hard on yourself."

I bit my lip. "I'm going to have to tell Mum about him. She'll want to know. I messed up with my job situation and didn't tell her straight away and she was really upset about that."

"Job situation?"

I focused on the wavy outline of the loch. "I was supposed to be a shoe-in for promotion at the publisher I worked for in Glasgow, but they ended up giving the job to a big name from the States."

"Ah."

"So, I took a sabbatical of around three months, so I could think about what I wanted to do and then your uncle offered me the manager post at Book Ends."

Tobias shook his head in disbelief. "Sorry you didn't get the job. That must've stung." He awarded me a look from under his thrusting lashes. "Maybe it was a blessing in disguise."

I feigned shock. "Steady, Mr Black. That sounded almost like another compliment." I gave him a long look. "Do you know, you're pretty easy to talk to? In fact, too easy." My lips performed a ghost of a smile. "You get my life story out of me without even trying. You should work for the security services."

"How do you know I don't?"

"You've got a point there."

There was a considered pause in the conversation. A sweep of emotions drifted across his compelling features. Tobias's dark looks grew serious again. "So, about your dad," he announced, returning the conversation back to its original topic.

I blinked, as though a momentary spell had been broken. "Yes. Of course. Well, I don't want him messing with my mum's head."

"What makes you say that?"

I played with my ornate dress ring on my right hand. "She's still in love with him."

I could see Tobias turning things over in his mind. "We can't help who we fall for."

Our eyes searched each other out again.

I snapped mine away first this time and concentrated on the magnetic waltz of the loch. What was happening? Were there two separate conversations taking place here? What a day this was turning out to be.

I changed the subject. "So, what about you?"

"Sorry?"

"Why leave the cosmopolitan buzz of Glasgow and return to somewhere that has almost as many wild birds as it does inhabitants?"

Tobias stiffened. "Like I said before, I fancied coming back – a change of scene." His emotional guard clattered down and he focused on the skyline again. "It's good for the soul."

I watched the locals and tourists weaving and winding down below, amongst the hotch-potch of shops. Tobias was a good listener, but when it came to revealing things about himself, he could do so much better.

I decided to try again. "And you've no idea why your uncle had a change of heart about helping you?"

Tobias shrugged. "No. I don't know. I think he must have weighed everything up and decided that as I was family and invested in the shop, he should help."

The odd small boats creaked and dashed against the water, slapping against the waves as they stayed moored below us close to the loch's jetty.

"It's just like you said before. Families," groaned Tobias.

I pushed myself away from the railings. "Tell me about it. Anyway, I'd better be off. Thank you for listening to me witter on. I appreciate it."

"Don't be daft. Any time."

Our eyes locked again.

I trained my attention on my bag, scooping it up from beside my feet and slinging it over my shoulder.

"What are you going to do now?" he asked.

"Go and speak to my mother," I sighed. "Tell her about my dad. And I'm not looking forward to it."

Chapter Sixteen

Mum sank down onto the sofa. "I don't believe this."

She was still wearing her suit from the shop's opening. "Are they sure?"

I nodded.

Grandpa had changed out of his best suit and was now back in his regular polo shirt and casual trousers. His attention flitted from me to Mum and back again as he entered the sitting room. "What's going on here? Maisie, are you alright?"

"It's Dad, Grandpa. He showed up at Book Ends this afternoon."

Before I could go on to explain, my grandfather erupted. "Are you joking? What the hell does he want?"

Mum's misty eyes widened. "He's got dementia, Dad. Niall."

Grandpa's jaw dropped. "Seriously? Bloody hell."

My grandfather and mother looked at one another, unsaid, stunned expressions travelling between them.

My grandfather let out a long, low sigh. Then he scratched

at his white moustache. "Well, even though I've no time for the man, I'm sorry to hear that. Is that why he's come back to Bracken Way?"

I flopped down in the armchair opposite Mum. My hair was escaping from its up-do and half my make-up had slid off. "Yes. It seems that way."

Grandpa continued to stand by his chair, appraising both of us. Then he took up his armchair and toyed for a few moments with today's newspaper lying on the occasional table he used for his mug of tea and his library books. "I wouldn't spit on Niall Dunbar if he were alight, but I wouldn't wish that on anyone."

I almost laughed at my grandfather's honest and brutal admission about my father, even under these startling circumstances.

Mum heaved a sigh and continued to stare past her wine-coloured curtains and out of the sitting room window at nothing in particular. "I know, Dad."

The ticking of the clock on top of the stone fireplace broke through the strange atmosphere.

My grandfather pushed and pulled at his newspaper for a few more moments. "Maisie, you and Lexie have to do what you feel is right. If you want or think you should speak to him or spend time with him, then it's up to you." He allowed his gnarly hands to still. "Whatever your decision is, I'll respect it."

My mum jerked her head away from the sitting room window to look across at my grandpa. "Dad, right now, I don't know what to say, let alone think or do."

I reached over and clamped a caring hand over my grandpa's age-spotted one. He gave me a reassuring pat.

"At the moment, Grandpa, I feel just like Mum. I don't know what that is or what to think. I mean, I feel sorry for him but as for everything else, I'm not sure."

I looked to Mum, but she was lost somewhere in the distance again, not hearing what we were saying.

My grandfather squeezed my hand. "Well, whatever you two decide, I'm here for you. And that's the honest truth."

It was a relief to escape into the quiet solitude of Book Ends the next morning. Day two of the grand re-opening and I hoped it would be another successful day of sales.

I flipped the door sign to "open" and meandered around the bookshelves, appreciating the rows of novel spines grinning back out at me. My imagination travelled around the varied covers, the photographs, the sketches, the images, the enticing titles.

I turned and stared up at the silent Mirror Image. It conjured up pictures of Tobias, confidently describing his heavenly portraits to discerning customers. Then it shifted again, pulling up more pictures of him as we talked yesterday up at the castle. His attitude towards me, when confronted with my dad and his revelation, had taken me by surprise.

I batted the images of him away into the dark recesses of my mind. Just a few weeks ago, I was blaming Tobias Black for attempting to steal the bookshop from his uncle. Now, I was thinking about the colour of his eyes!

I gave my brain a mental shake. I was vulnerable right now. He'd been kind to me and I was appreciative. Grateful.

I strode over to the counter and fired up the till.

After all, it's not every day your estranged father reappears from the States to deliver bad news.

I busied myself with tidying up the underside of the counter. Yes. That's what it was. Gratitude towards Tobias for being a shoulder to cry on.

Outside the bookshop, the weather was mild, but a gunmetal sky rolled overhead and the loch carried an irritated air.

Now this was more typical bank holiday weather! I wasn't concentrating as I faffed around with a block of post-it notes and they fell to the floor. "Bugger!"

I reached down to retrieve them.

The shop doorbell let out its merry tinkle.

I arranged my face into what I hoped was a welcoming smile and straightened up to greet who I assumed would be a customer. "Good morning. How can I help…" My voice died.

It was my father. Again.

He was wearing a pink T-shirt and beige chinos. His hair was freshly washed and still damp.

The uncertain edge to his debonair features took me by surprise. On TV, he'd appeared so smooth and unflappable.

His mouth twitched with a fleeting smile. "Good morning, Lexie."

Isn't it odd, questioned an inner voice. My father was standing there, more like a regular customer than my own dad. The realisation of that, made my heart sink a little with the sadness of it. "Morning."

"Busy day ahead?" he asked, mustering up a casual smile.

"I hope so, although it is a bank holiday Sunday, so it could go either way." I found myself pushing and pulling pens and post-it notes around on top of the counter, before I forced my hands still. "How are you?"

Duh! What a bloody stupid question!

If Dad thought the same thing, he hid it. "I'm not too bad thanks. Slept pretty well, all things considered. Think I'm still a bit jet-lagged." He fumbled around in his trouser pockets. "My room at The Drawbridge is very comfortable and breakfast was good."

Oh dear. This was painful. It was more like chatting to Mrs Hegarty or Flora Simmonds, rather than my own father. We would be talking about the weather and the state of the local roads next.

Dad glanced around himself, as though searching for something else to talk about. "How long has The Drawbridge been there?" he asked.

"It opened several years ago now. It used to be the union halls and social club…"

"For the local fishermen," supplied Dad, cutting in. "Good grief. Yes, I remember now."

Another awkward hesitation.

"I was thinking of going to pay your mother a visit."

The shop doorbell trilled again, interrupting our conversation and bringing with it the couple who'd been gazing at the display of books in the window. The young woman made straight for the section boasting a selection of the latest romantic comedies.

She slid two novels out and brought them up to the counter to pay for them. "Thank you so much," she said in a rich Welsh accent, before leaving with her partner, the Book Ends tartan ribbon handles fluttering on the gift bag.

Once they'd gone, Dad resumed the conversation. "And what did she have to say? Your mother? About me, I mean?"

"She was like me. Shocked."

"Like I said, I don't want people feeling sorry for me."

I let out an agitated tut. "You can feel empathy for someone, without feeling pity for them."

He glanced down at the bookshop floor and nodded.

"So, what do you want?" My question came out more sharply than I'd intended. But all this manoeuvring and sidestepping was exhausting.

He pushed his hands into his chino pockets. "I don't know. No. That isn't true. I think I do." He let out an agonised sigh. "Shit! Who am I kidding? I know what I want." He tapped over the wooden shop floor, looking more like a condemned man. "I know I've no right to ask this of you and your mother, Lexie, after abandoning you both the way I did."

He drew in a long, low mouthful of air. "But if there was any chance that both of you could find it in your hearts to forgive me, it'd mean the world."

I felt as if my emotions had been thrown into a washing machine and put on a crazy speed cycle.

Dad read my confused expression. "Sorry. I know all this must've come as a huge shock. It's a big ask."

I chewed my lip. "Dad, I think we need to take things very slowly. I can't speak for Mum."

"Of course."

I eyed a lady outside the bookshop windows, strolling past with her woolly little dog. "You said you're here for a few weeks?"

"Yes. I return to Washington on the 18th of June."

What should I do? What did I want to do? I didn't want to come across as unfeeling, but right now, I was struggling to make sense of everything.

"Can you speak to your mother?" asked my dad. "See what she says. Ask her if she feels she'll ever be able to talk to me?"

I rubbed at my face. "Yes, alright. I'll talk to Mum, but like I said, Dad, we can't just erase the past and act like nothing ever happened."

"I know. I know. Thank you." There was a hint of relief in his eyes. "Can you call me after you've spoken to her?"

"I'm closing the shop at four o'clock today, so I'll speak to her after that."

"Thank you. I do appreciate this, Lexie."

"Well, please don't get your hopes up or assume anything yet."

"I won't. But if there's a chance – even a small one – then it's better than nothing."

My eyes followed my father as he gave a stilted nod and left Book Ends.

My head felt like it was swimming with too many thoughts. I straightened up some of the books, even though they didn't need straightening. Behind me, the shop doorbell dinged.

I turned, wondering if it was my father again, but it was

Tobias. Gone was the smart, fitted shirt and satin blue waistcoat from yesterday. In its place, was a tight black T-shirt that sculpted his biceps and dark combat trousers. He hesitated in the doorway. "Did I just see your dad leaving?"

"Yes. He decided to drop by again."

"Ok." Tobias looked at me. "He doesn't give up; I'll say that for him. He reminds me of someone else I know."

I made a weird puffing noise. "I can't think who you mean."

Tobias angled his head. "So, your dad?"

"It's as I thought. He wants to make amends."

Tobias made sure the shop door closed behind him. He ambled over. "And what do you think about that?"

I picked at a groove in the counter wood. "I don't know. Would he have come back here to Bracken Way and asked for forgiveness if he hadn't found out he was ill?"

Now it was the turn of Tobias to make an agonised noise. "That's the million-dollar question and only your dad knows the answer to that one."

"Yes, but I suspect I do too."

Tobias studied me. "In the scheme of things, does it really matter why he came back? The fact is, he did."

He moved towards Mirror Image and began switching on the spotlights above his artwork, illuminating the various expressions of the myriad of people he'd captured on canvas. "I suppose the real question is, whether you and your mum are prepared to or feel capable of forgiving him."

I moved over to another of the bookcases and shuffled around a couple of biographies. "He hasn't been a part of my life for twenty-three years, Tobias. He was the one who chose to walk out on us. He put his career ahead of his family."

"And now that he's faced with his own mortality, he's sat there, thinking about the mistakes he's made in his life and how he can put at least some of them right."

I crinkled my nose up. "When did you become so wise?"

Tobias let out a peel of laughter. "You wouldn't say that if I told you about the mistakes I'd made in my life."

"Oh, yes? Like what?"

He flexed a brow and diverted the conversation back to my dad. "So do you think your mum will hear him out?"

I threw up my hands. "Right now, I've no idea. My head feels scrambled." I pointed to my forehead. "This is telling me one thing." I gestured to my heart. "And this is telling me something else."

Tobias nodded. "I can understand that. What do you think your mum will want to do?"

I pushed and pulled a couple more books around on the shelf in front of me. "I think I can guess. She'll make a few noises, but she still loves him."

I returned to thinking about the shock clouding in her eyes and could still hear the disbelieving gasp escaping from her chest, when she saw Dad appear on TV that lunchtime a few weeks ago.

Tobias's deep voice interrupted me. "So, you think she'll agree to hear him out?"

"I think so. I know her. She'll regret it if she doesn't."

Tobias had been leaning against his glass gallery counter. He pushed himself off it and strolled towards me.

"All the parents' evenings my mum attended on her own,

the school shows, nursing me when I caught chicken pox, waiting up for me when I went out on my first date... She was there for it all, juggling a job and being there for me." I swallowed. "I just can't forget and wipe out what he did, as though it never happened."

"Well, for what it's worth, your mum did an excellent job." Our eyes sought out each other. It was as if both of us were daring the other to breathe first. Then Tobias drew himself up.

My cheeks flashed with colour.

"Anyway," he announced, taking a step backwards to put some distance between us. "You have to do what feels right for you."

My attention drifted to the way his lashes fluttered against his cheekbones when he looked down.

"Excuse me?"

The doorbell clattered and a woman's harassed voice made us both spin round.

"I hope I'm not interrupting anything?"

We both made a big show of confirming that absolutely no interruption of anything important was taking place at all.

The woman in question appeared to be in her late fifties, with poker-straight ash-blonde hair skimming her shoulders, a heavy fringe, and she was dressed in an ankle-length, raspberry-coloured dress studded with pink flowers.

"How can I help you?" I asked.

She carried an anxious edge to her features, as she clutched her shoulder bag to her like a child hanging onto their security blanket. Her eyes took in Book Ends, before travelling up to appreciate Tobias's paintings.

She tapped towards one of my bookcases that housed an

array of our latest Scandi noir titles. "This is a wonderful set-up you both have here."

"Thank you," smiled Tobias.

She abandoned the bookcase and made her way towards him.

He gave me a discreet, "What's going on?" look when she continued to wander around for a couple more minutes, drinking in the books and the portraits.

The woman gazed up at Tobias's paintings, her appreciative stare softening at a portrait Tobias was trying to sell, of an elderly couple sat side by side in upholstered red velvet chairs. They were holding hands.

"You painted all of these?" she breathed, spinning round in her sandals to speak to Tobias.

"Guilty as charged."

She turned back, focusing her attention on the gliding colours and sweeps and smudges of the paint. "They're wonderful."

"Thank you."

I started to mouth at Tobias, "Do you know her?" when she turned back around, almost catching me in the act.

She looked at Tobias and then at me. It was as though she couldn't make up her mind which of us she wanted to address first.

She steeled herself, still gripping onto her handbag. "This is going to sound very strange," she began, "but I would like to talk to you both about a proposition."

My senses went on alert. Was she some sort of salesperson? "I take it you're interested in books and art?" I asked, wondering who she was and what she was about to say.

"Because if you are, you've come to the right place," added Tobias.

She hesitated from under her fringe, her expression taking in every aspect of the shop. She must have spotted Tobias and me swapping more puzzled glances.

"I'm sorry," she blurted. "I'm not expressing myself very well."

I noticed one of her hands abandon her handbag and fly to her throat. Her voice cracked and she paled. "It's been rather a traumatic time."

"Are you alright?" I asked her, concerned. "Would you like a glass of water or a cup of tea? I think you should sit down for a few moments."

She shook her fringe. "No thank you, but that's very kind of you." She steadied herself. "I know this is going to sound rather odd, but please bear with me."

Her next words tumbled out of her mouth in an excited, garbled rush. "I'm hoping that both of you might be able to help."

"With what?" I asked.

She marshalled herself and shot Tobias and me an almost apologetic smile. "My elderly mother is growing very frail. She has advanced osteoporosis."

Thoughts of my father entered my imagination. I glanced over at Tobias. "I'm so sorry to hear that."

"Yes, that must be awful," he added, his attention flitting backwards and forwards from me to the woman.

"Thank you," she sniffed. "She's eighty years old and a real character." She toyed with the strap of her bag, blowing out a puff of air. "It started in her hip and spread from there. The doctors were talking about kyphoplasty – special surgery for vertebral compression fractures – but at her age, the risk of something going wrong increases. There's always the threat that surgery like that could put pressure on surrounding bones and increase the chance of even more fractures."

The woman straightened her shoulders. "She's so no nonsense about it all, but she's been through enough."

My curiosity burned. Why did she want to speak to Tobias and me?

As if reading my mind, the woman composed herself again and explained. "There are things I know my mother always wanted to do but never had the opportunity. You're both young, so you have plenty of time to make your dreams come true, but as you get older…" She regrouped. "Time runs away with you and you never stop to appreciate the things that really matter."

Again, echoes of what my father had said earlier rang around my head. I forced back a pang of emotion as I recalled his begging to be heard and forgiven. How long did my father have left? I had no idea. How fast might he deteriorate?

He hadn't presented me with a bucket list. Did he even have one? If he did, I wondered what was on it. It hit me that I'd no idea what his favourite band was or did he prefer Italian food to Chinese? The stark reality that he knew next to nothing about me either, my own father, slapped me in the face.

I forced more questions about my dad away and made myself concentrate on the lady in the pretty floral dress again. "That's very true," I managed with a smile. "We take so much of our lives for granted."

Tobias gave me a long look, before turning his attention back to the woman. "So, madam, how can we help?"

She appreciated the books on the shelves and the alluring portraits again. "I know you must be so busy. I was just chatting to the lady who owns that lovely tea room up the street and she was talking in very complimentary tones about you both."

She drew herself up. Her dark eyes were imploring, verging on desperate. "I'm sorry. I'm wittering on like an idiot."

"Not at all," I assured her. "It's fine. Take your time."

She took a breath. "You're both being so kind and it's much appreciated."

I noticed her fingers knitting together on her lap. She swallowed and carried on. "The residential home where my mother is in Bracken Way is marvellous, but well, she's becoming frailer and time isn't on her side."

The woman seemed to realise she hadn't mentioned her name nor that of her mother in her urgency to explain. "I'm so sorry. I haven't introduced myself. I'm Maeve Marshall. My mother is Celeste Matthews."

Tobias and I introduced ourselves to her and encouraged her to carry on. She pushed out an embarrassed smile and continued. "Yes, of course. So, while I was sorting out a few of my mother's things, I came across a sort of a bucket list."

She gave her head a shake. "My mother is an amazing woman and has squeezed what I thought was a lot into her years but seemingly not as much as she would've hoped."

Tobias smiled at Maeve. "She sounds a wonderful lady."

"Oh, she is, but she can be a bit of a handful when she gets started."

I let out a laugh. "Good for her! I hope I'm a bit of handful when I'm that age."

Tobias gave me a look as if to say, "I suspect you could be a handful now," but I focused on Maeve and didn't acknowledge his charged glance.

"So, Ms Marshall, this bucket list of your mothers?" I asked, my curiosity rising.

The woman, her eyes shining with emotion, whipped her ash-blonde head to each of us. "Please. Call me Maeve." She carried on with her explanation. "There are two items in particular on Mum's bucket list which I know she's desperate to achieve before she…" Maeve gave a watery smile and took a moment to compose herself again. "I'm a widow, you see. I know what it's like to lose someone you love. Anyway, I'd be most grateful if both of you could try to help her achieve these two particular wishes on her bucket list. You will, of course, be generously paid for your time." Her expression was imploring. "I know you can help my mother with two of her dying wishes. I just know you can."

As soon as she'd spoken, Maeve appeared almost apologetic.

Tobias indicated towards the office door. "Let's go and talk in there, shall we?"

Octavia had just arrived by this time, so Tobias asked her if she wouldn't mind keeping an eye on both Book Ends and Mirror Image, until Chloe arrived. "We won't be long."

Then he encouraged Maeve to follow us.

I asked her again if she wanted a cup of tea or coffee, but

she settled herself in the swivel chair at our insistence and politely declined.

She kept her handbag sat on her lap, as though using it to shield her from something.

Tobias pulled across another chair for me and sank down in the other, so that the three of us were in a semi-circle, rather than both of us couched behind the heavy walnut office desk.

He shot me a brief look. "Please forgive me for asking but what items might be on this bucket list of your mothers that you think we can help with?"

Maeve's mouth, dashed with a faint touch of rosy lipstick, edged upwards.

. "When my mother was younger, she always wanted to have her portrait painted." She paused. "But my grandparents were strict Bracken Way churchgoers, who thought such indulgences were frivolous, so she never pursued it."

Maeve's dark, faintly-lined eyes fanned out at the corners as she addressed Tobias. "My mother was born and raised here and I know she's always been fascinated by the castle. She said when she was younger, she would make her way up to the railings and just stand there, admiring the view. She liked to go up there and be on her own for a while."

I nodded. That made so much sense to me.

Maeve relaxed her fingers a little. "My mum has written that she'd love to have her portrait painted in front of Bracken Way Castle."

Tobias considered this. "I'm sure that's do-able."

Maeve's mouth sprang open. "Are you sure? I mean… you must be very busy with other commitments at the moment, what with just having opened your new gallery."

"Nothing that my staff can't handle – my job is to paint, so I'm very open to commissions."

Maeve's face was almost bursting with relief and delight. "Oh goodness. That's wonderful. Thank you, Mr Black. Thank you so much! It'll mean the world to her – and to me."

"It's Tobias. And you're welcome."

Her eyes sparkled with emotion. "You must tell me your rates and I'll arrange payment straight away."

Tobias shook his head. "Please don't concern yourself with that at the moment. I'm far more interested in meeting my subject and getting to know her, before I begin painting her."

Happiness radiated out of Maeve's expression.

"The most important element in any portrait for me is the eyes. This is where I want the viewers of my paintings to concentrate on. Once I get to know Celeste a bit better, I can encapsulate who she is."

I managed to shoot him a curious glance when he wasn't looking. This was the second time that Tobias had managed to surprise me. Underneath that brash, "I can be an arrogant dick" bravado, there was a thoughtful, caring side.

My heart gave an odd little flutter as I studied him.

It stole the breath from my throat.

I jerked my head away and tried to act like I hadn't been staring at him in the first place. "Well, that's that sorted," I assured her, trying to keep an odd wobble out of my voice. "Now, did you say there was another wish on her list that you also wanted to discuss?"

Maeve offered Tobias another pink-tinged beam of appreciation, before turning her attention to me. "Yes, Ms Dunbar, there is."

"Please. Just call me Lexie."

She examined me with her joy-filled eyes. "Alright. Thank you. Well, several years ago, Mum told me that she'd written a novel."

"Wonderful," I enthused. "When was this? What's it about?"

Maeve smoothed down her hair. "Well, that's the thing. I'm not sure."

"Oh?"

Maeve shook her head. "She told me she began writing a book when she was around fifty years old, but she was very evasive when I asked her what it's about."

"That's an achievement in itself, writing a whole book," I said. "So, where do I fit in?"

Maeve edged forward, her sandals pressing harder into the carpeted office floor while she concentrated on what she was saying. "It's on her bucket list that she'd love to have her novel published."

My eyebrows darted upwards. That was a big dream, especially for someone who unfortunately didn't seem to have a great deal of time on her side.

Maeve read my expression. "I know it's a big ask, but even if you were able to read it and give her some pointers, that would be wonderful." She made a resigned sigh. "I'm not deluded and I know it's very unlikely Mum will be able to achieve most, let alone all of her final wishes, but even if she felt she were within touching distance of a couple of them or got a taste of what might have been possible for her, I know she'll be able to leave this earth happy."

Maeve flashed me an embarrassed smile. "Mrs Hegarty

told me you were a successful publishing editor in a previous life."

I could feel my heart throbbing in sympathy for both Maeve and her mother. It was a heartbreaking and yet strangely uplifting situation.

I managed to speak, although my voice was thick with emotion. It conjured up the mixture of pain and shock about my dad's health. "What you're doing for your mother is wonderful."

Maeve batted one hand in the air and swallowed a lump. "I must be mad!" She eyed me again.

I played with my bangle, dangling from my right wrist. "Maeve, I have to tell you that trying to get a book published can take a long, long time. There are options like self-publishing, but even that isn't a quick process."

She nodded, a pessimistic spark rearing up in her eyes.

"However, let me take a look at Celeste's manuscript anyway and we can go from there. As Tobias suggested, I think we should both meet this rather amazing mother of yours and explain our proposals to her. How does that sound?"

Maeve released both nervous hands, her voice brimming with enthusiasm. "That sounds perfect. Thank you so much. Both of you."

She clicked open her bag and dived in one hand. "Now, you must tell me how much your editorial services cost and I'll pay you. This young man here might have fobbed me off, but I won't allow you to do the same."

I watched her produce her purse; a fabric material stitched with autumnal leaves. Beside her credit cards poking out, was a small photograph of an older, handsome woman with thick white hair and fine, lined features, giving a shy smile to the camera.

I didn't want to take an hourly rate from Maeve. It didn't seem right, somehow. I didn't want to offend her either. Then an idea erupted inside of me. "If you're happy to make a donation to Dementia UK, we have a deal."

Tobias's thick-lashed gaze widened and stayed focused on me.

"Are you sure?" asked Maeve. "A charity donation? To Dementia UK?"

"And that goes for my portrait services too," added Tobias.

I whipped my head round to look at him sitting beside me.

"If you donate an amount to the same charity, consider my portrait services yours."

"Tobias," I started, my voice croaky with surprise. "You don't have to."

He brushed aside any further comment. "I know I don't have to. I want to."

Maeve's mouth wobbled. "People are being so kind. That's more than agreeable to me. I don't know what to say. Thank you both so much."

I found myself giving Tobias another long, sideways look. My stomach did a weird, flippy-flappy thing.

"That's settled then," announced Tobias, oblivious to the strange roller coaster effect he was triggering inside me. "Now, when do we get to meet this delightful mother of yours?"

Maeve shot out of her leather chair, like she'd been tasered. "Did I see on your shop door that you both close at four o'clock today?"

We confirmed in unison that we did.

Maeve was fizzing with anticipation. "Right then. Well, all things considered, how about we do introductions today around half past four?" Her smile wavered. "Time is of the essence."

Her words resonated with me. Pictures of my dad lodged themselves in front of my eyes. I forced them back. "That sounds perfect."

Tobias gave me a pensive glance.

"Wonderful. Right, I'll call Bracken Way Residential Home and tell them they can expect us to visit Mum this afternoon. I live in one of those stone cottages on the outskirts of town, so it'll take me no time to get there."

There were enthusiastic handshakes all round, before she swirled out of the shop.

When she'd gone, Tobias swung round to face me. "I wondered if all that talk about losing someone might be a bit too close to home? Are you ok?"

I turned over Maeve's conversation with us; everything she'd told us about her mother; her desire to help her and make whatever time she had left as memorable and happy as possible. "Yes, maybe a bit," I admitted.

The shop doorbell fizzed into action and a smartly dressed older man, in a trilby and tailored suit, made for Tobias's gallery and began browsing. "No rest for the wicked," said Tobias with a twinkle.

"You were so kind to Maeve," I blurted out to his broad, retreating back, as he made his way towards Octavia, who was chatting to the new customer. The words were out before I could stop them. "And like I said, you telling her to make a donation to Dementia UK instead of accepting a fee." My cheeks fizzed, struck by how touched I was. "That was very generous of you."

Tobias stopped, turned and flashed a brief megawatt smile that lit up his handsome face.

"See?" he said with a wink. "The wicked wolf isn't so bad, after all, is he?"

Chapter Seventeen

Bracken Way Residential Home was a Victorian-style affair at the other end of town, which had been extended at the side and rear, in order to accommodate more rooms.

It was white pebble dash, boasting a cheerful lemon-painted entrance and matching windowsills.

The gardens were an appealing mixture of Scots pine and ash trees interspersed by colourful flower beds, decorated with shrubs, tea roses, lavender and lobelia.

Tobias guided us both up the hedge-flanked driveway and past the brass nameplate, proclaiming where we were.

His car, an olive-green Land Rover, wasn't what I'd been expecting. I'd envisaged him behind the wheel of some sporty little thing with racing tyres.

My surprised expression must have betrayed me, because he examined me across the car roof before we set off.

"I got this because it's practical and excellent for transporting my painting garb."

I had raised my hands in the air in mock surrender. "I didn't say a word."

"You didn't have to. You have very expressive eyes."

The air between us zinged. He produced his car keys and I got ready to clamber in beside him. I realised my cheeks were glowing and I was grateful when he hit the fob so I could get in.

Maeve was standing by her car, an amber Golf, when Tobias edged into the visitors' car park and parked up at the front of the residential home.

No sooner had we got out of the Land Rover, than Maeve bore down on us, her dress flapping around her ankles. "Thank you so much for coming. After I came to see you both this morning, I drove straight up here to tell Mum. She's delighted."

"We're looking forward to meeting her," I smiled. "And I'm very interested to read her manuscript."

"You are too kind. Both of you. She won't let me see her book. Won't let me anywhere near it. Not even so much as a glimpse."

"Writing a book is a personal experience. Often, it can be easier to show it to a complete stranger, rather than family. I suppose it feels a bit less intrusive." I thought of my previous editing endeavours, the books I'd slaved over, carving and chiselling my author's words into something more polished and flowing. In some ways, it seemed an age ago.

"You're probably right," agreed Maeve.

Tobias asked Maeve to lead the way and we followed.

Two potted fir trees sat in fat ceramic tubs either side of the residential home entrance. A long hallway, carpeted in royal blue, snaked down, with heavy ornate wood-panelled doors feeding off from it left and right. I guessed that that must be where the residents' rooms were.

Some of the doors were ajar, revealing crisply made-up beds, dressers and small television sets. To the left, was a reception desk, where the three of us signed in.

The hallway was bright and inviting, with pale gold-painted walls and bold black and white photographs of Bracken Way as it was years ago.

A vase of vanilla lilies cast their heady perfume from where they sat on a nearby coffee table. There was the faint clatter of tea cups and the squeak of a trolley.

I could smell freshly baked scones and tangy strawberry jam and made a comment to Maeve about the delicious smells!

She glanced down at her watch. "Ah yes. They'll be clearing away afternoon tea. My mum's room is up here on the right."

We smiled back at a couple of elderly residents, before reaching Maeve's mother's room.

The door was closed. On it, was a white China plaque, decorated with apricot roses and her name, *Celeste Matthews*, was painted across it in italic script.

Maeve rapped on the door. "Mum, it's me. Are you decent? I've Lexie and Tobias with me, like I told you earlier."

"I've never been decent in eighty years," came the indignant reply. "Come in, my darling."

Maeve rolled her eyes at both of us, before she clicked open the door and stepped in. We followed suit.

And as with Tobias's car, Celeste's accommodation was another surprise I was about to receive today.

Instead of what I'd imagined of a floral bedspread, delicate ornaments and traces of Lily of the Valley, Celeste's room was the total antithesis of that.

Ahead of us, was a white and gold dressing table, on top of which sat a square mirror, studded with lightbulbs all the way round it, like something a Hollywood starlet would admire her reflection in. Draped over the top of the mirror, was a selection of floaty chiffon scarves.

Her wardrobe door was open adjacent to that, giving a tantalising glimpse of sparkly dresses, court shoes and spiky kitten heels resting in open shoe boxes at the bottom.

Several odd sleeves of what looked like embroidered jackets poked out.

In the centre of the room was the bed, topped with pastel scatter cushions and sitting there a few feet away in a wheelchair, wearing a coral dress and matching cardigan, was Celeste. Her hair was a crisp cloud of white, like a halo, framing her enquiring face.

She possessed dark eyes like her daughter. Riven lines gathered around her mouth, but her cheekbones were still high and proud and her forehead was surprisingly smooth.

Maeve bustled over to her mother, delivered a fond kiss on her cheek, before introducing us again.

Celeste observed Tobias as he closed her room door behind him and the three of us pulled up chairs which were already *in situ* and which one of the carers must have fetched, in preparation for our arrival.

Celeste reached out one elegant hand to her daughter and gave it an affectionate squeeze. "So, I take it my lovely daughter has told you both that I'm going to croak soon?"

"Mum! For pity's sake."

Celeste let out a raspy laugh at Maeve's appalled expression. "Well, it's true, so why beat about the bush?" She sat back against her cushions, her hooded gaze appraising us in turn. "So, this is the young man who's going to paint my portrait, is that correct?"

"Yes, madam. I am."

Celeste pulled a mock horrified face. "Please stop with the formalities. I know I'm a great deal older than you but I don't need reminding of it. Please call me Celeste." Her gaze shone. "Having my portrait painted by such a handsome fiend is going to be no hardship." She sighed. "If only I were fifty years younger, I'd be chasing after you."

Tobias grinned. "If you were fifty years younger, I wouldn't be running away."

Celeste winked at him playfully. "Handsome *and* charming. A lethal combination, wouldn't you say, young lady?"

I realised Celeste was addressing me. Colour crept up my neck.

Beside Celeste, Maeve was shaking her head in exasperation at her mother. "Eighty going on twenty, or at least she thinks she is."

Celeste gave me a warm smile. "And you must be Lexie, the young lady who's going to take a look at my car crash of a novel."

"I am indeed and I'm sure it isn't like that at all."

Celeste gathered her cardigan around her, despite the warm temperature in the room. Maeve frowned with concern.

Outside the window, late afternoon sunshine was forcing its way across the grounds and edging through the trees.

"Hopefully I won't peg it till you've been able to give me some feedback on my writing."

Tobias tried to bury a laugh and Maeve looked aghast.

It was as she turned to address her portrait plans again with Tobias that I noticed a small colour photograph of a stunning young woman in a solid silver frame on the dressing table.

She was gazing at the camera, her pale gold hair pulled away from her face in romantic waves. Her features were long and arresting, enhanced by lashed, hooded eyes.

Celeste followed my gaze. "That's me," she confirmed with an element of pride. "I was thirty-three there."

Tobias gasped, "Wow," and Celeste's lined mouth performed a small smile.

"Age is cruel but death is crueller."

Thoughts of my dad erupted inside my head like a volcano again. I knew I had to face things and confront the situation with him. Both Mum and me. We had to decide what we were going to do about Dad's request to talk, instead of just dodging and skirting around everything. Hoping to ignore the situation wasn't going to make things any better.

"…and so, I thought you might be able to tell me what you think of my writing. Maeve tells me you're an editor and that you work for a big publishing house?"

Celeste' s questioning voice made me blink and refocus. I sat up straighter. "Sorry? Oh yes. That's right. Or at least, I did."

Tobias studied me for a few moments. He spoke to Celeste again, as though he were allowing me some time to gather my thoughts. "Maeve said you'd like to be painted with Bracken Way Castle in the background?"

"That's right," agreed Celeste, knotting her fingers together as she sat there. She scowled down at herself. "Although with my body in this state and sitting in this damned thing, I won't be able to make the journey up there."

"That won't be an issue," reassured Tobias. "I can paint you and recreate the castle as the backdrop. You won't have to go anywhere."

The older woman's expression glowed. "Wonderful!" She slid the three of us a careful look. "I have this dress." She hesitated. "It's very special to me. I'd very much like to be painted wearing that."

"Of course. May I see it?" asked Tobias, intrigued.

Celeste indicated to Maeve. "Could you fetch it for me from my wardrobe please, dear? It's hanging at the back, in a black suit carrier."

Maeve got up and approached the wardrobe. She eased open the double doors, giving us a greater glimpse of its sumptuous, glitzy contents.

"You have so many stunning outfits," I remarked to Celeste.

Her voice was a lilting, soft Scottish burr. "Thank you my dear. Just a pity I'm too old and decrepit to get into most of them now."

Maeve's hand trawled over her mother's vast array of glamorous clothes, until it landed on one outfit concealed in a black cover towards the back. She unhooked it and returned across the room towards Celeste, lying it across her lap before she sat down again.

Celeste reached for the zip and attempted to unfasten it. Her gnarled fingers struggled, falling over each other. "Blast!"

"Here. Allow me," said Tobias, standing up. He grasped the zip and eased it down effortlessly with his long fingers. A snapshot of him doing the same to a dress I might be wearing zoomed through my imagination and I cursed myself. He looked very well versed in gliding down dress zips... I forced away the pictures in my head. *Good grief, Dunbar! What is up with you today?!*

I focused again on Celeste, as she started to angle the black cover zip open, to reveal swathes of silver thread. Celeste stared down at it, lost in her own thoughts for a few moments. A secret shadow of a smile tugged at the corners of her mouth.

She gathered herself and using her other hand, scooped out the flowing dress. Like a silvery waterfall, it slithered free from the black suit cover.

It was floor length, consisting of two layers. The first was tuille, laid over with long silver threads, like running rain drops. It had spaghetti straps, made out of the same shimmery silver.

Maeve's mouth dropped open. "Where did you get that, Mum? It's beautiful. I don't ever remember seeing that dress before."

Celeste offered her daughter an odd glance. "Oh, I got this a long time ago. No doubt you've seen it before, but don't remember."

"No, I would've remembered a dress like that."

Maeve continued to admire it as she sat beside her mother. "Where did you say you got it from?"

Celeste squirmed against her cushions. Her voice was

suddenly sharp, in stark contrast to before. "I didn't say. Does it matter when and where I got it?"

Maeve blinked at her mother. "No, of course not."

Celeste's hand smoothed over the material, as it sailed down and over her lap. It concealed her wheelchair. Her cheeks popped with embarrassed colour and she gave Maeve an apologetic glance. "Forgive me, sweetheart. I shouldn't have snapped at you like that. I'm a cantankerous old cow sometimes."

Maeve tapped her on the hand that was resting on the dress. "What do you mean sometimes?"

Tobias reached over. "May I?" and when Celeste said he could, he allowed the material of the dress to slide through his fingers. The way he touched it and appreciated the fabric with such tenderness was so sexy to watch, it was almost X-rated.

"This'll spring from the canvas," he said. "Against the backdrop of the castle, it'll make for a striking portrait."

"That's what I was hoping you would say, young man."

One of Celeste's fingers reached under one of the thin straps. She moved it this way and that, allowing the light to glance against the encrusted silver. "I have a matching bolero to wear over it. At my advancing years, who'd want to see my bony old shoulders?"

Tobias shook his head. "My portraits never lie, Celeste. You'll be seen as you really are and that's as an amazing woman."

"There's the smooth talking again," she said, with a wry smile.

"No, it's the truth and you'll see my paint brushes don't lie either."

"That's excellent. At least I won't be captured for all eternity in this wheelchair. I've splashed out on another one and have had it pimped-up, as you young ones say."

"Pimped-up?" I asked, not being able to conceal a grin.

"Oh yes!" Celeste was indignant. "A rainbow stripey cushion and pink glittery arm rests. That's the one I want to be in for my portrait. You can never have too much bling, dear girl!"

"Quite right too!" agreed Tobias. "It's your portrait, so if you'd like to be painted in your pimped-up chariot, then that's what we'll do."

Maeve's arched brows waggled. "I didn't know you got yourself another chair, Mum."

Celeste gave her daughter a look. "I don't tell you everything, darling, even if you are my daughter."

"Oh, I'm starting to see that!"

Celeste gestured to her wheelchair again, struggling to conceal her frustration. "This might sound ridiculous but there are times when I still feel like a young woman, trapped in this dried up, bony old body."

Tobias reached over and gestured to the gorgeous dress, still draped over Celeste's lap. "I believe that the eyes say everything. If you think you're still young, then that'll come across in the painting."

Celeste bit her lip. "I appreciate that very much, Tobias. Thank you."

Tobias studied her. "Now, what I was thinking was capturing you in watercolour. I can use vibrant shades and give a new dimension to your portrait." He gestured to the gorgeous dress, still tumbling over Celeste's knees. "And I can build up layers of colour to enhance your gown and that complexion of yours."

Celeste glowed with delight. "That sounds perfect. Thank you." She turned back to me. "Now, I hope you don't think I'm being rude, Maeve and Tobias, but would you mind if I had a private moment with Lexie, please?"

Tobias rose to his feet. "Of course."

Maeve remained seated by her mother and frowned.

"Please, darling."

Maeve disguised a sigh and followed Tobias out of the room. She clicked the door shut behind them.

I waited a few moments. "Is everything alright, Celeste?"

She didn't reply.

Instead, she leant over as far as she could in her chair towards a wooden bedside cupboard and pulled the handle of the deep, middle drawer.

Her hand tugged it open and she eased out a wodge of yellowing paper. It was typed upon and gathered together by a lacy ribbon.

"This is the book," she said. "I'm not silly. I know it isn't going to set the literary world on fire, but to have someone like you, a successful editor, read it through... well, I'd appreciate it."

"Successful editor," I muttered, almost under my breath. "I don't know if I'd go that far."

Celeste cocked her head of white waves. "But Maeve told me you worked at Literati Publishing."

I took the opportunity to give her a potted explanation about what had happened and how I wasn't appointed to the senior editor position.

Looking back on it now, it was as if the elation of seeing the end product – a polished manuscript, the excitement of my authors being published for the first time – had happened to someone else.

But it struck me as I sat there with Celeste, that the festering injustice about how Literati treated me wasn't anywhere near as painful as it had been. Time did heal. "Anyway, this isn't about me. I'm more than happy to read your manuscript and give you feedback on it. What's it about?"

My attention focused on the covering page, which said:

Love Never Dies

By Celeste Matthews

Celeste wriggled in her wheelchair. "A romance," she stated vaguely. "It's set here in Bracken Way."

"Ah yes. Maeve said you were born and grew up here."

Celeste's look was indecipherable. "Yes. Then I moved away for a while."

"That sounds just my cup of tea then."

I gestured towards her closed door and lowered my voice. "I hope you don't mind me asking, but why didn't you want to give me your book in front of Maeve?"

Celeste's fingers raked over the dress. She stared down at it with her milk chocolate eyes. After a few more moments, she raised her head. There was a faraway look to her. "Like I just said to my daughter, it's still nice to have one or two secrets of one's own."

Chapter Eighteen

Tobias insisted that he'd drop me back at Mum's house, so I gathered Celeste's manuscript under my arm and pulled my bag to me as I sat in the passenger seat of his Land Rover. "You were wonderful with Celeste today."

Tobias swiped off his smoky sunglasses and leant both his arms on top of his steering wheel. I noticed a faint smattering of dark hair. "I wish you wouldn't sound so stunned that I could be kind to someone. Anyone would think I was a cross between Godzilla and Michael Myers!" He pulled a grotesque face which made me laugh.

"You know what I mean," I said.

We exchanged smiles and I realised after a few moments that my attention was drifting to his mouth again.

I gripped tighter to Celeste's manuscript and clambered out.

Tobias pointed at the book in my arms. "I see you've some light reading for tonight."

"It's a romance. I suspect it may carry some

autobiographical aspects. Celeste was very mysterious about its contents." I gave the front cover a gentle pat.

Tobias continued to watch me from out of the passenger side window. "It wasn't just me who was lovely with her today." His deep, rumbly voice wrapped itself around me.

"Oh?"

"No." Tobias gestured again to the book in my arms as I stood there on the pavement.

My shoulders gave an easy shrug. "Oh, you know. I'm a wonderful person. What can I say?"

He continued to sit there, looking at me from out of the driver's side. He made no attempt to drive off. "Lexie…"

"Yes?"

My breathing sped up. Oh God. What was he about to say?

Tobias drank in my expression. He sat up straighter, his muscles tensing under his T-shirt.

An array of emotions crossed his stubbled face. My heart sped up. Then he sunk back in his seat. The moment evaporated. "Have a good evening."

I blinked back at him, disappointment stabbing at me. "What? Oh. Yes. Of course. Right. You too."

My deflated reflection smudged against the windows of his car. So, he hadn't been about to say something momentous then. I must've imagined it.

"See you tomorrow?" he called out, leaning across to get my attention from the open passenger side window. "I know it's a bank holiday, so I wasn't sure what you'd be doing."

I rearranged my mouth into a bright smile, even though my heart felt like a deflated balloon. "I'll be opening for a few hours. Might be able to capitalise on a few day trippers."

"I was thinking the same thing." He slipped his sunglasses back on and performed a casual wave. "See you tomorrow then. Bye, Lexie."

I stood for a moment on the warmed pavement, the lazy late afternoon sunshine glancing off his disappearing Land Rover.

I let myself into Mum's house with my spare key. Once I got myself sorted out, I knew I'd have to think about getting my own place. There were rumours the flat above the greetings card shop was going to be put up for sale, because the current owner was emigrating to New Zealand.

I enjoyed being fussed over by Mum and Grandpa, but they needed their own space like I did.

I dumped my bag in the hall, thinking about Tobias and what had happened – or *not* happened – just now. I was sure he was about to say something to me.

No. My imagination was playing tricks on me.

Had I been hoping he would ask me out?

I dismissed the notion. No. No. Not at all. We worked alongside one another. Not a good idea. Much better to remain acquaintances.

Nevertheless, I tried to ignore my gnawing disappointment. "I'm back," I called out to Mum and Grandpa. "Sorry I'm a bit later than planned."

I kicked off my ballet pumps and placed Celeste's book down on the kitchen table.

I was greeted by a delicious waft of cooking roast chicken and the surprising sight of Rhiannon, her bob scraped back from her face in a stubby ponytail, lashing potatoes with oil.

Mum and Grandpa had been despatched to the sitting room by Rhiannon.

"I'm cooking dinner for all of us."

I planted my hands on my hips. "That smells wonderful and thank you. But what have you done with Rhiannon?"

Rhiannon glided the roasting dish back into the oven and closed the door, waggling one oven glove. "Sunday roast is about the only thing I can cook, as Guy used to enjoy reminding me, so I expect you to eat every last scrap on your plate."

Guy Chambers was Rhiannon's social influencer ex-husband. He was also a motivational speaker and happened to be published by Literati.

"Yes, Mum."

She smiled and tugged off both oven gloves. "What's that?" she asked, nodding her head at Celeste's manuscript.

Before I could answer, her features lit up like a Christmas tree. "Is that what I think it is?"

"What?"

"That. A manuscript?"

She clapped one thrilled hand over her mouth. "You can be so precious at times!" She gestured to the manuscript. "It was only a matter of time. You're missing it!"

"I'm doing some freelance editing."

She grinned from ear to ear. "So how about we talk about your future over dinner?"

My brain managed to register what she meant. "What? Oh no. I'm doing some freelance work, but I've no intention of returning to publishing." I gave Celeste's manuscript a pat on the table. "As for this, I offered to read it for someone, just as a favour. It's a bit of a long story."

Rhiannon's joyous expression collapsed. "Oh. I see." She folded her arms across herself, exposing her tiny butterfly tattoo on her right wrist. "Look, Lexie, please don't think I'm trying to tell you what to do."

I shot out one hand and clutched the edge of Mum's kitchen table. "We've already been through this, Rhi. Like I told you, I'm advertising my services as a freelance editor, but as for anything else, it's a no."

"Yes, but for how long? Don't get me wrong. I do admire you for taking on Book Ends and doing something different, but you belong at Literati, Lexie."

I shook my head. "I did. Not anymore. I've moved on."

From the sitting room, I could see Mum and Grandpa ignoring the TV and focusing their attention on the drama playing out in Mum's kitchen.

Two spots of frustrated colour appeared on Rhiannon's creamy skin. "What do you mean? What are you talking about? You can't manage a bookshop for the rest of your life."

All I wanted to do was throw off my work clothes, shrug on something casual and relax. "Who says I can't? What's so bad about that, anyway?"

Rhiannon raked a hand over the top of her head. "Nothing as such, but it's not you." She let out a sigh. "I wondered whether your dad turning up out of the blue like that and his dementia might have something to do with this. It must've been an awful shock."

Rhiannon was choosing not to hear what I was saying. My doubts over my future at Literati and the frustration over not getting the senior commissioning editor role surfaced well before Dad arrived back on the scene.

"Not getting that senior position made me think about what I wanted to do and where I wanted to go with my life, Rhi. It has nothing to do with my dad."

Rhiannon's exasperation shone out of her.

I continued to lean against Mum's circular kitchen table. All Rhiannon could see was the Lexie-shaped hole at Literati.

Rhiannon chewed the inside of her cheek. "You should be editing your stable of authors." She sighed. "What are you hoping to gain from running a bookshop? This isn't you, Lexie."

"Isn't it? Maybe it is and you just don't want to accept it." I tried to steady my voice. "You know what books mean to me. I don't have to tell you how important I think reading is." I threw my hands around, hoping Rhiannon might begin to comprehend what I was trying to do. "At Book Ends, I hope I can encourage people who've never picked up a book before, to give reading a try."

Rhiannon's lips morphed into a disapproving expression.

I scraped out the nearby kitchen chair and sank down into it. Rhiannon pulled out the chair opposite me and did the same. Sumptuous sizzling and popping sounds came from the oven.

Mum and Grandpa remained in the sitting room, allowing us to have our frank exchange in peace.

"So, you're going to sell other people's books instead of helping to create them?"

"If you mean, am I going to continue managing the

JULIE SHACKMAN

bookshop, then the answer is yes. That's if I can turn around its fortunes in the next year."

The deep, rich aroma of the roasting chicken made my stomach groan with hunger.

As I sat there and reflected, I realised that I woke up every morning and looked forward to heading into Book Ends. Whether that had something to do with a tall, dark and brooding portrait painter was another thing.

I clapped my hands together on my lap. "You believed in me from the off and I'll always be grateful for that."

Rhiannon fiddled with her short platinum ponytail. "And I still do and that's why I'm talking to you like this. I think it's such a waste of your talent."

I eyed Celeste's stack of typed pages at my elbow. "Well, I'm going to put those editing talents to good use again with this and like I said, I'm doing some freelance work."

"You know full well what I'm getting at."

The oven let rip with a loud, incessant ping, to signal the roast dinner was ready.

Mum began to rise from her chair in the sitting room to come and help, but Rhiannon gestured to her to sit down again.

"If I ever felt ready to return to publishing, you'd be the first to know, Rhiannon. I promise. Now, let's pour some white wine to have with your gorgeous dinner."

Bank holiday Monday delivered a mist across the water.

I arrived in the bookshop and wandered around with my head on a constant loop of thoughts.

Celeste's situation drummed in my mind, as I switched on the till and credit card machine. Thoughts of my father materialised. I compared his diagnosis and his appeals to talk to Mum and me with hers. Both were facing their own mortality.

Celeste was adamant she was going to squeeze every last bit of enjoyment and fun out of the time she had left and my father, who had already achieved what he wanted in his career, was searching for forgiveness.

I stared out of the shop window, not seeing the tentative swishes of sunshine burning through the mist across the loch and the first fresh-faced locals venturing out along the main street. Soon, the day trippers would begin arriving with their bikes, canoes and frustrated, over-excited small children.

A stab of guilt over my dad surprised me. Here I was, planning to read Celeste's work and yet, I was still struggling to decide how I felt about my dad and what I should do.

I eyed my mobile staring at me from the top of my bag as it sat on the counter. Why the hell was I feeling guilty? I wasn't the one who abandoned their family.

I neatened up some historical romances. My mobile continued to glower at me.

Outside, a young woman with streaks of pink in her hair drew up to admire my display. We exchanged fleeting smiles through the sun-dappled glass.

She moved on. Still, my mobile sat there, intimidating me. "Oh, for pity's sake," I growled, relieved Tobias hadn't arrived yet and discovered me cursing into the air.

I moved over to the counter, dragged my phone out of my

bag and rooted around inside my purse for Dad's new business card.

After a rummage, I found it.

I hesitated, waggling the card in my right hand, as though I didn't know what to do with it.

What was I going to say to him?

Growing more and more frustrated with myself, I jabbed in his mobile number and began to pace around the bookcases that towered round me. I listened to my jewelled pumps clipping on the wooden floor as I moved.

This was no biggie, I reassured myself. I would just ask him how he was doing.

I waited, hooking a few strands of loose hair back behind my ears.

My mobile connected to my father's and the dial tone rung out for what seemed like an eternity before his voicemail message kicked in. It was as smooth and confident as always, the Scottish-American lilt evident in his accent.

He let out a husky laugh at the end of the recording and then the beep echoed in my ear, signalling for me to leave a message.

I opened and closed my mouth a few times and shut my eyes in frustration. "Er. Hi. It's Lexie. Thought I'd ring to see how you're doing. Anyway, see you later."

I hung up and dropped my phone back into my bag, as if it were about to take a bite out of my fingers. That went well. It sounded like I'd inhaled a ball of helium.

I busied myself with tidying more books. Dad was probably at breakfast or out for a wander somewhere – or chatting up one of the hotel receptionists.

I made my way round the bookcases, stretching to reach a couple of Tessa Dare novels, when I heard the shop doorbell jangle.

My heart did a weird jump.

Tobias?

I found myself smoothing my hair and straightening my shirt.

But when I emerged from around the corner, it wasn't him. It was his uncle. "Oh, hello, Trevor. How're you?"

He opened and closed his mouth. His dark eyes darted from me up to Mirror Image, where the lights were off and it was silent. "Good morning, Lexie. How are you?"

"'I'm not too shabby, thank you. I wasn't expecting to see you today."

"Er. No."

"Are you looking for Tobias?"

He swallowed and pushed his spectacles back up his nose, his attention on everything else except me.

"Are you alright?"

Trevor's expression swam with doubt. "Yes. I mean, no." He didn't seem himself. "Have you seen Tobias so far this morning?"

"Not yet, but he should be in at any moment… Trevor?"

"I should really talk to him," he rushed. "It's very important."

I studied him. "Trevor. Are you alright? Can I help?"

But he was already making for the shop door.

Chapter Nineteen

I watched Trevor hurry from the shop, without so much as a backward glance.

I frowned.

He wasn't himself.

What was that about?

Moments later, Tobias barrelled into Book Ends.

My stomach tied itself in knots. "Hi there. How are you?"

Tobias didn't reply. He carried the air of someone who wasn't quite sure where they were or why. His expression was grim. "Have you seen my uncle?"

"Yeah. He was here a few minutes ago, looking for you." I took in his stormy expression, black brows tightly knitted together. "Tobias, is everything alright?"

He didn't answer. He stared back at me, as though he was struggling to understand the question.

"Tobias. What's going on? Are you ok?"

He fiddled with the leather strap of his watch. He dropped his head. "Did my uncle say anything to you?"

"About what?"

He hesitated. An undecipherable edge fired through his eyes. "About me."

"No. He said he wanted to talk to you though."

I set down the pile of romantic sagas I was clutching on top of the counter. "Tobias? What is it? Trevor's behaviour did seem rather odd."

Tobias forced a troubled hand through his curls. "Family matters."

I shot him a concerned look. He still stood there. "Look. Whatever it is, you don't have to tell me if you don't want to." I gave him what I hoped was an encouraging smile. "But if you did, I promise you that it wouldn't leave this shop. You can trust me."

Tobias's chest heaved under his fitted, butter-coloured shirt.

"You listened to me moaning on about my dad and Literati, so if I can return the favour, you only have to ask."

Sweeps of anxiety kept crossing his handsome features.

"Anyway," I started, hoping to push some light relief into the situation. "I'm here for you. That's what I'm trying to say."

Outside, the bank holiday traffic was beginning to build, breaking up the view across the road to the loch.

Tobias remained standing on the bookshop floor, a confused look on his face.

"Well," I forced, wondering what on earth was going on. "You know I'm here if you do decide you want to talk."

I started off towards the counter to retrieve the two books I'd put down there, when Tobias's voice made me stop. "Lexie."

He moved towards me, his shoulders hunching over.

I stared up at him. "Yes? Talk to me. What's going on?"

He gave his stubbled chin an anxious rub. "I'm not too sure where to start." He let out a sigh. "You were right, as it turns out."

"Sorry. I don't understand. Right about what?"

Tobias propped himself against the counter. His jaw throbbed as he considered what to say. "I should've realised something was up, that it seemed strange at the time. You thought it was."

"What?" What was he talking about?

Tobias sighed. "That it was a surprise when my uncle decided to help me try to secure premises for my new gallery."

I eyed him. "Tobias, you aren't making any sense."

"Sorry. I know I'm talking in riddles. It's come as a huge shock, that's all."

I found myself reaching out a concerned hand and placing it on his. His lashes flickered as they studied my hand. I realised what I'd done and snatched it away again. Good grief! Why the hell did I do that? I cleared my throat, my hand still feeling the warm imprint of his. "What's come as a shock? Tobias?"

He pushed a chunk of his curls back behind one ear. "Would you believe that I've just found out my late father isn't my real father after all?"

I blinked up at him in shock. "What?" This confession made me search around inside my head for something more prophetic to say, but I wasn't sure what. Instead, I waited for Tobias to elaborate, but he didn't.

"Are you sure?"

"Yes."

Confused, I let out a long, low breath. "I'm sorry." I hesitated. "So, how did you find out? I don't understand."

He let out a gravelly croak of dark laughter. "No, I don't know that I understand it yet either."

He held me to the spot with his wounded gaze.

My heart lurched for him. "Tobias? What is it? Just tell me."

He shook his head, as though he were struggling to comprehend what he was about to say.

Tobias fought to keep his deep voice calm. He flashed me a look. "His name is Cormac, apparently. My real father, that is." He pushed a troubled hand through his hair. "But I don't know anything else about him. And I don't know if I want to."

A couple of passing locals and a few tourists drew up in front of the window.

I took one look at his mixed-up expression. "Tobias. Are you sure about all of this?"

He gave the briefest nod of his head.

"Jesus. I'm sorry. I don't know what to say."

He blew out some stunned air. "What is there to say?"

I slapped the book counter decisively. "Right. Let's get some air. We'll take a walk down by the loch."

"But what about this place?"

I made a dismissive snort. "We won't be out for too long. What time is one of your staff members coming in today?"

"Octavia is on shift from 10am. I'll text her and tell her we're popping out for a few minutes. She can keep an eye on everything."

I started round the counter. "Chloe will be in around then too. I'll drop her a text and say the same thing. Now come on. We can't talk in here. Someone could come in."

"Yes. Much-needed customers."

I ignored him and retrieved my bag. "Closing for half an hour this morning won't break the bank."

The loch was awash with sun that had banished the mist. A couple of small anglers' boats danced on the water, their masts piercing the sky like fine white needles. A couple of birds crested on the faint breeze.

I drew to a stop above the steps that led down to the shoreline. "So, this Cormac guy is definitely your biological father?"

Tobias appreciated the electric-blue skyline. He gave the sharpest nod of his head.

"How did you find out?"

"My mother told me last night."

I turned this over in my mind. "Jesus. Right." I was almost as stunned as Tobias was. "I'm so sorry, Tobias. It must've been an awful shock." I examined the whispering water lapping at the shore. "But how did the subject come up? Did you have your suspicions for a while then, that your late father might not be your biological father?"

Tobias squinted against the lemon sun. "No. I had no inclination whatsoever."

"So, what happened?"

He was silent for a few seconds. "After dropping you home last night, I decided to drive to Mum's. I wanted to take a look at a couple of her old family photo albums." Tobias then went onto say that he'd been commissioned to paint the portrait of a late military captain by his family. "I remembered I'd seen a couple of photographs of my late great-grandfather, Harold – he'd also been a captain in the army during World War One – and I thought that might help me channel the First World War time period and give me some extra inspiration."

Tobias's eyes looked pensive. "I know where Mum keeps her albums, so I started taking a look while she insisted on making me some dinner." He hesitated then recounted taking out the boxes from the bottom of her bedroom wardrobe. "It was while I was rooting around, that I accidentally knocked over a couple of her shoe boxes and that's when I found a small photo album wedged right at the back."

"And what was in this one?"

Tobias narrowed his eyes against the sun. "I thought it might be more family photographs of me, Mum, my late dad, Trevor, Naomi and Tamsin… the usual suspects."

I felt the sun sweep over and down my back, warming it through my summer shirt. "But it wasn't?"

Tobias looked rueful. "Well, yes it was but there were a few letters stashed in there as well."

Tobias shook his head, as though he wanted to dislodge the images. "The year was 1985, so a year before I was born, and the letters stuffed in there were from my aunt Naomi to her sister Caroline – my mum." Tobias admitted he didn't have time to read them all. "But from what I did read and from what my late aunt was saying, she was trying to comfort my mum, as she'd just found out that Bernard, my dad, wasn't able to give her a baby."

Tobias looked at me. "Then a couple more letters, which were more replies from my aunt to my mum, were going on about how much dad loved her and that he felt guilty about not being able to give her a family." Tobias looked bewildered. "It sounds like my parents had both been struggling to come to terms with not being able to have a child." He swallowed. "Then they mentioned some guy called Cormac a few times, saying he would've been delighted at the prospect of becoming a dad."

He pinned all his attention on me. "As soon as I read that, it was like my world imploded. This Cormac must be my father. Mum must've had an affair with him and I was the result."

Tobias rubbed at his chin, peppered with dark stubble. "So, I grabbed the letters and the album and went straight back downstairs. You should've seen my mum's face when she saw me holding them. She looked like her whole world had collapsed around her."

My chest deflated for him. "What did she say?"

Tobias's mouth drew into a solemn line. "She became defensive at first, asking me what I was doing and saying that I'd no right to be searching around her possessions. She looked shellshocked. So small and quiet."

A couple of prams spun past us as we stood there, lost in our own conversation, their wheels glittering in the sunshine, and the young mums pushing them savouring ice creams as they chatted.

I drank in Tobias and urged him to continue. "And then?"

"She asked me how many of the letters I'd read and I told her I'd seen the first three, but that was enough to realise what had been going on."

Tobias let out a weary sigh. "She burst into tears. She kept apologising over and over, saying she should've told me years ago about my dad not being my real father." He made a dismissive noise. "Her reasoning was that it never seemed like the right time to tell me. Then, when my father passed away, she didn't want to ruin the memories I had of him."

My empathy soared. "Did she tell you what happened?"

Tobias adjusted the collar of his shirt. "I asked her about this Cormac character, but she just kept crying, insisting that it didn't matter and that Bernard had always been there for me and that he would always be my real father."

Tobias closed his eyes for a few seconds as he recalled the encounter with his mother. "I started shouting, saying my whole life had been built on lies." He let out a bitter laugh. "It's like something you see on daytime TV."

I tried not to stare at the irresistible way Tobias's lashes spiked.

He started to scrape at the granite wall with one of his nails. "I asked her who else in the family knew about this. She said Trevor does, but not Tamsin." He shook his head. "Seems like we're at the back of the queue." He fell silent again for a few moments as he replayed his discussion with his mother. "Mum begged me to come back and hear her out, but I refused. I jumped in my car and went for a long drive. I'd heard enough."

I kicked a smooth caramel stone down by my feet. "You shouldn't have driven anywhere, feeling like that. You could've had an accident. You should have phoned me."

Tobias flashed me a look. "You've got enough going on in your own life at the moment."

I gazed up at him. "I know, but that doesn't mean I can't be here for you."

We swapped prolonged stares. Then Tobias concentrated again on the loch and the soaring hillside.

I considered how Trevor didn't initially offer to help Tobias, and how he then suddenly suggested that he launch his gallery in Book Ends. "That must be why your family relations have always been a bit fraught."

"That's putting it mildly."

Below us, a noisy family bustled on their way with two skipping little girls devouring ice lollies.

"So didn't your mum tell you why Trevor changed his mind about helping you with your art gallery?"

Tobias angled his strong jaw upwards. "I asked her that. Sounds like she begged him to. Guilt, probably, after everything that had gone on behind my back."

My thoughts shot back to Trevor dashing into Book Ends a short while ago, looking for Tobias. "No wonder he was so anxious to talk to you."

His expression darkened. "I bet he was. No doubt my mother was straight on the phone to him as soon as I left her house, warning him that I'd found out."

We exchanged glances, as the shouts and squeals from children on the loch shore rose up. "So, what are you going to do now?" I asked him.

Tobias considered my question. "I don't know how I feel or what I should do." He looked lost, staring ahead of himself, before twisting his attention back to me. "Shit. I'm sorry. You don't need to hear this. What with your dad being ill."

"Forget it. I think you've trumped me on this occasion for family drama."

Tobias managed a brief smile. "Do you know what you're

going to do about your dad? Are you going to talk? Jesus. We've even more in common than I thought."

Our eyes seared into one another. I forced my attention back towards the water. "I did ring him this morning, but he didn't pick up."

At that moment, my bag by my feet vibrated. I realised it was my mobile ringing.

I hesitated, but Tobias urged me to answer it.

I bent down and fished my phone out of my bag. "Hello?"

The Scottish-American infused voice entered my right ear. "Hi, Lexie. It's Dad."

I whipped my head round and pointed to my phone, mouthing to Tobias, "It's him." I gathered myself. "Hi."

Stilted pleasantries were exchanged, before Dad hesitated. "Do you think we might be able to meet up and talk?"

What was I going to do? What did I want to do? I felt empathy for him, because of his dementia diagnosis, but as for taking things forward, I had no idea. There was just this vacuum and I had no idea how to fill it.

I thought of Celeste, seizing life and savouring every minute of it while she still could. I thought of Tobias, towering there in front of me and attempting to deal with the revelation that the man he'd admired and loved all his life wasn't his biological father. I couldn't keep running away and dodging the situation. Life had its twists and turns and there was nothing we could do about it.

I had to decide how I was going to deal with my own issues.

I remembered that Rhiannon was travelling back to Glasgow before eight o'clock that evening. I had to stop fumbling around. I straightened my back. "We can meet up by Bracken Way Castle this evening, if you like. How does eight o'clock sound?"

I was certain I heard a rush of relief down the line, like a gust of wind that would often batter the loch and take everybody by surprise. "That's perfect, sweetheart." Dad faltered. "I don't suppose your mum might come?"

I shook my long, straight hair, even though he couldn't see me. "Sorry, Dad. She really feels for you but as for meeting up… well, she hasn't said she would. At least not yet. I don't think she's ready."

"You mean she might be at some point though?"

"I'm not answering for Mum. Don't ask me to."

I could hear his ragged, frustrated breathing. "I don't know how long I still have like this, Lexie. How long I'll still be able to remember and laugh, smile and cry over the memories I have."

A clump of my hair was sent flapping across my cheeks in the sun-drenched breeze and I whipped it away. "I know, Dad, but you hurt her. She loved you so much. You can't just expect her to forgive you in an instant. "

"I know."

Now it was my turn to sigh. "I think the two of us should just talk first and then take it from there."

"Alright," he conceded. "I understand."

I was about to hang up, when I heard my father's voice erupt again down the line. "Lexie. Wait."

I put the phone back to my ear. "What is it?"

Tobias kept his profile trained on the loch and the scenery but every so often would award me a soft look of support.

My stomach rippled.

I returned my attention back to my phone call with my dad. For a moment, there was a deafening silence. I thought the line had crashed. I put the other hand over my other ear, as a couple of bickering gulls, the loch and a gaggle of tourists triggered a melting pot of sound. "Hello? Are you still there, Dad?"

There was a crackle. "Yes, I'm here." His voice became thicker. "Thank you, Lexie. Thank you."

Chapter Twenty

R hiannon, Mum, Grandpa and I indulged in a cheeky Chinese takeaway, before my friend prepared to set off in her funky electric-blue Mazda for Glasgow.

She hovered at Mum's front door and gripped onto the long black handle of her shocking-pink wheelie case, which was bright enough to have been able to guide stranded ships home. Rhiannon didn't do discreet. "Now, I'm not going to go over old ground and repeat myself."

"Excellent. Good to know."

"But promise me that you'll think about what I said, Lexie. I don't think you realise what a talented editor you are."

Returning to work in publishing was the very last thing I wanted, but I had to placate her somehow. "If I tell you I'll think about what you said, will you stop nagging me?"

Rhiannon batted her warm hazel eyes, slicked with glittery blue shadow. "I can't make rash promises."

I gave her a nudge, a hug and watched her wheel her

clacking case towards her car. "Have a good journey. Let me know you get home ok."

Mum and Grandpa joined me to wave her off. Rhiannon waved back out of the driver side window as it began to melt away up the road. She interspersed her waving with the odd one-handed writing mime, which I think was supposed to represent editing. I responded by sticking out my tongue.

Mum and Grandpa vanished back inside and I stood taking in the quiet street and the orange silhouette emerging from behind the castle in the distance.

Then I disappeared back up to my room to get ready, both physically and mentally, for meeting up with my dad.

I tied my hair up into a messy bun and freshened my make-up.

When I had arrived home from work, I'd changed out of my work clothes, opting for my plain white T-shirt, slim-fitting jeans and my cream denim jacket. I tugged on my trainers, my fingers working the laces on auto pilot, while I thought about my father.

I finished teasing my hair and snatched up my phone from my bedside cabinet.

I felt nervous. I hadn't told Mum and Grandpa who I was meeting. Not yet.

My stomach swooped and dived as I made my way down past the huddle of shops towards the castle. Bracken Way had been a hive of holiday activity today, but now it was only the last few defiant bank holiday stragglers who were packing up cool boxes, picnic blankets and herding over-tired children into their cars for the journey home.

My stomach performed another apprehensive roll.

This was ridiculous! I could understand my feelings if I was going out on a first date with Tobias, but not meeting up with my own father.

A date with Tobias? Yeah, right. Not a good idea on any front. I needed relationship heartache like a hole in the head and affairs of the heart, with me, never seemed to turn out well. I hadn't been faultless though. I'd thrown so much energy into my job at Literati, I never had time for anything else. Love and romance didn't seem to sit well with my family. Even my own parents' marriage had been a disaster.

A dull ache ripped through my chest. Such a pity that real relationships couldn't be as magical as the ones my romance authors had written about at Literati.

The sunset bled amber, crimson and scarlet stains across the sky, as the castle shimmered into view.

It was almost eight o'clock.

My father was already up there waiting for me, hunched over the rail and lost in the horizon. His greying collar-length hair was getting a little too long, furling up at the ends. He was sporting a battered leather jacket, dark jeans and white trainers. He looked like he was about to audition as a drummer for a middle-aged rock band.

I strode more purposefully than I felt up the steps.

As if sensing me approach, he turned around. He tensed. "Lexie." The relief was evident on his tanned, lined face. "I wondered if you might change your mind about coming."

"I wouldn't do that. I don't like to let people down." *Not like you*, ground a hurt voice in my head. As soon as I said it, I wanted to bite the words back, even though a part of me was ashamed to admit I meant every word of them.

My dad looked like he wasn't sure what to do with his arms. They opened and closed several times. No kisses. No hugs. It would have been awkward for both of us.

Huge public displays of affection were out. Tentative, odd smiles were exchanged instead.

I stepped up beside him so that our profiles were side by side, appreciating the blue, craggy vista. The slight bump at the bridge of his nose mirrored mine.

"So, you wanted to talk to me?" I asked.

He nodded.

I breathed in the heathery tang dancing on the breeze. "How is… how are you? I mean, your condition."

Dad rubbed at his cheeks and contemplated my question. "Godawful some days, bearable on others. I have to face facts, Lexie. It's going to get worse, not better."

I leant on the rail. His words prodded and poked me. "What about treatment for it?"

"My consultant said it's a case of just slowing down the symptoms and its progression." I listened as my dad, his hair being sifted by the breeze, spoke about the limited options open to him. "He said he's starting me on a drug called Memantine, to try and improve the quality of my learning and memory."

"What else?"

"Some sort of antipsychotic to control the impending anxiety, depression and agitation." My father's lips twitched with sarcasm. "It all sounds fabulous, doesn't it? I can hardly wait." He stared straight ahead at the shimmery water. "I'm going to be rattling when I walk."

This disease was going to take everything that he cherished: his intelligence, writing ability, the core of who he was.

"I've made a monumental cock-up of my life."

His sudden admission made me crick my neck as I snapped my head round to look at him. "Not where your career is concerned, you haven't. We've read about the journalism awards you've won over the years. All the exclusive stories you broke."

Dad squinted ahead, as if in pain. "I'm not talking about my career. I'm talking about you and your mum. About being a parent and a husband. Making a successful, happy marriage."

Now it was my turn to look discomfited. "Well, I won't argue with you there."

To the left of us and a bit further down the road, the glowing lights from The Drawbridge hotel sprang into life, illuminating its tree fringed driveway and flowers.

"I'm so sorry," he blurted, whipping his attention round to look at me. "I know I've been such a shit father to you, Lexie."

"And a shit husband to Mum."

Dad accepted this with a fierce nod. "I've no defence. You're right." He jutted out his clean-shaven chin. "But I want to try and change that. I want to try and make things right."

I thought of the years he wasn't around. The struggle Mum had to keep our lives on an even keel. Her working as a secretary in the local solicitor's office and the mental and physical strain of being a single parent.

I didn't want to sound churlish or hard-hearted, but my emotions were battered and scattered all over the place.

"Please be honest with me, Dad. Would you have come back here, if you hadn't received your dementia diagnosis?"

Dad examined me from under his floppy hair.

"Would you?"

Colour flooded his face. There was a stony silence for a few moments.

"What I do know, is that my diagnosis has made me think about my life here in Bracken Way and how it was before I took off to London. It's made me think long and hard about you and your mum. And it made me realise what a selfish prick I've been."

I didn't disagree with that either. Every word he was saying was true; these were the conclusions I'd reached about my father years ago.

I noted the facial similarities between us even more so now, the arched angle to our brows and the quirk of our mouths, as we stared at one another. "So, what is it you want, Dad? Forgiveness?"

"Maybe I do. But I'd be more than happy if your mother could find it in her heart to let me apologise to her. Face to face. Even if she just granted me five minutes." Dad's generous mouth sunk. "Like I told you, I don't know how much longer I'm going to be myself and that's why I need to put things right before this… this bastard robs me of who I am."

Flickers of resentment lit up inside me. "We could have been happy, Dad. We could have been a proper family, if you hadn't been such…" I struggled to find the word.

"Such a self-centred bastard." Dad's eyes searched my face.

"I put everything else before you and your mother and I'll always carry that with me." He braced himself against another blast of fresh air dashing across the surface of the loch. "This might be my last chance to make amends."

The shore below us shimmered with water cascading over the pebbles and rocks.

His tone was creaking, desperate. "Would you speak to your mum again for me please, Lexie? Could you try to persuade her to just listen to what I have to say?"

I rubbed at my sleeves, covered in my cream denim jacket. The stiff breeze was whipping up, sending shivers down my back. What should I do? Should I just ignore my father's pleas and tell him to do one? Or should I give my mother the opportunity to speak to her ex-husband and hear him out? It could be the last chance she ever had of seeing him again. Seeing him again like this.

I drank in the frightened look in his eyes. It took me by surprise. Niall Dunbar, the intrepid, fearless journalist, looked mortal all of a sudden. Who knew?

I turned over my father's desperation. "I'll tell her I've met with you, Dad, and will ask her if she'll do the same. But you have to respect her decision." I gave my head a brief shake. "She loved you so much. When you walked away like that it broke her. I don't think she ever truly got over it."

His stare gleamed with fresh emotion. "I've been such a shit to both of you. I don't deserve love like that." He dragged a weary hand down his face.

"Look, I'll ask her to meet with you, ok? That's as much as I can do."

A defeated mish-mash of pain and hope took over his features. "I can't ask for or expect any more. Thank you."

We stood, side by side, with our bumpy nosed profiles.

"How are things with you?" he asked eventually. "I have to admit I was surprised to learn from Gilbert that you're no longer working in publishing."

I shifted from foot to foot. "Gilbert's been a busy bee, hasn't he, keeping you informed of local events."

Dad pulled an embarrassed face.

"The truth is, I was overlooked for a promotion I was promised at my publishers, hence the bookshop."

He stared down and out at the glistening pebbles and stones bleeding into the water. "Well, it's their loss. I want you to know that I'm very proud of you. Your mother's done a wonderful job."

"She had no alternative, Dad. She had to do it on her own. If it hadn't been for Grandpa and Grandma Pattie, I don't know what she would have done." I threw him a look. "What *we* would have done."

Dad made a desperate sighing noise. "I know. All the more reason to tell your mum how sorry I am and how much I regret what I did. To both of you."

"You met up with your dad? When?"

"Just now, Mum. Up by the castle."

Mum's jaw dropped. "Why didn't you tell me you were going to see him?"

I toyed with one of my earrings. "Because I didn't want to upset you and I wasn't sure what you'd think or how you'd react. And I wanted to hear him out first." I paused. "He wants to talk to you. He wants to explain and apologise."

Mum paced up and down her sitting room. She crossed and uncrossed her arms. "I don't know, Lexie. I know he's ill and I feel for him, but opening up old wounds after twenty-three years. Will it achieve anything?"

My grandfather, reposing in his chair, sat forward. "Och, Maisie, you have to do what you feel is right. I've no time for Niall Dunbar, after the way he treated you and Lexie, but if you refuse to speak with him and he returns to the States, it's likely you won't see him again." He let his words hang there, the inference clear. "Could you deal with that? Is that what you want?"

Mum hugged herself in the middle of her spotless sitting room. It smelled of apple furniture polish. "Oh God. I don't know what I want or what to think right now. Would he have given us a second thought if he hadn't been diagnosed with dementia?"

"I asked him the very same thing, Mum."

"And?"

"He said finding out about his illness has given him some much-needed clarity, put it that way."

She spun out and towards the kitchen. "I don't know. I honestly don't." She rubbed at her arms. "I've spent years trying to put him behind me and now he comes back and drags it all up again." She paced up and down on the kitchen linoleum. "I don't know if I want to revisit those memories anymore."

I followed her and lowered my voice. "Even after telling me you're still in love with him?"

Her dark blue eyes sparkled with emotion. "Especially because of that."

I stayed with Mum and Grandpa for a cup of tea, before insisting that today's events were catching up with me and I would go up to my bedroom.

I also explained to them that I had a new recruit coming to work part-time in Book Ends, a very pleasant stay-at-home husband and former English teacher, Daryl Hughes.

"Good," said Mum, pursing her lips. "The more, the merrier. You're run ragged in that shop."

I almost laughed at Mum's dramatic tone. "I'm not run ragged, Mum. I've got Chloe in full-time with me, which is a great help, but having Daryl in a few hours here and there will be an added bonus."

"Well, you can see you've lost a few pounds, sweetheart. It's probably all that walking and carrying books."

With Mum's advice to eat a proper breakfast ringing in my ears, I got ready for bed, exhausted and not even able to second-guess what Mum wanted to do or would do about my dad. It was a tangled mess and I could see she was trapped between what she wanted to do and what she thought she should do. It would've been easier if she still didn't love him, but I didn't point that out.

The orange street lamps glowed against my curtains as I clambered into bed with Celeste's manuscript. I was keen to press on and read it, making notes on structure as I went. I was aware of Celeste's situation and that was pushing me to make swift progress with it. I needed a distraction and some escapism from the real world for a while too.

I untied the lace ribbon, placed it on my beside cabinet and began to read, only for my mobile to ping on my bedspread. It was a text from Tobias:

Hope everything went ok with your dad tonight. Was thinking about you this evening.

I blinked down at the message. He'd been thinking about me this evening? Oh, he meant because of the situation with our respective fathers, I reasoned quickly. Don't you dare read anything more into it than that.

His message ended:

Anyway, see you tomorrow. Tobias x

My attention was drawn to the kiss.

I stared down at the "x" far longer than I should have done.

I chewed over what I should say in reply and came up with something, after a few attempts and deletes:

All went well, thanks but my mum is still not sure about what she wants to do with regard to meeting up with my dad. I know she feels so emotional and mixed up over it. As for Trevor, just take your time to decide how you want to play things. Think he's done the right thing by making himself scarce for now. Thanks for your concern. See you tomorrow.

Lexie. x

I jabbed in the kiss, deleted it, mulled it over for a few seconds and put it back again. Then I fired the text back to him.

Now stop dwelling on Tobias and keep reading Celeste's book, I urged myself.

Chapter Twenty-One

"My mum has been trying to speak to me," admitted Tobias the following Monday lunchtime. It was the beginning of June and there was an air of anticipation at the school holidays starting in a few weeks.

"I told her I don't want to see her right now, not until I can get my head around this." He let out an angry growl. "I also used getting everything sorted with my new flat as an excuse. When I think about them not telling me… my own family, for Christ's sake!"

I arched my brows. "Yes. Well. They maybe thought they were doing it for the right reasons."

Tobias didn't look convinced.

"Life has thrown a few curveballs our way recently," I sighed.

Tobias's expression darkened. "I couldn't agree more. I feel like mine has turned into one bloody great lie."

I pushed myself out of the chair, stationed behind the bookshop counter. "No, it isn't. You're still the same man you were before. And though I hate to admit it, a very talented artist."

Tobias's lips flickered for a few seconds. "You could've added how attractive and dynamic I am as well."

I felt my stomach flutter. "Let's not get too carried away, shall we?" I moved away. My heart zoomed in my chest like a rogue rocket. I shot Tobias a glance. "Trevor texted me to say he's gone away for a few days to a book festival in the Scottish Borders."

"How convenient."

I busied myself, gathering together my jacket and bag then proceeding to switch off the light.

"What are you doing for the rest of the evening, Lexie?"

I halted in my tracks. "I'm going to head back to Mum's to continue reading and editing Celeste's book. How about you?"

The dark tips of his lashes made his eyes glow. "Well, I was going to head home and do some more admin, but I got more done in here today than I thought I would." His eyes raked my face. "And it'd be nice to have some company and think about something else for a while, other than my car crash of a family and where I've packed my favourite sketching pencils."

He continued to stare down at me. "How about you come back to my place and I make us something to eat? I'm no Gordon Ramsay, but I've been known to make a mean stir fry. We can commiserate together over our relatives."

My head screamed No. We were both vulnerable right now. Both our lives were in a mess. *You don't need romance, Lexie, remember? And you certainly don't need any complications.*

Politely refuse, hissed an inner voice. *Thank him and go home. Focus on Celeste's book.*

But the reasons not to go and have dinner with Tobias were dismissed with full force by my skittering heart. It thumped harder in my ears.

"I'd like that," I found myself saying, unable to stop myself. "Thank you."

Tobias's new apartment reflected him perfectly.

It was masculine and uncompromising with wooden grained floors.

His sitting room consisted of a hexagonal black and glass coffee table and a charcoal leather sofa and two chairs, decorated with zebra-striped cushions. A bookcase ran the far length of the sitting room wall, housing everything from a Lewis Hamilton biography to Ken Follet.

The kitchen was similar in style, black and chrome with a dark rattan blind at the window. There was trendy cutlery, beside which sat another *Guardians of the Galaxy* mug and an *Iron Man* mobile phone holder in the corner.

Tobias must have caught me smiling. "I'm a bit of a Marvel geek," he confessed with a sudden, shy blush. "Star Lord is one of my heroes."

I struggled not to imagine Tobias looking sexy in a leather jacket, boots and tight jeans like Chris Pratt. I batted the pictures away. "I can understand why. Those films have a fantastic soundtrack."

I also noticed further down the hall, a framed print of a Ghost rock album. He caught me admiring it. "I'm a big fan," he smiled, gesturing to the picture. "I love listening to their music when I'm painting."

"Me too," I said. "Well, when I'm editing. And I thought you might be. I remember you wearing one of their T-shirts." Bugger! My cheeks zinged. He'd be thinking I was some sort of stalker!

I started to burble on about "Spillways", "Dance Macabre" and "Call Me Little Sunshine", explaining they were three of my favourite tracks of theirs.

"You've excellent taste. All great, but I love "Darkness at the Heart of my Love". There's something mystical and sexy about it."

Tobias's fingers brushed against my shoulders as he took my jacket and hung it up on one of the pegs in his hallway.

I could feel him studying me, so I kept my attention focused on one of the far kitchen windows, which overlooked one of the country roads out of Bracken Way, with fields sandwiched beside it and clusters of hedges.

Next to the kitchen, was what looked like a makeshift art studio, containing an easel, paint palettes, pots of brushes and various canvases. Some were blank, screaming to be painted on, while others carried almost completed pieces or works that had just been started; ghostly traces of silhouettes and features I could just make out, in faint pencil.

Odd boxes sat around, waiting to be unpacked and there were a couple of paintings lying against the magnolia wall in the hallway, poised for hanging. The apartment carried an air of newness and expectancy.

Tobias concocted a delicious stir fry infused with juicy chicken strips, slices of glossy red and yellow peppers and crunchy beansprouts. The sauce he created, dashed with a tangy hint of pineapple, enhanced it even more.

Across his marbled breakfast bar, we discussed everything over dinner, from how he got into painting in the first place (he trained at the Edinburgh School of Art and then Glasgow Art School) to my struggle to get a foot into the publishing industry.

He twinkled across at me, watching my mouth as we talked and it had all been so natural; we weren't dancing around each other anymore, but both able to let our guards down and behave how we wanted to.

I realised I didn't want to tear my eyes away from him.

His deep laugh; his dry delivery when he was telling a joke; the way his curls skimmed his shoulders; how he reached up with his long fingers and tucked his hair back behind his ears. Sitting there right now across from me, he reminded me of a sexy pirate.

Oh God.

I snatched up my glass of crisp white wine, buried my face in it and took a mouthful.

Tobias tipped his head to one side. "If someone had said to me a few weeks ago that we'd be sitting having dinner together like this, I wouldn't have believed them."

"No, me neither. Pistols at dawn, more like."

I watched him push his fork around his plate, before setting it down again. "Lexie, I know I often come across as a morose sod, but I want you to know something." He trained his mesmerising green stare on me again. "I've been thinking about you a lot. Far more than I should."

I gripped the stem of my wine glass tighter.

Had I just imagined him saying that? Was I willing him to say it and he hadn't? Worried that I might snap it or injure myself on the wine glass, I set it straight down again by the side of my plate. "You've been thinking about me?"

"Yes."

My heart galloped harder. I had to make a decision here. Was I going to take a step over the cliff or was I going to just stand there and admire the spectacular view?

Because I'd put so much time and energy into trying to advance my publishing career, I'd chosen not to get involved with anyone. I hadn't been interested. The risk of being let down too, by someone I loved, wasn't something I relished. Nobody seemed worth taking the chance on. I felt it was safer for me to fall in love with the heroes in my author's books and that meant I could focus on promotion.

But now, sitting here now on this Monday evening in June, with the dreamy sun cascading in through his kitchen window, this seemed to slot together like the last pieces of a puzzle that I had been struggling to make sense of.

I took another gulp of my wine and discovered my voice. "And if I'm being honest, I've been thinking about you a lot too."

Tobias's eyes glittered. "That's a relief. I was beginning to worry then."

More flirtatious smiles were exchanged.

"Tobias…"

"Oh, excuse me." His mobile rang out by the kitchen sink and he reached out one muscular arm to retrieve it.

His heated expression as he glanced up at me again made my knees feel as though they were made of water.

But his expression darkened when he saw who the caller was.

It was like a tower of bricks tumbling and crashing down. He whipped his head to one side, away from me. "I'm not doing this now. What do you mean? I don't need to do anything, Mum."

Awkward silence prevailed. I made a move to stand up, but Tobias shook his head and pointed at my stool, encouraging me to sit back down again.

I could make out the emotional female voice of his mother down the line.

"Ok. Tell you what. I will, if it means no more nagging and not having anything to do with this sham of a family!"

His jaw was set like concrete. "I'm busy for the next couple of days with Mirror Image, but I'll get back to you." He rung off.

Tobias dumped down his phone on the black marble breakfast bar. The excited air of anticipation between us moments ago had been sucked out of the room.

He glanced at me across the table. "I know I can't keep putting off the inevitable, but right now, I don't want to think about having to face my mother and uncle."

"I do understand, if it's any consolation." I flicked him a look.

His expression had lost the fire from earlier. "Relationships," he managed. "I don't think they're worth the hassle in the long run." He angled his eyes away. A conflicted expression was gripping his features. "Either personal or family." He shifted on his breakfast bar stool. It was as if the words were pieces of jagged glass in his throat. "You're a good friend, Lexie."

My stomach dropped to the floor.

What? What just happened? Had I just imagined the last five minutes?

Tobias pushed and pulled at his empty plate.

Burning hurt stacked up behind my eyes. Had I read it wrong? Was my radar out of kilter? Was it because of the phone call with his mum?

Tobias clapped his hands together. "Now, would you like some coffee?"

I managed to shake my head and scrambled from my stool. I couldn't stay here a moment longer. I felt an utter idiot. My insides were twisting. He'd clammed up. *A good friend*. But that was what I'd wanted, wasn't it?

I wanted to go home. I didn't want to be here anymore. Embarrassment caught in my throat. "No thanks. That was lovely. I had better be off. No rest for the wicked."

"I'll drop you back."

"No! I mean, no thanks. I would rather walk."

I darted out into the hall, snatched my bag and jacket and made for the door. I wanted to escape and not be anywhere near Tobias right now.

I walked home from Tobias's flat, my head and heart feeling shamefaced. He'd invited me over for dinner, flirted with me, we'd laughed and teased one another, he'd said he had been thinking about me and then he backtracked and hit me with the dear friend line.

I gulped in greedy mouthfuls of air tinged with the scent of flowers. My head was overloaded with confused thoughts.

My publishing career, my dad, now Tobias – why the hell

225

was I lurching from one mess to another? Where was I going wrong? What had happened to my common sense?

I reached Mum's house and scrambled for my key in my bag, eager to get inside and slam the door closed behind me.

It was as I was kicking off my shoes, trying not to look at my distraught image in the hall mirror, that Mum appeared from out of the sitting room.

"Had a good time?" she smiled. "I thought you might be back a bit later than this."

"Yes, thanks," I managed. I didn't want to have to explain or relive the evening. "Well, I've got work tomorrow. Didn't want to be late. How are things?"

Her voice was full of adrenalin. "I've been thinking long and hard about everything; about your father." She gulped. "Your grandfather told me earlier that I was letting my stubborn streak dictate what I should do."

"Mum?"

She let out a long rush of air, like a hissing balloon. "Your father will be heading back to the States soon and I have to decide what I'm going to do. Could I live with myself not meeting up with him? I've thought long and hard about that and I'm not sure I could."

Her words galloped out of her. She wrung her hands in front of her. "I've decided I'll meet your father and hear what he has to say." She gathered herself. "I have ghosts I need to lay to rest too."

Chapter Twenty-Two

The next few days saw Chloe and me showing Daryl, our new part-time member of staff, the ropes and familiarising him with everything. I was also busy with freelance editing in the evenings for a couple more aspiring authors, browsing through the latest bookseller magazines and thinking of ideas for new window displays for the shop.

I also pushed on with reading and editing Celeste's novel, which had me entranced.

Every evening, I found myself looking forward to losing myself in its spellbinding pages. It was somewhat wordy in parts and lacking in description in others, but the characters and plot were enthralling.

I also decided to be proactive about getting my living arrangements sorted, now that my Glasgow estate agents had just given me the good news that an offer had been put in from a young couple for my flat. I therefore made an appointment with the local estate agents here in Bracken Way, to go and see the two-bedroom flat situated above the local greetings card shop, For Every Occasion, which had just gone on the market.

The kitchen was smaller than my one in Glasgow, but the sitting room was more generous and it had wonderful views of the Bracken Way hills. It was also clean and comfortable, as well as only being a five-minute walk to work, which was a major plus point.

I decided to put in an offer straight away.

New-flat-hunting, as well as anything else I could think of to keep me occupied, meant spending less time thinking about Tobias.

I was grateful he was also busy with a flurry of new portrait commissions, which meant he wasn't around a lot of the time in Mirror Image. He was doing his best to avoid his mother and his uncle, who was back from his book festival event. Tobias warned them not to set foot inside the art gallery for the time being.

He seemed to think that avoiding the issue was the best option, rather than hearing what Trevor and Caroline had to say.

Much to my delight, Celeste, adorned in a cream knitted shift dress with a matching bolero jacket and a string of pearls, decided to surprise me with one of her carers, Joy, on the Thursday morning that week.

She appeared in her glitzy wheelchair, wreathed in smiles and pushed along by Joy.

I darted towards the shop entrance and assisted Joy and Chloe to angle Celeste's wheelchair into Book Ends.

"Isn't this marvellous?" appreciated Celeste, gazing around

herself. Her delicate hands clutched onto the arms of her wheelchair. "I hope the locals are supporting you, Lexie."

"Oh, they are. Business is good and I hope to build on the support we've had so far. In fact, business is so good, that we've had to take on another member of staff part-time." That would help me in trying to avoid Tobias too, I thought to myself with a stab of guilt. It would mean I could concentrate on more office-based work and promotional stuff.

And not have to have as many dealings with him, whispered a voice in my head.

"Well, if you'll excuse me for two seconds, I'll have a quick browse through your crime section," beamed Joy.

"If you need any help, don't hesitate to ask," called Chloe, flashing a wide smile.

"Will do." Joy hurried off, her sky-blue carer's uniform rustling as she went.

"And how are you?" I smiled down at Celeste in all her summer finery.

"Just about the same, dear. Fighting for every breath."

"Oh, please don't say that."

"It's true," she said with a wink. "But I won't be going down without a bloody good fight."

"Glad to hear it. Now, would you like me to take you on a tour of the premises?"

"That would be lovely. Thank you."

Celeste arranged herself and I began to angle her wheelchair towards the first set of looming bookcases, the spines beckoning us with their varied colours and author names.

Then Flora Simmonds came barging through the door, interrupting the peaceful reverie.

"Lexie, I have a favour to ask. Would you be able to put a poster in your window for me please? It's for the summer fayre at the town hall."

She tossed her floaty scarf back over her shoulder and eyed Celeste in her wheelchair. Her pale stare narrowed as she peered down at her. "Do I know you from somewhere?"

Celeste sat up a little straighter and clasped her hands in her lap. "I don't think so. Now, if you'll excuse me…"

Undeterred, Flora carried on. "No, there's definitely something familiar about you." She scrutinised Celeste again. "Are you sure we haven't met before? It's really annoying me."

"Not as much as you're annoying me," muttered Celeste out of the corner of her mouth.

But Flora didn't hear her. She still had the bit between her teeth. "How long have you lived in Bracken Way?" she asked Celeste, scanning her from head to toe.

Celeste's expression sharpened. "Long enough."

Flora continued to study Celeste.

She craned her neck for the umpteenth time as she stared down at her. What was her preoccupation with Celeste? Why all the questions?

"Everything alright, Flora?" I asked pointedly. "It's just I'd offered to take Celeste on a tour of the bookshop."

Without waiting for Flora's response, I started to wheel a relieved Celeste away from her interrogator.

That was until a sudden loud gasp echoed behind us. The half a dozen other browsing customers twisted their heads round to see what the matter was. Chloe, replacing receipt paper in the till, jerked her black corkscrew curls up. Had Flora taken ill?

Part of me expected Flora to be demanding immediate medical assistance, but instead, she was wide-eyed, unable to tear her attention away from Celeste.

One of Flora's hands flew to her chest and rested there, like an age-spotted star fish. "I knew it. Celeste! I knew I recognised her from somewhere, but I couldn't place her. Now I know!" Flora's face was illuminated in triumph. "It's her!"

Celeste's complexion drained of colour. Both of her hands reached down to grip the arms of her wheelchair.

Flora's smug face peered at each of us, delighted that she was the centre of attention and we were hanging on her every word. "It's her," she repeated again, jabbing one finger.

Irritation and concern for Celeste took hold of me. "Yes, you've already said that, Flora."

Flora levelled her stare at Celeste again, relishing every second. "Don't tell me you don't know who she is." I glowered at Flora, who let out an exasperated sigh. "For pity's sake. You live in Bracken Way and yet you've no idea about the history of the place or the infamous people who make up part of it." She let the word "infamous" roll off her tongue.

Celeste squirmed against her cushion.

"Let me introduce you then," proclaimed Flora, looming over Celeste in a wave of Chanel perfume and linen trousers. She paused, savouring every ounce of Celeste's discomfort. "This lady is the silver songbird."

Chapter Twenty-Three

Silver songbird?

What was she talking about?

Celeste's hands gripped tighter to the arms of her wheelchair. She struggled to recover herself. "I don't know what you're talking about."

"Yes, you do," insisted Flora with glee. "It is you, isn't it?"

I frowned, concerned by Celeste's sudden wan appearance. I bent over beside her. "Celeste, are you alright?"

She didn't answer at first. She didn't look at me, but instead trained her troubled attention on somewhere over by the other bookcases. Her voice was preoccupied. "Yes. Yes. I'm fine."

Flora wouldn't let her pursuit of Celeste drop. "There's no need to feel embarrassed," said Flora in a faux caring tone. "After all, it was years and years ago now." A triumphant smirk spread across her face. "Still, a bit of a girl back in the day, weren't you?"

Celeste rocked backwards and forwards in her wheelchair. She looked like she wanted to pass out. "I'm so sorry, Lexie, but I'm getting rather tired. Would you mind finding Joy for me please? I think we should head back now."

I glowered at Flora. I didn't want to leave Celeste alone with this woman a second longer than I had to.

Thankfully, I didn't have to.

Joy appeared, clutching the latest crime blockbuster. "I must treat myself to this…" Her voice faded when she noticed Celeste's expression. "Are you alright, sweetie? What's wrong?"

"Nothing," clipped Celeste, fiddling with her necklace. "I'm just feeling a bit tired."

Joy flicked Flora and me a puzzled look. "Ok. Let me buy this and then we'll head straight to the car and get you back."

Chloe served Joy, thanking her for her custom as she slid the novel into one of our gift bags.

"What happened?" whispered Joy to me, once she had paid for her book. "Celeste was fine and dandy this morning."

Flora, meanwhile, continued to lurk close by, shooting none too discreet glances at Celeste.

"Flora Simmonds – the woman in the linen trousers over there – made a remark to Celeste, which has upset her."

"What did she say?"

"She called her the silver songbird."

"What's that?"

"I've no idea."

Flora snapped her head up, as she pretended to examine the blurb of a new thriller. "I was only making idle chatter."

We both smiled at Celeste, who returned our support with a shaky smile of her own.

Joy, clutching her Book Ends gift bag, barged past Flora to get to Celeste.

I dashed to the shop doorway. Flora continued to hover inside, watching proceedings out of her narrowed, lined eyes, as I angled the shop doors open to allow Joy to navigate Celeste's wheelchair out of Book Ends and back onto the pavement.

Once outside, Joy peered down at Celeste, concerned. "Do you want me to give the doctor a ring?"

"Stop fussing. I'm fine. And you will do no such thing! If you ring him, the next thing I know, I'll be getting carted off to hospital and I won't see the light of day again."

Joy rolled her eyes.

"I'm just a bit tired, that's all. Nothing a G&T won't cure."

"Celeste, you always say that."

"Yes, and it always works."

Joy had managed to park her white saloon in one of the disabled bays just a little way back up the street.

After Joy had assisted Celeste into the passenger side and got her settled, I waited until she closed the car door. Celeste was still pale. She pushed out a shaky smile at me through the car window.

"I've no idea what all that was about," I murmured to Joy.

Joy frowned across the roof of her car. "Celeste can be very private when she wants to be. I'll try to choose my moment and then ask her."

I waited until Joy and Celeste drove off, before leaving the quiet, sun-washed street and returning inside Book Ends.

I awarded Flora a hard stare. She was swanning around, picking up odd books, glancing at them and then sliding them back onto the shelves. She had really discomfited Celeste. But why?

Indignation raged inside me. I marched over to where she was. "What was that remark you made to Celeste just now? Something about her being the silver songbird? It really upset her."

Flora blanched under my scowl. "I didn't mean to. I knew I recognised her from somewhere and then it hit me."

Pity something actually didn't, snarled a voice inside my head. I thought of the contented smile on Celeste's handsome, lined face vanishing and my anger reared up again. "You could see she was getting upset and yet you just carried on picking on her."

Flora's frosted mouth sprang open. "I did no such thing." She recovered herself. "It's not my fault if she's ashamed of who she was."

I blinked at Flora. "What are you talking about now?"

But she didn't elaborate.

Flora flapped the ends of her florally scarf draped around her neck. "Some people are overly sensitive."

My mouth flatlined with disapproval. "I don't want this bookshop used as some sort of local gossip hub. I'm certain Trevor wouldn't either. It's supposed to be welcoming and inclusive to everyone."

Flora fixed me with a stare. "It isn't gossip. It's fact."

I was struggling to keep a lid on my irritation with this woman. "What is?"

She pursed her lips and refused to answer. Oh, this was ridiculous!

I planted both hands on my hips and surveyed the

meandering customers inside and lingering tourists outside. I pushed my face closer to Flora's and hissed out of the corner of my mouth. "Whatever you know or think you know about Celeste, I'd appreciate it if you kept your opinions to yourself."

Flora gave a dismissive tut, but still took a step backwards.

My phone rang out from the counter, before I could add anything else.

"I'll get that for you, Lexie," said Chloe, firing chilly looks at Flora as she answered my mobile on my behalf.

"Yes. Well, some people don't deserve courtesy," Flora trilled, banging down another book she'd been holding. I watched her sweep out of Book Ends.

I stuck my tongue out at her retreating back.

Chapter Twenty-Four

That evening, I set up my laptop and after uploading some promotional pieces for recommended beach reads for the summer on Book Ends social media channels, I decided to do some investigating myself on this silver songbird reference that Flora made.

My growing optimism died. There was nothing.

I didn't know what to expect, but I had hoped there might be some sort of link or clue. I typed in a number of combinations, but still it didn't come up with anything. I looked up the history of Bracken Way, hoping there might be a mention somewhere, but that didn't throw up anything either.

I frowned at my laptop screen and decided to ask Mum, who was curled up on the sofa with the latest Jodi Picoult.

"No. Silver songbird, you say? Nope. Doesn't ring any bells with me. I'll mention it to your grandpa though. He's just getting ready to head off to bed. Give me a second."

"Thanks, Mum. That would be good. It seems to be a bit of a mystery."

I waited while I heard muffled conversations through Grandpa's bedroom door at the top of the stairs.

A few moments later, Mum returned. "He said he vaguely remembers some local gossip about a young girl in Bracken Way being called by that nickname years ago now, but who she was, he doesn't know."

"Does he know why she was called that?"

Mum relayed my question to Grandpa, by calling up the stairs.

He stuck his head round his bedroom door. "Och, it was supposed to be some scandal or other, but there were a few different stories going around. Then it became yesterday's news."

Well, for Flora Simmonds, it was still current. "Scandal?" I repeated, my curiosity rising. "What sort of scandal, Grandpa?"

A few moments later, my grandfather reappeared at the top of the stairs, looking like Noel Coward in his berry dressing gown. "What's all this about, little dove? Why are you asking? I need my beauty sleep!"

I gave him a brief account of what happened earlier in the day at Book Ends. "Flora called Celeste Matthews that name in the bookshop and there was a bit of a commotion." I paused. "So, do you know what this supposed scandal was, Grandpa?"

"Och, it was years ago now, lass. But if I recall right, some of the gossipy local lasses hinted some young woman from the area had got herself into a spot of bother." Grandpa let out a snort. "I never used to pay any notice to their tittle-tattle. That Flora Simmonds has always had a nasty tongue in her head, mind. She still floats around the town as though she owns it."

Grandpa heaved a tired sigh, wished me goodnight and then vanished back into his bedroom.

"I wouldn't pay much heed to that old bag Flora," muttered Mum. "You get to your bed. You need your sleep, young lady, running that business."

Friday was a busy morning in Book Ends and Mirror Image respectively.

Mum was meeting up with Dad in the evening and every so often my stomach rolled in sympathy for her.

Dad had rung me before I left for work, stunned, then relieved and delighted that Mum had called him and agreed to meet up with him. He had jumped at her suggestion of seven o'clock up by Bracken Way Castle. "Should I buy her some flowers, Lex? She still loves stargazer lilies, right?"

"You might end up wearing them, Dad. Best just to go empty-handed for now and take it from there."

I kept finding my head drifting away, thinking about my parents, so I decided to focus on updating the bookshop window display with a summery theme, to try and occupy my thoughts elsewhere.

I made it a sea of yellow- and blue-toned covers, side by side, with matching coloured buckets and spades I bought from the local gift shop.

I'd just finished arranging the books on top of two large sheets of lemon- and aqua-coloured paper, which I'd rippled to reflect the loch and shoreline, when I spotted Tobias out of the corner of my eye, strolling down the pavement.

My heart did a weird lurch, like a car being thrown into the wrong gear. I crouched lower in the bookshop window. I hated feeling like this, especially after he'd made it clear he viewed me just as a friend.

The sun was tangled in his curls and he was wearing a deep red shirt and pale trousers.

I dusted down the front of my cotton dress and clambered down and out of the window.

"Good morning," I smiled, hoping he couldn't hear my heart careering around.

He stared at me a little longer than usual, my dress billowing against my knees. "Morning." He loitered for a few moments, before stalking past me towards the gallery. "How have things been? Sorry I wasn't around yesterday. Bloody paperwork!"

"Oh, God," I groaned at the memory. "Awful! Flora confronted Celeste in here after she recognised her and called her the silver songbird. Then Celeste took an odd turn and demanded to be taken back to the residential home."

"So, all in all it went well then?" A small smile teased at his mouth. Then he frowned. "Silver songbird? What does that mean?"

"I've no idea."

He prowled around, firing up his new coffee machine, which he'd installed the other day.

Here we go again, I groaned to myself. *Skipping around one another.*

Despite what I'd thought on Monday evening over dinner, there couldn't have been any flirting. I must have imagined it. Or dreamt it.

I forced myself to dismiss any further notions of Tobias and me sharing anything other than a work-related, platonic friendship.

"Fancy one of my irresistible lattes?"

I blinked and dragged my attention back to Tobias, who was gesturing to his coffee machine. "Oh, go on. Thank you."

Tobias waggled one cup in each hand. He started to make them.

"Have you had any more thoughts about speaking to your mum?" I asked him.

His hands stilled, clutching the coffee mugs. "No. I haven't. Right now, I just want to blank it all out and concentrate on my art."

"But Tobias, you can't just avoid the issue. At some point, you're going to have to talk to her."

"So, back to this weird stand-off with Flora and Celeste?"

He didn't want to discuss it. I buried a frustrated sigh.

Tobias brows fenced as he turned it over in his head. "Celeste has never mentioned anything to me about silver songbirds when I've been painting her portrait. How do you like your latte?"

"Frothy please."

"The frothier the milk, the better," he smiled. Then he raised one finger. "Lexie, you've got a small piece of yellow paper stuck to your face."

I shot one embarrassed hand up to my right cheek. "Where?"

My fingers fumbled at my cheek.

"No, you keep missing it."

Tobias strode towards me, covering the floor in two long

strides and, as if in slow motion, he raised one hand and brushed it against my face.

My breath lodged in the base of my throat.

He looked down at me from under his lashes. His fingers left a tingling sensation. "There. Got it."

He opened his palm and a shred of yellow paper was sitting there. My skin felt the sensation of his touch, the warmth of his hands making me flush.

I pulled away from him as though he'd burned me. "Great. Thanks," I managed. "I might have started a new fashion trend, walking around with that on my face."

Tobias blinked at the sudden space between us. "Yes. Sure. No problem." He gestured to his posh black and chrome coffee maker. "Right. Two lattes coming up."

I hurried over to the bookshop counter and flapped around, trying to look busy but not doing anything.

Pull yourself together. You can't keep reacting like this.

As I shuffled around some change in the till, a thought occurred to me. Perhaps Tobias was a serial flirt? Maybe this sort of thing was just a game to him? What if he was one of those guys who would try and reel a girl in, get her interested and once she was, he'd become bored and move onto the next one? It made sense. The blowing hot and cold.

Annoyance and hurt were piling up inside of me. I wasn't his plaything. He could bugger off if he thought he could treat me like that. He might look like Jon Snow out of *Game of Thrones*, but that didn't give him the right to act this way.

Tobias returned, grasping two white mugs of steaming, milky lattes.

"Thanks," I smiled coolly, accepting one from him.

I concentrated on the intense scent of the coffee and took a couple more steps backwards, as if doing that would make a sudden wall appear between us.

I hoped he wouldn't notice.

Shit. He had.

Tobias's brows flexed over his mug. "Lexie, I hope you don't mind me asking, but don't you like my aftershave?"

"Sorry?"

"My aftershave? Only, I've noticed you move away from me a couple of times."

Oh bugger. Now what was I going to say? My mind struggled for a sensible reply. I let out a tinkly laugh. "Not at all." I tried to cover my tracks, but sounded like a raving lunatic instead. "Your aftershave is very nice. Very spicy. You must have imagined it."

Tobias didn't look convinced. "Thanks." He took a mouthful of his coffee. "How're things with your dad?"

"My mum is going to meet him."

"Great. Well, that's good… isn't it?"

"Yes. No. I mean, I think so." I cradled the white ceramic mug in my hands. "God knows how it'll go. My mum feels for him, but he's hurt her so much."

"Maybe they just need to be honest with each other." Tobias drew himself up as he spoke. A concoction of emotions rampaged across his handsome face.

"They've wasted so many years," I sighed.

Tobias gazed at me as he took another considered sip of his coffee. "That's true." A thoughtful expression settled on his features. Then I watched as Tobias moved towards me and reached for the mug in my hands. He took it from me and set them down together on the bookshop counter. I realised his generous lips were suddenly inches from mine.

I felt hypnotised.

Tobias looked like he wanted to kiss me. He raised his thumb and caressed my cheek. I couldn't help it. A moan escaped from the base of my throat.

"Lexie. I need to talk to you…"

The shop doorbell rattled out.

Tobias and I jumped apart.

A woman's voice rang out. "Tobias?"

I turned around.

Trevor had entered the shop, and next to him lingered a woman with blow-dried pale gold hair.

Tobias's expression hardened. "Mum. What are you doing here?" He motioned to Trevor. "Ah. I see you've brought backup with you? Making sure you both stick to the same story?"

The woman gripped tighter to her squashy petrol-blue bag. "We need to talk to you, Tobias. Both of us."

His eyes flashed. "There isn't anything else to say."

"But there is," implored Trevor, taking a tentative step forward. He pushed his spectacles up the bridge of his nose. He glanced at Tobias's mum next to him. "We can't carry on like this."

"You need to understand what happened," said Tobias's mum.

Tobias's expression turned to stone.

Trevor sighed. "You need to know the truth."

"What truth?" snapped Tobias. "What the hell are you talking about?"

Caroline Black looked in my direction, an embarrassed flush colouring her fine features. "Could we talk in private please, darling?"

Tobias shook his head. "No. Forget it. Whatever you have to say to me, you say it in front of Lexie." He faltered and gazed across at me. "She's a friend."

Ah. There it was. That dreaded phrase again.

Tobias's mum struggled to push out a smile at me. "Alright. If that's what you want."

She sucked in a mouthful of air, while I darted down to the shop door and swivelled the sign to say we were closed. At least none of Tobias's staff were due in yet and neither was Chloe or Daryl.

"I think you put two and two together and came up with five," she said to her son. "And I didn't have the guts to tell you otherwise."

Tobias pulled a dismissive face. "With what?"

"Those letters between me and your aunt Naomi."

She shot her brother-in-law an awkward glance. "Naomi and I were best friends, as well as sisters." She tried to gather herself. "And because Naomi and I were so close, that's why she offered to help your father and me."

Tobias's eyebrows fenced. "Help with what? What are you going on about? You're talking in riddles, Mum."

Her voice cracked and a sob caught in her throat. His mother lifted her face up to the bookshop ceiling for a few moments.

"Mrs Black. Are you alright?" I knew it was a bloody stupid question under the circumstances.

She gave me a brief smile through the threatening tears.

"No, I'm not but I have to do this. There's been enough secrecy over the years and it has to stop."

Trevor, standing beside her, snatched up her hand and gave it a supportive squeeze.

Tobias watched them linking hands. His eyes flashed. "I said, help with what?"

Mrs Black looked stricken. "Your dad and I were desperate to start a family. We thought it was just going to take a bit of time, but we'd been married for three years and I wasn't falling pregnant." Her face pleaded with her son for understanding. "I wanted to protect you," she managed. "Naomi did what she did with the best of intentions. I also wanted to protect my late sister's memory."

"What has Aunt Naomi got to do with any of this?" asked Tobias. He turned to me and then back to his mum. "What are you talking about?"

Mrs Black clamped her eyes shut, as though willing the whole sorry situation to vanish in a puff of smoke. She forced them open again. "Naomi wasn't your aunt, Tobias."

Trevor nodded. "That's right." Now it was his turn to shuffle on the spot, looking like he wished he were anywhere else but here.

Tobias looked aghast. His mouth sprang open and shut. "What?"

Trevor looked pained. He ground his jaw. There was a crackling, electrified silence. "Caroline isn't your biological mum."

"Your aunt Naomi was your real mother. Not me."

Chapter Twenty-Five

T obias let out a long, low breath. "Jesus." He stared, horrified. "Are you serious, Mum?"

Caroline could only manage a brief nod through her tears.

"Perhaps we should sit down," I suggested, reaching out to squeeze Tobias's arm. Concern for him ripped through me.

Tobias remained standing on the spot, shellshocked, as Trevor, Caroline and I swapped stricken looks.

"Tobias?" croaked Caroline.

He was fighting to straighten his broad shoulders. He moved stiffly towards the office and sank down in one of the chairs next to me, as if in slow motion. He was struggling to make eye contact with either Trevor or Caroline. "So?" he demanded. "Can someone tell me why my life has suddenly become like an episode of some daytime soap opera?"

Trevor's dark gaze was troubled. He shifted on the chair beside Caroline, before raising one finger and pushing at his round spectacles again.

Caroline dabbed her wet eyes with a hankie. "When Naomi

was seventeen, she met and fell in love with a local car mechanic, Cormac Munro."

Tobias's mouth hardened.

"They were besotted with one another and when she was eighteen, they got engaged, but at Christmas that same year, Cormac was killed on his motorbike. The weather had been atrocious and he hit a patch of ice on one of the country lanes." Caroline hesitated, gathered herself and then continued. "Naomi was distraught. She was in a state of shock, as you might imagine. Then, a few weeks after Cormac's death, she told me her period was late."

Caroline went on to explain that at first, Naomi was convinced that it was just the stress of losing Cormac. "But it turned out it wasn't. She was pregnant."

I shot a concerned look at Tobias seated beside me. His stubbled face was ashen.

Her hands tumbled over each other in her lap. "Naomi was adamant she wasn't going to have a termination, but in those days, single mothers... well... I don't have to tell you, I'm sure."

Caroline raised her damp face to the office ceiling and turned back to stare across at Tobias. "That was when Naomi suggested your father and I adopt you. We couldn't start our own family and we knew we could give you the life you deserved."

Tobias's jaw clenched.

Trevor flashed a cautious look at his sister-in-law beside him.

Caroline shuffled on her chair and dabbed at her face with

a floral stitched hankie she plucked from her bag. Her sky-blue eyes shone with tears.

The silence was palpable. It was as if we were sitting in a library, rather than a bookshop on a busy Scottish high street.

Tobias glanced at me and then back at his mother and uncle. "So, who knew about this arrangement?"

"Only immediate family," assured Caroline, her voice small. "Before Naomi's pregnancy became more obvious, she went to stay with our grandmother – your great-grandmother – near Aberdeen, and me and your dad rented a cottage close by and stayed there until after you were born, so we could help out and keep an eye on Naomi." Caroline reddened. "There was also the fact that I wasn't expecting, so it would've looked suspicious if I'd suddenly appeared back in Bracken Way with a newborn baby, having shown no signs of being pregnant." Caroline's desperation increased. "I fell in love with you the minute you were born."

Tobias drilled his attention into his mother. "So, if everything between both sisters was so perfect, why did it become so fractious when I was growing up then?"

Trevor squirmed as he sat there. "You can't legislate for people's feelings, especially after the birth of a baby. I think Naomi believed she could control her emotions and that everything would carry on as normal, but it didn't. At least, it didn't for her."

He opened and closed his hands several times as he talked. "Naomi and I met in 1988, two years after you were born. I was working in a little bookshop in Pitlochry and she came in, wearing the prettiest candy-pink summer dress. I couldn't take my eyes off her. She told me she was on a weekend break with her mother and started asking about Sylvia Plath, but I couldn't concentrate." Trevor's face was wistful. "I was too busy looking at her."

He appeared lost in happy thoughts for a few moments. Then he spoke again. "I'd always wanted to open up my own bookshop and so when we married, we eventually ended up moving here to Naomi's hometown, and then in 1993 we bought Book Ends."

Trevor said soon after they began dating, Naomi told him about the death of Cormac and having Tobias. "She assured me she'd be able to stay detached, that she had assumed the role of your auntie and could handle the fact she was your biological mother. But as time went on, Naomi said she realised she'd made a terrible mistake."

Caroline blanched beside him and dropped her gaze.

Trevor carried on. "Naomi wanted you back. I think us having Tamsin made her maternal feelings for you even stronger. She said when you were older, she was going to tell you that she was your mother." He leant further forward, still knotting his fingers together. "It started to cause so much tension between the four of us. Naomi was back and she started hanging around Caroline and Bernard more and more, so that she could see you and spend time with you." Trevor gave me a look. "Naomi would find any excuse she could. I can understand it. You reminded her so much of Cormac."

Caroline nodded in agreement. "You're his double, with the same curly hair. He was tall and handsome too."

Tobias scratched his stubbled chin, but his voice wasn't as brittle. "Sounds like something from Jeremy Kyle. Oh, I am proud!"

"It wasn't like that," snapped Trevor. "You make it sound like some seedy transaction." Trevor sank his weary head back against the chair. He stared upwards for a few moments. "You deserved a stable, settled life, Tobias, and Caroline and Bernard wanted to give you that. Naomi wanted to, but she couldn't. Not then."

Caroline's expression was pleading as she stared across at her son. "I couldn't lose you, darling. That's why so much awkwardness developed between the four of us." Her eyes shone at the memory. "I wasn't prepared to give you up. You were – *are* – my son. That's why Dad and I decided we had no option but to keep Naomi at arm's length."

Tobias eyed us, his mind whirring. "So that's why we moved away from Bracken Way to the south side when I was a kid? I liked it here. I had to leave all my friends."

Caroline rubbed at her eyes.

"I wondered why we just upped and left like that. You told me at the time it was because of work opportunities for Dad." Tobias ground his jaw. "But that was a lie. It was just to suit you then?"

Caroline stared in horror. "I was desperate for a child. I was desperate to be a mother to you and I knew Naomi was regretting giving you up. I was terrified. I couldn't lose you."

Tobias lounged back in his chair. "Sounds to me like you were all so desperate to get what you wanted, rather than give any consideration to me."

Tobias's expression was grim. He jumped to his feet. I could see thoughts swirling through his anguished eyes. He let out a grunt. "This explains everything. That's why you changed your mind about helping me relocate my gallery." Tobias's face bore down. "So, what was it?" he directed at Trevor. "Family guilt?"

"It's what Naomi would have wanted," insisted Trevor. "I'll be honest. I did get a shock when I saw you in Bracken Way a few weeks ago. It brought everything flooding back." Trevor coloured. "Seeing you was a reminder of so many things; it reminded me of Naomi and what I've lost, the pain and regret she went through after she surrendered you to Caroline and Bernard." Trevor faltered for a moment. "But what Caroline said made sense. We should've been honest with you years ago, Tobias. Naomi would've wanted me to help you find a location for your new gallery." He pushed on, as Tobias's dark brows knitted together. "She wanted to keep a connection to you. That's why she insisted you get a stake in the shop." Trevor indicated to Caroline. "When your mum—"

Tobias cut Trevor off with a hollow laugh that rang around the bookshop office. "But as it turns out, she isn't my mother, is she?" He glowered at the two of them.

Caroline's face was etched in panic at the sight of Tobias beginning to stride away. "What are you doing? Please, sweetheart. Don't leave."

"If you think I'm going to stay here a minute longer than I have to, you're deluded."

Trevor moved to speak again, but Tobias ignored him. He swung round to me and tried to stem his anger. The pain in his eyes stabbed at me. "I'm sorry about all this, Lexie."

Worry for him coursed through me. "No. Please don't apologise, Tobias. There's nothing for you to be sorry about."

But he was already walking out of the office.

Caroline's face crumpled and Trevor swiped off his

spectacles and rubbed his eyes. "We should've told him years ago," choked Caroline. "Naomi was right. I've been so stupid. When he found those letters I panicked."

"The four of us were stupid," sighed Trevor. "I was the one who kept telling Naomi not to say anything to Tobias. I insisted that if she did, there was every chance she'd never see him again. I warned her that you and Bernard might sell up and even take him abroad. Glasgow was a world away as it was."

Trevor turned to me, his long, sombre face etched with guilt. "I know it might not sound like it, but we all wanted what was best for Tobias." He threw his hands up into the air in a helpless gesture.

His dark brown eyes brimmed with anguish as he turned his attention back to Caroline. "Naomi wanted to give you the one thing you couldn't have. She knew you and Bernard would be such wonderful parents."

"I can only begin to imagine how it must have been for all of you," I said, glancing at the empty chair where Tobias had been sitting only moments before. "I know it's easy for me to say, but please try not to worry. It would be a shock for anyone. Tobias just needs time to come to terms with everything."

Once Trevor and Caroline had departed Book Ends in a flurry of concern over Tobias, I typed up a quick notice, printed it off in the office and then attached it to the shop door, explaining that Mirror Image Portrait Gallery would be closed for the rest of the day for personal reasons and apologised for any inconvenience.

I then spent the rest of my time not able to concentrate on anything except Tobias. My attempts at ringing him were met with an unanswered phone, before his voicemail kicked in.

I left a couple of messages, but he didn't call me back.

I trudged home at the end of the day, replaying the conversations from this morning over and over.

Families. Parents. What a painful, emotional mess they could make of things, when they put their minds to it!

Because I'd been so preoccupied by Tobias, Trevor and Caroline, my parents' meeting for a heart-to-heart had been relegated to the recesses of my mind.

I arrived back at Mum's, relieved to tear off my work clothes and jump into my jeans and a T-shirt. I kept recalling Tobias storming out of the bookshop, hurt and pain blazing out of him.

I didn't feel hungry, but thought I'd better try to eat something.

Grandpa had already eaten and was muttering over the newspaper crossword.

I rooted around in the fridge and after deliberating for five minutes, I decided I couldn't cope with a full-blown meal and opted instead for scrambled egg and salmon on a bagel. Mum would have been horrified. Good job she was out meeting up with my father.

I eyed my phone as I chopped up the fresh Scottish salmon to lay over the top of my scrambled egg. Still no response from Tobias.

My concern mounting, I picked up my mobile and decided to ring him again, before sitting down to eat.

I paced up and down the kitchen, my bare feet slapping against the cream-coloured linoleum tiles.

I was about to hang up, when there was a sharp click that took me by surprise. "Hi, Lexie."

I started. Part of me had been expecting his voicemail again. "Oh. Hi." I couldn't disguise the relief in my voice. "I just wanted to check you were ok. I rang a few times earlier."

"I had a couple of meet-ups with portrait commissions. I didn't have to, but I wanted to keep busy after… well, you know, this morning."

"I can understand that."

I continued to stride around and fetched a knife and fork from the cutlery drawer. "Tobias, I know this must have been the last thing you were expecting to hear and you can tell me to mind my own business, but I believe that the four of them were trying to do what they thought was best for you at the time."

He gave an unconvincing murmur.

"They should've told you years ago and not let you find out the way you did, but if it's any consolation, Trevor and Caroline are in bits over this. It's obvious how much they love you and how much Naomi and Bernard did too."

And could you be beginning to love him too? questioned a teasing voice in my head. The thought lit up in my chest but I ignored it.

Tobias's preoccupied voice interrupted my thoughts. "Let's face facts. They've made a right cock-up of the whole thing. You're being very diplomatic." He hesitated. "Lexie, thank you again for being there today for me. It means a lot."

I found myself gripping my phone tighter. My heart zinged. "Oh, don't mention it."

"No. Really. These past couple of weeks; well, I don't know what I'd have done without you."

There was another pause. My stomach swooped. This was ridiculous.

My mind was choked with images of Tobias. I could keep denying my feelings. No matter how hard I persisted in telling myself that I had no interest in Tobias, I knew I was lying to myself. He was running away with my heart and no matter how hard I tried to fight it, it was useless.

I couldn't carry on like this. What with Celeste's condition and my dad's revelation about his illness, life was precious and had to be grabbed with both hands. Happiness was a priceless commodity.

I recalled Tobias's words about me being a good friend, but right now, they didn't matter. What mattered was me getting how I felt about him out into the open. I thought I would burst otherwise. Ok, he might not feel the same way. Actually, scrub that. He'd told me he didn't. But I wanted him to know how I felt and I would just have to handle the consequences. I couldn't carry on, tucking away my feelings for him and pretending they didn't exist. No regrets. Celeste and Dad had taught me that.

My throat was dry. "Tobias," I stuttered, before I had time to change my mind. "There's something…"

"White or red?"

I froze. A woman's husky voice was chatting to him in the background.

"White or red, Tobes?" she repeated.

"Oh, white please," he answered, his voice muffled as I could hear him move the phone away for a moment. "Sorry, Lexie. You were saying?"

I drew up and stopped prowling around the kitchen. *Tobes?* Embarrassment shot through my veins. He was with someone. I struggled to stay composed. Had he found solace in the company of a woman? Why couldn't he have drunk wine with me?

My heart drummed in my ears. Oh God. And I'd been about to confess how I felt about him. Shame gnawed at me. Had I been wrong? Perhaps my notion that he was beginning to become attracted to me was my wishful thinking after all?

I should have listened to my common sense. Why the hell hadn't I?

Burning tears cluttered up my eyes, but I jammed my lips together to bite them back. I should have the word MUG stamped in neon lights across my forehead. Memories of us almost kissing earlier; the feel of his thumb softly brushing my cheek; the sexy curve of his full lips; came crashing through my head.

"Lexie. Lexie? Hello? Are you still there?"

I raked a hand through my hair, sending it whipping back from my face, like a straight, light brown flag. "Er. Hi. Yes. Sorry, look, I'm going to have to go."

"Oh. Ok. I meant what I said to you. Thank you so much for being there for me. I don't know what I would have done—"

I'd heard enough. I cut him off. "No worries. That's what friends are for. See you at work tomorrow." I jabbed at my phone, desperate to end the call. Why did I ever think that I might stand a chance of having a happy ever after? Ha! Editing romance had given me too high expectations.

A single tear trickled down my face, but I brushed it away. I'd spent the best part of the day fretting about Tobias, imagining him in bits, confused and hurt. Instead, he was with a woman, helping him knock back wine?!

I banged around in the kitchen, clattering plates. The bastard!

What had that almost kiss been? Was it just because he'd felt emotional? Confused, maybe? Was he a player after all? Had he seen an opportunity to kiss me? Or maybe I'd been some sort of temporary distraction? Hadn't it meant anything to him?

Well, whatever games he thought he was playing, there was no way I was going to neglect Book Ends. It was going to be difficult for a while, having to work alongside him, but I would just have to make the best of things.

I thumped another plate. I wasn't prepared to jeopardise Book Ends' future or my own, just because Tobias was behaving like a tosser.

The height of the summer season would be here before we knew it, and now I'd hired a couple of staff members I could take some time off, knowing there was sufficient help in Book Ends.

I wouldn't have to see Tobias as often. The less that happened, the better.

I found myself clinging to the hope that if Mirror Image continued to do well, Tobias would view Bracken Way as too self-limiting anyway and he'd look to expand elsewhere.

I jumped as my phone's ringtone interrupted my thoughts.

I snatched it up. Mum's image appeared.

Guilt tripped up my spine. I'd been so preoccupied with thoughts of Tobias and his mysterious woman just now, my parents meeting up had been temporarily relegated.

"Hi. How did it go with Dad?

"Good." There was an awkward silence. "I'm on my way back now."

"Good?" I probed.

Mum sounded weird. "Yes. Very."

I waited for her to elaborate, but there was just a strange silence. "Mum, are you alright?"

"Yes," she squeaked after a few seconds' pause. "At least, I think so."

My protective streak for my mum kicked in. "What's going on? Did he upset you? What did Dad say? What happened?"

Mum cut through. "Stop worrying, sweetheart. He didn't upset me."

"Oh, right."

"Quite the opposite."

I frowned as I slid the tea towel back over the handle of the oven door. "Why? What happened then?"

She took a long intake of breath. "We talked for ages. I've been with him all evening. He kept apologising for what he did to the both of us. In some ways, it was as if the past twenty-three years never happened." She halted, her words transforming into a whisper. "I can hear myself saying these things to you, Lexie, but I can't quite believe it myself."

A warning klaxon let rip in my head. "Mum? What are you saying? What are you trying to tell me?"

"Don't hate me," she begged, her voice growing more urgent, "Don't hate your father."

A wave of concern swamped me. "Mum? Will you please tell me what happened?"

There was a crackle down the line. "Your dad won't be returning to the States."

"What? Has he decided to stay in Scotland?"

Her voice softened like melted butter. "Yes. Here in Bracken Way."

It took a few moments for my head to catch up. "But where is he going to live?" As soon as I asked her the question, my stomach plummeted to the floor. A shocked gasp escaped from my throat. "Wait. No."

Mum ignored my reaction. "We've decided to give our relationship another go," she carried on, her disbelief creeping down the line. "We don't know how fast his dementia will progress, so we're going to grab every bit of happiness we can, while we can. Together."

My mouth opened and shut. This couldn't be happening. This was some sort of weird dream. I blinked a few times. Nope. I wasn't dreaming. I was still standing in Mum's sweet, cosy home, listening to her tell me that she was getting back together with my estranged father – twenty-three years after he'd left us.

"But Mum... but... have you thought this through? Do you realise what you're doing?"

"Yes. I've never been more sure of anything." Her voice was whipped up with emotion. "I've been looking into it and there will have to be a health and social care assessment carried out, to make sure his needs can be met at home.

Eventually, he might need to go into residential care." She paused and gathered herself. "But I'm not thinking about that right now. We'll need to organise for social services to come and assess what we need; what your father needs. That will be the first step."

"Mum," I faltered, my voice breaking and stuttering. I'd imagined them talking, a strained atmosphere at first, whirling with accusations, possibly giving way later to reluctant mulling over the good times, before swapping stories, the recriminations being replaced by tentative laughter. But I hadn't envisaged this.

I rubbed my face. "Look, Mum, this is commendable and I do admire you for it, but what you're thinking of doing is huge."

She continued, regardless. "Shower rails, widening doors, ramps; whatever it takes."

"Mum," I began again. "You need to think about what you're doing; what this means for you and for Grandpa."

"Your dad is going to live with us," she stated, her tone brooking no argument. "I'm lucky. I've got you, whereas your father has no one."

I bit back a swell of emotion.

"I'm going to take care of him, Lexie."

Chapter Twenty-Six

The weekend vanished, what with Mum's revelation about her and Dad getting back together and me trying to ignore my festering hurt over Tobias. And to think I was going to tell him how I felt about him as well. Whatever that almost kiss had been, it was clear it had meant far more to me than it had him. I had to try and face up to the fact that my feelings for Tobias weren't reciprocated after all.

Still, at least I'd received a phone call from the local estate agent on the Monday morning to tell me that my offer on the flat had been accepted. It was as if the stars were aligning at the same time.

Mum was being her usual, proactive self, making lists of who she should speak to at the council's social services department about Dad's requirements, as well as ensuring he was registered with a local GP and arranging for his American medical records to be transferred to Bracken Way Medical Centre. Dad, meanwhile, was making himself useful and was making numerous transatlantic phone calls to Washington, explaining to the TV station that he wouldn't be returning, and liaising with an American house removal company to transfer his belongings over here and have them put in storage.

Mum had even started reading up about distraction techniques to use when Dad became agitated or upset, such as playing music, making him a drink or going for a walk.

Mum rolled up her sleeves and took it all in her stride, even insisting on sitting in with my father when he had a Zoom call with his hospital consultant in the States.

It was no surprise that my grandfather was speechless about the whole turn of events. When Mum told him, he'd looked at her as though she'd just landed in a spaceship from another planet. Then pragmatic realisation took hold. "Aye. You know, part of me isn't surprised," he had sighed at her in his crumbly Scottish accent. "You've never stopped loving that man, even after all these years." He had rubbed at his pencil-thin moustache. "I hope he realises what a lucky bugger he is."

When Mum had left the sitting room, my grandfather had looked at me, resigned. "Your mother's mind is made up. What can I say?"

I crouched down by his armchair and hugged him. "You don't realise what a wonderful man you are."

"Och, I do," he replied with a twinkle. "It's just you and your mother don't tell me often enough."

I had laughed. "Well, once Dad is staying here, Grandpa, you're more than welcome to come and stay with me in my flat any time you like, for a bit of respite."

Grandpa blinked at me. "Your flat? Where are you going, lass? What flat?"

"I'm buying the one above the greetings card shop," I

explained. "I'm going to tell Mum now." I let out a laugh. "She won't want me to leave but under the circumstances, it's for the best." I gave a casual shrug. "Looks like everything happens for a reason."

Grandpa sat up straighter. "You kept your flat-hunting quiet."

"I didn't say anything in case it didn't work out. I love staying here but I need to feel that I'm moving forward and living with my mum and grandpa at the age of thirty isn't doing that."

He patted my hand with his. "I understand that, lass."

I smiled into his eyes. "You're welcome to come and stay any time you like."

"Only if I can bring my Dame Shirley Bassey record collection."

I assured him that as I was partial to a bit of Bassey myself, that would be more than acceptable.

Monday morning in mid-June continued to be busy, with the anticipation of summer.

We were delighted to see that book sales were in the ascendancy, as locals planned their beach reads and tourists browsed, looking for a bargain to lose themselves in on their journeys home.

Tobias texted me to say he would be in around lunchtime, as he was planning to head straight to the residential home to continue painting Celeste's portrait.

I fired back a brief reply saying that was fine, thanks for letting me know and that I would see him later. No need to ask if he had a good weekend, I thought with a stab of hurt.

Tobias appeared just before midday, adorned in an old, loose white shirt smeared with dollops of paint and a pair of tatty beige canvas trousers. With his hair curly and wild around his jaw, he looked irresistible, which irked me further.

I moved over to one of the wooden stands, where I housed a variety of bookmarks and began tidying it up. My stomach still insisted on a lurch when I saw him. Why couldn't his teeth and hair have fallen out overnight?

"Hi," I managed. "How're things and how was Celeste?"

"She was on good form. Flirting like mad and telling me about the good old days."

I paused, a fistful of crocheted bookmarks in my hand. "I don't suppose she mentioned anything about this mysterious silver songbird thing to you?"

He shook his riot of curls. "No, she didn't, but I asked."

"What did she say?"

"She got all antsy and changed the subject. I didn't want to upset her, so I didn't push it."

"That's understandable."

He wafted his hand down at his outfit. "Oh, don't worry about my garb. I'm not going to be working here dressed like Picasso. I brought a change of clothes. They're in the car."

I shrugged. "You're a grown man. You do what you like."

Tobias frowned at me.

"Good weekend, was it?" Shit! The words galloped out of my mouth before I knew it.

"Yes, thanks. Not very exciting."

"Oh?"

"No. Just making appointments and preparing the groundwork for more portraits."

I waited to see if he would elaborate or mention having company, female in particular, but he didn't.

"How about you?" he asked.

"Yes, good too thanks. My parents got back together."

Tobias's jaw dropped. "Seriously? Bloody hell! It's all happening for you. How do you feel about it?"

I made sure I didn't maintain eye contact with him for too long. It hurt too much. "Like my grandfather said, we weren't that surprised. You can't help who you fall for."

Tobias's attention lingered on my face. "Isn't that the truth."

I busied myself, feeling bruised. "Oh, and I bought myself somewhere to live. A flat."

"Well, that's great. Congratulations. Whereabouts?"

"It's the one above the greetings card shop."

"Nice and handy for work." He paused. "So, what happens now with your parents?"

"Dad's moving back in with my mum and grandpa. They're in the middle of sorting everything out now. Mum is in her element, making lists about lists and organising everyone."

Tobias smiled. "Your dad is a very lucky man."

My hand hovered over the wire rack. "Yes, he is. I just hope he realises how much."

I watched Tobias vanish into the office, but my attention was torn away by a tapping on the bookshop window.

It was Flora Simmonds.

Oh great! I hadn't seen Flora since her exchange with Celeste. I recalled the upset brimming in Celeste's eyes that day in Book Ends, when Flora had taken great delight in confronting her. My protectiveness towards Celeste had kicked in then. Now it was back with vengeance.

Flora swept in. "Had any more interesting visitors to Book Ends recently?"

I folded my arms, sending my bangle on my right wrist jangling. "Are you referring to Celeste Matthews by any chance?"

Flora widened her eyes. "Who? Oh, you mean, the silver songbird?"

I pursed my lips. She was trying to wind me up – and it was working. "Why do you call her that?"

Flora pretended to browse the nearby biography section. "Her maiden name was Finch." She angled round to me, raising her light brows under her powder. "You should ask her yourself about the heady days of her youth. Quite a tale."

She slipped me a tight smile and vanished back out into the street without buying anything.

Ask her yourself. Flora Simmonds's supercilious expression riled me.

Frowning to myself, I abandoned what I was doing and fetched my mobile from under the counter. I located Maeve's number. If Celeste had said anything about her confrontation with Flora to her daughter, I was certain Maeve would have mentioned it to me. Especially as it took place in Book Ends. They had a very close relationship.

And Tobias said she'd changed the subject when he'd mentioned it.

After several rings, Maeve answered.

I apologised for troubling her and exchanged some small

talk. Then I broached the subject. "I don't suppose Celeste has mentioned anything to you about a woman called Flora Simmonds?"

"No. Should she have?" Maeve hesitated. "Who's Flora Simmonds?"

"Never mind," I breezed. I didn't want to cause Celeste any trouble, so I backtracked. "It doesn't matter. Forget I said anything." I apologised again for troubling her. "Actually, I was thinking of heading up to the residential home at lunchtime to say hello to Celeste."

"Oh, Mum would love that," she enthused. "Thank you. That's very kind of you."

I rounded off the call.

Whatever was going on and whatever this silver songbird thing was, it seemed Celeste didn't even want to share it with Maeve, let alone anyone else.

Chapter Twenty-Seven

J oy took me through to where Celeste and a handful of
other residents were sitting in the summer room, gazing
out at the immaculate lawns.

"Were you able to ask her about what happened, Joy? With
Flora Simmonds?"

Joy arched her plucked brows. "I've tried to talk to her
about it a few times, but Madam just clams up. All she would
say was that Flora woman had been rude to her, but then she
changes the subject."

The afternoon sun was sliding behind the trees at the end of
the garden and birds hopped from branch to branch.

"Celeste? Lexie's here to see you."

I followed Joy further into the conservatory, which was
decked out with assorted potted plants and a couple of bright
paintings of Loch Bracken.

Celeste was seated in her wheelchair, with her back to us.

Joy assisted her to manoeuvre her chair around. "Can I get
you anything, before I leave you two ladies to it?"

Celeste twinkled up at the young woman. "Tom Hardy and a bottle of pink champagne please."

Joy rolled her eyes and laughed. "I think we're currently out of Tom Hardy, more's the pity." She gave me an encouraging smile and disappeared.

I took up residence on a squashy amber and yellow wicker chair opposite Celeste. "So, how are you?"

Her pale, pink-lined mouth flickered. "Did Maeve ask you to come?"

"No. Not at all. I wanted to." I hesitated. "Look Celeste, you can tell me to mind my own business."

"Oh, don't tempt me."

I pulled a jokey face at her. "But I've been thinking about what happened between you and Flora Simmonds."

Celeste sniffed and rearranged the pastel knitted blanket draped over her knees. "What about it?"

I cocked my head to one side. "Anyone could see she upset you. She would have upset me, interrogating me like that." I leant in a little closer to her. "Tobias said you brushed him off when he mentioned it to you and Joy said the same. So?"

"So?"

Celeste fingered the delicate knitted pattern on her blanket, which reminded me of snowflakes. "Good grief. This town never changes, does it? Everybody's always too keen to get involved in other people's business."

"It's not that. I'm very fond of you and I don't like to see you upset."

Celeste's mouth softened. "There are no secrets around here."

I let out a small laugh. "Are you only just realising that?" I paused, as a couple more of the elderly residents made their way out of the summer room, aided by carers. They delivered wishes of "Good afternoon" as they departed.

We were now alone in there, with just the June afternoon sun for company, lighting up the frames of the windows like they were panelled with gold.

Celeste examined me out of her bright, sharp eyes. At moments like this, it was difficult to comprehend that time was not on her side.

I hunched forward, the floral chair I was sat in creaking as I did so. "What was that about, Celeste, with Flora? And why didn't you tell Maeve what happened?"

Celeste's eyes opened wider with worry. "Does that mean you have?"

"No. I asked Maeve if you'd mentioned Flora to her, she said no, so I changed the subject."

Celeste flashed me a relieved look and glanced away, the gilded light glancing down the lines on her handsome face.

"So, are you going to tell me what this is about?"

After a few moments, Celeste shook her head, her silvery hair shimmering. "Oh, good grief! In the brief time I've known you, you never stop asking questions, do you, young lady?"

I gave a small, embarrassed smile. I must take after my dad more than I thought. "So, you *do* know Flora Simmonds from before?"

Celeste picked at the blanket over her knees. "Alright. Yes. Unfortunately, I do know her. She used to live close to me and my parents donkeys' years ago now. A right curtain- twitcher if ever there was one."

I sat back in my chair. The sunshine was giving Celeste an ethereal glow.

She was discomfited. She kept flapping her hands and settling them again. I could tell there was something she was holding back.

I sat forward again and decided to change the subject in the hope of distracting her. "I'm really enjoying reading your manuscript. It's great. Very well written."

Celeste's hollowed cheeks blushed. "Tish. You're just being kind."

"No. I'm not. It's the truth."

"Well in that case, thank you. That's very kind and a huge compliment from an editor of your stature."

"Once upon a time that was me," I half-smiled.

"It's still you," she insisted.

I waggled one brow. "Thank you, but I'm not here to talk about myself. I'm here about you."

She made a dismissive noise.

"I hope you're intending on coming to Book Ends again."

Celeste's smile evaporated. "I'm not sure about that."

I sat back and surveyed her. "Whyever not?"

She shrugged her slim shoulders. I waited to see if she was prepared to explain why, but she wasn't.

"I think it'd be a very great shame if you decided not to." I continued to look at her. "All this is because of Flora, isn't it?"

Celeste prickled in her wheelchair. "I don't know what you mean." She opened her mouth, before clamping it shut again a few seconds later.

I noticed Celeste lace her fingers tighter together. She squirmed underneath her pastel blanket, but said nothing.

"Celeste, I know I haven't known you for very long, but you don't strike me as the sort of person to give up on things easily."

She pushed out her chin.

I blew out a cloud of frustrated air. "If you don't return, if you hide away from town, Flora will think she's got one over you."

Celeste narrowed her eyes. "That's very underhanded of you, Lexie."

I shrugged. "Needs must." I kept my attention trained on her. This whole situation was so unfair. This poor woman was trying to enjoy the time she had left before she passed away and yet, because of the intimidating behaviour from another individual, she was apprehensive about doing the things she enjoyed.

Celeste remained quiet.

I glanced around, frustrated. "Alright. I'm sorry. I just wanted to see if there was anything I could do to help." I rose up from my floral chair and hooked my bag over my shoulder. "Good afternoon, Celeste."

I reached the open double doors leading out of the conservatory.

"Lexie. Wait."

I stopped, took a deep breath, then turned back to face the older lady.

Celeste was eyeing me with apprehension. She let out a long, slow sigh and pointed to where I'd been sitting opposite her only moments before. "Please. Don't go. Sit down."

Feeling the smallest of wins, I took a few steps back towards her and returned to the vacant chair.

"Tell me. Have you considered working for MI5?"

I gave her a small smile. She raised her eyes heavenwards with an air of defeat. "Alright. I surrender."

Chapter Twenty-Eight

Celeste rubbed her furrowed forehead, getting ready to tell me her story. "I was nineteen at the time. My parents were very strict. They wanted me to go into circumspect employment like being a secretary, but I had other plans. I suppose I wanted to rebel."

Celeste carried on, her voice getting stronger. "I always loved singing and had rather a good voice. Around here, some thought of me as a bit of a flibbertigibbet and so just to annoy them, I played up to it."

Her expression hardened. "Flora Simmonds never liked me. Lord knows why. I never did anything to her, but she was always so spiteful. I couldn't believe it when she came bustling up to me in the bookshop. I hoped she wouldn't recognise me."

Her mouth flatlined and she continued. "I took a job as a personal secretary to one of the local councillors. My parents were delighted as you might imagine, but my heart wasn't in it. A Glasgow talent scout happened to be on holiday in the area and heard me singing one evening in the local pub." Celeste's mouth morphed into a cheeky smile. "I used to do gigs once a week. My parents had no idea."

"So that's where the idea came from for your book? The showbiz background?"

I thought about the main character, Melissa, in Celeste's story, being a struggling singer.

Celeste nodded.

"So, what then?" I asked, almost toppling out of my chair, enthralled.

"Glynn Reid – he was the talent scout – well, he offered to be my agent." She let out a ropey laugh. "I remember him telling me I could be the Scottish Barbra Streisand."

"And then?"

Celeste sighed as she sat there. "Glynn got me a couple of spots singing at weddings in the area. Then he told me that the Stafford-Wells family wanted to surprise old man Wells with a big birthday party for his sixtieth."

"The same Stafford-Wells who used to live in that big house out on the coastal road?"

"The very same."

They had been like the local landed gentry in the area, but had moved out of Willow Bay House years ago, when the place began swallowing up money. They ended up selling the property and it was eventually transformed into an expensive pub and eatery.

"So, did you get hired for the event?"

Celeste nodded, as the residential home gardens were lit up by marmalade sunshine outside the conservatory windows. "I was bloody terrified, but Hope Stafford-Wells, his wife, paid me well and Glynn, as my agent, took his generous slice of commission. Still, for a young woman of that age at that time, the fee I received was very generous."

Celeste rubbed at her knees, still concealed by her pretty knitted blanket.

"Oh, please go on," I begged, my curiosity on fire.

She nodded. "Alright." Her eyes misted over as she carried on talking. "It was going to be a huge party and Glynn suggested I buy an expensive dress. I knew it had got to the stage where I had to tell my parents about my singing gigs. I was getting more and more work and it was only going to be a matter of time until someone else told them before I did."

Celeste paused and then carried on with her story. "My PA salary was modest and my parents refused to contribute towards buying an outfit."

I let out a gasp of indignation. "Not helping you or giving you any encouragement. I think that's awful… If that had been my mum, I wouldn't have been able to stop her going dress shopping with me."

Celeste's mouth drifted into a small, dry smile. "My mother thought that anything above the ankle constituted indiscretion and loose morals." She flapped one delicate hand. "Anyway, I managed to secure a few more pub and club singing spots and did some extra work at the council offices, so I had enough money to buy something snazzy."

"I bet you did! So, what was your dress like?"

Celeste's gaze became dreamy. "Do you remember the dress I asked Maeve to retrieve from my wardrobe that day you and Tobias visited? The one I'm wearing for my portrait sitting?"

I let out an appreciative gasp. "Yes. The silver dress! The one with what looks like silver raindrops on it? You must have looked stunning."

Celeste blushed to the roots of her wavy ball of hair. "I didn't scrub up too badly, it has to be said."

She explained that she'd spotted the beautiful dress in Glasgow, when she was travelling in one Saturday a couple of weeks before the party. "I'd seen a lovely crimson one in the window of this upmarket boutique, but it was after I went in to try that dress on that I saw the silver one on a mannequin in the corner."

Celeste described slipping on the dress, its gauzy underlay sliding down and over her head. "It was like putting on a waterfall," she mused. "I felt like Marilyn Monroe in it."

She smiled at the memory. "As soon as I tried it on and saw my reflection in the full-length mirror, I knew it was the dress for me." She pulled an embarrassed face. "And, of course, that also meant new shoes, a bag and getting my hair done. But I knew it would be worth it, or at least I hoped it would." Her voice faltered.

"Celeste?"

She composed herself. "I can remember standing up on stage in that glamorous function room up at the big house. It was all chandeliers and cream and yellow tablecloths, balloons and napkins. Everything shone like precious jewels, even the cutlery."

Celeste swallowed, before she managed to pick up the story again. The branches of the trees outside the windows waggled and dipped in the summer breeze. The air was warm and languid.

"I can remember belting out 'Happy Birthday' to Johnson Stafford-Wells and I'd just started singing 'Congratulations', the Sir Cliff Richard song, when I thought I was going to forget the lyrics, forget where I was, forget everything." Celeste's cheeks burned with colour. "There was the most handsome young man I had ever seen, who'd pushed his way to the front of the audience."

I craned forward, enchanted. "Who was he? What did he look like?"

Celeste's expression was gentle. "It turned out he was Reece Stafford-Wells, their son. He was twenty-four and had these stunning smoky-grey eyes almost like a mirror and a mass of floppy, light brown hair."

Celeste dropped her voice, even though we were the only two in the summer room. "He stood head and shoulders above all the other gentlemen there."

I digested this, desperate to hear more. "He sounds gorgeous. Did you speak to him? What happened?"

It was then that her soft, lined expression twisted into one of pain. "Oh, we spoke. We flirted, in between me singing my set for his father. It turned out to be the most magical evening of my life, wandering together in the grounds, talking and laughing together under the stars until…"

A thud of apprehension landed in my chest on Celeste's behalf. "Until?"

"Until Flora Simmonds spotted us together."

My jaw dropped to the floor. "Flora? What was she doing at the party?"

Celeste was back to fiddling with the edge of her knitted blanket. "She was there because she was after Reece. Her parents were real social climbers. Her father was the local bank manager and he took it upon himself to deal personally with the financial arrangements of the Stafford-Wells family."

A sliver of trepidation stabbed at me. "So, what happened? What did Flora do?"

Celeste fell silent.

Part of me couldn't help but compare the agony on her face with the pain I'd experienced on hearing the woman's voice in Tobias's flat that evening. I recognised that expression. "Celeste?"

She pushed some hair away from her face. "She used my past to ensure Reece wouldn't want to have anything to do with me."

I stared across at her. "What past? Celeste?"

She reached out a hand and placed it upon mine. She set her shoulders under her cardigan. "Two years before, when I was seventeen..." She drew up and readied herself. "When I was seventeen, I... I fell pregnant."

Chapter Twenty-Nine

C eleste tried to suppress her haunted look. "Flora took great delight in telling Reece, and after that the relationship was over before it even had a chance to begin." She struggled to inject some lightness into her voice. "They were different days then. Why would someone like him, from a monied, entitled family, want to fraternise with me after that revelation?"

My thoughts rocketed to Naomi and the similar situation she'd found herself in, when she fell pregnant with Tobias. "Oh God, Celeste!" My empathy twisted to burning anger. "Bloody Flora Simmonds! Who the hell did she think she was, taking it upon herself to tell Reece something like that? What a cow!" I shook my head in disgust. "And he needed to grow a pair and stand up for what he wanted. Talk about weak." I pulled myself up after my rant. "Sorry, Celeste."

She waved her hand in the air. "There's no need to apologise. You're right. He didn't have the balls to stand up to his parents."

At Celeste's mention of balls, one of the carers gave her a mock look of shock as she strode in to collect a couple of magazines from the coffee table and out again.

A memory about Flora's weird reaction to the mention of the Stafford-Wellses the day I discovered Book Ends was up for sale jumped up and down in my mind. "Oh God. That makes perfect sense!"

Celeste frowned at me. "What does?"

"One of Flora's associates was talking about Dame Alicia Kilroy, one of my former authors I edited for at Literati. It was the day Book Ends' closing down sign had been erected." I eyed Celeste with growing excitement. "This friend of Flora's commented about how much Dame Alicia's house looked like the old Stafford-Wells property. She'd seen an interview with Dame Alicia in a magazine and her house had featured in it."

"And?" pushed Celeste.

"At the mention of the Stafford-Wellses, Flora's mood changed in a flash. She became irritated and almost bit her friend's head off."

Celeste arched a brow. "I bet she did. Probably thinking about how she could have become Lady of the Manor."

I patted Celeste's warm hand. We were alone again. I gave her a supportive smile. "Celeste, you don't have to talk about it if you don't want to, but the baby – what happened?"

Celeste gathered herself. "I had her adopted. The father was a young musician in one of the bands I'd been appearing with at a few of the clubs." Celeste's eyes sparkled with regretful tears. "I wanted to keep her, but my parents wouldn't hear of it. When I told the baby's father I was expecting, I didn't see him for dust."

I grasped her trembling hand tighter, as the branches of the trees outside danced in the light. "Do you know what happened to your baby?"

She nodded her head and gulped. "Yes. I tracked her down about ten years ago now, but I never told anyone."

I stroked her fingers. "What's she like?"

Celeste's face took on a preoccupied look. "She reminded me a lot of Maeve. She was blonde like her, but a bit taller. Sporty-looking, so definitely not like me!" She attempted a smile. "From what I could see, she inherited her dad's love of the guitar, though."

Celeste gathered herself. "I discovered she was a musician in a folk band in Glasgow, so I found out when she and her band would be performing and I went to the venue."

I blinked at Celeste. "Did you speak to her?"

Celeste bit her bottom lip. "No. I wanted to. I remember standing outside that bar, surrounded by the city noise and the lights. I had all these things racing about in my head that I was desperate to say to her, but when the time came I couldn't do it." Celeste coloured. "I ended up jumping straight back in a taxi and coming home again."

Outside the residential home the hedges rustled in the sunshine.

"Well, it's a big step, isn't it?"

Celeste gave her head a resigned nod.

I stroked her veined hand. "What's your daughter's name?"

"Corinne. Corinne Young. That's her married name. She was Corinne Harvey. That was the surname of the couple who adopted her."

My eyes widened. "You've done your homework on her."

"Well, like I said, I can't take the credit. A very expensive but talented private investigator did that for me," admitted Celeste. "He was recommended to me by an old showbiz friend of mine who was having issues with her husband's infidelity. He tracked down Corinne for me." She linked her fingers together in her lap. "He reported back that she was a professional musician, married with two teenage daughters. Well, the girls will be older now, of course." She flushed pink. "I'm a grandmother. Imagine that."

I digested everything Celeste was telling me. "Does Maeve know she has a sister?"

Celeste flashed me an embarrassed look and shook her head. "I have been so, so foolish, Lexie. I should have told her years ago when she was a child, but my late husband wouldn't hear of it. He said it was in the past and it should stay there."

My thoughts returned to Tobias. In many ways, it was a similar situation. A family secret that had festered and bubbled away in the background for years, only to explode like a volcanic eruption.

Celeste's troubled mouth twisted up at one corner. "My husband thought he was doing me a favour by marrying me. The fallen singer. Damaged goods."

"Well, that's just ridiculous."

Celeste's shoulders disappeared into her dress. "After falling pregnant and then the Reece situation, I was glad to get away from here; try to put everything behind me and start over." Celeste shrugged. "I think my parents were embarrassed by it all and when they insisted we move to Edinburgh, I was only too glad." Her lips morphed into a sorry smile. "That was where I met Huntley, my late husband, a few years later."

"So, why did you come back?"

Celeste's lips gave a fleeting smile. "It was Maeve. Her and her late husband Ronnie holidayed here a few times, because of the family connection to the place, and then when he retired early from the police he said he wanted to move here and Maeve was delighted."

Celeste arranged her blanket. "Huntley's health was beginning to suffer and she didn't want to leave us in Edinburgh and so we all came back to the area a couple of years ago."

"Were you apprehensive about it? About coming back to Bracken Way after that?" I pursed my lips. "Flora could've told Maeve about Corinne. If she was capable of doing that with Reece, she would be more than capable of telling Maeve about the baby."

Celeste raised her face. There was an element of satisfaction to her features. "Not long after we arrived back in Bracken Way, we were told some rather juicy gossip about Flora's husband." Celeste paused. "So, a rather imposing friend of mine from the showbiz world made sure he bumped into Flora accidentally on purpose one day and advised her that if she so much as dared to utter a word to Maeve about her adopted sister, Bracken Way would know about her husband's affair." Celeste gave me a knowing look. "Flora thought she'd managed to keep that under wraps for years."

My eyes grew to the size of plates "Affair? Arthur Simmonds? Are you joking?"

"No. I know. Quite a shock, isn't it? Church elder, pillar of the community."

My lips made a long, low whistling sound as I recalled Flora's stout, pompous late husband. "He just didn't seem the type."

"They're often the worst."

I let this piece of latest stunning information sink in. "And do you know who she was?"

"She?"

"Arthur Simmonds's mistress."

Celeste gave me a knowing glance. "Not she. He."

I couldn't keep the shock from crossing my face.

Celeste nodded. "Do you remember Timothy Archibald, who used to own the local post office?"

I recalled the tall, thin, dapper man with a serious side sweep of jet-black hair. He had been a confirmed bachelor; a gentle giant. My mouth formed a series of surprised shapes. "Are you saying Timothy Archibald was Arthur's lover?"

Celeste nodded.

"Bloody hell! I'd no idea all this was happening in Bracken Way." I sat there, letting these revelations tumble through my head. "And what happened between Flora and Reece? I take it nothing did, if she married Arthur?"

"His parents married him off to a rich horsey type from Dumfries and Reece and his new bride moved to the south of France. Her parents owned a successful vineyard there." Celeste shook her head at the memories she was pulling up after so many years. "So, Flora's jealous conniving was all for nothing."

Good grief! I was struggling to unscramble the array of tangled, secretive and messy deceptions. I thought again about

Flora sneering at Celeste and the way she'd curled up her mouth as she'd called her the silver songbird. "So, the silver songbird nickname she gave you was because of your surname and your silver dress, I'm guessing?"

"That's right. What with my maiden name being Finch, and the silver dress I wore that night of the birthday party, I think she thought she was being rather clever." Celeste pulled a dismissive face. "Flora was crazy about Reece. The story I was told after we returned here, was that she married Arthur on the rebound, as she never got over losing Reece and all that went with him: the house, the name, the prestige."

Celeste dropped her voice an octave. Further out in the corridor, a loud TV set burbled out from an open door. The booming volume of it made me think of my grandfather. "Some say that's why Flora is how she is. It's why she's so bitter at life and what it dealt her. But the way I see it, you choose to make these mistakes. Nobody forces you."

"Yes, but a lot of people have tough and difficult lives and they don't go around bullying and picking on people!"

"That's very true, Lexie." Celeste let out a weary sigh, followed by a yawn. "Please excuse me but I think I'm in need of a nap. I have another portrait session with your gorgeous work colleague tomorrow and I need my beauty sleep."

"Of course. You go and get some rest. And thank you for confiding in me."

Celeste fluttered her blanket. "Thank you for listening. Now, would you mind very much escorting me back to my room please?"

"Of course not."

I rose out of the chair, grasped both wheelchair handles and negotiated Celeste back down the snaking, carpeted hallway. I thought again about how frail and tired she looked all of a sudden. I had to select my words with care. "Celeste, are you going to tell Maeve about Corinne?"

Celeste sat like a small bird. "Part of me doesn't want to, but I think I should. I don't want to die and leave a mess." She clasped her fingers together as I wheeled her along. Her voice was thoughtful, but edged with trepidation. "And if I'm going to try and speak to my adopted daughter before I pop my clogs, it's only right Maeve knows."

"Oh, please stop talking like that," I pleaded. I couldn't bear the thought of this wonderful woman, with the husky laugh and the cheeky spark in her eyes, not being here anymore.

I eased her wheelchair up to her door and angled it open, so I could push her inside. "So, you're going to make contact with Corinne?"

Celeste stared out of her room window, fringed with delicate checked curtains. "Yes. I have to, Lexie. I feel like I've no other option. I can't die knowing that she's out there and doesn't know that I still think about her every day and that if I could change everything, I would."

Her profile in her room was shadowy under the summer sun. "There hasn't been a day that I haven't thought about her."

I crouched down beside her. "I understand. It must have been tortuous, having to give up your little girl like that." I surveyed her downturned mouth and the worry lines feeding out from it. "So, have you thought about how you're going to make contact with her?"

Celeste nodded with renewed determination. "A letter. I'm going to write to her and ask if she'll come and see me. She lives on the outskirts of Glasgow."

I didn't want to put a downer on Celeste's plans, but I didn't want her to get too optimistic either. "What happens if she refuses? Or if she ignores your letter?"

Celeste sat very still. "That's Corinne's prerogative. In a way, I wouldn't blame her. But I have to at least try." An awkward little blush flashed across her face. "Lexie, would you help me write the letter? I now have an accomplished editor as a friend, so it makes perfect sense to ask you if you would be so kind as to assist me?"

I stood up and smiled down at her. "I'd be honoured to help you write it."

She attempted to conceal her apprehension. "Excellent. Thank you. That will be another weight off my mind." She angled her head to one side as she gazed back up at me. "So, onto jollier matters. Now, what's the story with you and that rather dashing painter?"

My cheeks lit up in furious crimson. "There is no story."

"If I were you, I'd soon remedy that," quipped Celeste, whipping off her blanket and tossing it onto her made-up bed with the sparkly cushions. "He's such a looker. Life is too short, my lovely."

She glanced around herself, even though she knew there was just the two of us in her room. "Now, before you go, please open that bedside cabinet for me, will you? I've got a secret stash of brandy in there. You're not driving, are you? Good. One for the road then!"

Chapter Thirty

I arrived at Book Ends the next morning, with my head still stuffed like a pincushion with everything that Celeste had told me last night.

Once I'd placated Celeste by having a glass of brandy with her, I'd made her promise that Flora Simmonds would not be the reason she didn't make the most of what precious time she still had.

Celeste had then celebrated by knocking back another brandy, drawing disapproving tuts from me.

I had beamed at her, clasping her hand in mine while juggling my brandy. "So, the silver songbird will be back?"

Celeste had pulled a comical face. "I'm more like the Brown Buzzard nowadays."

Tobias made his entrance at ten o'clock. I wasn't prepared to tell him anything that Celeste had told me. She had made me promise to keep everything under wraps for now and I wasn't going to break her trust.

I knew it had taken so much for her to confide in me as it was.

And anyway, it wasn't like Tobias and me were close. At one time, I had started to think things might have been moving in a different direction, but not now – not after Wine Woman, or his remarks about me being "a good friend" and him keeping his distance. That spoke volumes.

After a couple of phone calls, he gathered his mobile and his jacket, so he could head up to the residential home to see Celeste.

"How are things? With your mum and Trevor?" I asked him.

Tobias pushed a frazzled hand through his hair. He glanced around at his illuminated portraits. "Let's just say that it's a bit of a stand-off." He rubbed at his chin. "I feel like a fraud, Lexie. It's like I don't know who I am anymore and that I've been living somebody else's life."

My heart softened at the sight of him in front of me, so troubled. Shit! Even if he was involved with someone else, it didn't mean I could switch my feelings off, like a light. I wished I could. "You're still the same person, Tobias. You just need some time to come to terms with everything. Anyone would've been left reeling if they'd been told the same thing you were."

He managed to locate a faint smile. "Thank you." He fell quiet for a moment, before shooting me a look from under his sooty lashes. "Do you know how wonderful you are?"

I stiffened. *Oh, don't do this to me. Please. Don't be nice. I don't think I can take it.*

I angled myself away from him, so he couldn't see the glistening tears in my eyes. I think I preferred it when he'd been a rude prat. I forced my voice into something which I hoped sounded playful. "I bet you say that to all the bookshop managers."

Tobias lingered, but the sudden arrival of two teenage boys made him draw up. "Right." He looked hesitant. "Ok. Better go. See you later."

He vanished and I switched back to professional mode for the customers.

I relaxed that Friday night on my bed, a glass of white wine at my elbow and Celeste's manuscript propped up on my lap.

Mum, Dad and Grandpa had retired for the night.

As I prepared to read more of Celeste's book, I mulled over how my life was beginning to take more of a cohesive shape. The estate agents had rung to say the sale of my Glasgow flat was now almost complete and I was just waiting to get the official go-ahead, so I could move into my new place in Bracken Way.

I took a slow sip of the zesty wine. Moving back here hadn't been a backward step after all. It had been a learning curve, but a valuable one. Leaving Literati and taking a risk had been worth the worry. It had shown me that I was more capable than I thought.

I did miss some of my lovely authors, but my love of books and reading would always stay with me and Celeste's story was compelling. It could do with sharpening up in places, but it had a lot going for it. The story resonated even more with me now that I knew she'd drawn on her own painful experiences and her singing career, in order to write it.

I had just reached the end of chapter ten, where the protagonist, Melissa, was about to reveal some dark secret to her mother, when my mobile rang.

I reached over to the bedside table, careful not to send the loose, typed pages of the manuscript skittering everywhere across my bedroom carpet.

Rhiannon's name appeared on my phone screen. Would this be another valiant attempt from her to try and persuade me to start back at Literati again? Or was she just giving me a call to say hi and ask how I was?

It turned out it was a combination of both.

I told her about my parents getting back together. She let out a stunned gasp. "Jesus. What a woman your mother is."

"I know. I just hope Dad realises it too." Then I asked her about her ex-husband, Guy.

There followed a series of dismissive sniffs. "He never changes. Still a flash sod and making his new editor Theo wait for his latest self-improvement tome."

I took a mouthful of my wine. "And what's his latest book about?"

"Developing your creativity, in order to harness inner calm."

"Oh, some nice light reading then. Is it any good?"

"I've only read the first fifty pages, but nah. It's still the same flowery bollocks he always writes, but it's part of a three-book deal, the public love him and Literati thinks the sun shines out of his arse, so..." She grunted with disapproval down the line. "Anyway, enough talk about my dick of an ex. How is Book Ends doing?"

"It can be challenging, but business is brisk and yes, I love it."

There followed a somewhat strained pause.

"Alright Rhiannon, why are you really calling me at this time on a Friday evening?"

She feigned innocence. "I don't know what you mean."

"Oh, come on Rhi. Out with it."

"Alright. You rumbled me, although I was genuinely keen to check that you were ok." I could hear the cogs turning in her mind from here. "What's happening, Lexie?"

"With what?" I knew what she was referring to, but decided to delay the inevitable.

"With climate change," she groaned. "What the hell do you think I'm talking about? You and your career as an editor."

I took another mouthful of my wine and prepared to answer her, but she jumped in first. "Look, I'm going to be honest here. I'm surprised you've stuck with this bookshop manager job this long. I thought you might get bored."

"Nope. No boredom here," I trilled. "Quite the opposite." Pictures of Tobias, Celeste, my dad and Book Ends ran through my mind.

Rhiannon sounded more conciliatory. "Lex, I know you've had your hands full, but I remember in the dim and distant past what you said to me when you first joined Literati."

I shuffled on top of my bed. "What was that?"

"That a good editor is like a jeweller. They polish, craft and hone the work of a writer until it gleams."

I chewed my lip and glanced down at Celeste's manuscript still balanced on my lap. It was true. I had said that to her.

My head slumped back against my pillows. I listened to her exasperated sigh down the line, as I then confessed that I'd bought a flat in Bracken Way. I thought this was as good a time as any to tell her.

"I guess I'm not surprised," she conceded. "Look, what I'm trying to say is, I'm proud of you. Sodding annoyed I can't lure you back to Literati, but I'm still proud of you for taking a chance and sticking with it."

I stared back down at Celeste's typed manuscript, the words bleeding into one another.

My hand grazed the pages. Celeste had created this story out of nothing. She had carved pictures and sprinkled life and colour onto blank, white sheets of paper.

"Lexie? Are you there?"

I yanked my attention back to Rhiannon. "Yes, I'm still here. Sorry."

I straightened up, still stroking the manuscript.

Rhiannon sighed. "Ok, Dunbar. You win."

We rounded off the call, promising to speak to each other again in a week or so and then I took a huge gulp to finish the last of my wine. It hit the back of my throat.

The next morning saw a summer flurry of book purchases, predominantly bulky beach reads, thrilling crimes and spirited romcoms. Holiday season was on the horizon and there was a buzz of hyperactivity everywhere. I was grateful that I had both Chloe and Daryl in the shop to help out.

Tobias was secreted in the office, tackling admin and being interviewed over the phone by a prestigious art critic for a newspaper article.

I was about to place an order for another supply of the latest cosy crime sensation, when the shop door rattled open, bringing with it Mum, Dad and Grandpa.

It still seemed so surreal, seeing the three of them together, as though the past two decades had been a figment of everyone's imagination.

Mum was adorned in a floaty hemmed lemon dress; Grandpa was wearing an expression of bemusement and my dad was clasping Mum's hand. His hair was a little shorter. Mum must have persuaded him to get a haircut. It suited him.

"Just passing, so thought we'd drop by," smiled Mum, striding towards me and delivering an affectionate kiss to my cheek.

Dad stared around. "Looking good, Lexie." He moved around the bookshop, his tanned hands browsing the spines. "How long can I borrow the books for?"

His words made me prickle with alarm. Grandpa's bristly brows gathered.

"This isn't a library, Niall," said Mum smoothly. "It's a bookshop, remember? Book Ends? Lexie works here."

Dad studied our faces. "A bookshop?"

My breathing lodged with concern in my throat. I forced my mouth into an encouraging smile. "That's right. I'm the manager, remember, Dad?"

Confusion swam in my dad's eyes. Then it passed over, like a brooding cloud allowing the sun through. "Book Ends. My clever daughter."

Mum refused to allow her serene, contented expression to slip. "We can splash out on a takeaway tonight after you finish work, sweetheart."

"Sounds good."

Grandpa waited until I'd kissed my parents and they were back out on the sun-drizzled bookshop step, admiring the glistening ripples across the loch. He hung back for a few moments. "Your mother is being amazing. She refuses to accept defeat."

"And Dad?"

Grandpa stroked his moustache as he thought about my question. "I think he's so grateful to your mum. He's trying to stay positive for her, but…"

"But?"

He gestured over the shoulder of his light summer jacket. "Niall Dunbar is still in there, but I've noticed over the last few days that there have been more frequent bouts of him becoming confused." His posture sunk. "Your mother would never admit it, of course, but she must've noticed it too."

My grandfather puffed out his cheeks in frustration. "Yesterday, he thought I was one of his old newspaper bosses."

I wrapped my arms around myself. "Do you think Mum is in denial?"

"Aye, partly that I think but more desperation. She thinks if she stays positive enough, she might be able to turn the situation around for him." My grandfather stuffed his hands into his trouser pockets. "Social services are due round to carry out an assessment on the house."

Grandpa leant over the counter and kissed me on the cheek. "She just keeps repeating what the GP has told her; that your dad will have days where he's more settled and others when he'll be more confused. But I tell you, lass, she'll go down fighting it with Niall, that's for sure." He winked at me. "You and your mother have so much in common."

"Well, Grandpa, I think you've been wonderful about everything. I know how you feel about Dad and I don't blame you."

"Aye. Well. None of us know what's around the corner, do we?"

He left to join Mum and Dad, the Saturday morning sunshine glancing off his hair.

I was congratulating myself about how lucky I was to have such an amazing family, when a figure came thundering into the bookshop.

It was as she drew closer, I realised it was Maeve. "Oh, hi there. How are you?"

Celeste's daughter struggled to contain herself. "Alright thank you, or at least I was until my mother told me this morning that I have a half-sister." Indignation and shock radiated out of her. "But I don't need to tell you that, do I? You already know everything!"

"Sorry?"

Maeve scowled at me. "You had such a cosy chat with my mother. Care to enlighten me?"

"Celeste didn't choose to confide in me first," I insisted to her furious face. "It was because of Flora having a go at your mother about her being the silver songbird."

I stopped and bit my tongue. Shit! Had Celeste still not told Maeve about that as well? Don't tell me I'd just put my size six feet in it?

Maeve eyed me with disbelief. "Oh, don't worry. She just told me all about her singing too. Well, sixty years late, but still…" She let out a sarcastic laugh. "Is there anything she *hasn't* told you?"

"Please don't be like that, Maeve. Your mum was so upset about Flora and I asked her about it. I wasn't sure if she'd tell me anything."

"Well, aren't you lucky?" she smarted "I'm her daughter. I should've been the one she confided in, not the local bookshop manager!"

Then she performed a theatrical slap to her forehead. "Or should I say I'm one of her daughters. How stupid of me." Maeve's damp eyes glittered. "So, seeing as you're such an expert on my family, what would you advise we do now?"

"Pardon?"

Her tone was icy. "About Corinne. My sister who I knew nothing about. Do I open up my ailing mother to possible heartache or do I tell her to go to her grave, not having tried to make contact with her again?"

I prickled with embarrassment. "Maeve, I …"

Maeve's dark eyes filled with frustrated tears. "I thought we were friends, Lexie. You should've told me."

I remained standing there, staring after her as she dashed out of the shop.

"She didn't mean it. She's hurting over her mother."

I jumped at the sound of Tobias's rich, deep voice behind me.

He was leaning against the office doorway.

"How long have you been standing there?"

"Long enough to get the gist of what's been going on."

Tobias creaked the office door closed behind him and strode towards me. "Please try not to get upset. You haven't done anything wrong. You tried to help."

I averted my gaze from his alluring emerald one. "Yes. Well, it doesn't feel like that way. Right now, I feel as though I've made one enormous mess of everything."

Tobias disagreed. "You've done everything with the best of intentions and underneath it, Maeve knows that." He gazed down at me. "She knows Celeste doesn't have long and she's lashing out."

I rubbed an imaginary groove along the edge of the polished counter with one finger. "I feel so conflicted now."

"About what?"

"About everything. Celeste has asked me to help her write a letter to her adopted daughter. She's hoping they can meet before she... before somethings happens to her."

Tobias shot out both hands and placed them on top of my shoulders. I could feel the imprint of his fingertips. The breath felt trapped in my chest.

"If you want my advice, I'd let the dust settle with Maeve. She'll come round."

I struggled to speak as his hands continued to rest on both my shoulders. "You didn't see the look on her face."

The warmth of his skin seared into mine. But echoes of the woman's voice in his flat, talking about wine, bounced around my head again, the intimate way she called him "Tobes".

I took a deliberate step backwards. Tobias removed his hands and they fell by his sides. He offered me an odd look. "So has Celeste seen her adopted daughter?"

I refocused. "From a distance ten years ago. She's a

musician. Celeste had desperately wanted to talk to her, but she changed her mind at the last minute." I sighed. "Corinne – that's her name – lives on the outskirts of Glasgow and is married with two grown-up daughters."

"So Celeste is a grandmother?"

"Yep."

Tobias paused. "If Celeste is serious about wanting to reach out to Corinne, I don't think she should delay things. Time isn't on our side, unfortunately."

Did I hear him correctly? "Our"?

"You don't have to do any of this on your own, Lexie."

I dropped my attention to the bookshop floor.

"What with taking on this place, the shock of your dad's illness and then your parents reuniting… well, it hasn't been an easy time for you. I suppose what I'm trying to say in my clumsy way is that you shouldn't feel that you're alone."

I straightened my back and took a couple more steps backwards. His kind words were chipping away at my resolve, "Thank you, Tobias. I appreciate that. You're a good friend."

He stared down at me from under his arched black brows. "Of course. Yes. Right. Friends. That's what we are."

I turned back to the counter, so he couldn't see the pain swallowing me up.

The shop telephone rang, disturbing the awkward silence. I moved to answer it, relieved that I had something to do.

I couldn't see Tobias behind me, lost in his own thoughts too.

Chapter Thirty-One

"I'm off to take an early lunch," announced Tobias as he strode down the three steps from the gallery and into Book Ends territory. "I won't be long."

I wondered if he was going to meet Wine Woman. "Ok."

He didn't elaborate about where he was going, just draped his suit jacket over one arm and disappeared.

Pictures of the two of them gazing across the table at one another in some intimate restaurant made my stomach clench. I imagined her to be a coltish blonde, toned, with sun-kissed shoulders and dimples.

Stop, Lexie. Enough.

I glanced down at my watch. It was coming up for noon. I needed to keep busy, otherwise Wine Woman and Tobias would be tearing at each other's clothes over the starter, if my imagination had anything to do with it.

I'd promised Celeste I'd visit after closing the bookshop, so we could begin drafting a letter to Corinne.

I was very reluctant to start pulling together the letter when

Maeve was so upset and opposed to the whole situation, but I'd promised I would help Celeste.

A steady flow of customers ebbed in and out over the next hour, which kept me occupied and I decided to update the bookshop social media accounts with the latest competition I'd dreamt up for the kids – design your own bookmark and the winning entry would receive a twenty-pound book token to spend in Book Ends.

I didn't like to think about it, with the air laced with the smell of sun cream and everyone strolling past with dripping ice cream cones, but I was already beginning to give thought to suitable autumn and winter reads and the russet and amber colour schemes to adopt for my next window display.

I was flicking through the latest catalogues, noting down the up-and-coming new releases I wanted to order, when Tobias reappeared in the shop doorway.

I set down my pen and tried to feign casual interest. "Hi there. Nice lunch?"

Tobias thrust his hands into his trouser pockets. "I didn't go for an early lunch."

"Oh?"

"No. I went to talk to someone."

I was about to ask him why he was being so mysterious, when Maeve appeared from behind him. Awkwardness shone out of her.

I stared at Tobias and then at her. My brain was scrambling to put together the pieces. So, Tobias hadn't gone to lunch with any blondes – at least not today. He'd gone to speak to Maeve and smooth things over?

As if reading the confused thoughts whirling around inside

my head, Maeve moved towards me, one hand fiddling with one of her pearl earrings. "Tobias dropped by my house for a chat. He told me how upset you were over everything."

I gawped at Tobias. His mouth melted into a small smile.

Chloe took in the situation, gave my arm a squeeze and vanished into the office for a few minutes, to give us some privacy. Suki, meanwhile, grabbed her coat and bag and announced she was going out to get a sandwich.

Maeve approached the counter. "I'm so sorry, Lexie. I should never have spoken to you like that." She scooped a hunk of her hair back behind one ear. "You – well, both of you – have been so wonderful with Mum. Nothing has been too much trouble and I know she appreciates it so much. We both do."

She turned and offered an appreciative smile over her shoulder at Tobias. "All this with Corinne came as such a shock, especially when Mum admitted that my dad knew about her. Then when Mum told me she'd confided in you about it too, I reacted the way I did."

Her voice tailed off to an embarrassed whisper. She cleared her throat and gathered herself again. "Tobias told me about your parents getting back together and how selfless your mum has been about everything. He also said he's been dealing with some personal problems as well at the moment. Seems like everybody is dealing with something."

Maeve glanced down at the shop floor, before forcing her attention back up to me. "You're both contending with your own issues and yet, you're just getting on with things and finding the capacity to forgive and move on."

Tobias let out a mixture of a laugh and a cough. "I don't

know about that, Maeve. You're making me sound like a saint, which I most definitely am not!" He stared past Maeve at me, giving me a quick, devilish wink that made my stomach swoop.

"And neither am I," I half-laughed, recovering myself. "When my dad turned up in Bracken Way I was thinking and saying some very unladylike things!"

Maeve shook her blow-dried, highlighted blonde hair. "That's natural." She pushed out her chest and reset her thoughts. "Lexie, I understand if you don't want to after the way I've behaved towards you, but I'd appreciate it if you could still help Mum and me with composing the letter to Corinne."

My face broke into a relieved smile. "I'd be honoured to help in any way I can. I mean, it is a family matter so I don't want you to think I'm intruding."

Maeve looked appalled. "You're not. We both want you to assist." She blushed. "I'm not very good at this sort of thing and, of course, Mum is so close to the situation."

I nodded. "Celeste means a lot to me. She's a remarkable woman." I raised my eyes to Tobias. "Celeste means a lot to both of us."

Once Maeve and I agreed to meet up at the residential home at half past six so we could work with Celeste on producing the letter together, she departed, lighter and far more relaxed than when she had arrived.

I was too.

I opened and closed my hands, realising that I was alone with Tobias in the shop.

He pushed himself away from the front door and walked towards me. His eyes never left my face.

I could feel my breathing quicken. "I don't know what to say to you."

"About what?"

"Oh, stop being bashful. It doesn't suit you."

My legs dissolved as he broke into a dazzling grin that lit up his whole face.

"Tobias, that was such a thoughtful and kind thing to do."

He looked at me, his eyes glittering. "Underneath this devilishly handsome exterior beats the heart of an angel."

I laughed at his attempt to maintain a straight face. "Now you're just being ridiculous!"

We both remained rooted to the spot, drinking in one another and reluctant to leave. My thoughts were cartwheeling everywhere. What was going on between us? Tobias had made his feelings clear. He thought of me as a friend and yet, just when I thought this man couldn't surprise me anymore... I realised I wasn't speaking and was studying the planes and contours of his face. I recovered myself. "Thank you again, Tobias. Really. That was lovely what you did, smoothing things over with Maeve like that."

He gazed back down at me, his attention travelling from my loose hair, down to my mouth. My heart was jumping out of my chest. Could he hear the noise it was making against my ribs?

The sound of it thundered in my ears.

I was oblivious to what was happening outside Book Ends – the odd, freewheeling gull, the occasional honk of a car horn and the melting sun stroking the pavement.

An odd look flitted across his face, breaking the spell. Tobias took a step backwards and pulled his attention away from me. "It's no big deal," he insisted. "Anyone would have done the same."

"No, they wouldn't."

He shrugged his broad shoulders under his lemon sorbet-coloured shirt. His sleeves were rolled up. "Well, it's like you said before. That's what friends are for."

He delivered a brief smile and gestured to his art gallery. "Have you had lunch yet? I'll pop out and get us a sandwich from Mrs Hegarty's."

The moment was over, like it had never begun. "Er, no," I faltered, forcing a smile. "That'd be great. Thanks."

I dived under the counter to fetch my bag. "Here's some money. Get yourself your lunch from this as a small thank you."

I straightened up but he'd already gone.

Chapter Thirty-Two

"What do you say to the daughter you gave up as a baby? I've written easier letters in my time."

Celeste attempted to force some dark humour into the emotional proceedings.

The three of us were arranged in a semi-circle in her accommodation at the residential home, as early evening spread across the sky.

Celeste was sat in her wheelchair, decked out in layers of silk finery, while Maeve was to her left and me to her right.

Every so often, my attention would drift across towards her wardrobe. It was like a sumptuous dressing-up box and I was itching to take a closer look at what other gems were concealed within it.

Celeste's window was open and her apricot and gold checked curtains danced in the gentle evening breeze.

In front of us, she had insisted her finest tea set, a Royal Doulton Old Country Roses, was to be used. Accompanying it, was a plate of clotted cream shortbread.

"I'll spoil my dinner." I half-sighed at the sugar-coated wedges.

"Oh tosh," insisted Celeste. "A little bit of what you fancy does you good."

"You're a terrible influence."

She glittered at me with her dancing eyes. "So I've been told over the years. Go on, Maeve. Lexie. Get stuck in!"

I reached across for one of the shortbread fingers and held it up, ready to take a bite. "Are you both sure you want me here? I feel like I'm intruding."

"More tosh!" said Celeste with a withering expression.

"Absolutely," joined in Maeve. "You've been such a support to both of us these past weeks."

"That's very kind of you to say so."

Maeve leant forward and poured a stream of hot tea into the three dainty white cups, decorated with burgundy and lemon roses. The fine bone China let out a tiny rattle. "Here you go, Lexie. Now, let's get on with this letter, shall we?"

I bit into the shortbread and took a sip of my tea. "So how do you want to mention your health? Do you want to talk about that further into the letter?"

I thought Celeste was going to drop her cup and saucer. "There isn't going to be any mention of me dropping dead soon."

Maeve looked appalled. "Mum! Don't talk like that!"

Celeste hoisted her defiant shoulders upwards. "It's true. I don't want Corinne feeling sorry for me. I want her to agree to see me for the right reasons and not the wrong ones." She took a mouthful of her tea. "I want her to hear me out because she wants to, not out of pity."

"But Mum…"

Celeste flapped her lime-green silk dress hem. "No, Maeve. My mind is made up. There shall be no mention of my declining health."

She thrust her cup and saucer at her daughter. Maeve took it from her and placed it down on the table, shooting her mother disapproving looks which Celeste ignored. "Now, are we just going to sit here and gawp at one another?"

She clasped her fingers together in her lap, trying to disguise her nerves. "Maeve darling, could you fetch my Smythson writing paper and my pen from that desk drawer beside my bed please?"

Maeve did as she was asked. The three of us gazed down at the couple of blank sheets of expensive cream writing paper.

I tutted. "I should've brought my laptop, so we could've drafted the letter on that. I've left it at home."

"That isn't an issue," insisted Celeste. "We can use the scrap paper there to pull together the draft and then transfer the final version onto my best stationery."

Celeste, of course, took the lead, insisting on beginning to write the letter. Every so often, her bright, astute eyes would rest on Maeve and me, seeking feedback on what she was writing or just to consolidate it in her mind.

After a while, Maeve noticed her mother's fingers starting to tremble with the exertion. "Here, Mum. Please give me the pen."

Celeste reluctantly handed it to her daughter.

After an hour of more tweaking and polishing off the last of the shortbread, the completed letter sat in front of the three of us, composed of Maeve's small, considered handwriting.

My eyes trailed over what we'd produced. The scrap paper still bore our random scribbles and scorings out, but the final version on the thick cream writing paper was honest and heartfelt, not seeking pity but explaining in a raw and emotional way, what Celeste had gone through.

It read:

Dear Corinne,

I knew that this letter to you would not be an easy one to write, but I underestimated how difficult it would actually be.

I am sorry.

I realise this must have come as a very big shock, but I hope in some way, it may be a welcome one.

My name is Celeste Finch and in 1961, I fell pregnant with you. It was one of the scariest and most challenging times of my life. I was a struggling seventeen-year-old singer, with the odd club and pub booking if I were lucky.

Your father was a charismatic, handsome musician a few years older than me.

Stupidly, I thought we could make a go of things together. But it was not meant to be, so I found myself facing the prospect of becoming a single mother.

Despite the problems I was faced with, I knew I wanted to keep the little life that was growing and kicking inside of me. I was determined to make our lives together work.

Unfortunately, my church-going parents had other ideas.

As soon as I told them I was expecting, they ordered me to surrender you for adoption.

I pleaded with them; begged them to understand but they insisted that the "most Christian thing to do" was to have you adopted by a family who could give you everything you needed. According to them, I could offer my baby nothing.

I will never forget the smell of disinfectant in the hospital wards and the starched, scratchy bedcovers.

The sister in charge of the ward – there were three other young girls just like me – would parade up and down in her rubber shoes, proclaiming that "God would forgive us, if we repented."

I can remember that September morning you were born. It was crisp and bright, with autumnal leaves hanging from the branches outside the hospital window.

You were this gorgeous wriggling pink angel, with downy tufts of white hair and all I wanted to do was wrap you up in the shawl I had knitted for you and spirit us both away somewhere, where nobody could find us.

But everybody else insisted they knew what was best for both of us and so they took you away from me as soon as you were born. I was allowed the briefest hug with you and then you were gone.

My screams rang out around that hospital. I could hear this animalistic noise and wondered for a few seconds where it was coming from. It didn't take me long to realise it was actually me making that sound.

I never saw you again, until ten years ago, when I had a private investigator find you. I saw you go into a music venue in town, armed with your guitar, but I couldn't summon up the courage to speak to you.

I regretted my cowardly actions that night too.

I swear to this day, I can still smell your milky skin as I cradled you for those few seconds, before you were wrenched out of my arms.

So now, I am trying to make amends. I would be forever grateful if you would agree to come and see me. I am a resident of Bracken Way Residential Home.

Seeing my appeal to you written down makes it even larger and more prominent, but if you could find it in your heart to agree to speak with me, I would be eternally grateful, Corinne.

I realise what I am asking of you is a considerable and emotional request, but words cannot explain what it would mean to me to be able to see you and apologise in person.

Having you taken away from me in such a cruel way was something I regret I couldn't control as a naïve and fragile seventeen-year-old girl.

Now, I hope I am in a position to try and put things right – or at least attempt to.

Thank you for giving me the courtesy of reading this letter.

Yours sincerely, Celeste Matthews (née Finch)

I reread the letter a few more times, my throat closing up with emotion at its contents.

Maeve thought Celeste's decision not to include details of her failing health a mistake, but Celeste refused to even discuss it.

The writing paper rustled through Celeste's frail fingers as she folded it and slid it into the addressed envelope.

Once sealed, Maeve dug around in her purse and produced a first-class stamp.

"Are you alright?" I asked Celeste, noting her charged stare at the envelope lying on the table in front of us.

Celeste let out a broken gulp of air. "I'll let you know when or if I hear back from Corinne."

Chapter Thirty-Three

"You look shattered, lovey. I hope you're pacing yourself," warned Mum, bundling me into her arms.

"It's been one of those days," I sighed. I held her at arm's length. "The same goes for you too, you know."

"What do you mean?"

"You look exhausted, Mum."

She tried to brush it off. "Oh, I'm alright. You know me."

"Yes, I do. That's why I'm asking."

Mum pulled a jokey face.

"So, how's Dad today?"

Her smile wavered.

"Mum? What is it?"

She gnawed her bottom lip. "Today hasn't been such a great day, Lexie. You dad was confused again."

My chest fluttered with concern. "How bad?"

She was about to explain, when my dad materialised behind her from the kitchen.

"Hi, Mum." He grinned at me. "What's for dinner?"

"Dad," I faltered. "It's me. Lexie."

His brows grew stormy. "I hope you haven't made steak and kidney pie again."

Mum's face was desperate.

Resentment stole over his features. "Stop playing games with me, Mum. It's not funny!" My father examined me, looking lost for a few moments, before his confusion cleared. "Hello, sweetheart. How was the bookshop today?"

Relief swamped me. "Er… yes… good, thanks, Dad."

He planted a kiss on my cheek. "You're doing great. I'm so very proud of you." He winked at Mum and made his way to the bathroom at the end of the hall.

I waited until the bathroom door let out its familiar click.

"These episodes," struggled Mum in a hushed voice. "They're happening more and more." She swiped a frustrated hand down her face. "I feel so helpless. I don't know what to do." She jerked her head towards the sitting room opposite, where my grandpa was dozing in his armchair, the TV blasting out the weather forecast. "I knew it would be like this, but when you know the sort of man he was and what this dementia is doing to him." My Mum fought to remain stoical. "Your grandfather keeps telling me I'm doing everything I can and yet…" Her voice broke off.

"Mum, you are. Grandpa's right. The fact that you're even caring for him after everything… well, let's not go over all that again."

I scooped up one of her hands and gave it a squeeze. "I hope you've contacted the authorities to get some extra help. We knew it wouldn't be easy. And whatever you need from me, you know you only have to ask."

She clung onto my hand. "They're carrying out an assessment of this place and your dad next week and are going to provide details of respite care for when ..." She couldn't finish the sentence. "I read about sundowning and didn't take too much notice at first."

"Sundowning?"

"It's a term the medical profession uses about changes in behaviour that occur in dementia patients come the evening, usually around dusk. They can feel they're in the wrong place or that they should be elsewhere and their confusion gets worse."

I rubbed her arm. "And what have you been advised to do if and when that happens?"

"Talk calmly to him, hold his hand, make a cup of tea." Her voice failed.

"You're the most amazing woman, Mum. I mean it. But you mustn't think this is all on you. I want you to promise you'll ask for help any time. I don't have a confirmed moving-in date yet for the flat, so maybe that's a good thing."

She appraised me out of loving eyes "Thank you, darling. Your dad is right, you know. You turned out not too bad at all."

The rest of the week saw more healthy book sales and more commissions for Tobias from affluent holidaymakers, who, by Friday, were returning to Bracken Way to escape from the city pressures in their various luxurious lodges and holiday cottages.

I had launched a Book Ends Summer Reading Challenge,

with a list of exciting new titles which should entice the children and their parents in.

I was also busy arranging the transfer of my furniture and other belongings from my old flat in Glasgow, as the sale was almost signed off, to my new flat here in Bracken Way.

It was fortunate the current owner of my new place had now emigrated to New Zealand and was keen not to have the property sitting empty. I was therefore very lucky and grateful that he'd been so understanding about Dad and had given the go-ahead for me to move in, albeit with a limited supply of furnishings.

Mum and I had managed to make it look a little more homely in the last couple of days, with some cheap rugs, flowers, scented candles, a sofa bed and pictures for the walls. At least that would keep me going until the removal company I'd recruited were able to deliver my things from Glasgow.

Tobias finished jotting down the address of one of the Scandinavian-style holiday homes perched up on the loch hillside. "Another portrait request," he said, with a delighted grin that made my stomach turn to mush. I tried to ignore it.

"What is it this time?"

"A doting husband wants me to paint his wife for their thirtieth wedding anniversary." Tobias's black lashes twitched as he studied the details he had noted. "They sound like a Scottish version of David and Victoria Beckham, but hey, it's income."

"Yep. The bills have to be paid."

Drizzles of morning light seeped in through the bevelled windows of Book Ends. I closed my eyes for a few seconds, allowing the soft tickle of warmth to caress my face. It had seemed like such a long week. Just thinking about it all again and what I'd achieved in the last few days was making me knackered!

"I'd love to paint you."

Tobias's words made my eyes spring open. "Pardon?"

I looked at him and there was a glow highlighting his features. "There's an old-fashioned romanticism about your looks."

"Old-fashioned? Gee. Thanks for that."

Tobias laughed. "It's a compliment. With your long hair and fair complexion, you remind me of one of those elegant, untouchable Victorian ladies in a sweeping off-the- shoulder gown." He flicked me a look. "I would love you to sit for me, so I could paint you."

Visions of Tobias painting me flashed before my eyes: me sat there, struggling to be still and poised, while he concentrated on his canvas, his cheekbones hard and uncompromising. No. I couldn't. I wouldn't. Where did his mysterious female companion feature in all of this?

And how about preserving our working relationship? Still, it would be lovely to be painted for posterity, trilled an inner voice. A beautiful painting of myself, captured in my youth, would be something to gaze upon and remember when I was old. I thought of Celeste being painted by Tobias and it gave me a warm glow.

Tobias is offering to paint your portrait, not father your children, tutted an inner voice. That very image made my skin tingle. "That's a very kind offer," I croaked. "I'll think about it."

His eyes danced. "Sure."

Even though I'd no idea what was taking place right now

between the two of us, I didn't want this – whatever *this* was – to stop pirouetting backwards and forwards between us, but Tobias's mobile let out a series of insistent rings.

A good thing in hindsight.

"Excuse me," he rumbled.

He had just turned away and was chatting amiably to whoever had rung him, when Maeve entered. Her usually, bubbly, expectant expression was solemn. "Hi, Lexie."

"Morning, Maeve. Are you alright?"

She folded her arms. "Not really. Mum is far worse, though she won't admit it."

"Oh no. Has Celeste taken a bad turn?"

Maeve shook her straight fringe. "No. Nothing like that." She stuck out her bottom lip. "It's Corinne."

"What about her?"

"Mum received a reply this morning." Maeve's mouth contorted into a grim line. "She's refused to come and see her. She said my mother is sixty years too late and while she appreciates Mum making the effort to contact her, she has no interest in getting to know her."

My shoulders felt as though they were shrinking to the bookshop floor. "Poor Celeste. How has she taken it?"

"Oh, you know my mother," exclaimed Maeve with forced joviality. "She folded up Corinne's reply with an 'Oh well' and then asked if she could have a cinnamon scone with her afternoon tea. She's pretending to be all pragmatic about it, but you only have to take one look at her to see how wounded she is."

"I'm so sorry."

Maeve unfolded her arms and let one hand flap away my

apology. "You've nothing to apologise for. You thought we were helping her. We both did."

Outside the shop windows, a gull strutted up and down the pavement, past the gliding traffic.

"Do you think there's any chance Corinne might change her mind?" I asked.

"Not if that letter is anything to go by. It's very to the point. I've written longer shopping lists than that."

Despondency cluttered inside my chest, on Celeste's behalf. "If she knew your mum was ill, that might change things."

"And that's why my mother decided not to tell her. She didn't want her pity. Oh sorry. That's my phone ringing."

Maeve dived one hand inside her bag to collect her phone. She frowned down at the glowing screen. "It's the residential home." She shot me a concerned look as she answered. "Hello?"

The tinges of summer colour in Maeve's cheeks ebbed away. "What? When? Oh God. What happened? When did she do that?" Maeve's face was a mask of worry. "And she won't go to hospital?"

She paced up and down. "Right. I'm on my way now."

She finished the call and clutched at her bag.

"Maeve?"

"It's Mum," she struggled, preparing to head for the bookshop door. Worry clouded in her eyes. "She's collapsed."

Chapter Thirty-Four

Joy led Maeve, me and Tobias down the hallway and past the summer room, where a few of the residents were admiring the shadows playing on the lawns. Fresh gerbera and roses were thrusting out of vases on the windowsills.

Tobias had heard Maeve's panic and insisted he drive us here.

Celeste's door was open.

Joy encouraged Maeve in.

Maeve took one look at her mother and gave a disbelieving shake of her head.

"All I need is a stiff drink," carried Celeste's frustrated voice.

"You do *not* need a drink, Mum. Only water or juice."

Maeve turned and looked out of the room at Tobias and me hovering there. Relief swamped her features that we stayed and were there to support her. There was no way either Tobias or me would be anywhere else right now. She beckoned us both. "Please come in and see your ladyship."

Celeste was sitting up in bed, propped against a few pillows. She made me think of a diva movie star in her petrol-blue silk dressing gown and matching nightdress. She was also adorned in what looked like the whole contents of her jewellery box.

A coquettish smile played on her lips when Tobias and I entered. "Good grief. What is this? The cavalry?"

The young male doctor, who introduced himself as Dr Jenkins, rose up from where he'd been sitting on the corner of Celeste's bed.

"You had these two ladies very worried," explained Tobias. "I was too, when Maeve told me what had happened."

Celeste's expression was one of impatience. "It was nothing! Joy over-reacted. It was just a little stumble."

"It was not a little stumble at all, Mrs Matthews," piped up the doctor. "You collapsed."

Celeste was incandescent. "How do you know? You weren't here."

"Mum," growled Maeve. She shook her head with exasperation. "I see her tongue hasn't been affected."

I laughed and Dr Jenkins's brows rose at Celeste. "I was reliably informed." He pushed a lock of mid-brown hair out of his eyes. "Your blood pressure was rather low, but it's stabilised now. Do you know what might have caused it?"

Maeve's attention flitted over to Corinne's letter, which was lying on the bedside table.

Celeste gave the young doctor a look. "I thought you were supposed to know things like that."

Maeve delivered a sharp stare at her mother.

The doctor, however, just laughed. "You remind me of my own mother. An answer for everything." He pinned Celeste with his astute, sharp blue eyes. "I'd like to admit you to hospital as a precaution, Mrs Matthews."

"Absolutely not, young man! If I'm going to peg it, I want to do it here in my own bed, not surrounded by crusty old farts."

Tobias, standing beside me, choked back a bark of laughter.

"I'm feeling fine now. A bit embarrassed about causing such a needless commotion, but that's all."

"But Mrs Matthews…"

Celeste folded her freckled pale arms and stuck out her jaw.

The doctor heaved a sigh. "Alright. You can stay here." He swivelled to speak to Maeve and Joy. "Keep an eye out for any signs of concussion, drowsiness or vomiting. If you have any concerns about Mrs Matthews's condition, ring for an ambulance immediately."

They both confirmed they would without hesitation.

Dr Jenkins leant down and addressed Celeste. "And you behave yourself."

Celeste looked horrified at the prospect. "Dear me, no. What fun is there in that?" She made a contented sigh and rested her white, thick head of hair back against the pillows.

The doctor gathered his briefcase and suit jacket. "Could I have a quick word with both of you ladies please?" He indicated to Maeve and Joy.

Maeve nodded and stepped out into the corridor with Joy closing the room door shut behind her.

Tobias and I were left alone in Celeste's room with her, the faint traces of summer breeze gently billowing the curtains, bringing a freshness to the air.

"May I, Celeste?" I asked, patting a corner of her bed.

"Please do."

I sat myself down beside her and Tobias pulled over a chair. "So, what happened?" I asked her. "Or should I say, *why* did it happen?"

Celeste glanced up at me.

I pointed to Corinne's letter, stuffed inside the envelope. "Was it because of that?"

Celeste's attention followed mine. "Ah. So, Maeve told you I got the brush-off?"

"Yes." There was silence, except for the sound of birdsong outside.

"Is that why you collapsed?" asked Tobias gently. "Because of its contents?"

"No, of course not. I was being too cavalier with my wheelchair, that's all."

Her misty eyes lingered on the envelope and Corinne's elegant loopy handwriting. When she spotted me looking at it too, she pulled her attention away. "Now, if both of you don't mind, I'd like to rest my eyes for a few moments. Being a force of nature takes its toll."

"I bet it does," smiled Tobias across at her.

Celeste settled herself back against the pillows and before long, her eyelids fluttered closed and she was dozing.

A moment or so later, her door eased open quietly. Maeve was standing there, ashen-faced. She gestured for the two of us to follow her.

I eased myself from the bed, so as not to disturb Celeste,

Tobias rose from his chair and we followed Maeve back out into the hallway, leaving Celeste to slumber.

Tobias clicked the door shut at his back.

Dr Jenkins had departed by this time, but Joy was still standing there, looking troubled.

"What is it?" I asked, my stomach giving a concerned wriggle.

Maeve took a breath. "It isn't good news." She moved to speak, decided she couldn't and gestured to Joy to take over.

Joy's pink, round face broke into a sad smile. "The doctor said Celeste's becoming weaker, although five fire-breathing dragons wouldn't be able to get her to admit it." Her expression became graver. "She can't risk another fall. In her condition, fractures to the likes of thigh bones can cause serious issues to other parts of the body."

I rubbed my face. I didn't want to hear this. None of us did. But Celeste seemed so much brighter and her tongue was still working at full tilt. "So, what does that mean? What's the prognosis? How many months?"

Joy shook her head sadly. "Her heart is weakening." She hesitated. "I'm afraid it isn't months. Doctor Jenkins told us that it's weeks at best. I'm so sorry."

The silence was deafening, as the three of us tried to absorb this.

I was determined to hold it together in front of Maeve. The last thing she needed, was me dissolving into tears. I sunk my teeth into my bottom lip.

All at once, Tobias slid one hand down to mine and held it. The sensation and surprise of his warm, paint-gnarled fingers searching out mine made me want to sob.

My dad. Now Celeste. And I couldn't do a thing to stop it. I gazed across at Maeve, who was struggling to keep herself composed.

I hoped I could keep my voice on an even keel. "I suppose we just have to make sure she's as comfortable and content as she can be."

Tobias nodded his head. "I've put the finishing touches to her portrait and am having it framed for her now, so it should be ready any time to present to her."

A sudden burst of gratitude shone out of Maeve's lost expression. "Thank you." She looked bewildered again, stumbling around in her own private thoughts. "Do you think that letter from Corinne did have something to do with her taking ill like that?"

"The contents must've upset her, but there's no way to know whether it triggered Celeste's collapse or whether it was just a case of bad timing," commented Joy beside her.

Maeve's mouth set into a hard line. "I can't leave things like this. Dr Jenkins's prognosis has made that clear. I can't just sit here, do nothing and watch her wither away."

"So, what are you thinking?" I asked.

Maeve straightened her back. She flicked away a tear. "I suggest we go and talk to Corinne face-to-face. We have to try and make her change her mind about seeing Mum. You heard the doctor. She doesn't have much time left."

My brows rose in surprise. "Do you think it might work? That reply she sent to Celeste; you said it was very abrupt."

"It was, but Corinne didn't know about Mum's condition."

A niggle of worry took hold. "But Celeste made us swear we wouldn't tell her."

A long, low breath shot out of Maeve. "I still think that was a bad mistake. I know you did too."

"But you want to try to speak to her?" asked Tobias.

Maeve nodded, as a couple of other residents ambled past. "Ok, Corinne is saying she doesn't want anything to do with Mum, but if we don't give it one more try, Mum is going to pass away and I'll be sitting there wondering if I tried to do enough to reunite them."

She snapped her pleading gaze back to me. "This might be the last chance for Mum and Corinne to say hello and goodbye to one another." She gulped. "I know I'd regret it if I don't at least try." Maeve pinned me to the spot with her pleasing expression. "What do you think, Lexie? Are you in?"

I mulled over in my mind what Maeve had said. Celeste had weeks, not months. Time was running out. If this had been my mother in this dreadful position, I knew I would be thinking the same as Maeve. "If we do this, we shouldn't tell Celeste. If Corinne refuses to speak to us, that really will be it."

"I agree. So?"

I looked over at Joy in her pale blue carer's uniform. She shrugged. "It sounds to me like you've nothing to lose by trying to speak to her."

Maeve glanced at Tobias, who nodded in agreement. "Celeste always took chances in life, I'm guessing?"

Maeve's grief-tinged face lit up for a few seconds. "And then some."

"Right," I exclaimed. "I think we've just made our decision."

Chapter Thirty-Five

Maeve and I agreed to travel to Corinne's house on Sunday afternoon.

She pulled up outside my flat, looking summery yet assertive in a poppy-printed ankle-length dress and fitted red jacket.

I'd opted for something in a similar vein, but my dress was a floaty, hemmed lilac number that buttoned up the front. I had teamed it with my purple ballet pumps.

"Have you been to see Celeste this morning?" I asked Maeve, as she negotiated us away from Bracken Way and towards the north side of Glasgow, where Corinne lived.

"Yes, I have. I've just come from there."

"And, how is she?"

Maeve indicated, squinting up at her rear-view mirror as she drove us around a flower- studded roundabout. "She wasn't too bad. Still cracking waspish jokes. But the letter from Corinne was still propped up by her bedside clock. I think she's been reading it again."

I sighed at the thought of Celeste sitting alone in her room, torturing herself with that letter and the agonising memories attached to it. "You'll never get her to admit it, but it must have hurt her." I shot Maeve a side glance. "Did you manage to take a note of Corinne's address ok?"

"Yep. I pretended to be looking for a spare pen and when one of the carers came in to check on Mum, I jotted it down." Maeve nodded at her satnav. "One-seven-five, Montague Drive, White Woods, Glasgow."

The traffic didn't look too bad for a Sunday afternoon in June. The castle was long gone through the rear windscreen, as was the shiny line of the loch water.

Fields and parks opened out now, showing off jade grass, children streaming up and down and dogs dive bombing to catch frisbees.

Maeve gave me a quick glance as she concentrated on the road. "Lexie, do you think we're doing the right thing? Going behind Mum's back to talk to Corinne?"

"Are you having seconds thoughts?"

"No. At least, I don't think so. Oh bugger, I don't know!" She fell quiet, easing us up to a set of traffic lights. "I want to do what's best for Mum. I don't want her upset anymore."

I stretched out my legs as I sat back in the passenger seat and waggled my ballet pumps. "For what it's worth, no, I don't think what you're doing – what we are doing – is a mistake. I think it's essential."

Maeve glanced at me from behind her smoky sunglasses.

"If we don't try to reach out to Corinne again, then there definitely won't be any closure for your mum or for her. The way I see it, we've no choice."

My throat thickened, as I conjured up images of Celeste in bed and the osteoporosis taking a tighter and more malicious hold on her. "Maeve, you need to be the one to speak up and explain to Corinne what's happened."

Maeve nodded as she negotiated the traffic.

"Then it really is up to Corinne whether she's willing to carry on with her life, knowing she could've met her birth mother but deciding not to take that chance when it came her way."

Maeve listened, her hands controlling her leather steering wheel.

I smoothed the hem of my dress. I blinked back a couple of threatening tears. "It might not make any difference, you asking to speak to Corinne, but if we don't go to see her, you'll always be wondering."

Maeve forced out her chin. "You're right." She hesitated. "Has what has been happening with your dad made you think more about things?"

I allowed my attention to drift out of the passenger side window at a faraway herd of cows. They looked like clumps of solid black and white liquorice. "I'm not going to pretend our situation has been easy either. When my father first reappeared just over four weeks ago or so, I was furious at him. How could he think he could waltz back into our lives? But when we found out about his dementia I knew I had to make a decision one way or the other."

My fingers tugged at the neckline of my dress. "I could either turn my back on him or I could be there for my mum, who's still so in love with him. She was prepared to forgive my dad and help him and I promised I'd support her decision."

The corners of Maeve's mouth turned upwards. "I can understand that. And how do you feel about your dad now?"

My lips formed into a thoughtful "O" shape as I considered her question. "That's a tricky one. Right now, I feel sorry for him more than anything. The dementia is gradually stealing who he is."

Maeve angled the steering wheel to the right and took us up beyond the last of the country lanes, before the motorway spread ahead of us, like an outsized tarmac-black tongue. "Well, if you ask me, you, your mum and your grandfather have been wonderful about it."

"Thank you. I can't just forget what he did and act like it never happened. He was so ruthless about leaving Mum and me, but I suppose I'm just learning to compartmentalise it for Mum's sake." I let out a low laugh. "I still catch my grandpa giving my dad the odd killer stare though when he thinks nobody's looking."

Maeve laughed as she checked her mirror again and glided us onto the motorway. The red dot of Corinne's house was drawing ever closer on the satnav screen.

My stomach pirouetted with nerves. I hoped more than anything that Corinne could see her way to putting aside any preconceptions about Celeste and at least hear what Maeve had to say.

Corinne's house was a 1970s detached affair in a north Glasgow suburb, thronged by trees and a short walk from a plethora of dinky but expensive independent shops.

The front garden consisted of fat, ceramic pots of various plants and flowering bushes, leading up to a white panelled front door.

An attractive, rangy man in his early sixties, sporting Bermuda shorts and a deep tan, was busy mowing the front stretch of lawn.

Maeve eased her amber Golf into the kerb right outside Corinne's house.

The man looked up with a cursory glance, before returning to the matter of navigating the mower up and down the lawn again. It was hypnotic watching him create those Wimbledon stripes.

"Ok," exclaimed Maeve, reaching over to the back seat to retrieve her bag.

I reached down to my feet and scooped up my straw bag.

We both clambered out. The Sunday afternoon sunshine had slipped behind some tufts of cloud and a plane dipped lower, as it made its descent towards Glasgow Airport.

"Excuse me?" called Maeve over the top of her car roof. She made sure the doors were locked and moved closer, with me following up the rear. She whipped off her sunglasses and stashed them in her bag over her shoulder. "We're sorry to bother you, but we wondered if we might be able to have a word with Corinne Young, please?"

The man clicked off his lawnmower. "Corinne's my wife. I'm Fletcher Young. Can I ask what it's about?"

Maeve straightened her dress. "It's a bit delicate, Mr Young. I'm your wife's half-sister."

Fletcher Young's hazel eyes grew larger. "Right. I see." He eyed us both. "Is this to do with that letter my wife received last week?"

We both nodded.

He abandoned his fancy lawnmower and approached us,

so that he was now standing facing us from over the top of his hedge. "Please don't think I'm being rude, but I know my wife made it clear she has no interest in getting to know her birth mother."

"She did say that," conceded Maeve. She shot me a sideways look and then carried on talking. "But there's something we think she should know. My mother didn't want Corinne to feel coerced or emotionally blackmailed into seeing her, so she made us swear we wouldn't say anything."

Fletcher Young frowned from under his flop of salt and pepper hair. "Sorry? Not telling her what?"

Maeve blinked across at me, her eyes sorrowful.

"That Celeste is dying," I replied as steadily as I could manage. "She has advanced osteoporosis, and now her heart is failing. The prognosis is weeks at best."

Fletcher Young's eyes widened. "Oh, I'm so very sorry to hear that."

"Thank you," replied Maeve. "That's why we've come here this afternoon to explain to Corinne."

At that moment, the sound of a piece of Scottish folk music danced out of one of the open sitting room windows of the house. It was lyrical and fast, thrumming and drumming, like something out of a lively ceilidh.

Then the music stopped.

"Fletch! Fletch!"

A tall, angular blonde woman, like an older, sportier version of Maeve, came tapping down the front steps. She was clutching an acoustic guitar in one hand. She was dressed in khaki shorts, a loose-fitting short-sleeved shirt and was barefoot. Her hair was pulled away from her face in a high ponytail and her legs were bearing a toffee-coloured tan. Soft lines fanned out from her eyes. She gave off an air of being younger than she was.

"I think I've finally nailed that section for next week's concert. Oh."

She drew up, blinking at the sight of Maeve and me on the pavement. "Hello."

Corinne's husband fixed her with a reassuring, if somewhat strained smile. "Darling. These two ladies are here to talk to you."

"Oh? What about?"

He glanced over at us and then back to Corinne. "Your mum?"

Corinne stiffened. "Mum? What about her? Is she alright?"

He cringed under his deep, even tan. "No, sweetheart. You don't understand." His hands reached over and settled on top of his wife's shoulders. "They aren't here about Mary."

Corinne froze as another plane scarred the sky overhead.

"They're here to talk to you about Celeste Matthews. Your biological mother."

Corinne's face grew taut. "I've already made my feelings clear. I'm not interested."

Maeve held up one hand. "Believe me. I can understand how conflicted you must feel about it."

"Conflicted?" Corinne choked, flashing sudden white hot looks at us both. "I don't feel conflicted. That woman gave me up for adoption as soon as I was born. Why has she decided to track me down now?"

"My mother – our mother – did find you," admitted Maeve. "Ten years ago, now. She mentioned it in her letter to you."

334

Corinne glowered.

"She hired a private investigator to find you. She followed you to one of the music venues that you were performing at, but she just couldn't approach you in the end."

Corinne's full mouth grew tighter. "Yes, she did mention something in her letter about that." She gave her husband a look beside her. "Bottled out at the last minute."

"And she regretted that too," insisted Maeve. "It isn't true about her wanting to have you adopted. She wanted to keep you. She really did. But my grandparents wouldn't hear of it. It broke her heart saying goodbye to you."

Corinne flapped her hand as though defending herself from a swarm of irritating insects. "I just told you. I'm not interested. I want both of you to leave. Now."

Maeve took another step closer to the hedge partitioning Corinne's garden from the street pavement. "What, not even when we tell you that my mother has weeks to live?"

Corinne squinted over at us from her quiet, tranquil corner of suburbia. "Pardon?"

Maeve moved to explain about Celeste, but her voice dried up.

I gave her a brief smile of understanding and took over. "What Maeve is trying to tell you is that Celeste has advanced osteoporosis, and now her heart is struggling. She only has a matter of weeks left."

Fletcher Young turned to study his wife. She shot him an unfathomable expression. "I'm sorry to hear that. She never mentioned anything about being ill in her letter."

Maeve managed to compose herself again. "Would it have made any difference if she had?"

Corinne didn't answer. She bent down and scooped up her guitar from beside her. "Like I said, I'm very sorry to hear that."

Maeve waited, but any shreds of optimism in her eyes soon died. "So that's it?"

Corinne stared levelly over the low hedge at her half-sister. "What do you want me to say? I don't know her."

"And that's why we're here," ground out Maeve. "My mother wants to speak to you. She wants to apologise."

Corinne rubbed her face in frustration. "Like I said, my condolences, but it's too late."

Maeve's frustration bubbled over. "Shall I return to the residential home now and tell her that then?! I'm sure that'll make her day."

She started to say something else, but before she uttered something she might regret, I gave Maeve's arm a supportive squeeze and pointed her back towards her car. "Go and wait for me please, Maeve. I won't be a minute."

Her dark eyes were fired up. "But, Lexie, you know the truth."

"Celeste wouldn't want you getting yourself upset like this and having a barney in the middle of the street."

Maeve opened and closed her mouth. She swiped at her damp eyes with her bare arm. With a swirl of her dress hem, she marched back to her car. She jumped into the driver side and banged the door shut.

I edged a little closer to the hedge. "I do understand how difficult this situation is. My father walked out on my mother and me twenty-three years ago. I received the odd birthday and Christmas card. Then he returned recently from the States.

Just showed up out of the blue." I paused. "It turns out he has dementia."

Corinne listened. "I'm sorry."

"Thank you." I shrugged my shoulders. "Don't get me wrong. I have no illusions about who my father was. He chose his career over his wife and child." I paused and cleared my throat, as Corinne and Fletcher Young watched me. "But soon, he won't be that man anymore. He won't even recognise us."

I glanced over my shoulder. Maeve was glowering through the windscreen at Corinne.

"What I'm trying to say is, nobody expects you to forget what happened. It's like me with my dad. Don't let regret be the only thing you remember about her in the end." I managed a fleeting smile. "I'm sorry if we've upset you. That wasn't our intention. Celeste didn't want to tell you about her health, in case you decided to see her out of pity."

Corinne's grim expression fell.

"Anyway." I reached into my pocket and produced an old piece of paper and pen. I pulled out my phone and copied down Maeve's details and then jotted down my own. "Please take it and just think about what we've said. Thank you for your time and sorry for interrupting your day."

I walked back to the car.

Maeve's troubled, pale expression was still set across her face, as she pulled away and drove us back to Bracken Way.

Tobias appeared at Mirror Image on Monday morning, surprising me by arriving just after I did.

He was angling in a large covered portrait, concealed under a sheet of grey canvas.

He gave me a wink that made my stomach spin. "Would you like to take a look at Celeste's finished portrait then?"

"What a silly question. Oh yes please!"

Tobias shot me a jokey look. "Now be gentle with me please. Us artists have very tender egos."

"You have an ego but it sure isn't tender." I laughed at him.

He pulled a comical face and tugged away the canvas, while performing a verbal drumroll sound.

I clapped one hand over my stunned mouth. "Oh my God, Tobias. It's... it's breath-taking!"

In a palette of the softest hues, Tobias had brought Celeste to life. She was seated in her wheelchair, but it faded into the background, unable to compete with the knowing sparkle in her eyes; the soft lines captured on her complexion and around her mouth and the thickness of her white hair, falling back from her expectant face.

I felt as though I could reach out and touch the pearly detail on her icy gown, pouring to the floor and over her feet like a Highland waterfall. A matching bolero glittered over the top of her dress.

And rearing up behind her, like a grand old gent, was Bracken Way Castle, shadowy and mysterious in the background.

For a few moments, I wasn't able to say anything. It was as though I'd become hypnotised by the striking portrait and Celeste's thoughtful expression shining out from the painting.

He'd captured the cool but mischievous elegance of her, with delicate brushstrokes and vibrant hues.

"Well, don't keep me in suspense. What do you think? Do you think she'll like it?" asked Tobias, not able to disguise a glimmer of trepidation.

"Like it?" I studied the painting again. "It's stunning. She'll fall in love with it. Maeve will too."

Tobias's serious face split into a relieved megawatt grin. "Something tells me you like it as well."

"Stop fishing for compliments, Mr Black."

Tobias covered the portrait over again with the sheet of canvas and placed it behind the counter at Mirror Image. "Had any more thoughts about sitting for me?"

My heart revved up. "Oh well… I don't know."

Tobias tapped back down the steps from the gallery and leant against the office door frame. "If I can paint a portrait like that of Celeste, imagine what I could do with you."

Was he saying things like that deliberately? A deeper blush gripped my face.

He kept his handsome expression unreadable. "You know what I mean."

Was he teasing me?

My conflicting emotions swirled. This didn't sound like a good idea. Being so close to Tobias as he painted me. His gaze sweeping over me. Shit. What had I promised myself? That I would keep well away from him.

Oh, come on Lexie. I could handle it. I could. He would be painting me, not stripping off.

Oh no! Stop it! Don't go there. Think about stocktaking. Think about those annoying idiots who fold over the corners of book pages.

But Wine Woman… I still didn't know what the story was there. Was he seeing someone?

I mulled it over. I was overthinking this. It was just a portrait. What harm would that do? I was a grown woman. I wasn't stupid.

Stop being such a coward, I told myself. I could handle Tobias and my feelings for him. I could keep them in check. It wouldn't be a problem.

I set my back straighter. "Yes. Fine. Sure. Thank you. That would be great. But I insist on paying you. I'm not a freeloader."

Tobias approached me like a prowling tiger. "We'll talk about that later." In an instant, he flipped back to professional mode. "Right. Excellent. I'll check my diary and come back to you."

Then he stalked off, giving me a slow smile over his shoulder.

"When are you planning on going to visit Celeste again?" asked Tobias the next morning in the shop.

The sun was playing a game with the summer rain, washing Bracken Way in warm, dappled sun one minute, before tipping it down again.

"I thought I might go this evening," I replied. "Are you going to give her the portrait?"

"Yes, that's the plan."

"Then we can go together if you like," I suggested, before wishing I could bite my tongue off. I didn't want Tobias to get the wrong idea. "I mean, travel up there at the same time."

Tobias's mouth lifted. "I guessed that was what you meant."

Pictures of Celeste's manuscript floated into my head. "I wanted to speak to her about her book."

"Is it raunchy then?" grinned Tobias, with a wicked glint.

I laughed. "Not by today's standards. It's just it ends so abruptly, like she never bothered to finish it."

Tobias frowned. "But I thought she had."

"Me too. It's a pity as it's such a great story. I've suggested some revisions and sharpened it up here and there. It really is fantastic."

"Well, let's go up there together," confirmed Tobias. "I'll pick you up around seven o'clock?"

"Thanks. That's fine by me."

Tobias nodded. "I can't wait to see Celeste's face when she sees her portrait."

Celeste stared, opened-mouthed at Tobias's portrait of her, mounted in its thick gilt-edged frame.

He angled it this way and that in the centre of her comfy, sun-stippled room.

She turned to me and Tobias and then back at the painting, with its snowy whites, lavenders, ice pinks and the crumbly castle in the background. She kept clapping her hands together in delight. "I knew it would be wonderful, but I never imagined it would look like this."

Maeve, who we'd contacted and asked to join us up at the home so she could see it too, struggled to maintain her composure. "Thank you so much, Tobias. It's wonderful. You're so talented!"

Joyful tears shimmered in Celeste's dark gaze. "I don't

know how to thank you or what to say."

"You don't have to say anything," beamed Tobias. "I'm delighted by both your reactions. That's more than enough for me." Then he corrected himself. "Oh, there is one thing you could do for me, Celeste?"

"And what might that be?"

"I would very much like to display your portrait in Mirror Image, once you've had time to appreciate it, of course. It's good to ring the changes with my displays and I'm very proud of this one."

I grinned at Celeste's startled expression. It wasn't very often she was lost for words. "What? Me? In your gallery?"

"Why shouldn't you be?"

Maeve nodded hard. "That sounds a wonderful suggestion. What do you think, Mum?"

Celeste angled her wheelchair with the assistance of Tobias, so she could take another lingering look at the painting. "I think that would be lovely."

"Then consider it having pride of place," insisted Tobias.

There were contented smiles all around.

Celeste then swivelled her attention to me. "I know you've been very busy, Lexie, but I don't suppose you've had a chance to read more of my book?"

"As a matter of fact, I've read it all. But there's something I wanted to mention. You haven't finished writing it."

"Ah. Yes." She adjusted the set of pearls nestling against her throat. "I did plan to discuss that little issue with you."

I blinked at her, confused. "Why's that?"

Her lined eyes shone with hope. "Because I'd be honoured if you were to finish writing it for me."

Chapter Thirty-Six

I sat, rigid, on the edge of the chair.

"Me? Why?"

"Because I understand you're a very talented editor, Lexie. You wouldn't have worked with the likes of Sir Stephen Todd and Dame Alicia Kilroy if you hadn't been."

I was aware of three expectant faces examining me.

Someone must have been discussing me with Celeste. Maeve's cheeks brimmed with pink. There was the guilty party right there.

Celeste concentrated her gaze on me. "You're doing a wonderful job with Book Ends, but editing is still your day job."

"The bookshop is my day job now, although I do still keep my hand in with a bit of editorial freelancing." I couldn't help but smile. "Why don't you say what you think, Celeste, instead of beating around the bush?"

She cocked one pale brow at me. "Somebody has to say it how it is."

"Oh, there's no fear of that not happening with you around, Mum," groaned Maeve.

Celeste tipped her head to one side. Watery evening sunshine was sliding past her curtains. "Like I said, I'd like you to finish writing my book. As you can see, it isn't complete and I'm not going to be able to do it. It would mean the world to me if you did."

My throat dried up. "Now you're using emotional blackmail?"

Celeste shrugged. "Whatever works."

Tobias looked at Maeve and struggled not to laugh.

"I know you'd be able to finish the story beautifully and tie up all the loose ends."

Bewilderment coursed through me. "But it's your book. It's your story. I don't know how it should end. Why didn't you complete it?"

Celeste clasped her frail hands together. "Because I didn't know how it should end." She gazed up at me from her wheelchair, with her puff of white hair and appealing eyes. "Write the epilogue you'd be happy with; that would make the reader sigh and smile with contentment." Celeste was unrelenting as usual. "What do you think?"

My mouth kept falling open and shut. "But it wouldn't be factually correct," I persisted, floundering around for more excuses to use. "And it's written in your voice."

"Who cares? A lot of it is exaggerated anyway and as long as the ending is a happy one, that's all that matters."

I stood there, conflicted.

"Would you really deny a very ill woman?"

"Mum!" hissed Maeve. "You're shameless. Stop it!"

Celeste ignored her. "It's true. I think I'm entitled to use some emotional blackmail, considering my situation."

"Good grief," muttered Maeve to Tobias. "She has an answer for everything."

Celeste carried on. "You never struck me as a young woman who shied away from a challenge."

"I'm not." I made the mistake of looking in Tobias's direction. He arched one brow at me.

Could I do Celeste's book justice? Would I be able to write fiction? I was so used to editing other people's work, I'd never thought about sitting down and actually writing something like that myself. What if the ideas failed to materialise? What if I couldn't do it? "I don't know," I struggled.

Now it was Tobias's turn to jump in. "Well, you aren't going to know for certain unless you try."

"That's very true," chimed in Maeve.

"And if you get a move on with finishing it, I might even be able to read the end of it before I pop off."

"Mum! For pity's sake!"

Celeste winked up at a horrified Maeve.

"This is really unfair," I sighed, my attention zooming to each of them in turn. "All of you ganging up on me."

Tobias winked. "Uh-huh."

I stuck my tongue inside my cheek. This was a huge responsibility Celeste was bestowing upon me. I wasn't an author. But then again, I had edited a number of successful novels in my career. I liked to think I had a good idea of what worked in terms of writing fiction.

Tobias waggled his brows. "I think Celeste was hoping for an answer today, Lexie."

I dragged a hand through my hair. "Alright! Alright. I'll do it. I just hope the ending is to your satisfaction, Celeste."

She clapped her fragile hands together. "Wonderful! Thank you, darling. You've made this decrepit lady very happy. Now, who's for a celebratory whisky?"

Maeve was doing her best to dissuade her mother from indulging in alcohol and was trying to persuade her to opt for an Earl Grey tea instead, when her mobile rang.

She reached into it, sat on the table behind her. "Hello? Yes, speaking." Her mouth slackened and she began to make a series of odd noises. "Right. Yes. You're where? What? You mean, right now? Outside? Oh. I see. Give me a minute."

She clamped her hand over her phone and jerked her head at me. "Lexie, could I have a quick word please?"

"Of course."

Puzzled, I went outside while Tobias remained in the room with Celeste. I could hear them chuckling.

I clicked the door behind me. "Is everything ok?"

Maeve was hopping from foot to foot, like a small child who needed to pay a visit to the bathroom. "Yes. No. I think so." She brandished her phone at me. She was struggling to speak. "Oh my God. I can't believe this." She took a breath. "You'll never guess who that was. Corinne. It's Corinne on the phone." Her stunned face broke into a smile. "She's changed her mind about meeting Mum. She's agreed to see her."

I let out a shocked gasp. "You're joking?! That's great!" I gawped back at Maeve. "I wonder what made her change her mind? Oh, it doesn't matter. She wants to talk to Celeste, so that's the main thing."

Maeve nodded her blow-dried blonde head. "Yes, it is. It's just…" Her voice stuttered.

"What?"

Maeve made sure her hand was still clamped over her phone, not able to contain herself. "Corinne is here. She's in the car park right now."

Chapter Thirty-Seven

Maeve and I flapped around, looking like we were in a slapstick black and white movie.

"Oh bugger. She's outside? Right now? What should we do?" I asked her. "Should we tell Celeste that Corinne is here?"

"Maybe we should," hissed Maeve, her attention being pulled away from me and up the hallway. "Oh, I think it might be too late for that."

Fletcher Young was standing at the residential home entrance. Hovering in front of him was Corinne, clutching a mixed bouquet of pastel roses and lilies.

She stood, casting her eyes around for a few moments, until Maeve hurried over to her. I followed.

Corinne hugged the bouquet. "I'm so sorry for turning up like this."

Maeve tried to bite back a ball of emotion. "Don't be. It's wonderful you changed your mind."

They exchanged awkward smiles and then Maeve

encouraged Corinne to follow her. "Come on. Mum is going to be thrilled."

Fletcher gave his wife an encouraging nod from the doorway and vanished.

Corinne suddenly looked like she wasn't sure why she was there. She drew up. She was dressed in slim-fitting white trousers and a frilly, summery top. "Talk about impulsive," she said into the bouquet she was holding. "I did think about ringing you first and then I thought that if I did that, I might end up bottling it. So here I am."

Maeve brushed aside her concerns. "It's fine."

I issued Corinne with a supportive beam. "Celeste will be beside herself." I hesitated. "Can I ask what made you change your mind?"

"Not what. *Who*." She blushed, glancing back up the hallway to where Fletcher had been standing moments before. "My husband talks a lot of sense when he sets his mind to it."

We moved in unison down the carpeted hallway and clustered around Celeste's closed door. Corinne steeled herself. "Is this her room?"

From inside, we could make out the murmured conversation between Tobias and Celeste.

Maeve nodded. "Ready?"

Celeste placed one nervous hand across her stomach. "Right. Yes."

Maeve swept the door open.

Celeste angled her head as she sat in her wheelchair, chatting to Tobias. She stared at Corinne for a few seconds, a bemused smile on her face. Then one of her hands flew to her mouth.

349

"Hello, Celeste," managed Corinne, her voice cracking.

Celeste let out a stunned breath. "Corinne?"

Corinne nodded and gripped her bouquet of flowers tighter.

Celeste's eyes glistened. "My girl. Oh, my girl. Come here."

The next few minutes were a blur of stunned expressions, sobs and exclamations, followed by tentative handholding.

Tobias rose to help Maeve get Celeste comfortable in her armchair. Then he sidled up to me, as a tear-stained Corinne lowered herself in front of Celeste's armchair to talk to her.

"Do you think we should leave them to it?" he murmured.

"Yes. That's a good idea."

Maeve was about to vacate the room too, but Celeste wouldn't hear of it. She shot out one hand and gently took her younger daughter's wrist. "You two are sisters. We're family here. I have my girls. Both of them!"

Maeve promised to text me later with a full debrief and so Tobias and I exited and left them to it.

We both stood together in the hallway. Further up, there were bursts of radio programmes and TV shows emanating from cracks in half-open doors and the sweet scent of fresh flowers from the summer room.

Tobias made a satisfied sigh. "It looks like things might be sorting themselves out."

"Thank goodness." I breathed. "Right. The next thing on my list is to write the end of Celeste's book."

Tobias towered over me. "Well, before you do that, how about coming round to mine for a celebratory dinner?"

I gazed up into his chiselled face. It was as if I was struggling to think straight.

"And I can make a start on sketching you for your portrait."

One of my hands shot up to my loose hair. "Tobias. I'm not ready."

"What?"

"I've been busy all day and talk about putting myself through the wringer."

"I know you have, but you still look lovely."

Heat seeped up my neck. "Yeah right. I believe you. Thousands wouldn't."

Tobias arched one dark brow. "So, you're going to turn down the opportunity to taste my legendary roast chicken?"

Oh no. Don't do this to me.

I found myself wrapped up in his stare, unable to escape. In truth, I didn't want to. I thought about Celeste, still trying to squeeze every moment out of life. Oh, bugger! It was a bite to eat and an opportunity for Tobias to paint me. That was all. "Yes," I heard myself say. "That sounds delicious."

The roast chicken was succulent and the roast potatoes were golden and crisp. Not content with a swathe of vegetables, Tobias also added a huge Yorkshire pudding to each of our plates.

When I'd finished eating, I felt like my stomach had ballooned to three times its normal size. That would look good in my portrait.

I said as much to Tobias, who kept a straight face as he said, "Don't worry. I can always get a bigger canvas."

I picked up one of his monochrome cushions and pretended to throw it at him, which elicited a wicked smile.

We cleared away the dinner plates, stacked them in his dishwasher and were now nursing cups of delicious smelling Italian coffee.

Tobias fetched a large sketch pad and pencils from his makeshift studio in another room. He arranged me on his sofa. "Now, please try not to move. Do you mind if I play some music while I sketch you?"

"Of course not."

Tobias ordered his Alexa to play "Life Eternal" by Ghost. The haunting, heart-wrenching lyrics swam around me.

He sat himself down in an armchair opposite me. His pencils began to skitter across the white, blank page as he looked up at me and then dropped his gaze again, to concentrate.

I sneaked my coffee cup from the table in front of me and took a few quick gulps. The combination of the music and being in such close proximity to Tobias was making my heart quicken. "I wonder how things went with Corinne?" I muttered to him out of the corner of my mouth.

"I'm sure she'll ring you." He shook his head, as he studied the shape of my face. He dropped his eyes again to sketch. "Now, stop worrying about other people for once and concentrate on yourself."

I reached out and picked up the coffee again for another speedy mouthful. Tobias was looking with a critical eye at what he'd drawn so far. He didn't realise I was admiring him.

His thick arched brows were fixed in concentration and his inky lashes jutted forward as he looked down at his sketching.

I raised my coffee cup to my lips. "So, how do you work? With your sketching and painting, I mean?"

"I try to capture the likeness of a person, or their essence. Simple and bold." He flicked me a look and I tried not to dissolve in a puddle. His hand danced across the pad, the pencil moving this way and that.

"And when do you start painting a portrait?"

"When I'm satisfied that I've got my subject how I want them."

Another intense, dark look at me, which made me swallow. Was he doing this on purpose? If so, it was working.

"When I'm about to start painting an actual portrait, I set up my palette and rub the canvas with a neutral oil medium. That means that the linen is slightly saturated and the canvas tends to receive the paint from my brush more easily."

He returned to looking at his pencil sketch. He raised his gaze again. "I like all the edges to be soft in my work – like where the hair touches the skin."

I bit back a ball of something in my throat. It was as if the air was being sucked from my body. How could he do that? Make an innocent remark sound so erotic?

I risked a look at him, expecting him to be focused on his sketch pad, but he wasn't. He was studying me from under those intent, dark brows. He shifted as he sat there. "It was because of a failed relationship."

"Sorry?"

The captivating ballad had finished and morphed into a rockier track.

Tobias hesitated. "Why I decided to move back to Bracken Way." He shrugged. "I found out just over a year ago that my

353

then-girlfriend was having an affair with my now ex-business partner. My ex-girlfriend is an artist too." Tobias's mouth hitched up at one corner. "I thought I'd managed to put it all behind me, but then she goes and shows up again, begs me to take her back, starts texting and phoning, turning up at the gallery I owned in Glasgow all the time." His voice tailed off and he gave a dry smile. "I think she was missing the lifestyle rather than me."

I processed what he was revealing to me. "And you decided to get away?"

"Yep. Oh, don't get me wrong. I no longer have feelings for her, but I didn't need the hassle."

I opened my mouth and was about to say something.

"You're moving again!" he called, startling me.

"Oh! Oh shit!"

In slow motion, my cup jumped in my hands. I scrambled to catch it, but my fingers tumbled over one another. Thankfully, the coffee wasn't as hot as it had been ten minutes ago.

The white cup upended on my lap, sending its dark beige contents spilling all over my tangerine summer dress. "Bugger! Bugger!"

Tobias dumped his sketch pad on the chair he was sitting in and dashed over to me. He ordered Alexa to turn off. "Are you alright? You're not burned, are you?"

He crouched down in front of me, before racing through to his black and chrome kitchen. Seconds later, he returned with a clean cloth, soaked in cold water.

"I hope it didn't go on your furniture."

"Oh, don't worry about the sofa. I'm more concerned about you."

I accepted the cloth from him. "I'm fine. The coffee was cool."

"Thank goodness for that."

I dabbed at my dress, trying to soak up the worst of the coffee stain. I jerked my head up. Tobias was crouching in front of me. I appreciated his full, quirky mouth.

He continued to gaze at me. "Are you sure you're alright?"

"Yes. I'm fine, thank you," I squeaked.

Our lips were inches apart now and neither of us were in any hurry to pull away. Then something nudged at the corners of my mind. It wouldn't leave. It was gnawing at me. What about the almost kiss from before?

What about that female voice I heard that night, talking to Tobias and offering him wine? I remembered the hurt and jealousy jabbing at me and it threatened to strike again.

Guilt took hold of me. "Wine woman," I murmured. Aloud. Oh shit! Great! I blushed beetroot and couldn't look at him. I must have sounded like an utter idiot!

Tobias looked confused. "Sorry?"

I pulled back from him and dragged an embarrassed hand through my loose hair. Me and my big mouth! I had to tell him, otherwise he'd think I was crazy. "When I spoke to you one evening a few weeks back, there was a woman's voice in the background, talking to you about wine." I cringed. "Oh God. I must sound like a suspicious, moody teenager. I'm sorry."

Tobias frowned for a few seconds, before his face cleared. "Hang on. She didn't call me Tobes by any chance?"

I nodded, as I continued to dab at my dress. I couldn't look him in the eye.

"That was Theresa Day, my old art lecturer from college."

I jerked my head up from my soiled dress to look at him.

"She drops by to see me once a month. She was a real art hero of mine. Still is. She always brings a bottle of wine with her." Tobias's lips threatened to break into a smile. "She's sixty next week, lives with her long-term biker partner and they have a blended family of five kids between them."

Oh no. What an idiot. I wanted Tobias's sofa to swallow me up.

Tobias continued to examine me as he knelt there. "Hold on. Is that why you've been skirting around me? Because you thought I was seeing someone?"

My neck heated up. "I haven't been skirting around you."

Tobias waggled his brows, arguing the point.

"Ok. Maybe I have. A bit. But so have you with me."

He stood up and sat down beside me. I could smell his spicy aftershave. "You're right. I have. I'm sorry." He rubbed the back of his neck. "Like I just told you, my track record hasn't been great relationship-wise." He offered a small, embarrassed sigh. "I know I've been an unpredictable idiot." He paused. "I think that's because I always seem to be the one who gets hurt."

Tobias's mouth slid into a shy smile. "But when I talked to Celeste about you earlier, I realised what a dick I'd been."

I stared at him as he sat there beside me. "You talked about me? Why?"

"Because I'm sure she's part witch. She knew straight away

that I liked you and she told me not to waste a second of my life and to just go for it."

I couldn't drag my eyes away from him. My heart was thumping so loud I was sure he'd be able to hear it. Was this really happening? All the wasted time and the dodging about with one another; the sidestepping and the hesitation. "Oh, Tobias. I've tried to ignore my feelings too. I thought that us working together would be a problem." I fiddled with the cold cloth and then dumped it on the table.

Tobias lifted one finger and placed it on my lips. "I've wasted enough time. Right now, all I know is I'm going to have to kiss you, otherwise I'm going to lose my mind."

Tobias inched closer to me. His lips found mine and traced them, soft and tentative at first. Then the kiss deepened, his tongue teasing mine as he slid a hand into my hair pulling me closer.

I kissed him back, pressing myself against him. A low growl escaped from his throat.

We both slid backwards against the sofa, a tangle of limbs.

"Oh, not now!" groaned Tobias against me, as my mobile rang out disturbing the peace. We kissed again, before reluctantly parting. I picked up my phone, my lips still burning with the delicious feel of his mouth.

It was Maeve. "Are you alright?" she asked. "You sound breathless."

Tobias nuzzled against my neck, the coarseness of his stubble gently grazing my skin. Ripples of excitement shot down my spine.

"No, I'm fine," I managed. "Just dashing for my phone. So, what happened? How did it go with Corinne?"

"It was a bit odd to begin with, as you might imagine. We kept bursting into tears and then ended up talking non-stop, but I think we all felt the better for it. In fact, I know we did."

"That's great. Do you think Corinne will try to see Celeste again?"

"She said she wants to. She mentioned popping up at the weekend for another chat. She was showing Mum photos of her granddaughters." Maeve hesitated. "Thank you, Lexie, for what you've done. You and Tobias. Your friendship has been invaluable."

Hearing her words, Tobias nestled in again against my neck and stroked my hair.

"You've done so much for me and for Mum and we won't forget it." I heard her smile down the line. "Now, enough soppy talk, otherwise I'll set myself off again. I'll let you get back to your evening with Tobias. You're a lucky girl! Goodnight."

She rung off.

I stared, bewildered, down at my phone. How did she know? I laughed to myself and snuggled back in beside him. "Aren't you supposed to be sketching me?"

Tobias's grin was wolfish as he leant forward and kissed me again. "Oh, there's plenty of time for that."

Chapter Thirty-Eight

I arrived back at my flat that evening, after Tobias insisted on dropping me home.

There had been more greedy, breathless kissing in his car, before I reluctantly parted ways with him.

I felt like a besotted teenager, giddy with the thoughts of seeing him again – it was heavenly.

I got ready for bed, flitting in a dreamy state from my bedroom to the kitchen to make myself a camomile tea.

Once in bed, I thrashed around, unable to sleep. Thoughts careered around my head like an out-of-control train. Mum coping so well with Dad; Corinne turning up like that; Celeste's expression when she saw her; the years falling away; then Tobias sketching me, before we kissed... I could still feel the solidity of him against me; my fingers furling and tangling in his dark curls... Oh, this was useless!

I threw back the covers, made a second cup of camomile in the hope it might help me to fall asleep and set up my laptop in the sitting room.

My promise to Celeste to write an ending to her book echoed around my head.

My fingers hovered above the keys. The cursor flashed on the screen. I could make out my faint silhouette.

I could do this. I would write the epilogue for Celeste.

I reached for my mug, took a measured mouthful and set it back on the coaster. I began to type, the rattle of the keys reverberating around my quiet flat.

Adrenalin and determination spurred me on.

I became lost in what I was writing, thoughts and ideas pouring out of me, until I realised my eyes were feeling gritty, so I got up and strode around my flat to stretch out my tired arms and legs. Then I returned to the ghostly glow of the screen and began typing again.

I wasn't aware of the time. My fingers continued to produce sentence after sentence, paragraph after paragraph, like I was possessed and was unable to stop for breath.

As I carried on writing, I realised with a surprised jolt that I was actually enjoying this; breathing life into the characters and chiselling out their lives.

I refused to stop, exhilarated by the way the story was running with me and coming together.

It was only when I typed *The End*, that my fingers finally came to rest on the keys and I slid back against my sofa and slipped into a dazed sleep.

What the hell had I been thinking last night?

I opened one apprehensive eye, then the other and squealed at my reflection in the hall mirror.

My skin was pasty and there were purple smudges of weariness under my eyes. My original plan had been to sashay into Book Ends that morning, bowling Tobias over with my glossy, mermaid complexion and looking ethereal in one of my prettiest dresses.

Instead, I'd sat up writing half the night and now I looked like Freddie Krueger in a frock.

Desperate, I applied a couple more coats of black mascara, slid on some of my brightest pink lipstick and smudged blusher on my cheeks. I secured my hair back from my face in a high, bouncy ponytail. If I smiled a lot, that might disguise the psycho killer bags under my eyes. Then again, I might freak Tobias out even more if I was grinning like an idiot at everything.

I slid my laptop case over my shoulder. It had been worth it though. I might have a face like a burst balloon, but I'd written the epilogue of Celeste's story! That it was for her made the realisation that I'd been able to write fiction and had enjoyed the chaotic, frantic process, sweeter still.

I decided I would drop by straight after work and read it to her.

The grey drizzle couldn't dampen my spirits as I huddled under my cherry blossom umbrella, walking towards Book Ends.

The pavements, roads and roofs were glistening with July rain. Parents were praying for improved weather in the meantime!

My stomach soared as I reached the shop entrance. I could

see from the outside that Mirror Image was still in darkness. Tobias hadn't arrived yet.

I tightened my ponytail and located the shop key in my bag.

"Well, good morning."

Tobias was head and shoulders behind me, his towering silhouette wavering in the shop windows.

A shiver of anticipation raced up and down my spine.

I turned. "Good morning."

His hair was in damp curls, skimming his broad shoulders. He offered me a lazy smile. "How're you today?"

"I'm very good, thanks. You?"

I unlocked the door and he raised his arm above me and pushed it open. We exchanged private smiles. "Never better," he said.

The air in the shop crackled as we went about our usual routine, firing on our electronic tills and switching on the spotlights.

"Did you sleep well?" he asked.

"Not so much."

"Me neither."

He came striding towards me in his black trousers and navy shirt. "I couldn't stop thinking about you. It got so bad; I ended up working on one of my commissions for a bit."

We glanced around to make sure no customers had snuck in while we weren't looking. Chloe, Daryl and Octavia were due in soon too.

Tobias slid one arm around my waist and pulled me to him.

"Funny you should say that," I said, stroking the collar of

his shirt. "I did a similar thing last night. Well, not painting, obviously."

"Oh?"

"I sat up most of the night and wrote the epilogue for Celeste's book."

"Really? I'm impressed." Tobias lowered his mouth to mine and grazed my lips with his. "Do you think I might have given you some inspiration?"

I pretended to ponder the question. "I'll have to think about that one."

Our mouths became greedier for one another and I became lost in him – until my ringing mobile cut through the passion.

We both let out frustrated groans.

Maeve's number appeared.

"Good morning," I chirruped, happiness exploding in my chest. "How's things?"

My blood froze at the sound of Maeve choking back tears. "Oh, Lexie," stammered Maeve. "It's Mum." She struggled to sound coherent. "She's slipping away."

Chapter Thirty-Nine

I reached for Tobias's hand as we made our way towards the residential home entrance. My laptop was suspended over my other shoulder.

It was bruising and bumping against my side, but I didn't care.

Maeve was standing looking lost at reception. The three of us exchanged silent, tight hugs.

"I've tried to get hold of Corinne, but she isn't picking up. I did leave a message though." She rubbed at her watery eyes. "It's as if she knew deep down Corinne would come and see her. She's hung on till then." She raised her damp face. "Now that she has some peace, it's like she feels she can let go."

Hot tears were on the verge of spilling down my cheeks. "Can we see her? I wrote the epilogue of her book last night."

A breakfast trolley trundled past, the crockery rattling like false teeth on top of it.

"Oh, how wonderful. Mum will be thrilled."

I glanced up at a solemn Tobias beside me. "Maybe I could

read it to her. I want her to know I did it. For her. That's why I brought this." I indicated to my laptop case over my shoulder.

Maeve's usually immaculate blow-dried hair was pulled back from her haunted face in a severe, low ponytail. "I'm sure she'd love that."

As we approached Celeste's closed door, Joy emerged from another room. "She's looking forward to seeing you both." She nodded in silent sympathy and vanished.

Maeve reached for the handle and creaked it open. "You two go ahead, I want to grab a quick cuppa. Can I get either of you anything?"

Tobias shook his head. "No thanks. Take your time. We'll call you if anything changes. You need a breather."

Maeve patted Tobias's shirtsleeve. "You've got a good one here, Lexie."

Celeste was in bed, supported by a bank of clean, fresh pillows. Her white hair had been brushed and was falling back from her face. She appeared more fragile, yet there was an inner calm about her.

Her weary eyes fluttered open. "Oh, look who it is. The best-looking couple in Bracken Way."

I blushed and Tobias smiled. "Is it that obvious?" he asked her.

Celeste hitched her eyes up to the ceiling. "You two have been sodding around one another since day one. If I'd been fit, I would have clunked both your heads together."

"No need for that now," said Tobias, stroking my hand.

Celeste patted her bed covers and ordered Tobias to fetch over a chair. "Better late than never. I'm delighted." Her voice was far more paper-thin than usual. "Guess who came to see me at the weekend?"

"Who?" I asked, my voice thick with emotion.

"One Flora Simmonds."

"No!" I gasped. "What on earth did she want?"

"To apologise for everything over the years."

I stared at Celeste. "And did you accept her apology?"

She nodded against the pillows. "I made her work for it, but yes, I did. It would have been churlish not to. I think she was worried I might come back and haunt her." She slid a faint smile over at Tobias. "I might be dying, but I've had one hell of a life. A far better one than she ever had, by the looks of it."

"Don't say that," I blurted, snaking my fingers around hers.

She gave them a weak squeeze of affection. "So, what have you been up to apart from the obvious?"

Tobias grinned at her.

"Celeste!" I sighed and shook my head. I pointed over to my laptop which I'd placed in the other empty armchair when we came in. "I've been writing the end of your book."

Her tired eyes brightened for a few moments. "You did it?"

"I promised I would."

Tobias retrieved the laptop for me and set it up on the bed.

"Would you like me to read it to you?"

"Is the Pope Catholic?"

Tobias rested his stubbled chin on my shoulder. "I think that's a yes."

I located the file and pulled up the document on screen. The words I'd written shimmered in front of my tear-cluttered eyes. I cleared my throat and began to read aloud.

Celeste lay back staring at the creamy aertex swirls on her

ceiling, while I described how Melissa secured a record contract, became pregnant and married the handsome musician Vince who had stolen her heart. I also spoke of how she was able to fight and keep the child who her parents and authorities wanted adopted.

I continued to read, my words washing over her, transporting her to another place and time.

Her sunken mouth glided into a serene smile, as I neared the end of the story. I described how Melissa carved out a life for herself, her husband and her family and how successful and happy her two daughters were.

I read the final few sentences. Tobias listened too, every so often murmuring his support. I could feel his soft breath in my hair.

I bit back a ball of emotion as I finished reading. "And the silver songbird flew high. Even as the years moved on, the love she gave and the love others had for her endured... The End."

Maeve entered the room just as I fell silent. She drew to a sharp halt. Her face fell at the sight of her mother lying there so still.

Tobias took me in his arms, his expression grave. "She's gone, Lexie. She's gone."

Chapter Forty

The next couple of weeks were a painful yet contented blur.

Celeste's funeral was a reflective, celebratory affair, attended by so many locals of Bracken Way, as well as former showbiz colleagues from far and wide.

As she'd requested, her ashes were scattered on top of the hill at the castle, overlooking the oval mirror of Loch Bracken and the majestic, heather-riddled hills beyond.

Corinne and Fletcher attended. She was brimming with regret that she hadn't listened to her voicemail until after Celeste had passed, but Maeve appreciated them attending the funeral and they promised to keep in touch. It was what Celeste would have wanted.

Not having a force like Celeste around anymore was a very difficult thing to adjust to. But having Tobias, the bookshop, not to mention Mum, Dad and Grandpa to focus on, was keeping me occupied.

Since the grand re-opening, the bookshop continued to

flourish, as did Mirror Image. However, the torrential rain darkening the clouds in mid-July meant that the bookworms were not as keen to venture out and I found myself quieter than usual that afternoon.

Tobias was out on a commission and I'd been taking the opportunity to polish and edit Celeste's book.

I picked up my phone and, for what felt like the hundredth time, read the text that Maeve had sent me a few days ago.

It would be a fitting tribute to Mum, if her book could be published, Lexie. What do you think the chances are?

I turned over Maeve's words in my head and found myself scrolling for Rhiannon's number. If Literati did go for it, I would ensure Maeve was financially compensated on Celeste's behalf.

Rhiannon answered after a few rings. I'd already messaged her just after Celeste passed away.

"How are you? How is everything?" she asked, her voice tinged with concern.

"All a bit odd," I admitted. I glanced down at my laptop screen on the counter. "Would Literati like to take a look at a new novel?"

There was stunned silence down the line. Then an eruption. "Did you just say what I think you said?"

"Maybe."

"Oh, stop teasing me, Dunbar! Have you started editing again?!"

"Yes and no."

"Sorry?"

"Celeste wrote a book years ago. It's great. She didn't manage to finish it, but I have on her behalf."

I could hear Rhiannon's thoughts whirring down the line. "What's it about?"

"A struggling young singer in a small Scottish town in the 1960s. Think *Beaches* crossed with *Steel Magnolias*."

Rhiannon started breathing harder. "Oh my God. I'm hyperventilating! It sounds great. Autobiographical?"

"Bits of it are."

Rhiannon's breathing grew sharper. "And you edited it and wrote the end, you say?"

"I did. Her daughter Maeve would love to see it published. I thought it might have legs for a series – a prequel and then a third about her two daughters."

"Right. How quickly can you email it over to me and I'll pass it onto one of the commissioning editors? If they were keen and wanted to commission a series, would you be willing to write it?"

My breath quickened.

"Lexie? Are you still there?"

I pulled myself together and thought of Celeste's faith in me. "Yes. I would."

Rhiannon sighed with pleasure. "Wonderful. Ok. Can you email it over to me now please?"

A frisson of nerves shot through me like an electric current. "I'll send it straight away."

"Great! Oh God, I can see the press release about this beauty already!"

I laughed. I just hoped it lived up to Rhiannon's expectations.

. . .

I was preparing to leave my flat the next morning for Book Ends, when Rhiannon's number lit up my phone. I didn't even have time to say hi, before she launched into an excited tirade.

"Can you check your emails on your phone if I forward this on to you right now?"

I clicked on my inbox, to see an email to Rhiannon from Verity Edwards, one of the commissioning editors at Literati:

Hi Rhiannon,

Hope you're ok?

Thanks to you, Lexie and the late, great Celeste, I've been up all sodding night reading that book. I look dreadful but what a wonderful story! The characters are compelling and I couldn't stop turning the pages.

I will send it back for Lexie just to address a couple of minor tweaks and then I'm getting it straight to acquisitions. I'll keep you posted.

As promised, Rhiannon returned the manuscript with only a couple of suggested minor changes to be made, which I worked on that evening and then returned it to her before heading to bed.

I was prepared for a glacial wait. I knew only too well how slow the publishing industry could be.

But just as Tobias had persuaded me the following evening to go out for dinner, an email arrived in my inbox. I was putting the finishing touches to my hair and didn't take any notice. It was only when Rhiannon called me moments later, fizzing with excitement, that I wondered what was going on. "Have you had a chance to read Verity's email yet?" burst out Rhiannon. "Guess what? An offer already! A three-book deal with us for a silver songbird trilogy. The sales team bit Verity's hand off, they think it's got huge potential!"

I gripped the phone, emotional visions of Celeste wavering in front of me. She would be thrilled.

"Lexie? Lexie? Are you ok?"

Tobias, who had been patiently waiting for me in my sitting room, appeared.

"Literati want to publish Celeste's book. They want a trilogy."

Before I knew what was happening, he whirled me around, planting a fierce kiss on my thrilled, stunned mouth.

"Yes," I beamed up at him, through the promise of delighted tear as I gripped my phone. "Everything is simply wonderful."

Epilogue

Twelve months later

Time had moved on, but the memories of Celeste stayed.

The trilogy of the *Silver Songbird* books was eagerly anticipated. The first novel hit the Kindle Top 20 and stayed there for weeks. The second in the series is about to be published.

With Maeve's approval, I donated all proceeds from the first book to the Silver Songbird charity for troubled teenagers that she had started up in Celeste's memory.

Maeve and I are still close friends and I know we always will be.

Tobias, Trevor and Caroline managed to reach an understanding. Tobias said it's still a somewhat surreal situation for him, but that he's beginning to comprehend why Naomi did what she did. He understands why the four of them made the decision they came to, but he's still coming to terms with the shock of finding out who his birth mother really was.

Mirror Image is keeping him occupied and the commissions are stacking up, so he's delighted.

As for Book Ends, there will always be a desire for books. At the moment, I'm managing to juggle my writing and editing with the bookshop, but thank goodness we recruited Chloe and Daryl when we did. They are proving invaluable!

Trevor is more than happy with how his beloved bookshop is faring and said his dear Naomi would be too.

Dad's condition will never improve, sadly. Some days he's more lucid than others. There's been more of a definite deterioration in him, but with Mum at his side, he's battling on and that is all any of us can do. She makes the most of the respite care that the local hospice offers and has made a few new friends with other people who are caring for loved ones with dementia too.

Grandpa is the same as ever – still betting on the horses when he thinks Mum isn't looking – but has been a rock to Mum and me and for that we are always grateful.

I am on deadline for book three, which isn't too pressing… except when you are planning your own wedding, that is!

Tobias and I were in agreement that we wanted to get married at Bracken Way Castle. It'll be like Celeste is able to celebrate our big day up there with us. Roll on 31st May next year, when I become Mrs Dunbar-Black. (I wasn't going to go with the double-barrel, but Rhiannon is convinced it will look good on future book covers.)

Tobias has promised he's going to present me with my portrait on our wedding day. I can't wait to see it!

As for Rhiannon, she's decided to give it another go with her ex-husband, Guy. Goodness knows how long it'll last this time, but she said he makes her laugh and brings excitement into her life, so who's to say she's wrong not to take a chance on them again?

As a silver songbird once told me:

You grab happiness with both hands when it comes along – and never let go.

Acknowledgments

Huge thanks as always to my wonderful editor Jennie Rothwell at HarperCollins for being so talented, enthusiastic and patient! Thanks also to Dushi Horti and the other amazing team members at One More Chapter, who really are a fantastic group of people.

Grateful thanks to my terrific agent Selwa Anthony. To know you're always in my corner is a blessing. Thanks also to Linda Anthony, for always being there for me.

Love always to my boys.

To Chris Martin (no, not that one!) for "giving" Tobias his "one eye open" line.

And finally, a huge thank you to the musical maestros that are Tobias Forge and Ghost. Lexie and my Tobias are also fans – they have excellent taste! I'm now obsessed and suffer writing envy when listening to their amazing lyrics. They accompanied me on my journey with this story. Thank you.

I was late to the Ghost party – but what a party!

ONE MORE CHAPTER

One More Chapter is an
award-winning global
division of HarperCollins.

Sign up to our newsletter to get our
latest eBook deals and stay up to date
with our weekly Book Club!
<u>Subscribe here.</u>

Meet the team at
<u>www.onemorechapter.com</u>

Follow us!
 <u>@OneMoreChapter_</u>
 <u>@OneMoreChapter</u>
 <u>@onemorechapterhc</u>

Do you write unputdownable fiction?
We love to hear from new voices.
Find out how to submit your novel at
<u>www.onemorechapter.com/submissions</u>